Valerie Wood was born in Yorkshire and now lives in a village near the east coast. She is the author of *The Hungry Tide*, winner of the Catherine Cookson Prize for Fiction, *Annie, Children of the Tide, The Romany Girl, Emily, Going Home, Rosa's Island, The Doorstep Girls* and *Far From Home*, all available in Corgi paperback.

Find out more about Valerie Wood's novels by visiting her website on www.valeriewood.co.uk

D0766632

Also by Valerie Wood

THE HUNGRY TIDE
ANNIE
CHILDREN OF THE TIDE
THE ROMANY GIRL
GOING HOME
ROSA'S ISLAND
THE DOORSTEP GIRLS
FAR FROM HOME

and published by Corgi Books

EMILY

Valerie Wood

CORGI BOOKS

EMILY
A CORGI BOOK : 9780552147408

Originally published in Great Britain by Bantam Press,
a division of Transworld Publishers

PRINTING HISTORY
Bantam Press edition published 1999
Corgi edition published 2000

3 5 7 9 10 8 6 4

Set in 11/12pt New Baskerville by
Phoenix Typesetting, Burley-in-Wharfedale, West Yorkshire

Corgi Books are published by Transworld Publishers,
61–63 Uxbridge Road, London W5 5SA,
a division of The Random House Group Ltd,
in Australia by Random House Australia (Pty) Ltd,
20 Alfred Street, Milsons Point, Sydney, NSW 2061, Australia,
in New Zealand by Random House New Zealand Ltd,
18 Poland Road, Glenfield, Auckland 10, New Zealand
and in South Africa by Random House (Pty) Ltd,
Endulini, 5a Jubilee Road, Parktown 2193, South Africa.

Printed and bound in Great Britain by
Cox & Wyman Ltd, Reading, Berkshire.

Papers used by Transworld Publishers are natural, recyclable
products made from wood grown in sustainable forests.
The manufacturing processes conform to the environmental
regulations of the country of origin.

For my family with love

Acknowledgements

I would like to thank Professor D. M. Woodward, Hon. Archivist, Hull Trinity House, Trinity House Lane, Hull, for information on Trinity House School; Sheila Gardiner for a book list; and Peter Burgess for information on Hull gaols.

My thanks again to Catherine for reading the manuscript.

Books for general reading

Marjorie Barnard, *History of Australia* (Angus & Robertson, Australia, 1962).

Robert Hughes, *The Fatal Shore* (Collins Harvill, London, 1987).

N. V. Jones (ed.), *A Dynamic Estuary* (Hull University Press, 1988).

Chapter One

'Leave me a dozen eggs and yon hen and tha can tek 'little lass.'

The child stared, first at her mother, who had spoken, and then at the tall, thick-set youth who carried a square wicker basket with a speckled hen poking its beak over the top and she knew that her future was being decided.

The youth's eyebrows shot up and then down and then up again. 'Nay, I can't! She said I had to fetch 'little lad.'

Her mother shook her head in the determined manner which the child knew so well. If this was to be a battle of wills, she knew who would be the victor. ''Lad can't go. I need him here. Tha can tek Emily. She'll be a good worker when she's big enough.'

And so it was decided. Emily was sent to put on her boots and shawl, whilst the hen and eggs were handed over in exchange. 'I'm not sure,' she heard the boy say as she entered the house. 'She'll have summat to say.'

Her father was sitting in a chair by the fire, his head against the chair back, pale faced and his eyes half closed. Emily put on her boots and then stood by him. He gave a slight nod and she lifted each foot in turn so that he might fasten up the laces as he usually did, for she had not yet mastered the art of tying them with knot and bow without them coming undone.

'Must I go, Da?' she ventured, clasping her hands in front of her.

He swallowed, the movement seeming to cause him pain for he closed his eyes for a moment before answering. 'Aye.' His voice was husky. 'If thy Ma says so. There. I've put a double knot so's they won't come undone. Tha'll be fine, don't worry.'

'Will I come back?'

He stroked her blond head so like his own and then patted her cheek. 'I don't know, maybe not. Go on now, don't keep him waiting, it's a long journey.'

Still she hesitated and glanced towards the open door, where her mother, outside it, was impatiently tapping her foot. She looked around the small sparse room. There was nothing else she needed to take, no possessions or essentials, nothing that was hers alone. 'We've got an old hen,' she whispered. 'We don't need another.'

'Come and give thy Da a kiss and get off.' Her father drew her towards him and she leaned and kissed his thin cheek.

'Shall I see thee again, Da?' Her lip trembled as she spoke and she kept her eyes on his, willing him to say yes.

'Get off now, lass. Go on. Don't be asking questions that I can't answer.'

Her father, who had always known the answer to every question she ever asked, was reluctant to answer this one. She picked up her woollen shawl and walked slowly to the door, then looked back. Her father had his eyes closed again and his cheeks were wet. 'I could stay and look after thee, Da.'

He opened his eyes and she saw that they were glistening. He put up his hand and made a gentle movement for her to go; she turned again and left the room.

Her mother fussed in an unaccustomed manner, pinning her shawl and refastening the buttons on her dress. Then she gave her a little push. 'Go wi' Sam now and be a good lass. Do as his Gran tells thee.' She offered no kiss as her husband had done, nor any explanation as to why or where she was going.

Emily looked up at Sam, but he kept his eyes on the ground and didn't look at her. He had a round, weather browned face and wore a thick grey cotton smock and cord breeches and a floppy brimmed hat on his brown hair. He picked up the empty wicker basket and prepared to move off. 'Go on then, Emily,' her mother said again. 'Don't keep him waiting.'

The cottage stood at the end of a track with a small copse behind it. It was part of the estate where her father had been employed until he became ill six months before. Emily plodded behind Sam until she reached the end of the track and then looked back. Her mother was standing by the open door of the cottage, one hand shielding her eyes from the light, the other on her hip. Emily waved, but her mother made no answering sign. She took a few more steps and looked again. Her mother had gone, the door was closed and there was no-one standing by the uncurtained window. The only movement was a curl of smoke above the chimney pot from her father's fire.

They journeyed out of the hamlet, Emily following in Sam's large footsteps and noting the women who stood in cottage doorways to watch them pass. They were almost at the limit of the estate when she saw a familiar figure coming towards them. It was her brother, Joe, who since he was eight was helping with the harvest to earn money now that their father was ill. Emily had overheard her parents talking and agreeing that Joe was to be depended upon. 'There's nowt else for it,' her mother had said. 'Else we're for 'poorhouse.'

'Hey, Em! Where's tha going?' Joe's face was streaked as if he had been crying, but his voice was curious.

She shook her head. 'Don't know. Ma said I had to go wi' Sam.' Sam had stopped a little way off and was waiting for her. 'Why's tha not at work?'

He looked away from her and put a fist to his eyes. 'I've lost 'job. Mayster said they didn't want anybody my age now they've finished 'harvest, even though overseer said I was a good worker for a little 'un.' Joe was small for his age no matter how he stretched himself, not much bigger than Emily, who was only five.

Sam waved for Emily to come and she said hurriedly, 'He wanted thee but Ma said no; she said I had to go. We've got a new hen,' she added, unsure whether to be proud or sorry for the barter. 'Tell Da tha saw me, Joe.'

He nodded and set off in the direction of home, then turned back and called, 'Shall tha be coming back, Em?'

'Don't know,' she shouted back. 'Don't be asking me questions I can't answer.'

They walked all morning and into the afternoon, leaving behind her inland home, crossing the coach road which led towards the town of Hull, and skirting by a tree-lined track, a towered and turreted manor house set within a vast parkland, which was scattered with grazing sheep and cattle. They crossed over meadows and farmland and by the time they reached the bustling market town of Hedon, Emily was almost crying with tiredness.

Sam stopped at an inn and bought a tankard of ale for himself and a cup of water for Emily. They sat in the inn yard and he put his face up to the warm sunshine. 'Not far now.' Those were the first and only words he had spoken to her and she looked up at him and blinked, then as he lifted his tankard to take a gulp of ale she put her head down on the wooden table and closed her eyes.

He shook her awake. 'Come on, I'll give thee a piggy-back.' He helped her up on to the table and turning his back to her bent forward for her to climb on. She hitched herself up and, putting her arms around his neck, smelt the familiar, comforting aroma of warm grain, new-mown hay and damp earth gathered within the roughness of his clothes and promptly fell asleep.

When she awoke the sun was setting behind

them, suffusing the sky and land with a scarlet glow; the garnered fields were lit as if by a thousand lamps and sheep grazed amongst the stubble. She gave a small gasp at the immenseness of the wide landscape. Her own hamlet of cottages and barns and farmhouses was surrounded by woods and small copses, and she had never ventured beyond its limits. Here, the only signs of habitation were the occasional farmstead in the far distance. She lifted her head and sniffed. The air smelt different. Fresher, sharper, with a hint of saltiness. 'Sam,' she whispered, 'have we come to 'end of 'world?'

'Tha great daft lump!' The old woman lifted her scrawny arm and aimed a blow at Sam's head. He ducked with a dexterity which suggested that it wasn't the first time such a blow had been directed towards him. 'I telled thee to fetch 'lad. What's tha brought 'little lass for? She'll be of no use nor ornament!'

'Missus wouldn't let me bring him,' Sam blustered. 'She said she needed him. She said little lass'd be a good worker when she's growed,' he offered in mitigation.

'And who pays to keep her while she's growing?' the woman shouted at him. 'Didn't tha think o' that, tha daft beggar?'

Sam shuffled his feet and lowered his head. 'Sorry, Gran,' he muttered.

The woman turned her attention to Emily. 'Does tha know who I am? Did tha ma tell thee?'

Emily shook her head, not daring to speak in case she should evoke a torrent of abuse like Sam had just received. Perhaps, as it was obvious the old woman didn't want her, she would be sent home again, though she doubted if she could walk back so far again tonight. The darkness was closing in and for the last few miles when they had turned off the road to take small rough tracks before reaching their destination, she had clung to Sam's hand in case he should lose her in this vast empty landscape, which was punctuated only by isolated farms and cottages and the soaring spire of a church in the distance.

'Hannah Edwards, thy fayther's auntie.' The old woman's eyes pierced her face. ''Onny relative he's got left. That's why he's sent thee here. Is tha a good lass?'

Emily nodded. Da always said that she was, though she was often in trouble from her mother. 'What do I call thee?' she dared to ask.

'I'm glad to see tha's got a tongue in thy head.' Hannah Edwards pursed her mouth and considered. 'Tha can call me Granny, same as our Sam.' She turned towards the door. 'Better come in then, seeing as tha's here.'

The one-roomed cottage, like her parents' home, was built of mud and straw and rounded cobblestones of varying sizes, but with a roof, not of tiles but of barley thatch. It felt warm and welcoming to Emily, with a bright fire burning and the brass knobs on the door and cupboards gleaming. In a corner of the room was a curtained alcove, where she could see the legs of a bed, and on the fire a kettle was steaming and in the coals beneath potatoes were cooking in their skins.

'Sit down at 'table but don't start until we've said prayers.' Granny Edwards sat at one end of the scrubbed wooden table, Sam at the other and Emily sat in the middle, where a place was already laid. In the centre of the table was a large pot of soup and a loaf of bread. She bent her head as she saw Sam and his granny did and peeped from one eye to watch the old woman muttering softly.

'Amen,' Granny Edwards said in a loud voice. 'Amen,' repeated Sam. They both looked at her and waited.

She glanced from one to another, then tightly closing her eyes and clasping her hands together, repeated fervently, 'Amen!'

Granny Edwards nodded, apparently satisfied with her show of faith, and proceeded to ladle the soup into large brown bowls. Emily took a sip, it was hot and salty and unlike anything she had tasted before. She hadn't eaten since breakfast and following Sam's example she dipped in a slice of bread and finished off the bowlful.

'Tha's got a good appetite,' Granny Edwards muttered. 'Tha's going to tek some feeding.' She pointed a spoon at Sam. 'Tha'll have to tek on some extra work. If tha'd brought 'lad he could've found work on 'farms. This bairn can do nowt.'

'Our Joe's just lost his job,' Emily pronounced. 'Mayster said he was too little to work. I'm nearly as big as him,' she verified, 'and I'm good wi' hens and cleaning cupboards.'

There was silence as this pronouncement was digested, then the old woman's face softened. 'Lost his job, has he? So there's no money coming in!'

She shook her head in commiseration. 'That's hard on thy ma, very hard.'

'And on my da,' said Emily. 'He can't work 'til he's better.'

Granny Edwards rose from the table to fetch the potatoes and patted Emily's arm. 'God will look after thy fayther, never fear,' she said softly. 'It's thy ma and brother who need our prayers now.'

Chapter Two

Emily kept a discreet distance until she came to the conclusion that Granny Edwards's irascible nature hid a lion heart. It was to the widow Hannah Edwards that neighbours trudged down rutted muddy lanes and marshy tracks for advice, whether on why the jam wouldn't set or what to do with a wayward son or daughter, and the same son or daughter would come to her door to complain of overbearing parents. These last were given short, sharp shrift and sent home with the proclamation to thank God they had parents at all and were not homeless orphans as some poor bairns were.

Emily, listening from a chair in the corner often wondered if this last statement applied to her, for she often caught sympathetic glances coming her way as this pronouncement was made. The days slipped into weeks and she adapted to the routine of the household, and, having stated that she was good with hens and cupboards, was given the task of feeding the hens every morning and gathering the new-laid eggs, and keeping the food and pan cupboard tidy, at least as far as she could reach.

Sam worked every day, either in his garden, where he grew potatoes and other vegetables and tended the fruit bushes, or as a casual labourer on the local farms, where by his strength and willingness, he was assured of work.

'He's an 'andsome lad, our Sam, but not right sharp,' Granny Edwards announced to Emily one day, 'but he's a good lad and a hard worker.'

'Where's his ma and da?' Emily asked, having spent several nights beneath her sheets laboriously trying to work out Sam's relationship to his granny and therefore to her. 'Are they dead?'

'Might just as well be,' Granny Edwards muttered, more to herself than Emily, 'for all we ever see of her. No,' she confirmed, her fingers industriously clicking at her knitting, 'his ma's not dead, but she went off when Sam was twelve months old and I've ne'er seen her since. As for his da, well God knows where he is, or who he is, for I'm sure I don't.'

Emily gazed at her; so Sam was one of the poor orphans that Granny talked about and not her after all, she decided, for she had both ma and da and she resolved to be kinder to Sam than she had been.

The cottage sat barely a mile from the banks of the Humber. From there they could smell the salt of the sea, feel the sharp wind on their faces or be shrouded in a sea of fog, which drifted in from the estuary and chilled them to the bone and made them hurry to pile up the fire with driftwood which Sam collected from the river banks and dried ready for use.

Sam walked across the marshy land every day to Cherry Cob sands, returning always with some treasure. He brought home eel, shrimps or mussels, sometimes a bunch of samphire which grew on the marsh, or a rabbit caught by a ferret which he kept in his pocket. His mind was a little slow, but his ability to catch, fish, net or snare was sure, and he always brought something home for the pot, which his granny had ready and waiting.

Emily begged time and again to go with him. 'I won't be a bother,' she pleaded, 'and I'll keep ever so quiet while tha's fishing. Please, Sam, let me come.'

He'd glanced at Granny Edwards, who shook her head. 'Not yet. 'Tide's fast and watter's deep. Too deep for a bairn like thee.'

'But 'other bairns go, I've seen them.' She had watched the snake of youngsters wending their way across the marshland towards the mudflats. 'And they go on their own.'

Granny weakened slightly. 'They're older than thee and know where to go and where not. Maybe when tha's growed a bit.'

So she left it at that until a month had passed, but now winter was coming, a thin film of frost began covering the marshy land and the wind blowing in from the estuary was sharper and keener. They filled a sack with straw and pushed it into the window aperture so that no draught could penetrate and brought out a heavy blanket to cover the door. Driftwood was carried inside and Emily tied bundles of dry kindling with straw and stacked them in a corner of the room. Martinmas had passed, when the farm workers, ploughmen, dairy-maids and labourers stood by the market cross in local towns and bid for the next twelvemonth's work. Sam went to the town of Patrington and came home with a huge beam on his round face to say that he had been taken on as a regular labourer at one of the neighbouring farms. 'I'm not sleeping in, Gran. I'll come home every night.'

His granny gave a satisfied nod, pleased with him even though it meant her getting up at four-thirty each morning to make sure he had a breakfast of gruel or oat dumplings before he set out on his several miles' walk. His midday meal he would eat at the farm and on his return a dish of rabbit stew or mutton broth and barley bread would be waiting for him before he finally tumbled wearily into bed.

Time hung heavily for Emily now that Sam had gone to regular work. She fed the chickens and swept the yard and did a few jobs of work, but when those were done and the old woman sat dozing over her knitting by the fire, Emily would stand outside and wonder what to do next. There were no children in the immediate vicinity and the ones she had previously watched going to the river bank no longer came through the day. By teatime dusk was closing in and there was not a soul to be seen in that vast, awesome landscape. She missed her brother, Joe, for they had always played together, and she wondered if he had managed to get another job of work.

So she stood one midday, after eating her dinner of bread and cold bacon, and looked across to the far reaches of the skyline. The winter sun was bright, glistening on the patches of frost which hadn't cleared and outlining the stark bare branches of elm and ash in the distance. Granny Edwards had fallen asleep by the fire and the afternoon loomed long before her. Then Emily made a decision. She would go to the river. She could walk and just take a look, no more than that, and then come straight back home. Nobody will know, she pondered, and when I get back I can tell them that I was big enough to go by myself.

She slipped back inside for her shawl and to check that Granny was still sleeping, which she was, her mouth slack in a gentle snore and her knitting idle in her lap. Emily gave a little satisfied shrug and crept out again. The hens scuttled out of her way and she skipped along towards the track at the top of the dyke which she knew Sam always took to go to the river.

Though it was but a mile, it seemed much longer, for the track was muddy and stuck to her boots and slowed her down. Sometimes the path disappeared into a morass of mud and taking care not to slip down into the deep, water-filled ditch, she jumped down into the soggy grass. She kept on walking and thought she could hear the murmur of the tidal waters beyond the distant, low, green bank.

On she tramped, lifting her mudborn boots from the sucking ooze until she finally reached the bank. She scrambled up, crushing nettle and dead heads of sea aster beneath her feet and pushing her way through prickly, red-berried thorn and bramble; and there before her triumphant gaze lay the shining mudflats, which shimmered in the winter

sun and harboured hundreds of curlew and
redshanks which searched and fed on the crus-
taceans beneath the mud. Beyond the mudflats lay
the broad waters of the Humber and the banks of
Lincolnshire on the other side.

She heaved a sigh of satisfaction. She had got
here by herself, without assistance from Sam or
anyone else. 'I am big enough,' she declared aloud
and jumped down on to the grassy shore and found
herself almost knee-deep in water. The grass which
looked so firm from the bank was marshland with
hidden pools and rivulets. The mud beneath the
water sucked and oozed around her legs and with
difficulty she splashed and pulled and made her
way back to the bank, where she found a dry patch
and sat down to take off her boots. She tied them
together with her laces and hung them around
her neck, wrung out the hem of her dress, then,
cautiously and gingerly watching where she put
her feet, she walked towards the river.

The tide was out and the quaggy mud sucked
between her toes, but she ventured further until
she reached shallow water and stepped into it. It
was icy cold around her ankles and she quickly
came out again, though she lingered on the edge
and searched for pebbles to throw into the water,
but found only a few shells and some chunks of
driftwood, which she threw into the waves,
disturbing the bobbing gulls and shelducks which
were resting between the crests. A fleet of ships,
with their canvas sails filling in the sharp breeze,
was sailing downriver towards the mouth of the
Humber on their way to the sea, and she waved her

hands to them, wondering where their journey was taking them.

'I'd like to go on a ship,' she murmured and she bent to peer downriver towards the spit of Spurn peninsula, trying to see as far into the distance as she could. There seems to be no beginning or end to it, she thought, where does it go to or come from?

The curlews called their flute-like cry and above her redshanks flew, whilst behind her on the banks, woodpigeons rustled and foraged amongst the berries and haws. She played for a while, splashing in the pools and collecting small pieces of drift-wood to take home for the fire, until she began to feel a chill. The sun had gone, disappearing behind a thick bank of cloud and a mist began to drift in from the river; it settled on her hair like raindrops and her shawl felt damp. The tide too was rushing towards the shore. It gushed and babbled, trickled and frothed and percolated into all the muddy pools and gullies, absorbing them into one.

She decided to return home, for she wanted to get back before Granny Edwards awoke from her sleep, but she had mistaken the time it had taken her to come and the time she had spent by the river, and as she pulled and tugged her wet boots back on to her cold red feet, she realized that the light was going, the mist was getting thicker and that she must run if she was not to be found out.

Behind her she could hear the rush of the tide as the waters of the estuary travelled their journey, but in front of her, as, frowning, she endeavoured to locate her path home, there seemed to be only a lonely silence in that isolated vista. She shivered, the stillness wrapped around her, cocooning her in a thick, damp curtain. She shook her head to dispel it and turned again to the river to welcome its rushing sound, but the gesture increased her isolation as she realized that her only way was forward, to march into the silence and break it by her own presence.

'Sam,' she called bravely, 'Granny Edwards! It's me, Emily. I'm coming.' Her words echoed around her, swirling like the mist, which was becoming thicker by the minute. She stepped forward. She must run. But which way? She had lost the defined path and the dyke which she had followed here, and there was only hummocky grassland and patches of watery waste, which once more sucked and snatched at her boots.

She wandered for what seemed like hours and the darkness descended and the mist became thicker and colder. She stumbled straight on at first, but not coming across the dyke she then veered right, searching for the slight incline which would indicate its presence, but she heard again the sound of the river, louder now than before and a faint *creak, creak* which was eerie to her ears, and peering through the darkness she saw the outline of masts and a huddle of small boats moored in a creek, their masts and rigging creaking as they swayed gently in the water. On the far side of the creek a dim light glimmered, but she couldn't see a bridge or road and she was afraid of falling into the water. She shouted again and again, but there was no answering shout and she turned and struck out once more back the way she had come.

Tears started to fall, but she stumbled on. She was cold and hungry for it was long past her supper-time. Her hands still clutched the driftwood which she had collected and her wet skirt rubbed against her legs making them cold and sore.

'Sam,' she shouted, 'Granny Edwards! It's me, Emily!' She listened, but heard nothing. 'Da! Da! I need thee. Come and get thy little Em. I'm onny a little bairn.' She sank down on to the wet grass and started to sob. 'Da. I want my da!'

She laid her head down on the grass and as she did, found that it rose in a slight incline. She reached out with her hands, discarding the drift-wood, and stretching up realized that the ground rose higher. She clambered on hands and knees up the incline and came to the top. Below her lay the dyke, the waters rushing and gurgling from the river through the fields and wetlands and towards home.

She hurried on, slipping and sliding, but keeping to the edge nearest the field so that if she fell she would fall into the land rather than into the water. Then she stopped. There was a sound. Muffled, but there it was again. Someone was shouting. Voices were shouting her name.

'Sam,' she shrieked, 'Sam! It's me, Emily!'

Again came the call. 'Emily! I can't see thee. Keep shouting!'

'I'm on 'dyke. Come quick.' Her voice rose in sudden panic now that help was near. 'Come and get me. I'm lost.'

The voices grew louder and soon she could make

out distant shapes looming through the fog. Lanterns sent out an eerie, fluctuating light and soon she saw the broad figure of Sam running towards her. 'Emily! Come on, tha's all right now. I've got thee.'

He picked her up, crushing her in his arms. 'Don't cry, Em. Tha's safe now. We'll soon have thee home.'

Another man wrapped a blanket around her and two young lads with him gazed at her curiously. 'Tha should have asked us,' one of them said. 'We'd have taken thee down to 'river if that's where tha's been.'

She didn't answer, but looked with streaming eyes at the small crowd who had been searching for her and started to shake, with cold and fear at what might have happened to her and relief at being found.

'Will Gr-Granny Edwards be mad at me, Sam?' she whispered as they neared the cottage. 'I never told her where I was going.'

'Aye, I expect she will be,' he answered bluntly, 'but she'll be glad that tha's safe, so don't bother too much if she rattles on at thee.'

But Granny Edwards didn't rattle on at her, she seemed curiously subdued as she took off her wet things, Sam turning his back as she stripped Emily down to nakedness, and with a rough towel rubbed her vigorously all over until she was glowing, then, wrapping her in a warm blanket and with her feet in a mustard bath, she sat her by the fire. 'Here now, drink this down and tha'll soon be right as rain.'

She put a spoonful of honey in a small tankard

and half-filled it with ale, then taking the poker from the coals she plunged it into the liquid. It sizzled and steamed and withdrawing the poker she grated a nutmeg into the ale and handed it to Emily. 'Tha'll mebbe not like 'taste, but drink it down anyway.'

Emily sipped it, the taste was bitter but with an overlying sweetness and she felt the heat trickling down her throat, warming her. 'I'm sorry,' she whispered, 'I didn't mean to be a bother.' Tears started to spout again and her mouth trembled as she spoke, 'I wanted my da. I shouted for him, but I knew he wouldn't hear. He's too far away.'

Granny Edwards drew her chair nearer to Emily. 'Aye, he is far away, but I reckon maybe he did hear thee and that's why tha was found.'

Emily looked at her, not understanding. 'I might as well tell thee 'news now, as wait till 'morning,' the old woman said and looked at her with sorrow in her eyes. 'I got 'message this afternoon. They woke me up from my nap and I knew tha'd gone off somewhere, but I had to wait till Sam came home to look for thee, even though I called and called.'

Emily hung her head; so she would have been found out even if she hadn't got lost and been late home.

Granny took hold of her hand in an unaccustomed show of affection. 'I got 'message to say that thy da died two days ago. He's in heaven now I have no doubt, for he was a good man. And thy ma and brother have gone to 'poorhouse.'

Chapter Three

Emily's grief was deep, for now she knew that she wouldn't see her dear da again, whereas, if she had previously thought about it at all, which she meditated guiltily hadn't been very often, she had felt that her stay with Granny Edwards would be temporary and that she would eventually return home.

'If tha's good and say tha prayers every night,' she was assured, 'then tha'll meet him again at heaven's door.'

Emily sniffled. 'Does that mean I have to be good every day for ever, Gran?' she asked doubtfully, for if that was the case then she feared that she would not be there to greet him. It was very hard to be good all of the time.

'Tha shall go to chapel wi' me on Sunday,' Hannah said determinedly. 'We'll pray for his soul and for thy ma and brother's bodily comfort and trust in God. And, we'll ask Him to look down on thee,' she sighed deeply, 'and me too, to give me patience and fortitude to bring up yet another bairn.'

Emily looked skywards when she was out of

doors. She wasn't sure that she wanted someone watching her the whole time. Just suppose, she thought, just suppose I do something bad by accident, will God think I did it on purpose and still punish me?

She was dressed in a clean dress and warm shawl on the following Sunday and followed Hannah, who in her best black dress and cloak strode out down the four-mile road towards the village of Thorngumbald, where she attended chapel every Sunday, wet or fine, sun or snow. She had never suggested taking Emily before and neither did Sam attend. Emily was quite excited. Perhaps there would be other children there whom she might play with or talk to, perhaps those who visited the river, though, she considered, perhaps she had better not mention that subject just yet or Granny would start muttering again that 'she might have drowned and in my care at that'.

Hannah shook her umbrella in the air. 'We'll have a fresh going on now that tha's here for good.' She looked down at Emily. 'Thy ma sent word to ask if I'd be thy guardian. Well, what could I say?' she muttered under her breath. 'Can't see this bairn going to 'poorhouse along with 'other one.'

'Tha'd rather have had our Joe, I expect?' Emily ventured.

The old lady stopped abruptly. 'Why, I never said that! When did I say that?'

'When I came. Tha shouted at Sam and said he should have brought Joe.'

'Huh! Tha's got sharp ears for a little 'un.' She walked on and then glanced down. 'No, I reckon tha'll be all right. Tha's willing enough and not a bad lass. I expect we'll get along.'

Emily smiled and skipped along after her. The praise was sweet. She'd try to remember to include Granny Edwards in her prayers.

As she came out of the chapel clutching her new prayerbook, she looked curiously at the small group of children who were gathered there waiting for their parents to finish their conversation with other members of the congregation. They were scrubbed and clean, the boys with well-brushed hair and shiny faces and the girls neat in black stockings with starched pinafores over their dresses. Emily waited for Granny Edwards, who was in earnest discussion with the minister. She kept nodding over to Emily and the minister too looked her way and shook his head in a commiserative kind of way. He shook a finger as he spoke and they both turned their heads towards the building next door.

A young boy came across to Emily. 'Thou's little lass that got lost down by 'river!'

Emily nodded in agreement. 'I shan't get lost again,' she said defensively. 'It was only 'cos it was foggy.'

'It's allus foggy down there.' He looked down at his boots. 'If tha likes, we'll tek thee next time we go. Mebbe next Sat'day if it's fine.'

She looked towards Granny Edwards, who was bearing down on her. 'I'll have to ask,' she whispered. 'If she says I can, I will.'

The boy scooted off towards the group of other boys and girls who were waiting for him and she turned to ask the question, but was forestalled by Granny, who was saying, 'Well, that's got that settled. Minister says he'll put in a word for thee wi' schoolmistress. Now our Sam is in regular work we'll be able to manage. Tha's nearly six, so all being well tha'll start school after Christmas.'

She couldn't wait to start. Some of the children who called for her the following Saturday said that they went to the Thorngumbald school. The boy, Dick, who had spoken to her outside the chapel, another boy, Jim, and two girls, Dora and Jane. The girls were both aged seven and were only allowed so far from home under the safe keeping of the boys, who were eight and had been threatened with the strap if they came to any harm. The other boys in the group said that they didn't go to school because their parents hadn't any money, but in any case, said one, 'Larning is a waste o' time, I already know how to plough.'

Granny agreed that Emily could go with them as long as they were back before dark. The morning was sharp, frost lay across all the marshland and when Emily took a deep breath she could feel the icy air freezing her nostrils.

That winter morning was the start of friendships and quarrels and of a discovery of life on the river bank, when they dug in the mud for crabs and shrimps, fished for flounders and gudgeon with homemade rod and line, or stole eels from the baskets laid out on the mudflats. They chased foxes and rabbits and whispered together if they spotted a solitary heron or stood silently watching the mass influx of wildfowl, brent-geese and waders.

They clambered in and out of the small boats moored in Stone Creek, which in daylight was peaceful and no longer threatening as it had been on the night she had been lost. They made believe that they were sailing away over vast oceans and the girls had to be lookouts and bailers whilst the boys were captain and mate who planned the voyage. They were only disturbed by the shouts of men on the shore to, 'Get off those boats, tha young peazans!' and they scuttled away laughing to find other pleasures on those lonely shores.

That first winter came on hard and fast and the other children stopped coming for almost a month when the fields were thick with snow and the road was impassable and even Granny couldn't make her usual visit to chapel. Sam stayed on at the farm, for he couldn't get home and Emily and Hannah made the best of their time together. The pump in the yard froze and to get water for their cooking they had to break off icicles which hung from the door lintel.

They brought in more wood and kindling which Sam had stacked by the house wall and the cottage was warm if smoky. Hannah taught Emily to knit and to bake, and sat during the long winter evenings and spoke of her own childhood spent much as Emily was doing, in the depths of the Holderness countryside. She told her that after she married, her husband was made manager of a farm and she had taken over the running of the house, feeding as many as eleven to fifteen men three times a day as well as bringing up her own daughter.

'Old Mr Francis ran the estate then and later,

when his father died, young Mr Francis said I'd allus have a roof over my head, and even after Mr Edwards died he kept his promise. He let me have this house for onny a peppercorn.' She sighed. 'I don't know what'll happen to our Sam, though, when owt happens to me.' She glanced up from her knitting. 'And let's trust in God that afore I go tha'll be in service or wed.'

As soon as the road was clear, Emily was prepared for school. She was wrapped in new flannel bodices which Granny had made and in thick wool vests, which she had helped to knit and which itched and tickled as she got warm. Two new pinafores were made from cotton sheeting and new boots ordered from the cobbler in the market town of Hedon were delivered by the carrier.

'I'll tek thee this once and meet thee half-way home this afternoon,' Granny said as they set out on the long trek. 'So tek notice of which way to go.'

Emily clutched her bag, which contained her dinner of bread, a hunk of cheese and an apple, a piece of chalk and a clean handkerchief, which she had hemmed and painstakingly embroidered with the initial E.

She was eager and quick to learn and soon she could write her name, Emily Hawkins, and was mastering her numbers. The mistress was strict and made them sit up straight and speak clearly and properly, for, she said, she couldn't understand their rough country speech. Dick jeered at Emily's cleverness because he stumbled over his reading and writing, though he could add up quickly enough, but like the other boys he longed for spring, summer or autumn when they could help on the farms and had ready excuses for not going to school.

By the time she was eleven Emily was head and shoulders over the other pupils both in ability and height. Her hair was long and blond and was kept firmly under control in two plaits. Her shape was changing and she started to stoop to hide her swelling breasts. One morning she arrived at school in time to see Jane hand their teacher a note, and at dinnertime when Emily and Dora went outside to eat their dinner and go to the privy, Jane stayed behind and sat with her head on the desk and the teacher said not a word in admonishment.

'What's up with Jane?' Emily asked. 'Is she poorly?'

Dora shook her head and whispered in her ear. 'She's started her flux!'

'Started her flux?' Emily asked. 'What does that mean?'

'You know!' Dora blushed and would say no more until they were well away from the flapping ears of the boys.

Emily that day learned the facts of life from Dora, or at least as much as Dora knew, which wasn't much for she hadn't been told either, except by an older girl, and Emily walked home in a daze, pondering on whether to impart her new-found knowledge to Granny Edwards, for as she was so fond of saying, she hadn't had much learning and Sam was no scholar and that was why she had sent Emily to school.

Every spring they renewed their weekend visits to

the river, but as they got older sometimes Jane and Dora couldn't come. They now had more tasks to do at home, smaller children to look after, bread to make or kitchen floors to wash, and Emily found that she was increasingly irritable with the boys' behaviour as they clowned around in their last days of childhood before leaving school.

'You're always showing off,' she grumbled as they fought with one another, or tried to stuff a dead rat down someone's shirt, or dared each other to jump from one boat to another without capsizing it. They were noisy and boisterous, they chased rabbits down holes and pelted birds with homemade cata-pults. They generally went home wet and muddy and sometimes they manhandled Emily too when she complained of their stupidity, pushing her to the ground and holding her down with their sweating, panting bodies until abruptly they would let go of her and run off, their faces red and unable to look at her.

'Can I look down tha frock, Em?' an older boy said one day. 'I'll give thee a bite of my apple if tha'll let me.'

She stared at him, then felt herself blush. No matter how she pushed them down, her breasts always protruded. 'No you can't. It's rude.'

'Aw, go on.' He came nearer and tweaked the buttons of her dress. 'Just a quick look.'

'No.' She turned away, but he grabbed her and placed a hand over one breast, clutching it tightly. She swung out with her fist and caught him under his chin, making his teeth chatter, and he dropped his hand and looked away.

'Some lasses let us,' he muttered. 'They think it's a lark.'

She walked away, not looking back. Her cheeks burned and she felt a pulse throb in her throat. She was embarrassed, humiliated and confused. I'll never go with them again, she vowed. Never, never, never.

Instead, whenever Sam had time off she went to the river with him and he taught her how to fish. He borrowed a boat from Stone Creek and they rowed upriver, keeping close to the shore and watching out for hidden mudbanks. She gazed at the shore in all its seasons as they pulled hard, seeing the lonely salt-marsh flatlands and me-andering creeks from a different view, empty of habitation except for the winter-feeding wader birds; a thousand curlew which rose in sudden flight, the dunlin, plovers and gulls. Once she caught a young salmon on its way back to the sea and she carried it home in triumph. Sometimes, if the wind was not too strong and the tide was low, they would row down towards Spurn Point, the curling tongue of land which retreated from the sea to dip into the Humber mouth. The tidal flow carried them down on its journey to the sea, around the bulging Hawkin's Point of the reclaimed land of Sunk Island, to tip them ashore on a narrow fringe of marsh and mud and sand, where buck-thorn scrub and sea lavender grew and they would slop through the oozing mud of the river's edge, then race up and over the sandy dunes, Emily's legs going at double the pace of Sam's lumbering long stride, vying to be the first to view the mighty

German Ocean on the other side of the bank.

During Emily's last winter term at school Hannah was unwell. She had caught a cold which attacked her chest and dosed herself with honey and marshmallow root, but wouldn't stay in bed no matter how Emily and Sam tried to persuade her. Reluctantly, Emily went to school one morning and told the teacher she wouldn't be coming back until Granny Edwards was better. 'She needs me at home,' she explained to the startled mistress, who was unused to her pupils taking the initiative. 'She doesn't know that she does, but she does.' She stayed until dinnertime and then went home.

In the evening Granny took to the bed which she shared with Emily. 'I'll give Sam a note for 'doctor to come,' Emily said to her. 'You're not getting any better.'

'That tha'll not! I've never had a doctor in my life.' She tried to rouse herself from the pillow, but sank back again. 'Only once has he been over this doorstep and that was when our Sam was born.'

'Time he came again, then,' Emily said firmly.

'Oh, do as tha likes.' Hannah closed her eyes wearily. 'I haven't 'energy to argue with thee.'

When the doctor came the next day he listened long and hard at Hannah's chest, moving aside the thick embrocated flannel that was covering it. He pursed his lips and gazed at her. 'Well, Hannah,' he began.

'Don't be telling me owt I don't already know,' she croaked. ''Good Lord will decide whether I go or stay.'

'That's true.' The doctor closed up his bag.

'There's nothing I can give you. Just stay in bed and try to rest.' He turned to look at Emily. 'And this is a niece I believe? We haven't met before.'

'Aye, almost a niece – my late nephew's daughter. I've brought her up as my own.' Hannah wheezed and coughed and sweat stood out on her forehead. 'She's been a good lass, I hope she'll manage on her own.'

A sudden fear clutched Emily. Was Granny Edwards going to die? To leave her and Sam? She followed the doctor out of the room to the door, where he paused and lowered his voice. 'Mrs Edwards has pneumonia. Give her plenty to drink and wash her with a cool cloth if she's feverish.'

'Will she die?' Emily stared at him with wide eyes. 'She won't, will she?'

He patted her shoulder. 'Everybody does, child, sooner or later. There's no cure for death.' He picked up his bag. 'I'll come again.'

Emily boiled water, which she cooled to make Granny a drink, then whilst she was sleeping she prepared a meal for Sam. She skinned and jointed a rabbit which he had caught and put it into a pot with potato and onion and placed it over the fire to cook. She swept the floor and polished the brass knobs and filled up a bucket with water from the pump. Then she carried a basket outside and filled it with wood for the fire. When she had finished she carried a chair next to the bed, where Granny was now sleeping, and sat down to watch over her.

When Sam arrived home Emily was fast asleep and he had to waken her, the fire had burned low and she hastened to build it up. 'Your dinner's ready, Sam,' she said, lifting the lid off the pot and carrying it to the table, 'and I'll make some tea in a minute.'

Sam lifted the curtain and looked down at his granny. 'She don't look very good,' he said ponderously as he sat down at the table. 'One of 'hosses at 'farm was wheezing like that and 'master shot it.'

Emily drew in a deep breath. 'What'll we do if she dies, Sam?'

He paused in the action of lifting a fork to his mouth, then placed a piece of rabbit in his mouth and laboriously chewed and swallowed. He put his fork down in his dish and considered. 'Well,' he said slowly, 'we'll have to bury her, I expect.'

They sat up with her all night. Sam dropped asleep in the chair by the fire, but Emily, sleepless and anxious, never closed her eyes, but bathed the old lady's face frequently and trickled water through her lips. At four o'clock she roused Sam for his breakfast. She brewed a pot of tea, made his gruel and cut him a thick slice of bread. She sipped her tea as she sat by the bed and whispered to Sam that she thought the fever had passed. That the worst was over. He looked down at his grandmother and blinked his reddened eyes.

'Aye,' he breathed. 'Mebbe so.' He leaned over and kissed the pale cheek and stumbled out of the door.

Emily pottered around all morning, unable to settle to any job of work. She kept looking at the still figure in the bed, but Granny Edwards lay quietly sleeping so she didn't disturb her. She went outside to feed the hens and collect the eggs and looked up at the immense pale blue sky and took several deep breaths of crisp, cold air. She gathered up more wood in the basket and as she straightened up from the woodpile, she saw a horse and trap with the doctor and a woman in it coming along the lane towards the cottage.

The doctor nodded at her as he climbed down from the trap. 'Sam called and left a message this morning on his way to work. This is Mrs Scott. She'll do what is necessary.'

Emily stared first at one then the other. Called and left a message? What message did Sam leave? That Granny Edwards was much better? Why did he do that when the doctor had said he would call? She looked at their solemn faces and especially at the woman, who cast her a sympathetic glance as she passed inside the door, and felt a sinking despair. Granny Edwards is sleeping, she wanted to say. Don't waken her. Then a chill washed over her. Sam had known, that's why he had kissed her when Emily had never seen a kiss between them before. It had been a kiss of goodbye.

Chapter Four

A neighbour brought his cart and helped Sam lift
the plain wooden coffin into it. Emily had gathered
teasels and seed heads, wild grasses and stalks of
barley and strewn them over the top. It seemed
fitting, she thought, that the land that Hannah
Edwards had loved should send its harvest with her
to her last resting place. The neighbour climbed
into the driving seat and Emily and Sam followed
behind, to be joined along the muddy road by
farmers and their wives, labourers and young maids
who had known Hannah Edwards.

Mr Francis was waiting at the chapel, standing
slightly apart from other members of the congregation, and Emily glanced curiously at him when
Sam touched his forehead to him. His hair, though
dark, had white streaks, as did his beard. He was
tall and broad in his bearing. 'He's not young like
Granny made out, Sam,' she whispered, 'though
he's not really old,' and she wondered whether he
would allow Sam to stay on at the cottage even
though he didn't work for him.

She worried over this all through the service
and even as with wet eyes and trembling lips she

watched the coffin being lowered into the grave, a persistent question pounded through her head. What will happen to us?

As she and Sam began the walk back home they were joined by some of the women who had attended the funeral, women who had been acquainted with Hannah through the chapel. Most of them carried wicker baskets with white cloths on top. Emily glanced over her shoulder several times to see if they were perhaps moving off in another direction over the fields, but still they followed on behind until they came to the cottage.

'We've taken 'liberty of bringing a few victuals,' said one as they approached the door. 'Nowt much, but Mrs Edwards would have wanted a good tea made on her behalf.'

'Aye,' said another. 'Hannah would have put on a good spread for any of us in similar circumstances.'

Emily thanked them and invited them in, where they divested themselves of their outer garments, though keeping on their hats or bonnets, and proceeded to set the table, first with a white starched cloth with an embroidered cloth over it, and then from their laden baskets they produced boiled ham and tongue, boiled eggs and celery, cheese and pickle, cheesecake, jam tarts and plum bread and all manner of other tempting food.

Emily rushed to place the kettle on the fire and opened the cupboard to bring out plates, cups and saucers, knives and forks, then, not to be outdone, brought out the cake tin wherein lay a fruit cake which she had made only a few days before. One of the women looked over it approvingly. 'Hannah allus did have a good hand at bakin',' she commented.

'Our Emily made that,' Sam chimed up from his chair by the fire. 'She's a good baker. Granny showed her how.'

There was a sudden silence and all eyes turned to Emily. 'How old are you, Emily?' one of the women asked.

'I'm thirteen,' she answered and wondered why the women looked significantly at each other.

After they had said grace and eaten their fill, some of the women cleared away and prepared to leave whilst two or three others settled down as if to stay. Emily thought that they had been very kind and considerate, but wished now that they would go and leave her to her thoughts, in particular to the one which was questioning why Mr Francis, on commiserating with Sam on his loss, had told him that he would call round to see him later in the day.

'Now then, Sam,' one of the women, Mrs Turner, said, 'can tha make thyself scarce for five minutes? We want to have a word wi' Emily.'

Sam stared open-mouthed, then slowly got to his feet. 'Aye,' he muttered. 'I'll go and chop some wood.'

'And fetch some more water, Sam,' Emily directed, contemplating that she might have to make more tea when Mr Francis called.

'It's a bit delicate, like,' Mrs Turner looked Emily squarely in the eye when Sam had gone out of the door, 'but it has to be said, and we're onny thinking o' thee after all and what's best to be done.'

Emily folded her hands in front of her and waited. Whatever could they want to say to her?

'You see,' said another woman, 'you're thirteen! You said so yourself.'

Emily nodded. That was what she had said.

'And Samuel,' Mrs Turner raised her eyebrows, 'why he must be going on twenty-six!'

'He's twenty-four, Mrs Turner,' Emily said. 'He's just had a birthday.' She waited for a further statement, but none came, the women only gazed at her. 'So –,' she glanced from one to another. 'What –?'

Mrs Turner lowered her voice to a whisper and glanced over her shoulder to the door, which was closed. 'He's a man is Samuel! Might not act like one, but nevertheless he is.'

Emily laughed. 'I know that, Mrs Turner, but I don't understand what you mean.'

'I'm meaning', Mrs Turner was a little huffy, 'that he's a man wi' bodily needs and you're a lass and tha can't stay in 'same house! Not just 'two on you together.' She drew herself up and folded her arms beneath her ample bosom. 'That's what I'm meaning!'

Emily felt herself grow hot and her cheeks crimsoned.

'Tha'll have started 'flux, I expect?' another woman whispered. She pursed her lips. 'Can't be too careful when there's men about.'

Emily swallowed, but said nothing. She didn't know what to say, didn't really know what they were saying. She only knew that Samuel wasn't really a grown man, he was still like a child in many ways.

'So what we suggest', Mrs Turner appeared to be speaking for everyone else in the room, 'is that tha should apply to go into service. It's coming up to Martinmas. Tha can go to Hedon or Patrington and try for a kitchen maid on one of 'farms.'

'But who'll look after Sam?' Emily blurted out. 'He can't manage on his own!'

'Why bless you, child,' said one who hadn't spoken before, 'we'll all take care of Sam if he stops on here. We'll keep an eye on him, do a bit o' baking and that. We'd do that anyway in memory of Mrs Edwards as well as for himself.'

Mrs Turner rose to her feet. 'So that's that then. Come Martinmas tha'll try for a place? Patrington might be best, there's some good houses and farms that might take thee. Go presentable as if tha's prepared for hard work, no fancy frills or furbelows, 'cos that won't do at all.'

'Thank you for coming.' She escorted them to the door and on opening it saw Sam sitting morosely on a log with his chin in his hands. 'I'll think on what you've said.'

Mrs Turner turned towards her. 'Nay, lass, tha'll have to do more than think on it. Nobody will have owt to do wi' you if tha stops here wi' Samuel. Tha'll be thought a fallen woman, young as you are!'

When the women had gone, Sam came into the house and sat down by the fire. He stared into the flames. 'Don't know what Mr Francis is going to say when he comes,' he muttered. 'He'll want 'house back I expect, now that Gran's gone.'

Emily glanced around the room which had been her home for the last eight years. She had been to the house where her schoolteacher lived. A brick-built dwelling with wooden floors and rugs scattered upon them, there were curtains at the window and a maid to answer the door. Here, in Hannah Edwards's house, the furniture was plain and useful and set on an earth floor, which in the winter was cold and damp underfoot. The fire in the hearth which now burned with crackling dry wood sometimes filled the room with acrid smoke when the wind blew in the wrong direction or if the wood, gathered from the river bank, was wet. But for all its simplicity she viewed it with affection. Here she had learned to sew and bake and had learned her lessons and read from her school books to Granny Edwards, who, in turn, had taken such pride in her achievements.

'The women said I should go into service, Sam. They said I shouldn't stop here with you. That it wasn't right.'

Sam stared at her. 'Who'll cook me dinner, then?'

She permitted herself a small smile. Sam knew what was important to him. 'The women said they would look after you. They'd bake for you, and I expect they might do your washing, though you'd have to pay them.'

His face filled with dismay and his lips pouted. 'But they wouldn't be here to get me up in a morning and have me gruel waiting or me dinner on 'table when I got home, now would they?'

'No, Sam,' she said gently, 'they wouldn't. So we shall have to think of something else, won't we?'

He shook his head. 'No. I think it's best if tha

stops here, Em, if we can. Tha can't be going off to service and leaving me on me own.'

She sighed. The women didn't know Sam. As far as he was concerned, she would simply be taking Granny Edwards's place in looking after him. Those were Sam's bodily needs; there were no others.

Roger Francis came as dusk was falling. Emily saw him riding along the rutted lane and rushed to comb her hair and take off her apron. Sam rose from the table as he entered and touched his forehead.

'Good evening, Samuel. Good evening – Emily, isn't it?'

'Yes, sir.' Emily bobbed her knee. Granny Edwards must have spoken of her to Mr Francis for him to know her name. Today at the chapel was the first time she had met him.

He sat down as invited and she and Sam stood uneasily before him. 'You're a relation of Mrs Edwards, I understand?' He had a quiet voice and his manner was hesitant.

'She was my father's aunt, sir. She's looked after me since I was five, when my father died.'

'And what of your mother? Is she living?'

'I don't know, sir. 'Last we heard she and my brother were in 'workhouse.'

He looked grave, then said, 'Sit down, Samuel. You too, Emily. We need to have a chat about what's best to do. You know that I let Mrs Edwards stay on in this house for her lifetime? But', he glanced at Sam and then at Emily, 'it's a good-sized house, too big for a single man and, besides, I can't let you stay,

Samuel – not on your own, especially as you don't work for me. It, erm – it wouldn't seem fair to my other tenants.'

'Sir,' Emily spoke up boldly, 'the women who came to the funeral today said that I shouldn't stay here on my own with Sam, on account of us not being proper relations,' she added, and saw Mr Francis's eyebrows rise. 'But Sam can't look after himself, so I was wondering, sir, if you don't think me too forward in suggesting it, is, would you take Sam on at one of your farms and let him live in so that he doesn't have to worry about his food and washing?'

Mr Francis folded his arms and looked at her, and she thought his eyes looked kind. 'And what would you do?' he asked softly.

'The women suggested that I should apply as a kitchen maid, sir. I'm old enough at thirteen.'

She guessed that if Mr Francis were to take Sam as an estate worker he would stand by him on account of Hannah Edwards. He was the kind of gentleman, she decided, who would take care of his workers if they were loyal and hard-working, and Sam would be both these things, she had no doubt.

Mr Francis remained silent, as if mulling over the idea, and gazing at Sam, who stared back at him, his lips clenched in a tight line. Then Sam spoke, 'On 'farm they said I was a good worker and would keep me on after Martinmas if I wanted to stop.'

'Did they? And do you want to stop, Samuel? Or would you like to come to one of my farms?'

Sam glanced at Emily. 'I don't rightly know, Mr

Francis. What does tha think, Emily? What would our gran say I should do?'

'I think she would have liked you to work for Mr Francis,' Emily said. 'I think she would be very pleased if Mr Francis should offer you work.'

Roger Francis gave her a smile, as if amused at the way she had turned the responsibility upon him. 'But you would have to live in at the farm, Samuel. You can't stay on here by yourself,' he repeated. 'I need the house for someone else.'

Sam nodded. 'Aye. But what about our Em? What's to become of her when I'm not here to look after her? Gran wouldn't want me to leave her on her own.'

Emily felt a lump in the back of her throat and tears prickle her eyes. She dashed them away. 'I'll be all right, Sam. Don't you worry about me.' She turned to Mr Francis. 'When do you want us to leave, sir? Could we have until Martinmas? It's only two weeks away.'

Roger Francis stood up. 'Of course. Give notice on the farm, Samuel, and tell them you're coming to me.' He hesitated for a moment as he looked down at Emily and then said, 'And I'll find out if Cook needs anyone else in our kitchens. If she does, you can come to us without going to the statute fairs.'

She beamed at him. She had been dreading standing in the market squares waiting for some farmer's wife to like the look of her. It was like bidding for a young heifer or sheep, she thought. She bobbed her knee again as she let him out of the door. 'You're very kind sir, thank you.'

'You'll have to work hard if you come, Emily. There'll be no favours given.'

Startled, she drew herself up. 'And none expected, sir, thank you.'

He patted her on the shoulder, his hand resting lightly as he murmured, 'I don't suppose you'll stay very long in the kitchens; but it's a start. It's a start.'

Chapter Five

Emily gave the hens to Dick and sold the few pieces of furniture to some of the village people for just a few coppers, and handed the money over to Sam. He looked down at it in his hand and then handed it back to her. 'Tha'd better keep it, Em. I'm all right for brass and if 'mistress doesn't want thee at 'big house, tha'll need money till tha finds somewhere else.'

That was the worry, she thought. If Mr Francis had forgotten to ask the cook, then she might have to go to the statute fairs after all. They had already started; both Jane and Dora had gone to the town of Patrington to try for positions as kitchen maids.

She packed Sam's belongings into his wooden box ready for him to take that evening when he moved to his new farm, and put her few belongings, a clean apron, Sunday dress and petticoat, into a parcel and then started to clean the house thoroughly. She brushed the walls and swept the floor and cleaned the window and swept the yard. When she had finished she swilled her hands and face beneath the pump, brushed her hair until it shone and tied it into a bun at the nape of her neck.

She changed into a clean shirt and brushed down her skirt.

Sam had gone down to the river bank. 'Just for one last look,' he said, so she put on her shawl and set off to walk to Mr Francis's house, which was a few miles further inland, midway between the river and the sea. She had only a vague idea of where it was, for it wasn't an area she knew, and had reached the village of Thorngumbald when a carrier's cart caught her up and the driver offered her a lift.

'Where's tha heading, lassie?' he asked. 'Hedon market?'

She shook her head. 'No, I'm going to Mr Francis's house to try as a kitchen maid.'

He nodded. 'Elmswell Manor, that's a fine estate,' he said, 'and a good man to work for, though they say missus is a tartar. Where's tha from?'

She told him briefly about Hannah Edwards and Sam and about having to move from the cottage. He'd known Mrs Edwards he said, everybody had, and he knew Sam, who had been abandoned by his mother. 'Good riddance to bad rubbish.' He spat a chew of tobacco out into the road. 'She never did tell who Sam's father was. Trollop, that's what she was, bringing shame on her family.'

He dropped her off at some crossroads and gave her directions. 'Turn right here and go up to 'top of 'road. Turn right at lane by 'second oak tree and carry on until 'road forks. Take right-hand fork and that'll bring thee up to 'house.' He leaned forward. 'Go to 'back door and ask for Cook or housekeeper, don't be fobbed off wi' any of young maids. Treat Cook wi' respect 'cos she rules roost at that house. What she says goes – don't forget.'

She thanked him and set off down the long road. Half-way along she saw the figure of a girl in front of her. As she drew nearer she recognized who it was. 'Jane,' she called. 'Jane, is that you?'

Jane turned round. 'Where 'you going, Emily?' She gave a sudden smile. 'I've got a job as kitchen maid wi' Francises! They took me on at Patrington.'

Emily took in a breath. 'Oh! That's where I'm going! Mr Francis said he would speak for me.' Inwardly she groaned. If Jane had already been taken, they surely wouldn't want her as well; this might well be a wasted journey.

'Dora didn't get took on, she's going to try at Hedon and if nobody wants her there, she said she's going to Hull!'

The two girls stared at each other with wide eyes. 'To Hull?' Emily didn't know anyone who worked in the busy fishing town further up the estuary. 'But she won't know anybody there!'

'No, but she said there was plenty of work and if she can't get into service she'll try some of 'shops or factories.'

Perhaps I could do that if I don't get taken on here. Emily mulled the idea over in her mind. But Hull! It's a long way. A long way? she argued silently. A long way from where? There's nothing or no-one to bind me here. Granny's gone and I shan't see much of Sam once we both start work. I could go anywhere.

She thought then of her mother and brother as she tramped with Jane at her side, down the long

54

country road. There had been no word or letter since she had been told of her father's death. No message to say if they were alive or dead. I am quite alone in the world, she thought. But rather than feel melancholy, she took heart, for she knew that whatever she did she did for herself alone.

'I'm not sorry to be leaving home,' Jane was saying. 'Ma's having another babby and our Jenny can take a turn at looking after 'em all. Scrubbing floors won't be any hardship to me after looking after four little bairns. Catch me having any, I don't think!'

They approached the gates of Elmswell Manor and spoke only in whispers as they walked up the drive. 'We have to go to 'back door,' Emily said.

'I know that, silly. Where else would we go?'

The dignified grey-brick house was larger and grander than either had ever seen before. It stood three storeys high with Greek Doric columns to the entrance and a wide courtyard at the rear.

They knocked on the back door and a girl answered. 'Jane Dawson,' Jane muttered. 'I've been took on as kitchen maid.'

The girl opened the door wider to let her in, but partly closed it as she looked at Emily.

'I've called to see 'cook or 'housekeeper,' she began, but the girl interrupted, 'We don't need anybody else.'

'Mr Francis asked me to call,' Emily said firmly. 'He was going to speak for me.'

The girl hesitated. 'He particularly asked me to ask for Cook.' Emily thought a small white lie wouldn't harm.

'Better come in then.' She led her through a small lobby, then into a back room, where buckets and mops were hanging on the wall, and through another door into a large steamy kitchen, which was crowded with young maids, some in coarse aprons who were either mending the fire in the cooking range or scrubbing pans, and others who were dressed in grey with white aprons and caps and preparing trays with crockery, and several young men who seemed to be scurrying here and there, with either a silver teapot in their hands or a bucket of coal. Jane was standing with her back against a wall with a scared look upon her face, whilst a woman clad in a white apron and cap energetically rolled pastry on the table.

'Mrs Castle!' The girl hesitated. 'There's somebody to see you.'

Cook didn't look up from her task. 'Who is it? You know I'm busy at this time.'

'Emily Hawkins, Cook.' Emily spoke up for herself. 'Mr Francis said he would ask –.'

'Aye, he did, but I don't need anybody else in 'kitchen.' She glanced up at Emily and put down her rolling pin. 'I've just taken a maid on.' She nodded over to where Jane was standing and then looked searchingly at Emily. 'Who did you say you were? Are you from these parts?'

'Emily Hawkins. I lived with a relation, Hannah Edwards, over near 'Humber bank. Only she's just died and I've had to move out of 'house.'

The cook sat down heavily on a wooden chair. 'Ah! Aye, I heard she'd passed on. And what about 'lad? Samuel? Where's he gone?'

'Mr Francis got him work on one of his farms, but he's living in 'cos Mr Francis wanted 'cottage back.'

'Well aye, he would. It was a good little house.' She breathed in heavily. 'So what sort o' relation are you? You've got 'family look.'

Emily was surprised. She had her father's colouring, fair skin and blond hair. Who else did she look like? 'Granny Edwards was my father's auntie,' she explained yet again. 'She looked after me when my da died, my ma and brother went to 'workhouse,' she added in case she was asked.

'I'll speak to Mrs Brewer, she's housekeeper.' Cook got up from her chair and placed the pastry in a dish. 'She can take you for upstairs if she's a mind. She's allus saying she hasn't enough staff.'

'Thank you. Shall I wait?'

Cook looked up. 'Janet!' she called to the girl who had answered the door, 'run upstairs and tell Mrs Brewer she's wanted in 'kitchen as soon as she's got a minute. And you, young woman,' she signalled to Jane, 'get your coat off and your apron on and start washing them pans.'

Mrs Brewer agreed to take Emily. 'You can start tomorrow. Be here for seven o'clock, you needn't come earlier as you have a long way to travel, but every other day except on your days off, you'll have to be up at five-thirty to clean the fireplaces and light the fires before the family are awake. Will that be a hardship? Are you used to getting up?'

Emily smiled. 'It won't be a hardship, Mrs Brewer. I'm up at sunrise every morning. Thank you very much.'

She waved goodbye to Jane and almost skipped

down the drive. Her first position, with pay. Mrs Brewer had said she would get five shillings when she started tomorrow, the rest she would get at the end of the year. She would be given three grey dresses, white aprons, caps and stockings, and was expected to keep her boots clean and polished.

She was tired by the time she reached home. Sam had built up the fire and was sitting in the one chair which she had kept. 'I'll have to be off, Em. I said I'd be at 'farm for suppertime. I've built 'fire up for thee in case tha's stopping tonight. Did tha get job?'

She took off her shawl and hung it on a nail behind the door, then looked round at the empty room. 'I did. I start tomorrow at seven o'clock.'

'I'm glad, Em. Mr Francis is a fine gentleman. Look how he's allus looked after Gran. And now he's given me this job on 'farm. I could stay there for ever. We're very lucky.'

'Yes,' she said thoughtfully. 'I suppose we are.'

He lumbered towards the door. 'Well, I'd best be off then. I might see thee at 'market or somewhere, sometime.'

She nodded. 'I hope so, Sam.'

He turned back towards her. 'I'll miss thee, Em, just like I miss our Gran.' His blue eyes suddenly filled with tears which spilled over his cheeks. 'I'll miss thee a lot.'

She rushed towards him and put her arms around his waist and her face against his chest and smelled the aroma of earth and grain and remembered the time when he had carried her on his back all those years ago. 'I'll miss you too, Sam, such a lot. You've been like a big brother to me. You've taught me such a lot.'

'Have I?' He wiped his face with his sleeve. 'I didn't know I'd done that. Well, fancy!' He gave a tearful grin. 'Just fancy me larning anybody owt.'

'You're a good man, Sam.' She too wiped away a tear. 'Don't let anybody tell you you're not.'

'I won't,' he said solemnly and picked up his box. 'And thou's a good lass too, just like our Gran allus said.' He opened the door. 'Cheerio then, Em. I'll be seeing thee,' and he marched away without once looking back.

It was late afternoon but not yet dusk as the day had been bright and sunny, with very little cloud, not like a November day at all, so she decided that she too would walk to the river bank for one last time. She kept to the top of the dyke and walked swiftly and surely. She knew her way well now.

The tide was full and the river washing over the salt marsh, so that she had to stay on top of the dyke rather than go down to the water's edge. There was a stiff breeze blowing which caught her hair and on impulse she untied the clips which held it back and let it fly free. There were ships sailing down towards the mouth of the river, their canvas sails spread, and she put her arms up and waved as she used to when she was very young. I'm no longer a child, she thought. I have to do grown-up things from now on. But just this last time I want to run and shout just as I used to with Dick and Jim and Dora and Jane.

She jumped down from the dyke and into the marshy fields and with her arms outstretched and her blond hair flying she ran in great circles, whooping and shouting as if to the companions of her childhood, who had also gone to the adult world. Above her mallards flew over and then great flocks of geese and as she saw the pale sun dropping and the sky darkening, she climbed soberly back up to the top of the dyke and looked over the water, shining darkly with colours of red, silver and gold. 'Goodbye, river,' she called. 'Goodbye, childhood. Goodbye, Granny Edwards. Goodbye, Sam.'

Chapter Six

She sat on the hard chair by the fire; her body ached and her head jerked forward from time to time as she dropped into an intermittent slumber. Eventually she roused herself, built up the fire again with the remaining wood and went outside to fetch in some straw from the hen house. There was a sharp nip of frost in the air and she could smell the coldness of winter. She laid the straw on the floor in front of the fire and draped her shawl over it so that she wouldn't itch from fleas, then, taking off her skirt and blouse, she lay down to try and sleep.

The night was long and she lay looking into the flames or watched the flickering, dancing shadows on the walls and ceilings. Outside she could hear the screech of owls and the bark of foxes and as she drifted off into sleep she could hear the echo of Granny Edwards's voice gently chiding and Sam's deep voice in answer. She dreamed she could hear her name being called and the clatter of pans being put on the fire.

She awoke with a start. A wind had risen and was rattling the door sneck, the fire had died down and there was no more wood inside. She sat up and put her shawl around her and went to the door and opened it. It was not yet dawn, the sky was merely lightening with a pale milky hue and a cluster of stars still glimmered. She stretched; she was stiff and aching and she went to the pump and splashed her face and hands, the cold water instantly dispelling her tiredness.

Her bag was by the door and she rooted around in it for her hairbrush. She brushed and brushed her hair and twisted it into a bun so that it was neat and tidy. She dressed again and prepared to leave. Just one glance back, she thought as she walked away, and as she looked for the final time she could almost visualize Granny Edwards standing by the door watching her, just as her mother had watched her leave home all those years before. She straightened her shoulders and put her head up. Come on, Emily, she told herself. Another life is ahead of you. Who knows what is going to happen next?

The work was no harder than she expected, she loved the elegant rooms and the sweep of the staircase and she took great pride in her work. She was up at five-thirty as Mrs Brewer had told her she would be, and with the other housemaids had all the fireplaces in the downstairs rooms cleaned, the fire-irons polished and the fires relit by half-past six. Then they took off their dark aprons, washed their hands and put on their white aprons, ate their own breakfast in the kitchen and prepared the breakfast trays for Mrs Francis and her daughter Deborah, to be taken upstairs at half-past nine. The dining table was laid for Mr Francis and any visitors who might be staying. If there were no visitors then Mr Francis breakfasted alone at eight o'clock, helping himself from the dresser in the dining room, where he ate simply of smoked fish, toast and marmalade and coffee, before going about his business on the estate.

'He's very easy to look after is Mr Francis,' Mrs Castle said as they ate breakfast at the big kitchen table one morning. 'But then he allus was, even when he was a young man.'

'Have you been with the family a long time, Mrs Castle?' Emily was curious; the cook seemed to know all that happened in the household and yet she had never seen her out of the kitchen.

'Aye, since I was just a nipper like yonder lass.' She pointed over to Jane, who was sweating by the range as she stoked the embers. Jane was always the last to eat as she had to make sure everyone else had food on their plates and that the fire didn't go out. 'I started as a kitchen maid, just as she has, so don't look so glum, Janey, you might get to be cook when I'm dead and gone.' She gave a great rumble of a laugh. 'But don't bank on it yet 'cos I'm not planning on going for a long time.'

'We don't see much of Mrs Francis or Miss Deborah,' Emily added conversationally, 'except when we take 'breakfast trays up.' Rarely had she seen Mrs Francis downstairs; she seemed to take little interest in the running of the household, seemingly content to leave it to Mrs Brewer, and as for her daughter, Deborah, Emily only ever heard her voice echoing through the house, usually petulant and grievous.

Mrs Castle gave a searching look at Emily. 'It's not our place to see them we work for.' She touched her nose, 'We keep this out of everything,' she patted her mouth, 'and we keep this buttoned up. And', she went on, 'anything we hear we keep to ourselves.'

Emily was suitably chastened. 'I didn't mean –'

'I know,' Mrs Castle interrupted. 'It's onny natural to be curious about them you work for. But there's things you'll hear or see that you won't understand, so it's best if you don't hear or see 'em, if you follow my meaning.'

She leaned across the table and lowered her voice. 'Try to be invisible, Emily. That's 'best thing to do.'

'It's not fair,' Jane grumbled as they undressed and climbed into the bed they shared in the topmost room. 'I've got 'worst job of all. I'm at everybody's beck and call. And just look at my hands.' She held out her raw and chapped hands for Emily's inspection. 'And I miss my ma, and I even miss Jenny and all 'other bairns.' She burst into tears. 'I wish I was at home.'

Emily put her arms around her. 'Don't cry, Jane. It's not easy for you to leave everybody. It's worse for you than me, 'cos I haven't left anybody behind, only Sam, and I know he'll be all right at 'farm.'

Jane sniffled and wiped her nose on a handkerchief she took from under her pillow. 'My ma allus said she didn't know how Sam managed so well considering he had no ma or da, and especially as he wasn't very bright.'

Emily bridled. 'He might not be very bright, but

he can grow vegetables and catch game and he never wanted for any money 'cos he works hard.' But she started to wonder as she lay next to her sleeping friend, how it was that Granny Edwards and Sam hadn't finished up in the workhouse as her mother and brother Joe had done. Granny Edwards was a good manager, I expect, she thought sleepily as she turned over and tucked her hand beneath her cheek. That would be the reason.

She opened the curtains in Mr Francis's study one morning, and looking out at the winter landscape she was surprised to see him mounting his horse and riding away. The groom looking up at the window saw her and gave a wave. She raised her hand and turned to start her chores. Wonder where he's going so early? It's not yet a quarter to six and still dark. But she remembered Cook's advice to not see or hear anything and dismissed the question from her mind. She finished the study and, first knocking on the door, she entered the sitting room. She put down her dustpan and brush and went across to the window to open the curtains.

'Who are you?'

The sudden voice startled her and she jumped. 'Oh! I'm sorry, ma'am. I didn't see you there.' Mrs Francis was sitting in a high-backed chair hidden from Emily's view as she'd come in through the door.

'What's your name? Are you new? Have I seen you before?' The questions were abrupt, requiring an immediate answer.

'Only when I've brought up breakfast, ma'am,' she stammered. 'Emily Hawkins is my name and yes, I haven't been here long. This is my first position.' She stood in front of Mrs Francis, unsure of whether to withdraw or wait for dismissal.

'Fetch me a cup of tea and toast,' Mrs Francis demanded. 'You can do your chores later.' She shivered. 'I'm cold. Get someone to light the fire.' Her face was pinched and her eyes looked tired. She still wore her bedgown and robe and a cap upon her head, from which dark hair strayed out.

'Yes, ma'am.' Emily hurried downstairs in search of Janet. 'Be quick,' she said. 'Make some tea and toast for Mrs Francis and we have to light 'fire straight away. She's in 'sitting room!'

'What's this? What's this? Madam's up?' Mrs Castle took charge. 'You must take up 'tea and toast, Emily, if that's what she said. Janet, go up now and light 'fire. Come on, quick as lightning or you'll know what for!'

Emily set a tray as Jane toasted the bread. 'Mr Francis must have disturbed her,' she commented. 'I've just seen him ride off.'

'Have you now?' Mrs Castle set a silver teapot down on the tray. 'Well, never mind that, off you go and mind you don't spill. And ask 'mistress if she would like you to pour,' she called after Emily as she went up the kitchen stairs to the hall.

She didn't know why she felt so nervous in front of Mrs Francis. She had felt no qualms or apprehension with Mr Francis, he had a quiet gentle manner, but there was a look about Mrs Francis which disturbed her. It's because she is tired, I expect. She can't have slept well. 'Would you like me to pour the tea, ma'am, or shall I leave you?'

Janet had made the fire and quietly slipped away.

'Pour,' she said, scrutinizing Emily, 'and when I have finished you can come upstairs and help me back to bed. I won't want breakfast, so make sure that no-one disturbs me.'

'Poor lady has a lot to put up with,' Mrs Castle remarked when later a relieved Emily came back into the kitchen after helping Mrs Francis to bed and drawing the curtains tightly so that the early morning light didn't disturb her. There were just the two of them in the kitchen. 'Pop 'kettle on, Em, and we'll have a cup o' tea afore others come in for breakfast.'

'Mrs Francis doesn't seem very happy,' Emily said, temporarily forgetting Mrs Castle's former entreaty not to discuss her employers.

Mrs Castle appeared to have forgotten it too, for she nodded and said, 'Aye, it's not a happy family in spite of all its wealth and land.'

'What was Mr Francis like when he was a young man?' Emily asked as she poured boiling water on to the leaves. 'He was handsome, I expect, but was he so quiet as he is now?'

'No! He was as jolly a young fellow as you could find anywhere, allus laughing and joking and then – and then', her voice tailed away as she remembered, 'well, like I say, it doesn't do to gossip. No good comes of it. But all I'll say, Emily, and this is between you and me, they've had misfortune in this family and through no fault of anybody's as far as we can tell. The hand of God must have been there.' She looked pensive as she sipped her tea. 'Or mebbe it was Devil's work. Who knows?'

They heard the sound of a voice calling and Mrs Castle jumped to her feet. 'Quick. Go upstairs! That's Miss Deborah. Don't let her disturb her mother. Find Mrs Brewer if you can, she'll take care of her.'

Deborah Francis was standing at the bottom of the hall stairs in her bedgown and without her robe, her dark hair unbrushed and hanging about her shoulders. 'Where's Betty?' she complained as Emily appeared. 'I want Betty.' She stamped her foot, which Emily thought a very childish thing to do, especially as Miss Deborah was no longer a child but must have been all of twenty-one or -two.

'Betty, Miss Deborah?' Emily didn't know of a Betty.

'Betty! Betty Brewer, silly. Who are you, anyway?'

Deborah Francis was often asleep when Emily had taken in the breakfast tray, quietly opening the curtains and then slipping out of the room again.

'I'm here! I'm here!' Mrs Brewer bustled down the stairs. 'Whatever are you doing up so early, Miss Deborah? It's not yet eight o'clock.' She took hold of her mistress's arm. 'Come along, back upstairs and we'll have a nice cup of tea, all tucked up in bed.'

'Mama's door is locked, Betty. I can't get in,' she said petulantly. 'I knocked and knocked but she won't answer.'

'Hush now.' Mrs Brewer soothed her as she led her upstairs. 'Mama is not well this morning, we must let her have her rest. You can see her later.'

Deborah Francis turned half-way up the stairs. 'Who is that girl, Betty? I don't know her.'

'Emily. She hasn't been here for very long. You'll soon get used to seeing her about.'

Emily looked upwards and gave her young mistress a slight smile. She seemed younger than her years. Almost childlike.

'She's pretty, isn't she, Betty? She's very pretty.' She stopped again on the stairs. 'Is she prettier than me, do you think?'

'Not at all.' Mrs Brewer was appeasing as she ushered her onwards. 'Nowhere near as pretty as you. Quite plain in fact.'

But Miss Deborah had taken a fancy to seeing Emily again. Mrs Brewer came into the kitchen later in the day and asked Emily to take tea into Miss Deborah in the sitting room, when normally Mrs Brewer would have taken it in herself. 'She will have you bring it, Emily. She wants to take another look at you. Be patient with her, won't you? Try not to aggravate her.'

Why would I aggravate her? Emily wondered. And why does she want to see me?

She wanted to see her in a good light. That is what she said. 'You looked quite pretty this morning when I saw you, Emily,' she said. 'But I wondered if it was a trick of the light. Mama says that it can be. Stand by the window and turn around, please.'

Emily put the tray on a small table and obligingly turned slowly around, then she bobbed her knee and said, 'Will that be all, Miss Deborah?'

'No. Pour the tea and tell me who you are and where you are from.'

Emily poured the tea into a dainty china teacup

and handed it to her. 'I'm Emily Hawkins, Miss Deborah, and I lived with my grandmother until she died.' Near enough, she thought, no need to tell her all about Granny Edwards.

'And where are your parents? Or are you an orphan?' Deborah stared at her from wide-set blue eyes.

'Yes, miss. I'm an orphan, I think.'

'You only think? Why don't you know?'

'My father is dead and I don't know where my mother or brother are.'

'You have a brother?' Deborah put down her cup and clapped her hands joyfully. 'Just like me. I have a brother too.' She put her head on one side and considered. 'Only I think he might be dead!'

The door slowly opened and Mrs Francis appeared, her face was pale and her eyes had dark shadows beneath them. 'What is all this chatter, Deborah? I've told you that you mustn't gossip with the servants.'

Emily bobbed her knee. 'I was just leaving, ma'am,' and was relieved to see Mrs Brewer coming through the door.

'Miss Deborah wanted to talk to Emily, ma'am,' Mrs Brewer explained. 'I thought you wouldn't mind.'

Mrs Francis sank wearily into a chair. 'No,' she said. 'I don't really. It is a distraction, I suppose.'

Mrs Brewer indicated that Emily should leave the room, and bobbing her knee she left.

'Is she trustworthy, Mrs Brewer?' Mrs Francis turned tired eyes towards the housekeeper. 'Or will she tittle-tattle?'

'She seems very reliable, ma'am, and she has no immediate family, so she has no-one to gossip with apart from the other servants, and they are all discreet.'

'She has a brother, Mama, just like me,' Deborah interrupted, then looked vague. 'Or – I'm not sure if she said he was dead.' She shrugged. 'She's an orphan, anyway.'

Mrs Francis gazed vacantly out of the window. 'That's all right then,' she sighed.

Chapter Seven

All through the winter Emily was at the mercy of Miss Deborah's every whim. It must be Emily who helped her dress, Emily who brought her tea, Emily who should walk with her in the snow-filled gardens and if Emily was unavailable, busy with other chores, then Miss Deborah had a vicious tantrum of screaming which sent the whole household into a spin.

'We should be thankful I suppose that Emily is a patient, resourceful girl,' Roger Francis remarked to his wife as he handed her into the carriage, as once more they had managed to allay a difficult bout of temper from their daughter over a visit to a neighbour.

'There's something about her that I can't quite make out,' Mrs Francis began, 'but she's patient with Deborah, I agree. She tires everyone else so, with her constant chatter and questions.' Mrs Francis barely looked at her husband as he placed a rug around her. 'I am at the end of my tether. I don't know how much more I can stand.'

Mrs Francis hadn't wanted Deborah to go with her on the visit, but in a fit of resentment Deborah had insisted and had started to shout and scream when told that she couldn't. Her father couldn't calm her and neither could Mrs Brewer. Mrs Francis suggested that she be given a sedative, but Mr Francis demurred. Mrs Francis had stormed up to her room and in desperation Mrs Brewer had sent for Emily.

'Miss Deborah! I wonder if you would play the piano again,' Emily had dared to ask. 'I heard you the other morning and it sounded so lovely. I've never heard it played before.'

'Never heard the piano!' Deborah stopped shouting. 'What nonsense, Emily! Of course you have. Everyone plays.'

Deborah was a poor musician, but Emily didn't know that. She simply thought that the sound coming from the instrument was magical. She shook her head. 'I've never heard it, miss.'

Emily felt Miss Deborah's eyes staring into hers and wondered if she was going to have another fit of temper at her temerity. But she gave a sudden laugh. 'Good gracious, girl.' She unconsciously mimicked Mrs Francis's voice. 'Come over here and I will show you.'

Roger Francis was watching by the fireplace as his daughter sat at the piano and arranged her music and fussily told Emily where she should stand so that she could take particular notice. Emily glanced towards him and saw that he was watching, not his daughter, but her. He gave her what seemed to be a sad smile and then turned away.

'Tell Mama I can't go with her,' Deborah called after him. 'I can't be bothered with ladies' gossip today.'

Roger Francis watched from his library window as the carriage bearing his wife rolled away down the drive, leaving wheel marks on the fresh snow. He stood vaguely gazing into space and only half-listening to the discordant jangle of music coming from the drawing room, where his daughter entertained the maid Emily. He looked down at his desk at the pile of papers lying there and as if with a sudden, swift decision, crossed the room and pressed the bell by the fireplace.

'Tell Brown to saddle up a horse,' he told Janet. 'I have to ride into Hull.'

By the early spring Emily was weary of her mistress's demands. 'I think I'd rather be scrubbing 'kitchen floor instead of you, Jane,' she said as they climbed into bed. 'There's no wonder that Mrs Francis is always tired. Miss Deborah is exhausting.'

'Hmph. I don't think you'd like to swap,' Jane said cynically. 'You get excused all kinds of jobs just 'cos Miss Deborah wants you with her.'

'I still do my other chores,' Emily retaliated. 'I still get up as early as you. Anyway, you wouldn't like it being constantly badgered; do this, Emily, do that, Emily, come here, Emily. I'm prettier than you, Emily.' She put her chin in her hands. 'Thank goodness she doesn't get up early, at least I can have some peace when I'm cleaning out the fire grates.'

The next morning she lit the library fire and laid the sticks ready in the drawing room for lighting later, and crossed the hall to the sitting room. She heard footsteps upstairs and, glancing up, saw Mr Francis crossing the landing. She hurried down the kitchen stairs to tell Cook that Mr Francis was up and would probably want an early breakfast and then rushed back upstairs to the sitting room to clean and light the fire.

She drew the curtains and a smile lit her face, primroses were appearing just below the window and there was a haze of green on the trees in the meadows. Soon she would have a day off and she would go for a long walk, maybe even go as far as the river bank if she had time.

She bent to brush out the dead wood ash from the hearth, leaving a small amount to relight the new fire. She hummed to herself as she worked and didn't hear the door open, but she stopped abruptly and looked over her shoulder as someone brushed against her and she felt her hair tumbling around her shoulders.

'Miss Deborah!' She rose to her feet in dismay. Her mistress was standing behind her, only half-dressed and triumphantly waving Emily's hairclips in her hands.

'Miss Deborah, I shall get into trouble, please give them back.'

Deborah snatched at Emily's hair, which shone like silk and reached almost to her waist. 'It's like a curtain, Emily.' She danced around her. 'I shall insist that you always wear it like that.' She stopped abruptly. Then she came a step nearer and gently touched Emily's cheek. 'You are lovely, Emily.' Her mouth pouted. 'Mrs Brewer says you're not prettier than me but she's lying. She's lying.' Her voice rose and she turned as the door opened and her father came into the room.

'Papa! Look at Emily!'

Mr Francis did look at Emily, and Emily didn't know what to do as Mr Francis gazed at her with her hair hanging loose about her shoulders. She saw an Adam's apple move in his throat as he swallowed hard.

Deborah stroked Emily's cheek again. 'Look at Emily, Papa. Isn't she lovely? Mrs Brewer says she isn't, but she is. Isn't she?' Her voice was insistent.

'I am looking at her, Deborah. Yes she is.' His voice was soft. 'She's very lovely indeed. Mrs Brewer was wrong.' He took a deep breath and, with his eyes still on Emily, said, 'Now be a good girl, Deborah, and give Emily her hairpins back so that she can fasten up her hair.'

'No! I won't! She can buy some more. I shall wear these in my hair.' She stuck the pins in her own dishevelled hair and screaming with laughter she ran out of the room and up the stairs.

'I'm sorry, Emily. My daughter can be difficult sometimes,' he began, but she said swiftly, 'It's all right sir, I can borrow some more and get mine back later.' But her eyes were drawn to the open door and the stairs beyond and the figure of Mrs Francis in her nightclothes coming downstairs.

'What are we to do with her? There is no consideration for me.' Mrs Francis's voice was tense as she came through the door. 'A decision must be made.' Then she saw Emily standing facing her husband as if they had been in conversation. Her already pale face whitened even further and she put her hand on the door to steady herself. 'It can't be.' She stared hard at Emily and then her husband and then back to Emily. She shook her head as if to clear it. 'Not her daughter? Not here?' She stared at her husband with such a look of hatred that Emily shivered. 'You wouldn't do such a thing!'

'Don't be ridiculous!' he burst out. 'You're mistaken.'

'I think not,' she said slowly and deliberately. 'I always thought there was something familiar about her.'

'You are mistaken,' he repeated, then turning to Emily he dismissed her and she thankfully hurried downstairs to the kitchen, where she burst into tears.

'Whatever's wrong? What's happened to your hair?' Mrs Castle rubbed her floury hands on her apron and scurried across to the dresser, where she delved into a drawer and brought out a handful of hairpins. 'Come here, let me pin it up for you.'

She sat Emily on a chair and wound her hair into a bun. 'Janey, go and get some more coal for 'fire. Go on! Don't stand there gawping.'

'Now then,' she said, when Jane had left the room, 'this is Miss Deborah's doing, isn't it? She's at 'bottom of this?'

Emily nodded and wiped her tears and explained what had happened. 'I'm frightened of losing my job, Mrs Castle. Mrs Francis wasn't pleased with me. She said something – I don't know what she meant – about me being somebody's daughter!'

'Did she?' Mrs Castle put in the final pin and patted her shoulder. 'Well, no point in worrying about owt until it happens. And if she does want you to leave, well I'm sure that Mr Francis will give you a reference.'

Emily stared at her. 'But – I haven't done anything! I've done what I can for Miss Deborah. I don't understand!'

'I told you!' Mrs Castle rinsed her hands in the stone sink, dried them and then dipped her hand into a bag of flour and sprinkled it on to the table. 'I told you that there would be things that you wouldn't understand. This is one of them.'

Emily took a deep breath. 'Miss Deborah – is she –?'

The question lay unspoken between them. Mrs Castle glanced towards the door. 'She's not mad, if that's what you mean, at least not as mad as her brother. But', she tapped a finger to her forehead, 'there's summat a bit loose in 'top storey.'

Emily whispered. 'Her brother? She mentioned her brother.'

'Aye. He's her twin. He's in 'asylum for 'insane, poor fellow. But Miss Deborah's just a bit wild, though sometimes you might think she's heading 'same way.' She pounded a hunk of dough. 'It runs in 'family unfortunately.'

Mrs Francis always looks as if she's on the edge of something, Emily pondered, though you would think that living with Miss Deborah would be enough to drive anybody over. 'From Mrs Francis's side?' she said urgently as she heard Jane fumbling with the door latch.

'Bless you, no!' Mrs Castle stopped her pummelling. 'From Mr Francis's family. Onny nobody told him till it was too late!'

＊　　＊　　＊

Mr Francis sent for Emily later in the day. She knocked on the library door and entered to find him sitting by the fire in his high-backed leather chair. He looked tired, she thought, his blue eyes were heavy and rather sad, but he greeted her with a smile and invited her to sit down opposite him. She hesitated. 'Do sit down, Emily. Don't be afraid. I need to talk to you about my daughter.'

She perched uncomfortably on the edge of the chair. It doesn't seem right, she thought. I should be standing up.

'What I have to say is not because of anything you have done, you must understand that. We have been very pleased with your work.' He tapped his fingers against his beard as he considered. 'But my wife – Mrs Francis and I – in view of Miss Deborah's attachment to you, which, although it seems amicable at the moment –'. He got up from his chair and started to pace up and down. Emily too stood up. 'It could turn. She – she gets these attachments to people, but then turns against them.' He looked almost pleadingly at her and she felt so sorry for him. 'She is rather – delicate, I'm afraid, prone to moods.'

'I understand, sir.'

'Do you, Emily?' He shook his head. 'I think not.'

'What do you want me to do, sir? Would you like me to leave?' Better get it over and done with, she thought, but where will I go?

He nodded and appeared relieved. 'It would be for the best all round, I think.'

'Would you give me a reference, sir? I won't

be able to get employment without one.' It's not fair, she deliberated. How has this happened to me?

'I'll do better than that.' He sat down again. 'I have talked to Mrs Francis about this and we have agreed that this situation is not your fault and therefore we must do what we can for you.'

Mrs Francis wouldn't care what happens to me, Emily thought. She is not in the least interested in any of her servants. But she listened as he explained what they were willing to do. 'Mrs Francis has a second cousin who lives in Hull. She often has difficulty in getting good servants and I thought that if you were willing to work in the town, I would write to her suggesting that she takes you – perhaps as a lady's maid rather than in general service?'

How odd, she thought, that Mr Francis should be doing all of this. I always thought that the mistress of the house dealt with servants.

'So, what do you think? Could you bear to tear yourself away from the country and live in a town?' He smiled gently and she thought how handsome he must once have been.

'I don't know, sir. I've never been to a big town, although I've been to Hedon market.'

His eyes crinkled. 'Hull is nothing like Hedon. It is a big, bustling place. It's full of sailing ships, seamen and tradesmen. It's noisy with lots of people. It has theatres and music halls, shops of every description, and a big fair every year, much bigger than the village fairs. But', he added, 'you have only lived in the quiet of the country. You may not like it. I don't want to persuade you against your will. If you don't want to go then we will think of something else.'

She considered. What other option had she? 'Could I think about it, sir? Just for an hour?'

'Of course.' He pursed his lips. 'I would rather you didn't talk to the other servants of the reason for your leaving, perhaps you could tell them that you are considering another situation?' He saw her hesitation. 'Except perhaps Cook or Mrs Brewer? They would understand. They have been here a long time.'

Mrs Castle and Mrs Brewer were sitting at the kitchen table having a glass of ale when she went slowly downstairs. Mrs Castle had obviously primed Mrs Brewer about the situation, for she looked directly at Emily and asked bluntly, 'I suppose they've asked you to leave?'

She nodded. 'Yes. Mr Francis has asked me if I want to go to someone in Hull. He'll give me a reference.'

Mrs Castle snorted. 'That'll be mistress's doing. The further away the better.'

Emily turned an enquiring eye on her. 'Mr Francis said I could discuss it with you and Mrs Brewer but not with 'others. I don't know what to do,' she pleaded. 'What shall I do?'

'Go, my lovely,' Mrs Castle said, and Mrs Brewer nodded in agreement. 'It was a mistake you ever coming here.'

'What do you mean?' Emily asked in astonishment.

'Mr Francis suggested that I came. I didn't ask him for employment.'

'I know that.' Mrs Castle looked down at her glass and swirled the bubbles around. 'I didn't say it was your mistake. It was his. The master's.'

Chapter Eight

Brown the groom drove her in the trap to Hedon, where she was to catch the carrier into Hull. She had said goodbye to Mrs Castle and Mrs Brewer and Jane and the other staff and also to Mr Francis, who gave her a shilling. He pressed the coin into her hand and said earnestly, 'If ever you need help, Emily, do not hesitate to contact me.'

She thanked him and as she was about to leave, she said, 'I worry over Sam, sir. I hope he'll always have work.'

He seemed to hesitate as if there was something else he wanted to say, but merely nodded and murmured, 'Don't worry over Samuel. I'll make sure that he is all right.'

Of Mrs Francis and Deborah she saw nothing, they were busy in their rooms with two of the maids, supervising the wardrobes they would need for an unexpected holiday they were taking and Miss Deborah appeared to have forgotten of Emily's existence already.

'I'm sorry tha's going, Emily,' Brown grinned at her. 'I was hoping that in a bit I'd ask thee to walk out wi' me.'

She blushed and turned her head. 'I'm not quite fourteen yet,' she said.

'I know. I'd already asked Cook how old you was and she said even if you was old enough you'd still be too good for likes o' me! But I expect tha'll soon find some fellow in Hull who'll be good enough,' he added.

'I don't know.' It wasn't something she had thought about, although she was aware of Brown's cheeky grin and saucy comments, and some of the other men who worked about the house and grounds who winked at her or sometimes pinched her cheek. Jane, she knew, already had her eye on Brown. She had said as much already. 'I'm going to get married and move out of here just as soon as I can,' she had said, and even when Emily had told her that she would only be exchanging one kitchen floor for another, she said she didn't care, at least it would be her own floor and not somebody else's.

They passed the school at Thorngumbald and she pointed it out to Brown. 'I expect tha was glad to leave there,' he said. 'I never went to school, but I was allus good wi' hosses so it didn't matter.'

'Oh, no,' she said. 'I liked it. I was sorry to leave, it was only because of Granny Edwards being ill that I left.' She smiled. 'We learned about 'rest of 'country and where the rivers went, and about other parts of the world. Did you know', she said enthusiastically, 'that ships from Hull travel all around the world, even to 'Arctic and America and Australia?'

'I know that,' he said scornfully. 'Didn't have to

go to school to learn that! My da told me that, years ago.'

Suitably chastened, she dropped into silence as they travelled along the road. There had been rain overnight and there was a fresh clean smell of burgeoning growth, of buds and blossom about to open. A spring greening of barley covered some of the fields, where formerly sheep had grazed on winter turnips, whilst in others men and horses were drilling the corn beds on the heavy clay. Rooks were building their nests high in the trees and she could hear the bleat of newly weaned lambs.

'I'll miss all of this,' she murmured, almost to herself, as Brown pointed with his whip to where two Jack hares were up on their hind legs, squaring up to each other.

'You will.' He urged the pony on towards Hedon. 'Hull is full o' fighting men and foreigners and dirt and noise. I wouldn't swap places wi' you for another ten bob a year.'

He lifted her bag down from the trap when they reached the Market Place and then put his hand up to help her down. 'Wilt tha give us a kiss then, Emily?' he grinned, keeping his hand on her waist. 'Just this once.'

'All right,' she agreed and put her cheek towards him. But she gave him a sharp push away when he sought her mouth with his and she felt his slippery tongue in her mouth. 'Stop it!' She slapped his arm. 'You're horrid!'

He laughed and smacked her rear. 'No I'm not! Tha'll get worse than that from 'fellows in Hull, so don't think tha won't!'

She turned away, her cheeks burning with shame. Poor Jane, she thought, if he's the man she wants to marry!

It was the middle of the afternoon when she arrived in Hull and the carrier deposited her at the Black Swan in Mytongate, from where she walked to the Market Place. She had expected the town to be busy, but she hadn't expected such a cacophony of noise, of people shouting, of traders calling their wares, of dogs barking, and the rattle and jingle of harness from the horses which clip-clopped down the cobbled road pulling carts, traps and coaches. She asked the way to Parliament Street, where Mrs Purnell, the cousin of Mrs Francis, had her home.

'Cut across by Holy Trinity Church, love, then down Whitefriargate and then you're there,' said the woman she asked. 'No more'n a couple o' minutes.' She looked Emily up and down. 'You from 'country? A servant lass?'

'Yes. I'm going to Mrs Purnell,' she volunteered, thinking that as in the country everyone would know who was who. 'Is it always busy like this?'

The woman laughed. 'This is nowt! You should see it in a morning. Can't move for folk. Listen,' she bent towards Emily, 'tek care. There's allus somebody on lookout for a green lass like yourself. Not that I suppose you'll get out much if you're working for posh folks like them in Parliament Street. They'll want their pound o' flesh, I don't doubt.'

She waved a cheery goodbye and Emily, feeling heartened by her friendly manner, pressed on the way she had been told. Parliament Street was a street of tall houses with scrubbed white steps leading up to doors with shining brassware, just off the main thoroughfare of Whitefriargate, which was filled with busy shops. She stopped to look at the hats and gowns, the embossed silks and cottons which were displayed, at the shoes and boots made from the softest leather and then looked down at her own clumsy boots, her flannel skirt and shirt and her thick wool shawl. I'll never be able to afford any of these things, she mused, but at least I can look. I have never, ever seen such things before.

She looked at the piece of paper in her hand to check the number of the house and then walked down to the end of Parliament Street to find the rear entrance. There was a cramped, narrow passageway behind the houses with a high wall bordering another building, and after checking the number again she opened a gate into a small yard, went down the steps to the kitchen door and rang the bell.

'So why did you see fit to leave Mrs Francis's employ?' Mrs Purnell, a stout, rather jolly-looking woman, with several wobbly chins which escaped from the strings of her silk cap, interviewed Emily herself. She was nothing at all like her aloof relation, Mrs Francis. She wore a magnificent gown of ruched maroon silk which emphasized her size and spread all over the sofa on which she sat drinking tea.

'It was thought best, ma'am. Miss Deborah had taken a fancy to me and wanted me by her side all of the time. It was difficult to do my work.'

'And I suppose she had a tantrum if she couldn't have you with her, was that it?'

'Yes, ma'am.'

'I see that this letter which was sent ahead of you comes from Mr Francis, not my cousin. Why is that, do you think?' She stared from small brown eyes at Emily.

It was rather strange, Emily agreed, but she answered, 'I didn't see much of Mrs Francis, ma'am. I – I don't think she was well, and Mr Francis gave me employment in the first place,' she added.

'Hm. Well, I wouldn't be in good health either if I'd had a son and daughter like hers.' She considered Emily. 'Turn around, girl, let me have a look at you.'

Emily swivelled slowly around for inspection.

'You're young and your clothes are dreadful,' Mrs Purnell commented. 'But you're neat and your manners are good, so I suppose I can soon shape you. I'll give you a month's trial and see how you fare. My other maid had to leave – got into trouble with some fellow.' She shook her finger at Emily. 'I'm quite lenient, but I don't stand for that kind of thing, not with my servants. Still,' she continued to gaze at Emily, 'you're too young yet for that sort of behaviour. Be a good girl and I'm sure we'll get on.'

'You're rather young for a lady's maid,' Mrs Anderson the housekeeper sniffed, on being told she was to be employed. 'And why 'mistress has to choose country girls, I really don't know. They don't know 'first thing about style or fashion. Can you sew?' she said abruptly.

'Yes.' Emily was apprehensive. The atmosphere in this kitchen was quite different from the one at

88

Elmswell Manor, which was ruled by Mrs Castle and Mrs Brewer in a strict but fair manner. Here Cook lazed by the fire with a glass of ale in her hand and her table was littered with cooking utensils which no-one was attempting to clear. 'I have to do general work as well,' she explained. 'Mrs Purnell said so, until I'm properly trained.'

Mrs Anderson seemed pacified by this and took Emily to the top of the house, where she was shown into a boxlike room beneath the eaves. 'This is where the other maid slept, it's 'only room left so it's no use complaining.'

I wasn't going to, Emily thought. There doesn't seem much point. The bed was narrow and pushed up against the wall, leaving just enough room for a small chest of drawers on which there was a jug and bowl for washing and a candle holder with a stub of candle in it; above the bed was an embroidered text with the words: *'A Servant Girl's Prayer. Dear Lord, make me Chaste and Penitent. Make me Obedient and Dutiful to my Master's Wishes and Desires. Amen.'*

'Do I share with anyone?' she asked, hoping the answer would be no. There was hardly room for one let alone two people.

'No. This is yours, so keep it clean and tidy. And no visitors allowed, especially not male!' She lowered her voice. 'I don't believe in maids having a room to themselves. It's better that they share, then there's always somebody who knows what they're getting up to.'

Emily stared uncomprehendingly. 'I'm very tidy,' she said, 'and I don't know anybody who would call.'

Mrs Anderson turned to leave. 'Not yet you don't, but you will.' She stopped and looked again at Emily. 'With that pretty face you'll soon have a host of admirers, so keep them at arm's length. Especially 'gentry,' she added darkly, 'they're worse than anybody.'

There appeared to be only Mrs Purnell living in the house, with a cook, a housekeeper, two kitchen maids and two housemaids, Dolly and Susan, to look after her, and Arnold, who drove the gig when Mrs Purnell went calling and who fetched and carried in a general kind of way. But Mrs Purnell loved to entertain and a constant stream of visitors came for luncheon or supper, when they played backgammon or crib.

'If you think we're busy now,' Dolly had commented after an afternoon when Mrs Purnell had entertained six ladies for tea, 'you wait till Mr Hugo comes home. It's all parties and dancing, and you should hear 'racket they make. Sometimes even 'neighbours complain.'

'Who's Mr Hugo?' Mr Purnell had died some years before. That much Emily knew when Mrs Purnell had described herself as a poor widow. 'Is he a son?'

Dolly nodded. 'He's gone abroad.' She'd glanced towards Mrs Anderson and lowered her voice. 'We don't know why, but we can guess!'

'Door, Emily!' The bell on the wall jangled one morning and Emily straightened her cap, smoothed her apron and hurried up the stairs to the door. In the month she had been here, Mrs

Anderson now said she preferred Emily to answer the door, as she was more likely to look presentable to visitors than either of the other maids, which Emily accepted as a compliment and Dolly and Susan sanctioned as one less chore to be endured.

She unfastened the latch and opened the door, expecting to greet Mrs Purnell's usual group of ladies. A tall, slim young man dressed in naval uniform, with thick dark hair and his hat in his hand, stood on the doorstep. 'Good morning, sir.' She bobbed her knee.

'Good morning. Is Mr Hugo Purnell at home?'

'I'm sorry, sir. Mr Hugo is away at present. May I say who called?'

He rubbed his hand across his chin, where a dark stubble was about to grow into a beard. 'Philip Linton. I had hoped to see him,' he murmured. 'When will he be back, do you know?'

She shook her head. He seemed rather perplexed, she thought. 'Mrs Purnell is at home, sir. Would you like me to ask?'

'I would. Thank you.' He gave her a sudden smile, which changed his sombre expression to a merry one. 'If Mrs Purnell is not too busy, would you give her my compliments and ask if I might see her?'

She invited him in and scurried to find Mrs Purnell, who was having coffee alone in her sitting room. 'Fetch him in,' she exclaimed. 'He's just the man to brighten my morning! He's so handsome! Didn't you think he was handsome, Emily?'

Emily smiled. She was getting used to Mrs

Purnell's odd ways and knew when not to overstep the mark by becoming too familiar.

'Well? Do you think he's handsome or not? Don't tell me that you're still a child and didn't notice!'

'He is very handsome, ma'am. Very – upright in his bearing.'

Mrs Purnell chortled. 'Very upright! Well yes, I suppose he is. That's because he's a Trinity House man. Hmph.' Her mouth turned down. 'A navy man, just as my Hugo should have been. Go on then, send him in!'

'Mrs Purnell will see you now, sir, if you would like to come through.' She put out her hand for his hat and her fingers brushed against his. He smiled at her and she gave him a shy smile in return.

'Have you been here long?' he asked. 'I don't remember seeing you before.'

'Just over a month, sir.' She put his hat on the hall stand and led him to the sitting room. He was handsome, she thought. He's the first handsome man that I've noticed. She felt a prickle on the back of her neck and her cheeks flushed as she felt that his eyes were on her as he walked behind her.

She opened the door to the sitting room. 'Mr Philip Linton, ma'am.'

Chapter Nine

'How nice to see you, Philip, and how very handsome in your uniform, but you've missed my boy, I'm afraid.' Mrs Purnell smiled coquettishly at her visitor. 'He just upped and went a couple of months ago, said he was tired of the dull life here and was going abroad. Italy, I think he said.'

'Oh!' Philip Linton mouthed his regrets at missing Hugo, but privately he was very annoyed. Hugo owed him money and had vowed he would let him have it by March at the latest. Here they were almost in May and the blackguard had gone. He doubted that he would get it back. Others had lent him money too, he had heard, but they'd never seen it again. 'I don't suppose you know when he'll be back, ma'am?'

'Would he tell his mother! No, I have no idea at all. He will be admiring the treasures of Rome I wouldn't wonder.'

And not just the art treasures, Philip mused. He had an eye for other kinds of beauty too, had Hugo Purnell.

'Between you and me,' Mrs Purnell said indulgently, 'I think he has gone to escape some young woman's clutches! He wouldn't have gone off in such a hurry otherwise. Will you have coffee, Philip?'

She rang the bell and asked Emily to bring another pot of coffee and a plate of biscuits. 'Talking of treasures,' she chatted after Emily had left the room, 'I think I've found one. Such a good girl. It's so difficult to find staff nowadays and even harder to keep them. Not that young men like you have that problem! Put the tray here by me,' she said when Emily came back. 'Your parents,' she continued, 'they are well, I trust? And your sisters? They will soon be of marrying age, I suppose.'

He smiled. 'Not quite, ma'am. Anna is seventeen, Louise only fourteen. And yes, my parents were well when I last saw them.'

'And what are you doing back in Hull? Not still studying?'

'Yes, ma'am. I'm taking further navigational examinations next week, then I will be travelling to Portsmouth. I hope to be given orders soon after.'

'Ah!' She sipped her coffee and gazed at him from above the rim of her cup. 'Hugo doesn't owe you money, does he?'

He hesitated. The loan was between him and Hugo, not his mother, but he needed the money. His pay as a lieutenant was adequate but only just, and though his family would give him a loan if he wanted it, he preferred to be independent and was loath to ask his father to help him out. Besides, he would be given a lecture on lending money to unsuitable friends. Not that Hugo was a particular friend, just someone he had known for a long time.

'How much does he owe you?' she persisted. 'Come along, you might as well tell me.'

'Fifty guineas, ma'am.'

'Fifty guineas! Whatever would he need that kind of money for? He can never have spent his allowance already!'

Philip didn't answer. Hugo always had plenty of money when his allowance came, but he spent it. He spent it on gambling, wine and women. He had always spent money, even from the age of ten when he and Philip had first started at Trinity House as young cadets. But Hugo found the studying too arduous and he had had several brushes with the Brethren, mostly over non-attendance or being improperly dressed; he never wore his velvet stock and his uniform of blue tailed dress coat and white stand-up collar was usually crumpled or dirty; his tall beaver hat was battered and dusty having been kicked around on the way to school and he constantly missed church parade on a Sunday. He only just scraped into the upper school and eventually he was called before the headmaster and asked to leave, whereas Philip finished his schooling in marine science and was apprenticed to a master mariner to continue his career.

'I wish he'd stayed on at Trinity House,' Mrs Purnell sighed. 'I don't know what he will do with his life. I hope he marries someone rich,' she added, 'for his own money won't last long at the rate he's spending it!'

Philip fidgeted. He wished he hadn't stayed, he had no desire to hear any more about Hugo Purnell and if he never saw his money again, well, so be it.

'You will get your dues, Philip. I will go to the bank this afternoon and arrange a promissory note. Where are your lodgings? I will have it sent round.'

He thanked her and said she mustn't trouble herself, he would call again before he left town. But she insisted. 'I will send Emily,' she determined. 'Say no more about it!'

Later that afternoon, Emily took off her white cap and apron, put on her cloak and bonnet and looked in the mirror. She was quite pleased with what she saw. Mrs Purnell supplied her maids with black skirts, crisp white blouses, and a grey cloak and bonnet, and Emily felt she looked very presentable. She held the package firmly in her hand, for Mrs Purnell had emphasized most strongly that it was very important and must not be lost or mislaid on any account, and set off to find Mr Linton's lodgings in a terrace just off Savile Street, which was situated, she had been told, at the side of the New Dock.

It was a soft, warm afternoon and Emily thought ruefully of how lovely it would be in the countryside that she had left. The young fledglings will be starting to fly, the perfume of the bluebells will be everywhere, and oh, she thought, the frogspawn will be floating like jelly in all the dykes and ditches. She remembered how she and her young friends used to gather it in a bucket to take home and watch the tadpoles turn into frogs. Though she was fairly well settled in Mrs Purnell's employ, she missed not having a garden or meadows to look at and she missed the clean sharp air of the river bank.

She didn't know the area in which she was now

living, as, apart from one or two occasions when she had been sent out to buy ribbons and cottons from the nearby shops in Whitefriargate, she hadn't had the opportunity to explore. I'll deliver the message safely, she mused, and then, because Mrs Purnell is out until evening and I won't be needed, I'll have a little look around.

'Afternoon, miss. Nice day!' A man standing on the bridge over Junction Dock, greeted her.

She nodded and smiled. 'Yes, lovely,' she agreed, and walked on. Mustn't talk to anybody strange, she thought. At least not until I have delivered the message. She changed the package from one hand to another, it seemed to be burning a hole in her palm, she held it so tightly, and she wondered vaguely what was in it.

She saw the huge dock as she crossed towards Savile Street and the mass of ships' masts and rigging, and heard the clatter and ring of porters' sleds as they unloaded cargo. She smelt also the strong odour of blubber and wrinkled her nose, for this was a whaling town and the products of the whale kept the whole town and its industry prosperous.

She hesitated as she determined her directions, then crossed over the street to where she could see a narrow terrace of houses. 'Are you lost, miss?' Another man spoke to her and she shook her head and hurried on. She didn't like the look of him. He was scruffily dressed with a scraggy beard and a woollen hat pulled over his head. She turned into the terrace, for this was the one she wanted, and looked up at the house doors for the right number. Then, startled, she half-turned as she felt a rough hand around her wrist, the package was snatched from her hand and she was given a blow to her shoulder, which sent her sprawling to the ground.

Philip put down the book he was studying and glanced at the clock on the mantelpiece. He yawned and stretched and got to his feet. Mrs Purnell had promised to send the promissory note that afternoon but hadn't said what time. He hoped it wouldn't be too long as he had business of his own to attend to. He walked to the window and looked out and saw the young maid, whom Mrs Purnell had described as a treasure, turn the corner and look up at the houses as if looking for a number.

He also saw two men turn the corner behind her, and in an instant he knew from their demeanour and dress that they had no business to conduct in this respectable terrace, and as he took breath, he saw their assault on the maid. He flung himself down the stairs and out of the door, shouting, 'Stop thief,' as he ran along the terrace. By the time he reached the girl he realized that the men would have vanished beyond the main street, disappearing into the mêlée of dock workers and seamen around the dock area.

'Are you hurt?' He bent down towards her. 'It's Emily, isn't it?'

Emily sat up, dazed. 'Mr Linton! The packet's gone! Those men –! What will Mrs Purnell say? Oh sir, I'm so sorry!'

He looked at the pale oval face and the blue eyes fringed by dark lashes and mused that she had the face of an angel. He helped her to her feet. 'Come inside for a moment, I'll get my landlady to make you a cup of tea. You're hurt,' he added, as she winced.

'I've wrenched my shoulder, I think,' and she held up her hands too and he saw her bleeding fingers and palms, which she had grazed as she fell.

He escorted her into the house and called for his landlady. He couldn't take Emily up to his room, that was one rule which couldn't be broken. But he knew that Mrs Summers wouldn't mind if he took her into her own sitting room. 'Mrs Summers, there has been an accident! Have you hot water and bandages?'

'You poor lamb!' Mrs Summers was all sympathy when she saw Emily's dishevelled state and heard what had happened, and she rushed to put the kettle on the fire.

Philip sat next to Emily and poured the hot water into a bowl and then cooled it, testing with his fingers to make sure it wasn't too hot, then he gently bathed her hands. He smiled at her and said, 'This is good practice for me, I have just been reading how to treat injuries. Don't worry,' he assured, as he saw a trickle of tears on her cheek, 'those thieves won't be able to use what was in the envelope. It would have been in my name.'

There was relief on her face, though she flinched as the water touched the wounds on her hands. 'I'm glad it wasn't money, sir. Mrs Purnell said to be particularly careful, and the envelope felt very thick.'

'Oh!' He groaned and closed his eyes in exasperation. The silly woman had never sent cash!

'It can't be helped,' he said lightly. 'It might have been money, but it seems I wasn't meant to have it.'

'I'm so sorry, sir. Could I – could I pay you back out of my wages? But it won't be until the end of the year.'

'No, Emily, you can't.' How long it would take her! 'And you don't have to keep calling me sir.'

'Begging your pardon, sir.' Her cheeks suddenly flushed. 'But I'm only a servant girl.'

'And I am only a sailor,' he said, hoping he hadn't embarrassed her. 'So we are equal. My name is Philip Linton.'

'Yes, I know, Mr Linton,' she said solemnly. 'I do remember it from this morning.'

'Yes. Yes, of course you do!' He felt suddenly foolish. The servants at his home had been with them for years and everyone had their place, but they were used to his informal manner.

I'm not used to dealing with young women, he thought, apart from Anna and Louise. But, servant or not, she was incredibly lovely, softly spoken with a hint of country and such beautiful silky hair. But young, he pondered, and probably very vulnerable. 'I'll walk you back to Mrs Purnell's and explain what has happened,' he insisted, wrapping a bandage around her hand, and thought that if he had called for the note himself then this would not have happened. 'I don't want you to get into trouble, it wasn't your fault. I saw exactly what happened.'

She demurred, saying that there was no need and that Mrs Purnell would be out until evening, but he insisted anyway and put on his jacket and escorted her along the terrace and into Savile Street.

'Do you know the area?' he asked. 'You don't sound like a Hull person.'

'I'm not, sir – Mr Linton. I'm from Holderness. It's a country district, east of Hull,' she explained. 'I've lived by the Humber for most of my life and then I went to work for Mr Francis at Elmswell Manor.'

'I know of Holderness, a very isolated place, I believe. And so you decided to come and savour the delights of the town, did you?'

She shook her head. 'I didn't really decide, it was decided for me.' She paused, thinking back to when she was sent to Granny Edwards as a child and of when Mr Francis suggested she might work for him, and yet again when she was sent to Mrs Purnell's. 'I don't think I have ever made a decision for myself, things just seem to happen.'

He nodded. 'Sometimes they do. We are not always in charge of our own fate. Would you like to see the ships?' he asked suddenly. 'Look, we're practically there.'

She hesitated. Would it be right, walking along with a young gentleman? Suppose Mrs Purnell saw her? 'I – er, I don't know,' she stammered.

'It's really only a detour,' he persuaded, wanting her company a little longer. 'A sort of long way round to where we are going anyway.'

Well, she thought, I was going to explore a little. Perhaps it might be all right. 'Yes please,' she said shyly. 'I would like that very much.'

They walked slowly around the perimeter of the dock and Philip pointed out the types of ships, the schooners with their sharply pointed bows, the specially strengthened whaling ships, the coal cutters and barges and he pointed out especially the oldest ship in the dock, the *Truelove*, the three-masted barque which had been captured during the American War of Independence and which was still plying the Arctic waters in search of the whale.

She noted that Philip Linton was greeted by cadets of Trinity House, smart in white duck trousers and gleaming brass buttons on their navy monkey jackets. She felt their admiring eyes upon her and some particularly paused and touched their hats, but Philip merely returned their greeting and walked on, not stopping to converse. They continued the circuit of the dock and came to the top of Whitefriargate.

'Thank you very much, Mr Linton,' she said. 'You have been very kind. There is no need for you to trouble yourself further. It's only a little way now.'

'Oh.' He sounded disappointed. 'But it is no trouble. No trouble at all,' and he insisted on continuing until they came to Mrs Purnell's house, where they mounted the steps and rang the front-door bell.

Mrs Anderson answered the door and her eyes grew wide when she saw Emily and Mr Linton standing there and Emily's hands in bandages. 'My compliments to Mrs Purnell,' Philip said, 'I'm afraid Emily has met with an accident. She was set upon by two ruffians,' he elaborated. 'I saw it happen from my window. She was very brave,' he added and deliberated that indeed she had been;

had the incident happened to either of his two sisters there would undoubtedly have been screaming and hysterics. 'I think she needs to rest for a while,' he said, keeping a poker face. 'She has had quite a shock.'

'Yes, sir. Very well, she can go to her room.'

'Thank you very much, Mr Linton,' Emily turned to him and saw the mischief glinting in his eyes. 'I'll explain to Mrs Purnell what happened.'

'Do,' he said, 'and tell her I will confirm it if she desires.'

She managed to escape the questioning of Cook, Dolly and Susan by pleading a headache and a request to lie down, which Mrs Anderson could hardly refuse as Mr Linton had suggested it also. 'It's as well that Mrs Purnell isn't back yet,' she grumbled. 'There'd be no lying down, headache or not, and don't be getting ideas above your station,' she cautioned, as Emily climbed the stairs. 'I saw the look in his eye and that can only mean trouble for a lass like you.'

Emily took off her cloak and bonnet and lay down on her bed. How kind Mr Linton had been, he had treated her so well, as if she was his equal. And he was handsome, she smiled to herself, Mrs Purnell was quite right. His dark eyes were merry and his mouth – she checked herself. I mustn't think of such things. It's not right. He's a young gentleman and I'm just a servant girl. He was only being kind, Emily. Don't be so foolish.

That she was foolish, Mrs Purnell was convinced. 'You should have kept it hidden beneath your cloak,' she grumbled later in the day when Emily confronted her with the news of the lost packet. 'I trusted you.'

Emily paled. Mrs Purnell surely didn't think she lost it on purpose, that she had been careless. 'I asked Mr Linton if I could pay it back out of my wages, Mrs Purnell, but he said not.'

Mrs Purnell gave a great shout of derision. 'Pay it back! Do you know how much was in there?'

Emily shook her head. 'No, ma'am.' How could she have known when Mrs Purnell hadn't told her.

'Fifty guineas! That's how much! How long do you think it would take you?' Mrs Purnell stared at her with a hostile expression, then seemed to relent. 'Go along. I suppose it wasn't your fault. I'll see Mr Linton about it. And send Mrs Anderson to me,' she called after her. 'I've heard there's cholera in the town so I've decided we shall go to Scarborough for the summer.'

Chapter Ten

One of Mrs Purnell's friends had another friend who knew an eminent doctor who had advised, in confidence, that there had been a case of cholera at the workhouse, which backed up against the houses in Parliament Street. Mrs Purnell had turned pale at the disclosure, she couldn't abide the thought of disease, and the news that cholera was practically at her door was enough for her to make an instant decision. Her friend, Mrs Marshall, was taking a house in Scarborough and invited her to share it. 'We can share a cook,' she said. 'Mine is excellent, and we'll take our own maids.'

Emily and Dolly were to go with her, and Cook and Mrs Anderson were to stay behind in Hull. 'I wish I could go,' Susan grumbled. 'There'll be nowt to do here.'

'There'll be plenty to do, my girl.' Mrs Anderson overheard her. 'We shall spring-clean the house from top to bottom whilst 'mistress is away. I'll be sure that if cholera strikes here it won't be because of any dirt in this house!'

'I heard say it's 'cos of dirty water.' Cook roused herself from her chair by the cooking range. 'But I don't believe that. 'Water looks clean enough to me.'

'Mrs Purnell and Mrs Marshall are going to travel by train.' Dolly butted in. 'I heard them talking when I took 'tea in. But you and me, Emily, are going by coach with 'luggage.'

'By train! I've never seen a train!' Emily was impressed. 'Oh, I wish it was us going on it, Dolly.'

'Dirty, noisy things,' Mrs Anderson snorted. 'They'll not last, mark my words. They're a novelty, that's all.'

Though she might have wished for the adventure of a train journey, as Emily stepped into the hired coach which was taking them on the long journey to Scarborough, she felt a thrill of excitement to be travelling in a proper coach, like a proper lady, even though she and Dolly were hemmed in by boxes and cases full of items which Mrs Purnell had deemed were absolutely essential for her summer stay at the spa resort.

'It can be very breezy at Scarborough,' she'd advised, so Emily packed her own warm shawl and an extra winter shift. 'It can also be very warm.' So Emily also packed lightweight cotton blouses, and for Mrs Purnell she packed two dozen dresses, some grand for the formal parties she would attend, and some simple, of plain brocade or satin, with fewer frills and ribbons, which would be worn for card parties or afternoon tea. She packed two warm coats and one thinner one, as well as a cloak with a hood and numerous hats.

The coach with Emily and Dolly in it set off two days before Mrs Purnell's departure by train, in order that they could unpack and iron and prepare for their mistress's arrival. Mrs Marshall's servants were to do the same, arriving at around the same time.

'You'll like Ginny, Mrs Marshall's maid,' Dolly chatted as they rattled and bumped out of the streets of Hull towards the coast road. Dolly had been to Scarborough before and was very excited to be going again. 'She knows all that's going on with 'grand folk as well as servants, who's seeing who and who's getting married and all that.'

Emily barely listened to Dolly's chatter as they drove across the North Bridge and out along a different road from the one she had driven down with the carrier when she had first come to Hull. Then she had come along the Hedon turnpike, which ran alongside the river; now she was travelling along the Holderness road, which would eventually lead them to Bridlington, another coastal town. Her heart warmed as they left behind the town of Hull and adjoining hamlets and travelled through undulating countryside so reminiscent of her former home, and yet she was saddened as she thought of the childhood she had left far behind.

After travelling for about an hour, they came to a small village and passed a large, handsome building of red-brown brick, with a gabled front porch. 'That's a workhouse for 'poor,' Dolly said idly. 'Poor beggars. Fancy being stuck out here with nowt to do.'

Emily sat forward and put her nose to the window. 'Where are we? Where are we?' Her question was urgent for the countryside seemed familiar. Dolly shrugged. 'Ask coachie,' she suggested.

Emily pushed down the window and leaned out to call up to the box. The driver had slowed down as he passed through the village and so heard her as she shouted to him.

'Skirlaw,' he called back. 'Yon's Skirlaw's workhouse, built specially for poor folk.' He grinned at her. 'Want me to drop thee off?'

She managed a smile, but she gazed back at the building with a sense of misery swamping her. Could this be where her mother and brother had spent their days? She felt it most likely, for she was sure that this was the coach road she and Sam had crossed over, towards the narrow lanes and byroads on their journey towards the Humber and Granny Edwards's cottage. I might have been at the workhouse too, she pondered, if Ma hadn't sent me off with Sam; and for the first time ever she suddenly realized that her mother, by sending her away, had been saving her from a life of poverty and degradation.

Hot tears spilled down her cheeks. I thought you didn't care for me, Ma, she silently wept. I thought you cared more for our Joe than you did for me. I thought it was only Da who loved me. And it wasn't, but you never said. You were the one who made the decision that I should leave when you knew that Da was going to die. If only I had known!

Dolly looked curiously at her. 'What's up, Emily? Not feeling sick are you? We've miles to go yet.'

Emily shook her head and managed a watery

smile. 'No,' she sniffled. 'I was just thinking how lucky I am.'

They drew into an inn yard in Bridlington, and whilst the driver went into the inn for a drink and the post boy watched over their luggage, they took a short stroll to stretch their legs. 'Mustn't go far,' Dolly said. 'We're responsible if owt goes missing and Mrs Purnell wouldn't half have summat to say.'

So they kept the coach within their sight and merely strolled outside the inn yard and watched as other coaches pulled in and the occupants descended. 'There's Ginny!' Dolly exclaimed. 'That must be 'Marshalls' carriage. Yoo-hoo, Ginny!' she called to one of two maids, who were standing by an old-fashioned carriage and stretching themselves.

'What an old boneshaker!' Ginny came across to them. She was a cheerful-looking young woman, older than either Emily or Dolly, with dark hair and rosy cheeks. 'I have my doubts whether it'll reach Scarborough, especially up and down them hills that are coming.' She smiled at Emily. 'I haven't seen you afore, have I?'

'I'm Emily,' she replied shyly. 'I came to Mrs Purnell in the spring.'

'Ah, so you haven't been to Scarborough afore? Well, what a treat in store for you.' She appraised Emily in an admiring way. 'We shall have to keep an eye on her, Dolly. With that face she'll have a score of admirers chasing her.'

Dolly gave a jealous pout. 'She's too young, can't you see?'

Ginny shook her head. 'That won't make any

difference to 'young bucks at Scarborough! They'll be fighting over her, if I'm not mistaken!'

They left the harbour and fishing cobbles of Bridlington behind and continued on their way to Scarborough, slower now as the road became steeper, but always keeping the sea within their sight. Between Reighton and Hunmanby they saw that Mrs Marshall's coach, which was in front of theirs, was having difficulty getting up and down the hills and several times, as they approached a steep incline or hazardous corner, the two maids got out of the coach to walk and make it easier for the horses. 'Blooming old coach,' Ginny called to them as they drove past, 'it must weigh a ton!'

They couldn't stop to pick the others up, for their horses were struggling too, and besides there wasn't room to squeeze another pin into the coach, let alone two more maids. 'We always get rickety old hired carriages,' Dolly grumbled. 'Owt's good enough for us. Now when Master Hugo travels to Scarborough, he drives a curricle, red and black it is, with two spanking hosses. What a sight. You should just see him!'

The sun was beginning to dip as they topped a rise and saw below them the blue-green waters of Scarborough, with the ancient castle standing proudly on the headland which divided the two bays. Emily drew in a deep breath. 'How beautiful it is! Look at the castle on 'top of the hill, oh and the sea is so blue.' She pushed down the carriage window and breathed in again. 'Oh, and that smell! I never thought I would smell 'sea again!'

'I thought you hadn't seen 'sea afore?' Dolly said

curiously. 'I thought you was from 'country!'

'So I am,' she laughed and told Dolly of when she and Sam used to row down the Humber almost to the tip of Spurn. 'We used to run over 'top of 'dunes to be first to see the sea. Oh, how I love it,' she exclaimed. 'How I love it!'

They continued on into the town until they came to the rented house in Merchants' Row. Mrs Marshall's manservant, Johnson, helped their coachman to unload the luggage and lift it into the hall and then climbed wearily back into the carriage to make the return journey to Hull. 'See you in a couple of days, ladies.' He winked at Emily. 'Behave yourselves now, don't get into any mischief!'

'Fat chance,' Ginny muttered as she surveyed the pile of boxes waiting to be unpacked. 'Come on, Lizzie,' she said to the other maid, 'let's get moving and maybe we can have a stroll after supper. Would you like to come?' she called as Emily and Dolly went up the stairs with a heap of gowns over their arms.

Emily glanced at Dolly. 'Will it be all right?' she asked. 'Are we allowed?'

'Nobody here to stop us,' Dolly grinned. 'There's no Mrs Anderson to say what we can or can't do. Come on, let's look sharp and get this lot unpacked. We can do 'ironing in 'morning.'

It was still light as the four of them strolled along the foreshore towards the pier and the lighthouse, and Emily breathed in the salty air and gazed into the dark water at the cobles and fishing vessels which were moored there, then lifted her head to watch a coble coming in from the open sea with its lugsail rippling in the evening breeze.

'Watch out for t'nets, ladies, don't catch them pretty feet and fall.' A group of pipe-smoking fishermen was sitting amongst a pile of lobster pots. Some of them were mending nets and others were gutting fish. It was a young man who had spoken and the other men laughed. 'Watch out for this young lover more like,' an older man called and got up from his seat on an upturned wooden bucket and raised his salt-stained hat. 'Tha'd be better off with an older man, ladies. Somebody with experience.'

'Aye,' Ginny bantered back. 'And wi' a lot more besides, I wouldn't wonder. Good evening to you, Jack.'

'And to you, Ginny. It's good to see thee again. Tha's brought some new friends, I see.'

'Mrs Marshall and Mrs Purnell are sharing a house this summer so we're all together,' Ginny explained.

'So tha'll be needing some extra fish?' He lifted a pair of silver mackerel, the scales glinting in the lamplight. 'Tek these for thy supper and I'll bring a parcel round first thing tomorrow.'

'And who's this with an angel's face?' The young man who had spoken first came and stood by Emily. 'Won't you introduce us, Ginny?'

'This is Emily,' Ginny said. 'And she's onny for looking at, not for touching. She's onny a bairn so keep thy hands off, young Ben.'

He smiled and doffed his hat, giving a small bow. 'Charmed to meet thee, Emily.' He took her hand in his. 'I shall wait for thee, Emily. For ever if need be.'

He was tall and fair, and his smile flashed in his face, brown from the salt air, and Emily felt flattered that such a handsome man had singled her out.

'Don't tek any notice of what they say, Emily,' Ginny advised as they retraced their steps. 'It's all said in fun and they're all married men, except for young Ben, and he's all but.'

'Oh!' Emily was disappointed. It would have been nice to go back to her bed and dream, not of an unattainable Mr Linton, as she had been doing for many nights, but of a young man of her own class who appeared to be smitten with her. It seemed that it was only a joke after all.

But it was young Ben Thompson who called most days with freshly caught fish, and he would hover at the kitchen door and give Emily a wave if he saw her; but Mrs Marshall's kitchen maid, who usually answered his knock, was of a sullen nature and didn't respond to his banter, nor would she pass on messages of good wishes to Emily as he requested. Sometimes Emily saw him if she went on an errand into the town and she deliberately walked along the harbourside in the hope of seeing him and having a few words.

She was strolling along one day after collecting a parcel for Mrs Purnell, then stopped to lean on a railing and listen as she heard the sound of the band striking up across on the pier, when Ben rushed towards her, his face flushed and his words breathless. 'Emily,' he gasped, 'other fellows challenged me, 'cos they knew I was scared and hardly dare tell thee.'

'What?' she laughed.

'Just that – tha's so beautiful! I've never seen anybody as beautiful as thee.'

She blushed and looked away. 'You're just fooling,' she said, remembering what Ginny had said.

'No. No, I'm not,' he pleaded earnestly. 'And I know tha's young, but next year, mebbe – mebbe tha'd come out wi' me?'

'You've got a lady friend, haven't you?'

He bent his head. 'Aye, I have – but, but I'd give her up if I thought –!'

She drew herself up and looked him in the eye. 'Don't do anything you'll be sorry for, Ben. I might not come back next year.'

He grasped her hands. 'I can't sleep for thinking about thee, Emily. I'll wait, I promise.'

She released her hands and left him and walked with a spring in her step and a smile on her lips at the notion that someone's sleep was disturbed by thoughts of her. Several men touched their hats as she passed by and young gentlemen from the Grammar School and menservants gave her a smile and she responded with a nod of acknowledgement.

'What 'you looking so pleased about?' Dolly grumbled when she got back to the house. 'You'd better look sharp with that parcel 'cos mistress is going to a concert and wants ribbons out of it to put on her gown.'

'Where have you been, Emily? Gossiping, I'll be

bound.' Mrs Purnell reached for the parcel. 'Now, I want you to sew this ribbon across the bodice, criss-cross it like so, like the dress we saw in that shop window yesterday, but be quick because the carriage is coming at five.'

She watched as Emily took out the sewing box and selected a matching thread. 'I want either you or Dolly to come with me; we shall have supper after the concert is over and then play cards, so we shall be late. I don't mind which of you comes.' She smiled graciously as if she was giving them a treat. 'You can choose between yourselves.'

'Well, I'm not going,' Dolly decided when Emily told her. 'I've been before and it's boring. You've to hang around for hours while they listen to 'music, and then when they play cards it's fetch me my wrap, fetch me some coffee, go here, go there. Then you've to look out for 'carriage when they want to go home and it's dark out there at 'Spa, and it's cold.' She stared defiantly at Emily. 'You've not been afore. You can go. Besides,' she gave a pert grin, 'I've got other fish to fry.'

Mrs Marshall wanted Ginny to come too and Emily was pleased about that, not having been to the Gothic Saloon before, and as she and Ginny sat next to the driver as the carriage rumbled over the iron bridge to the Spa building, she felt privileged to be there. She settled Mrs Purnell into her seat and Ginny did the same for Mrs Marshall, they took their wraps and agreed they would come back at the interval, and then returned to the foyer, where they gave the wraps to an assistant in the cloakroom.

'We can relax for an hour now, Emily. They won't

115

want us till coffee time. Let's go and see who's here and who's not.'

They went out on to the terrace and milled around with the other servants, who were laughing and chatting as they waited for the interval. The music struck up and one or two couples started to dance. 'How lovely it all is,' Emily laughed. 'And Dolly didn't want to come!' The evening was warm, the sun was still shining and far out in the surging waves they could see people bathing from the bathing huts and hear their shouts of laughter. Children were playing on the sands, which were golden in the sunlight, and Emily felt as if she really was on holiday.

Ginny pointed out various people to her. Servants of this person or that. 'She's with Mrs Stanley of Beverley,' or, 'She's with Mrs Morley of York,' or, 'There's the Honourable Mrs Owstwick with her two daughters.' Emily was amazed that Ginny seemed to know everyone who was worth knowing.

They leaned on the low wall and looked down at the people walking below. 'The Brodericks are not coming this year, nor are the Francises; you worked for them, didn't you, Emily? Mrs Francis and her daughter have gone abroad. Ah!' said Ginny, 'and my favourite of all! There's Commander Linton with Mrs Linton and their two daughters. We don't often have 'pleasure of seeing him at Scarborough.' She pointed out a tall, bearded man walking arm in arm with his wife and two daughters. 'Perhaps he's retired from the sea. They live up on 'Wolds,' she added, 'and – they have the handsomest son that you would die for. But too young for me,' she said sorrowfully, 'even if there was the remotest possibility, which there isn't!'

'Oh,' Emily breathed, all thoughts of Ben Thompson flying away. 'Philip Linton, do you mean? I've met him. Do you think he will be here?'

'Shouldn't think so for a moment. He's gone off to sea, or so I heard.' She raised her head and looked along towards the Cliff Bridge. 'Though – perhaps I'm mistaken about that. Yes, I am. Look! There he is. The gentleman himself!'

Chapter Eleven

Emily stood mesmerized as she watched Philip Linton striding across the bridge towards them. Then she took a deep breath and prepared herself as she saw that he had noticed her and, with only a slight hesitation in his stride, he turned and came towards her.

'Emily!' He gave a slight bow. 'How very nice to see you again. I – er, I never expected –,'

'Mrs Purnell made a sudden decision to come to Scarborough.' She gave a slight curtsy and turned to Ginny, who was standing next to her with a polite though slightly amused expression on her face. 'This is Ginny, Mrs Marshall's maid. Mrs Purnell and Mrs Marshall have come together,' she explained, adding lamely, 'They're sharing a house.'

He greeted Ginny politely, who bobbed her knee, then with his eyes still on Emily he indicated vaguely towards the sound of the music. 'I had arranged to meet my family for the concert, but I seem to have missed them.'

Emily was tongue-tied, she wanted to tell him that Ginny had just pointed them out, but she didn't want him to think she had been gossiping about his family, so she remained silent with her eyes slightly lowered.

Philip pointed towards where some of the servants on the terrace were merrily dancing. 'They're enjoying themselves!'

Emily agreed. 'It's lovely music.'

He nodded. 'It's from *The Magic Flute*. Do you know it?'

She shook her head. 'No, sir. I haven't heard it before.'

He looked at her and she felt as if her heart was about to stop as he took hold of her hand. 'I'm not much of a dancer, but shall we join in?'

She was lost for words and looked for advice from Ginny, who merely shrugged and gave a wry smile and turned her eyes to the antics of the dancers, who were laughingly trying to keep in time to the birdlike music of the flute.

'Please do, no-one will mind,' he persuaded and led her out to the other dancers. 'There's a hidden story behind the music,' he explained softly. 'It's a fairy tale. Of magic, of comedy – but it is also a love story.'

She felt the pressure of his hand on hers and felt weak and giddy with emotion as he guided her round and round, but soon she started to laugh with merriment and as she did, so did he. The music stopped and the dancers broke into spontaneous clapping, but he kept hold of her hand. 'How lovely you are, Emily,' he whispered, his eyes on her face, and it seemed to her that they were the only ones there with just the sound of the sea breaking below the Spa wall and the cry of the sea-gulls above them.

'Ahem!' Someone close by was clearing his throat and as they both looked up, Emily thought she would die of humiliation as she recognized Philip's parents and sisters watching them. His father had an amused laugh in his eyes, but his mother was stony-faced, whilst his sisters gazed in open curiosity at Emily.

'Father!' Philip stammered. 'Mother! I was looking for you. I thought you must have gone inside.'

'No. We decided that the evening was far too pleasant to be spent indoors.' Commander Linton gazed at Emily. 'I don't think we have had the pleasure of this young lady's acquaintance.'

'Erm, no. Father, Mother, may I present Miss Emily –?'

'Hawkins, sir.' Emily bobbed her knee deferentially to Commander and Mrs Linton, and then in an afterthought to their daughters also. She was glad that she was wearing her crisp white blouse with her grey skirt, but felt a stray strand of hair creeping from beneath her bonnet. 'I work for Mrs Purnell, sir, ma'am.'

There was silence for a moment, then suddenly the music struck up again and Commander Linton gave a grin which made him look just like his son, and said genially, 'How do you do! Delighted to meet you, Miss Hawkins.'

Mrs Linton inclined her head but no smile lit her face as she said, 'I haven't met Mrs Purnell. Would she approve of her staff behaving in this way?'

Suddenly Ginny was at Emily's side. She gave a neat curtsy to Commander and Mrs Linton. 'Good evening, sir, good evening, ma'am. How nice to see you again at Scarborough.'

Mrs Linton's face softened. 'Ginny! So you are here too?'

'Yes, ma'am. Mrs Marshall and Mrs Purnell are sharing a house this year. They're at 'concert and said we could enjoy 'music while they were inside! This is Emily's first time at Scarborough,' she explained and gave an encouraging nod at a flushed and nervous Emily.

'I see!' Mrs Linton looked Emily over and inclined her head, then glanced at Philip. 'Well, shall we get along?'

They all moved away, Philip lingering last of all and turning for one last backward glance as the music faded and the maids and the men entered the door to do their superiors' bidding.

Emily wept as she climbed into bed that night. How humiliating to be caught in such a manner, and what would Mr Linton's parents say to him about dancing with a servant girl in public? And yet as she wept, there was a small spring of joy which would keep bubbling up no matter how hard she pushed it down. She thought she could still feel the sensation of his hand on hers, and mused on the brief moment that his hand had lightly touched her waist as they danced. Oh, how wonderful he is, she romanticized in a flight of fancy. And he said I was lovely! Perhaps I am, she thought dreamily. I feel as if I might be. She smiled in the darkness and pretended to be asleep as Dolly climbed into bed beside her. I don't want to talk, not tonight. Tonight I only want to dream.

'What on earth were you thinking of, Philip? What if the girl's employer had seen her!' Mrs Linton made no bones over her disapproval. 'She could have been dismissed on the spot.'

'Yes, I didn't think – it was just the music and everything,' he said unconvincingly. And not only the music, he thought. When I saw her there I just wanted to dance with her.

'Do you know her?' His mother continued her questioning. 'Have you met her before?'

'Yes. I'd called to see Hugo Purnell and she answered the door.' He omitted to mention the loan that he'd made to Hugo or the subsequent meeting with Emily at his lodgings.

'And you asked her to dance with you on the strength of one meeting!' His mother was aghast.

'Oh, come now, Constance. Don't make a mountain out of a molehill.' His father peered from over the top of his newspaper. 'She's an extremely pretty girl. If I'd been twenty, I would have asked her to dance too.'

Mrs Linton looked disapprovingly down her nose at her husband, but a flicker of amusement twitched her lips, so Philip hastily seized the opportunity to say, 'I was just being impetuous, Mama, and had she been of a different class and not a servant you would have been planning a wedding!'

'Had she been of a different class, you would not have had the temerity to do it!' she said scornfully. 'Now be off with you.'

He planted a kiss on her cheek and departed, leaving his parents to finish their after-supper brandy alone. A ritual they had always followed for as long as he could remember.

'I could be worried about that incident.' Constance Linton was thoughtful as she sipped her brandy, a spirit her husband had introduced her to when first they were married. 'There was just something about them!'

Her husband shook his head. 'I told you, she's just a pretty girl, a damn fine looker, I must say. Besides he'll be meeting plenty of other young women whilst he's away, any amount I should say.'

'I do not wish to know,' his wife replied. 'No. I mean it,' she rebuked him as he gave a jovial laugh. 'I do not wish to know what you common sailors get up to when you are away from home!'

'Well, not much chance of me getting up to anything any more, now that I'm back in harbour.' He sat and pondered, his newspaper forgotten. 'But I'm really pleased that Philip is doing so well. Wouldn't Mother be delighted that he is following in the family footsteps?'

She smiled. 'Yes, I'm sure she would have been. She would have been very proud. As proud of Philip as she was of you.' She looked at him and then raised her finger. 'I know what you're going to say! And don't say it! You've come a long way from your mother's beginnings if what she said was true.' She gave a laugh. 'They were so eccentric those two, your father and mother, I don't believe a word of anything they said!'

'You would never have married me, would you,'

Commander Tobias Linton stretched his legs in front of the fire and grinned, 'if Mother really had been a gutter snipe as she said, and not a Dutch princess or whatever else it was they said about her, and if Father really had been a smuggler before he was a naval captain?'

She leaned back in her chair. 'Of course I wouldn't, Commander! When I was the most sought-after young woman in Yorkshire? Would I have risked my reputation to marry a man with such dire connections?'

He looked across at her and smiled. If he was sure of anything in this life it was of his wife's love, it had sustained him over many dangers and hardships. But he understood his wife's anxieties for their children, especially Philip, once he had left to join his ship. There were many dangers for a young officer and not just at sea. There were women in wait too, undesirable women who could fell a man instantly if his wife only knew, not that he would dream of telling her. An innocent dance with a young servant girl was the last thing she should worry about.

Chapter Twelve

They stayed in Scarborough until the beginning of October and although Mrs Purnell was reluctant to leave, Mrs Marshall, who had leased the house, was eager to return to Hull as the social season there would be about to begin.

Emily too was reluctant to return to the cramped streets of Hull. She had so enjoyed the sea air and the warm weather, which had not induced the flies and smells in the way it did in the town. She would miss too the sound of the sea as it washed to the shore, and in particular the last two weeks when the wind had changed and become more blustery, driving the waves with great force over the harbour wall, making the small ships in the harbour dip and plunge like corks and the pedestrians on the foreshore scuttle out of the way to avoid a soaking. She found it exhilarating and exciting and whenever she could she volunteered to run errands so that she might brave the elements.

'I think you're mad,' Dolly proclaimed one day when Emily had been on an errand in the rain and came back to the house, wet and breathless but her face glowing with health. 'Won't catch me going out in weather like this.'

Mrs Anderson remarked on her complexion on their return to Hull. 'You look well, Emily,' she said. 'Better than us here. Some of us have had a bad time. I haven't told mistress yet, but we've lost Lily, the new kitchen maid, to cholera. We've had to fumigate her room and burn all her clothes.'

Emily and Dolly were both shocked. The girl had been young and not very healthy and seemingly had gone down with the disease rapidly, and they both agreed that they were glad they had been away. Mrs Purnell was both distressed and angry and immediately wrote a letter to the governors of the workhouse in Parliament Street, blaming them for the loss of her servant and the inconvenience of her having to find another.

'My son will be home in December,' she told Mrs Anderson in Emily's presence. 'I have had a letter from him, so make sure his room is well aired and a good fire burning when he does come. He'll feel the cold after Italy.'

Mrs Anderson's face tightened. 'Yes, ma'am. There has been a small fire lit every day while you were away in case he returned.'

'He has some good news for me, he says,' Mrs Purnell chatted in the casual way she sometimes did to her servants, when there was no-one else around to confide in. 'I can't think what it can be. Unless,' she became quite girlish and her false curls bobbed beneath her lace cap, 'unless he has met someone whilst abroad. What do you think, Mrs Anderson, you know him well after all these years? Do you think he might have found someone marriageable? Oh –!' Anxiety creased her face. 'I just pray it won't be someone foreign.'

Emily, sewing buttons on to a pair of Mrs Purnell's gloves, glanced up at Mrs Anderson and thought that though her expression appeared impassive, she seemed to be in some kind of emotional turmoil.

'I'm quite sure that Mr Hugo will choose someone suitable when the time is right, ma'am,' she said tightly. 'He always seems to know how to go about things.'

'You're right, of course. Well, we'll arrange a few parties and some young people to come over as soon as he gets back. What fun we will have, I've missed him so. The house is far too quiet without him.'

Emily was quite looking forward to seeing Mr Hugo and the thought of having young people in the house, with perhaps music and dancing, filled her with expectation. Not that she would be able to participate, of course, but the atmosphere in the house would, she was sure, be much lighter and brighter. She also mused on the idea that Mr Linton might appear at one of the functions, as after she had danced with him on the terrace of the Spa, to her great disappointment, she hadn't seen him again and Ginny had told her that she had heard he had been recalled to join his ship.

It was half-way through December when Mr Hugo finally arrived home, his arrival heralded by a loud banging on the door and a shrill ringing of the doorbell. Emily opened the door to find him standing on the doorstep with a manservant and an array of bags and boxes and a smart-looking curricle drawn by two black horses out in the street.

'Hello! And who are you?' He was tall and dark with a long sharp nose and a thin mouth. Not really as handsome as I'd expected, Emily thought. Though he's very merry.

'I'm Emily, sir.' She bobbed her knee.

'Emily! That's a very plain name for such a pretty girl.' He surveyed her admiringly. 'I must say my mother knows how to pick the beauties. Turn around, Emily. Let's have a look at you.'

She cast a scared glance at Mrs Anderson, who had followed her into the hallway after hearing the commotion. Mrs Anderson gave her a brief nod to comply, so slowly she turned for his inspection. 'Well, you'll do! Won't she, Mrs Anderson? I've seen some handsome women whilst I've been away but there's no-one to touch the comeliness of a fair English rose.' He pinched Emily's cheek. 'Believe me, Emily, I know.'

She didn't know why she felt apprehensive at his attention, for after Ginny's warning not to take men's admiration too seriously, she had simply smiled and accepted compliments, and there had been many whilst at Scarborough. She had thought no more about them, apart from Mr Linton's whispered words, and she really did want to believe him. But Mr Hugo made her feel very uneasy and she didn't know whether it was the accidental touch of his hand on her rear as she went upstairs with his bags, or Mrs Anderson's hoarse whisper to keep her bedroom door locked.

*   *   *

'I'm waiting Hugo, to hear the news you have to tell me.' Mrs Purnell viewed her son affectionately. 'You said in your letter there was something.' He had been home for three days and still he had not divulged his secret. 'Have you – have you met someone whilst you've been away?'

'I might have.' He poured himself a brandy and a sherry for his mother. 'You'd like that, wouldn't you, Mother? But I'm not sure whether to tell you now or at the party on Saturday.'

'Oh, but you must tell me now,' she gurgled. 'I must be the first to know.'

He laughed. 'You and her father!'

She looked shocked. 'You mean you haven't asked him yet? What are you thinking of? He might not agree.'

'Oh, he'll agree, there's no doubt about that.' He looked smug. 'She'll kick up a fuss if he doesn't.'

She put her hand to her heart and took a shuddering breath. 'You haven't – you haven't done anything wrong, Hugo? She is from a good family, isn't she?' The thought of scandal or of him making a poor marriage with someone unsuitable filled her with dismay.

'She's eminently suitable, Mother. She has money, she's from a good family – one of the best in the area. The only thing she hasn't got is brains and I'm not too bothered about that.'

No, Mrs Purnell agreed. Brains were not as important as breeding for a wife. But there was something he wasn't telling her. She knew her son well enough to know when he was holding something back. 'So, who is she? Do I know her or her family?'

He smiled faintly but looked away. 'I'm sure you will be pleased, Mama, when you get used to the idea.' His voice was placatory. 'You know her well. It's Deborah Francis. Daughter of your cousin and Roger Francis.'

Mrs Purnell's face turned ashen. 'You can't be serious? You *can't* be serious! You know the history. There is madness in the family! Think again, Hugo.' She shook her head disbelievingly. 'Not her! Anyone but her! Besides her father would never agree. He's very protective towards her, to both of his children. He won't allow it!' She tried to be convincing, but the look on his face told her she had failed.

'Listen, Mother.' He knelt beside her and whispering softly he topped up her glass of sherry. 'He will agree. We've concocted a story to make him agree. No, I'm not going to tell you what it is. But listen to what I have to say. She is the richest young woman of marriageable age in the district. No-one else will take the risk of proposing marriage because of her background, but it doesn't put me off. I don't intend to give her children so there will be no imbeciles in the family, you may be assured of that – and she's very attractive. You haven't seen her since she was a child. I tell you, she is a lovely young woman, a little excitable, I agree, but quite a beauty.'

He hesitated. 'I met her mother, of course, and she saw how attached Deborah was to me. I think I can safely say that she will be quite agreeable to the marriage. If anyone can persuade Roger Francis that his daughter should marry me, his wife can.'

'He *can't* be serious!' Roger Francis confronted his wife, a letter held limply in his hand. 'He says that he met you and Deborah in Italy and that he is sure that you approve of his intentions toward our daughter!'

He stared glassily at his wife. 'He surely knows of the situation here? His mother must have talked about us. How can he possibly think of marriage? It's out of the question!'

His wife gave a grim laugh. 'I fear you will find that Deborah has different ideas. She is quite besotted with him. It was quite embarrassing at times.'

'She has these phases of adoring particular people,' he said angrily, 'but it passes when she gets bored with them. She can't possibly marry.' He threw down the letter. 'He's a fortune hunter! Don't tell me he's not!'

'I'm quite sure that he is.' She looked away into the middle distance. 'But I'm afraid we have no alternative but to allow it.'

'What do you mean? Eleanor? What do you mean?' He sank down into a chair, but then got up again. 'What has happened? Speak, for God's sake!'

'Do not raise your voice to me!' She glared angrily back at him. 'I found your *precious* daughter and Hugo Purnell in a compromising situation as we were returning home.' She put her head in her hands. 'I had searched all over the ship for her and was about to call the Captain, when I suddenly thought of asking Hugo Purnell to help me look for her. I had left them together having coffee on the deck about an hour before.

'I need some time to myself,' she added resentfully before he could protest, 'I can't be watching her the whole time! Anyway,' her voice dropped, 'I knocked on his cabin door and when he opened it, I saw that Deborah was there. She was sitting on his bed. She'd taken her shoes and stockings off and was swinging her legs and looking very pleased with herself!'

'Blackguard!' He spat out the insult. 'Do you think that he –?' He couldn't bring himself to ask the question.

'How would I know?' She looked at her husband with loathing in her eyes. 'You're the one who would know that! You and all whoring men.'

'Eleanor! Enough!' The hurt showed in his anxious face. 'God knows I have tried to make amends.'

'Well it's too late now; for you and for her,' she spat out. 'When I questioned her about what she was doing there she just smiled sweetly and said, "Nice things"! Then later she told me that she was going to marry him. I cannot take any more,' she whispered. 'This tour was a nightmare for me. If you do not agree to this marriage and we find that she is with child, then I shall insist that we send her to join her brother in the asylum.'

He sank down into his chair again and rubbed his forehead. His hands trembled. 'I'll have to speak to Purnell. I'll try to find out, explain the situation in case he doesn't realize it. I mean, she shouldn't have children in case –.'

'In case they inherit your line of madness!' There was no sympathy in her voice, no compassion.

'You are being so unfair, Eleanor,' he said wearily. 'You know that I hadn't been told. I would never have had children had I known. My parents have a lot to answer for,' he said bitterly. 'They were ashamed, I know, but they should have told me.'

Hugo Purnell arrived the next day and Deborah greeted him with squeals of delight, throwing her arms around him. 'Hugo! Papa – this is Hugo. Isn't he so handsome? So adorable? And he wants to marry me. Don't you, Hugo?'

Hugo bowed politely to Roger Francis and then kissed Deborah's hand. 'I would like to speak to your father alone, Deborah.' He spoke gently but firmly to her. 'You and I will talk later.'

'Go and find your mother, Deborah, and tell her that Mr Purnell is here.' Roger Francis ushered his daughter away and coldly invited Hugo Purnell to join him in the library.

'First of all, sir,' he began without preamble, 'if what my wife says is true, and I have no reason to doubt her word, then I must tell you that I consider your conduct towards my daughter most reprehensible.'

Hugo opened his mouth to protest, but Roger Francis continued, 'You must have heard of her condition and I consider that you have taken unfair advantage of her vulnerability. What do you have to say, sir?'

Hugo gave a lazy smile. 'Your daughter, sir, prac-tically threw herself at me, there was no conniving for her affections on my part. During the whole of my time in Italy I was besieged by her attentions.' He raised his eyebrows. 'You must know how warm and affectionate she can be towards those she takes a fancy to.'

Roger Francis conceded this with a slight nod of his head.

'However, sir,' Hugo rubbed his hands together, 'I must confess that my affections, which are quite genuine I assure you, were rather carried away on our journey home – Mrs Francis will have told you of the rather embarrassing incident? I did not intend inviting Deborah to visit me in my cabin, but she just arrived at my door.'

'She has the mind of a child,' Roger Francis broke in. 'You took advantage of her!'

Hugo smiled thinly. 'Believe me, sir, she is not a child, far from it.' He stared him in the eyes. 'But I have an affection for Deborah. I would take care of her if we were married. We would live with my mother, therefore she would have a constant companion.' He appeared to hesitate, yet Roger Francis felt the hesitation was contrived. 'And if I may be so bold, Mr Francis, she would not be at the mercy of undesirable philanderers who, without honourable intentions, might take advantage of her – erm, passion, should I say, which if you will forgive me sir, can stir the fire somewhat.'

'I consider you a scoundrel, sir, to speak of my daughter in such a manner.' Roger Francis was full of cold fury. 'And I would like to receive your assurance that you have not violated her innocence!'

Hugo said nothing but merely patted his fingertips together, then, raising his head, he said, 'I have said I am willing to marry her. To do the honourable thing. What more can I offer?'

The door burst open and Deborah flew in, followed by her mother. Hugo gave her a small bow. 'Charmed to meet you again, Mrs Francis. I trust you are well?'

She ignored his pleasantries and looked towards her husband. 'What has been decided?'

Deborah looked from one to another. 'Have you been talking about me, Papa? With Hugo? We're going to be married! I'm going to have a cream silk dress with pink rosebuds embroidered all over it, and a sweet little pink bonnet, and what else did we say, Hugo? I can't remember.' She went up to him and put her arms around his waist.

He gently extricated himself from her grasp and looked significantly at her father. 'You must discuss the finer details with your parents, Deborah. It's in their hands now.'

Chapter Thirteen

'Emily! Come here.' Mrs Anderson beckoned to her. 'You were in service with the Francises. Can you tell me why Mrs Purnell is not pleased with 'news that Mr Hugo is to marry their daughter?'

'Marry Miss Deborah?' Emily received the news with a mixture of relief and foreboding. Relief that perhaps Mr Hugo would not pay her quite so much attention if he was married; several times he had caught her alone on the landing and seized a kiss, but she had a foreboding that she might see more of Miss Deborah and be the butt of her attention again. 'Well,' she began doubtfully, remembering Mrs Castle's advice not to see or hear anything in an employer's household, 'she is a little excitable sometimes.'

Dolly snorted and put her finger to her forehead. 'I heard as she was a bit –!'

'Well, it's a mystery.' Mrs Anderson was perplexed. 'But 'news is enough to send 'mistress to her bed when you'd think she would be delighted.'

'*Delighted!*' Mrs Purnell had exclaimed when Hugo told her that he had a letter from Roger

Francis saying he accepted the proposal of marriage on his daughter's behalf. The letter had been formal and without compliments. 'I am *not* delighted,' she emphasized when Hugo complained of her negative attitude towards the tidings. 'Of all the young women you could have chosen you have to choose someone who is unhinged!'

'You will like her, Mother,' he insisted. 'She is charming and merry, full of life. She will brighten your day considerably.'

'Brighten my day?' She frowned suspiciously. 'What do you mean, brighten my day?'

'When I bring her home,' he said cheerfully. 'You will get along so well, I'm convinced of it.'

'You are not thinking of bringing her here to live?' She gazed at her son in marked trepidation.

'But of course.' Nonchalantly he stretched and smiled. 'Where else would we live? I couldn't possibly live in the country, and besides this place is too big just for you; and you would miss me, now wouldn't you, if I went away?'

And it was then that Mrs Purnell took to her bed whilst Hugo went about making arrangements for his wedding to Deborah Francis and ordering the decorators to come in and paint and paper the bedroom which he had designated as suitable for his future wife.

'What do you think, Emily? Come and see. Will the new Mrs Purnell like the choice I have made?' He took hold of her arm as she walked by and pulled her into the room, which still smelled of paint. A new mahogany tester bed had been installed, its drapes covered over with sheeting. A mahogany writing table had been placed in the window, whilst on the marble washstand a jug and washbowl in white and decorated with pink flowers stood beside an ornate oil lamp.

Hugo took the pile of laundry that she was carrying and placed them on the bed. 'Come and look at the painting I bought in Italy. Charming, don't you think?'

'Yes, sir,' she murmured, trying to remove herself from his grasp and with some dismay, reasoning that a painting of a nude woman wasn't really a suitable subject for him to be pointing out to her.

He stood her in front of him and held her shoulders as they observed the painting. 'She has a fine body, don't you think, Emily?' His hands dropped to her waist. 'Plump, but not too plump.' His fingers strayed across her breasts as he whispered, 'Much like you, I would imagine? Nicely rounded, just the way a man likes a woman. Not just skin and bone.'

She struggled away. 'Sir, Mrs Anderson will be looking for me.'

He moistened his lips with his tongue. 'Ah, yes. Mrs Anderson. We mustn't forget Mrs Anderson, must we?' He slapped her rump. 'Off you go, then. I'm glad you approve of the room, Emily.'

She dashed away, quite forgetting the sheets until much later and not daring to go back for them until she heard him go out and the front door slam behind him.

'Master's in a bit of a mood, isn't he?' Dolly said. 'Looks as if he's lost a guinea and found sixpence.'

Emily said nothing, but wished with all her heart that Christmas would soon be over and the New Year begun and Mr Hugo and Miss Deborah married so that she might feel safe again.

Mrs Purnell, Hugo and Emily travelled in the carriage to the wedding, whilst Wilson, Hugo's manservant, travelled on top next to the coachman. It was a bitterly cold February day and the roads were deeply rutted and hard with frost. 'What a god-forsaken spot,' Mrs Purnell complained. 'Does anything ever happen out here?'

'Now you will realize why I don't want to live here.' Hugo bit his nails and stared at Emily sitting quietly in the corner. 'Roger Francis offered us a house, but I turned it down.'

'I didn't know he'd offered you a house,' his mother said sharply. 'You should have taken it. You could still have kept some rooms at my house.'

'Our house, Mother,' he corrected her. 'Anyway, I don't want to be too near my in-laws and I want to be where the parties are and the clubs, not stuck next to a field of potatoes or turnips.' He glanced at Emily. 'You're a country girl, Emily. What did you do for excitement?'

She considered and thought of her childhood. There hadn't been any time for excitement since then, not once she had started work. 'I used to row down the river, sir. Towards Spurn. And once I caught a salmon.'

'You caught a salmon!' he said dryly. 'What a thrill. Lucky old salmon!'

'Not an old one, sir,' she said seriously. 'A young

one. It would be returning to 'sea to feed and grow before coming back again to spawn.'

He yawned. 'Really! What a mine of information you are, Emily. Who would have thought it?'

She was thrilled to be coming back to Elmswell Manor and Mrs Castle and Mrs Brewer both greeted her warmly, though Jane only looked up from scrubbing pans and nodded to her. 'How you've grown!' said Mrs Castle. 'They must be feeding you well.'

'Not as well as you, Mrs Castle. Cook doesn't bake half so well as you, but we went to Scarborough last summer,' she said eagerly. 'And it was so healthy there. The air was good, just like it is out here,' she added wistfully.

'And I expect you'll be looking after Miss Deborah again.' Mrs Brewer observed her. 'How do you feel about that?'

'Is no-one coming with her?' Emily asked in dismay. 'I thought someone might be.'

Mrs Brewer shook her head. 'Well, I've looked after her all these years, but I'm getting too old to be a lady's maid, and I haven't been told any other arrangements.'

Emily unpacked Mrs Purnell's gown for the wedding and hung it so that the creases would drop out, and then went into her own adjoining room. It's so good to be back, it's like coming home, she thought as she gazed out of the window at the familiar winter landscape. I wonder how Sam is. I must ask Mr Francis if I get the opportunity.

The opportunity came the next morning as she escorted Mrs Purnell into the drawing room to await the bride and her parents before they set off for church. As she came out into the hall, Mr Francis came down the stairs. 'Emily! How nice to see you. Have you settled well in Hull?'

'Yes thank you, sir, quite well.'

He smiled and prepared to move on. 'Sir,' she said shyly, 'I was wondering how Sam is. If he is still at 'same farm.'

'Why yes, of course. He's very happy there, quite one of the family. They've become very fond of him.'

'Oh, I'm so glad. Would you – could I ask that you send him my best wishes, sir?' She was being forward she realized, but she didn't think that he would object. 'I would write to him but he can't read. He didn't have any schooling.'

She thought that sadness brushed his face, but he nodded and said he would pass on her greetings if he saw him. He turned away, but then turned back as if with an afterthought. 'You can always send a message through me, Emily, if ever there is anything urgent that Samuel needs to know.'

She thanked him and mused that Mr Francis was always very proper, he always gave Sam his full name.

The servants stood in the hall to greet the bride and groom and wedding party as they returned from church. Emily watched the faces of the family as they entered the hall and wondered why everyone except Deborah and Hugo seemed so solemn. The bride was very animated and talkative and her father seemed to be anxious about her. She looked very lovely and Emily drew in a breath when

141

she saw her hooped dress of cream with a scattering of pink silk rosebuds over the top silk layer. On her head she wore a pleated bonnet with pink ribbons and she carried a prayerbook.

'Emily,' she squealed, 'I'm coming to live in Hull. You will be able to look after me again just as you used to. Won't she, Hugo?'

'Indeed she will.' Emily felt her heart sink as Hugo's eyes held hers. 'I'm sure Emily will look after you very well indeed.'

Mrs Purnell's expression was one of frozen indignation as she heard this and as she passed Emily, she muttered, 'I am the one who pays your wages, don't forget that, Emily. You are paid to look after me!'

Emily bobbed her knee. 'Yes, ma'am. I won't forget.'

Relatives and friends of both families arrived for the celebration and the wedding breakfast was served. There was a lot of laughter and noisy chatter from Hugo's friends, whilst the friends of the Francises, who were fewer in number than the Purnells, were more circumspect. After the tables were cleared, a pianist and fiddlers arrived and soon the great house was throbbing with music and dancing began.

Emily, although she was there to attend Mrs Purnell, helped the other servants by giving out glasses of wine to the guests, and she felt quite lively as she revelled in the music and watched the dancers. She felt a hand on her shoulder and turned. It was Mr Hugo, who had had rather a lot to drink.

'Marvellous day, Emily,' he slurred. 'Isn't it simply grand? I don't know why I didn't think of getting married before. What do you say, Forbes?' He clung on to Emily as he called across to a friend.

'What do I say about what?' Forbes too, seemed to be the worse for drink and Emily tried to edge away, but was held fast between them. 'I wouldn't say no to a little romp with this filly.' He reached out to grab Emily by the waist, but Hugo pulled her away.

'Oh no, you don't,' he grinned. 'Not this one. You definitely can't have this one!'

'Is everything all right?' To Emily's relief, Roger Francis approached and cast a disparaging eye over Hugo and his friend. 'I think it's time you took a rest, Emily.' He didn't look at her, but continued to stare at Hugo. 'You have been on your feet all day. Go downstairs and I'll tell Mrs Purnell where you are, should she need you.'

She thankfully scurried away to the safety of the kitchen, telling herself she shouldn't be so foolish as to feel afraid, that it was only men's tomfoolery and that Mr Hugo was being thoughtful in rescuing her from the clutches of his friend.

It was almost midnight before the guests who were not staying overnight put on their cloaks and greatcoats and entered their carriages. There was a sharp frost, keen enough for snow and the horses' hooves crunched and skittered on the gravel drive as they pulled away.

'My word but I'm tired.' Mrs Purnell climbed wearily up the stairs with Emily's assistance. 'I shall sleep well tonight.'

Emily helped her undress and into her bedgown

and filled a glass with cordial as was her custom, before helping her into bed. A soft knock came on the door. 'See who it is, Emily, and if it's the housekeeper tell her I have everything I need.'

It wasn't the housekeeper, but Hugo with a glass in his hand. 'Is Mother in bed?' he whispered. 'I've brought her a glass of champagne to settle her for the night.'

The wine in the glass he held in his hand frothed and bubbled. 'Oh, take it away, Hugo. I've had enough, I have my cordial,' his mother said wearily as he entered the room. His face was flushed and he walked rather unsteadily.

'I insist,' he said. 'It will help you sleep. Come along now.' He sat down next to her on the bed. 'Don't think I shan't look after my dear mother just because I'm a married man!'

'Will you, Hugo?' she said plaintively. Then taking a sip, remarked, 'I think you will have your hands full looking after your bride.' She took another sip. 'It tastes rather odd.'

'It's the best that Roger Francis's money can buy.' He bent forward and whispered, 'We're rich, Mother. A handsome dowry and great expectations when Francis pops off.'

She drained her glass. 'Don't be vulgar, Hugo! Now off you go and let me get some sleep. Emily too, she must be tired.'

'You're not tired are you, Emily?' He came towards her and patted her cheek. 'What a good girl you have been. Such a treasure.' His eyes slid from her face and down her body. 'We're so pleased to have you,' he whispered, 'aren't we, Mother?'

'Mm! What?' Mrs Purnell had slipped down on her pillows and closed her eyes. 'Put the lamp out, Emily, when you've finished.'

Hugo reached out again and stroked Emily's face, his fingers firm against her skin, then he leaned forward and kissed her on the mouth. 'Well,' he breathed, 'I must be off to attend to my little wife's needs.'

'Goodnight, sir.' Her voice trembled as she opened the door for him.

She felt extremely agitated and Mrs Castle remarked on it when she finally went down to the kitchen to say goodnight. The servants were all very tired, but they still had the task of clearing up after the guests and the family, and not all of them had yet gone to bed. 'You get off, Emily, you look all in,' Mrs Castle said. 'It's not your job to help out here. You've been a good lass, though, and we appreciate it.'

'I am rather tired,' she murmured, but felt that she was not so much tired as apprehensive.

'Mr Hugo and Miss Deborah are just going up, Mrs Brewer.' One of the maids came down the stairs to report. 'She said as would you go up? Then that's just about everybody gone, thank goodness.'

'You mean Mr and Mrs Purnell, don't you?' Mrs Brewer corrected firmly. 'Don't forget they are married now.'

One of the maids sniggered as a footman whispered in her ear and Mrs Brewer gave them a frosty stare and rebuked them, 'And we will not have any coarse comments from you, Smith, if you please.'

The girl put her hand over her mouth to try and contain her giggles as Smith, undeterred, raised his eyebrows and rolled his eyes suggestively.

Emily went up the back stairs and along the corridor and entered her own door rather than going through Mrs Purnell's room. When she had left her she had been fast asleep and snoring softly.

She undressed and put on her nightshift and lay on her bed. That's over with then, she sighed. But what next? Do I stay with Mrs Purnell and risk Mr Hugo's pawing and Miss Deborah's tantrums? She couldn't think of her former mistress as a married woman. She looked childlike even in her wedding gown, small and slight, and it seemed as if she was playing at being married. Emily sighed again. Or do I look for another position and ask Mrs Purnell to give me a reference? Yes, she pondered. I think I will. I think it will be intolerable working there any more.

Mrs Brewer had undressed Deborah and put her into her new white bedgown and robe and as Hugo knocked and entered she collected her mistress's wedding gown and put it over her arm. 'Goodnight, sir, goodnight, ma'am.'

'Wait!' Deborah called her back. 'I think you have forgotten something, Betty.'

Mrs Brewer turned, a frown wrinkling her forehead. 'Have I, ma'am?'

Deborah put her chin in the air. 'You have forgotten my new name!'

'Oh! I beg your pardon. Goodnight, Mrs Purnell. Goodnight, Mr Purnell.' A bright spot of colour touched Mrs Brewer's cheeks as she left her young mistress with her new husband.

'Mrs Purnell! Doesn't that sound fine!' Deborah bounced on the bed, her pale legs showing.

'Indeed it does, my darling. Now come along and let me help you into bed.'

'Oh, I'm too excited to sleep,' she said and bounced off the bed again. 'I could stay up all night.'

'Could you?' he murmured. 'Well, don't forget we have a long journey home tomorrow.' What an idiotic idea getting married in the coldest month of the year when the roads are bad, he deliberated. We could have been off to Italy again if we'd waited until the spring instead of just going home to Hull. Then he smiled. The Francises must really have believed their precious girl had lost her innocence to marry her off so quickly.

'Look at me, Hugo, do I look pretty?' She spun around in a circle. 'Do you like my new bedgown?'

'It's very pretty. You look extremely sweet.'

'Hugo,' she came up close to him, 'will you do those nice things to me?'

He gazed down at her. 'Which nice things are those, Deborah? Remind me.'

'You know,' she giggled. 'Like you did on the ship, before Mama came in.'

'Ah,' he said. 'Those nice things! Yes, of course I will.'

She put her hands to her mouth and her eyes grew wide. 'Do you know, Hugo,' she whispered, 'I do believe that it was rather naughty of us! When I told Mama, she was very angry and said I mustn't do it again.'

'You told your mama, did you?' he smiled.

'You said I could!' she exclaimed. 'You said that I should tell my mama everything.'

'Of course,' he said smoothly. 'Every good girl should tell her mama. Before she is married, that is. But you mustn't tell her everything now. Now we have our own secrets!'

She breathed in delightedly. 'All right. Now will you do those naughty things to me?'

'I will, if you promise that then you will go to bed.'

'I promise.' She sat in a chair and wriggled. He knelt down beside her and putting one hand beneath her gown, he felt for her small round breasts and tweaked her nipples. With the other he held her foot and kissed her toes. 'How's that?' he said softly.

'Bliss,' she laughed. 'Absolute bliss, Hugo. Will you do it every night?'

'I can't promise.' He took a deep breath. 'Only if you're very good.'

She closed her eyes. 'Oh I will be,' she said dreamily. 'I will be good.' She opened her eyes and gazed at him. 'I feel quite sleepy now. It's a very pleasant way of drifting off to sleep. Would you like me to stroke your feet, Hugo?'

'No, thank you. It isn't something that I especially enjoy.' He pulled her up from the chair. 'Come along now, you promised. Into bed with you.'

Obediently she snuggled down beneath the sheets. 'Goodnight, Hugo. Will you be quite comfortable next door?'

'Perfectly comfortable, Deborah. I shall go down for a glass of brandy before retiring. Sleep well.'

'And you, dear Hugo. I'll see you in the morning.'

He closed the door quietly behind him and with a short sharp breath he leaned against it. 'Sleep well!' he muttered. 'There'll be no sleep for me tonight. Not unless I get some release.' He looked up and down the corridor and listened. It was quiet, with only the sound of the servants shuffling about on the floor above as they prepared for bed.

He crept down the corridor and, pausing for a moment outside his mother's room, he pressed his ear against the door and gave a small satisfied smile when he heard the gentle snore. The sleeping draught had worked its magic. He tiptoed on and, reaching the next room, he gently tapped on the door.

Emily was drifting off to sleep when she heard the sound and awoke with a start. Mrs Purnell must be calling her. She threw the bedclothes back and was padding to the adjoining door when the knock came again, but it was from her own door, leading out to the corridor.

She picked up her shawl and put it around her shoulders and opened the door a crack. There was no-one out there. She opened it wider and put her head out and was immediately pounced upon and pushed back into the room. 'Mr Hugo!'

'Ssh.' He put his hand over her mouth. 'Don't make a noise.'

'Sir, your mother – Mrs Purnell!'

'Is sleeping like a babe,' he whispered as he pushed her further into the room. 'She won't hear a thing. But just in case –'. Holding Emily firmly, he propelled her towards the adjoining door and turned the key. 'There. Now there's no need to worry, Emily. We won't be disturbed.'

'Sir.' She started to shake. 'I'd rather you left. If you are found in here I'll be dismissed.'

'Ah, but I won't be found. There's no Mrs Anderson here to spoil our fun!'

'Mr Hugo!' She backed away as he lifted her nightshift. 'I'm a good girl, sir. I've not –'.

'I know that, Emily.' His eyes gleamed. 'Do you think I can't tell?'

'Your wife, sir – Miss Deborah.' Tears began to fall as he pulled off her shift, exposing her nakedness.

'Is a child,' he muttered and bent his head towards her breasts, his hands roughly exploring her body. 'Always will be. She's no good to me. I need a real woman. One like you, Emily.'

'But I'm not a woman, sir.' She started to cry and he grinned and pushed her on to the bed.

'Not yet, you're not.' He unfastened the buttons on his trousers and pulled out his shirt. 'But you soon will be! Lie back,' he said sharply as she tried to raise herself, then his tone changed to one of firm persuasion. 'I've been waiting for this, Emily. You can't begin to realize how happy you are about to make me.'

Chapter Fourteen

After he had left, she cried and cried as she scrubbed her aching body with a wet flannel in an effort to remove all vestiges of him.

He had said not a word as he dressed, and on reaching the door he suddenly turned and she thought for one terrifying moment that he was coming back to violate her yet again. But without even looking at her, he had taken some coins from his pocket and thrown them on to the table beside the bed.

She hadn't slept again, neither did she get into the bed, but sat on the edge, gently rocking and weeping. As she had lain beneath his pounding, assaulting body, she had cried for her mother, and for her father, for her brother Joe, for Sam and Granny Edwards and for anyone who had shown her love or kindness in the past. But for the present, she grieved, there was no-one in the world who could help her. The face of Philip Linton flashed across her subconscious, but she had brushed the image away. He might have been kind and attentive once, but he would be no longer, not now, if ever he should discover that she was defiled.

A bitterness swept over her. I will be regarded as low and unchaste. No-one will believe that I was taken against my will.

As dawn was breaking she wrapped her shawl around her and crept downstairs to the kitchen to make herself a warm drink, and found Jane stoking up the oven fire. She looked up as Emily opened the door. 'You look rough this morning, Em. Didn't tha sleep?'

Emily shook her head, not trusting herself to speak.

'Hey, Em. I've got summat to tell you now we're on our own. Just let me get this black pig stoked up.' She threw some sticks on to the dull flame and riddled the ash. 'Do you remember I said I was set on marrying Brown? Well, he's agreed at last.'

Emily tried to show some enthusiasm by nodding her head, whilst remembering Brown's stolen kiss which had so repulsed her, and his significant words.

'Although', Jane whispered, 'I had to give in to him in the end. It was 'onny way he'd promise.'

'What do you mean?' Emily whispered back.

Jane stared. '*You* know! A bit of hanky-panky. Onny it was more than hanky-panky, 'cos he's got me pregnant.'

Emily felt sick. Pregnancy was the one thing she hadn't thought of. 'I'm so sorry. What – what will you do?'

'Don't be sorry.' Jane laughed. 'It wasn't that bad and it was worth it. At least I'll be able to get out of here. I shan't tell 'Francises yet,' she said conspiratorially. 'Then they'll give me a shilling or two when they ask me to leave. I'll go to me ma's until we get wed, then he'll have to keep me.'

Emily filled a jug with hot water for Mrs Purnell's bathing and made a pot of tea, putting two cups and saucers on the tray and carrying them upstairs to her own room. She drank a cup of tea, all the time listening for movement from her mistress's room, but there was only the sound of snuffling and snoring.

A tap came at the door and she cautiously opened it. Mrs Brewer stood there. 'I thought you'd be awake, Emily. We shall have breakfast shortly if you want to join us. I expect the family will sleep in this morning.'

'I'm not hungry, Mrs Brewer, thank you,' she said. 'I'm just having a cup of tea and waiting for Mrs Purnell to wake.'

'You look pale, Emily. Are you not well?'

'I've started my flux, Mrs Brewer.' Tears came into her eyes as she told the lie. 'I'm sorry – I'm sorry.' She pointed to the stained sheets.

'Oh, don't worry.' Mrs Brewer nodded sympathetically. 'They'll boil. There'll be plenty of washing to do when everybody's gone. It'll take a week!'

Emily was starting to wash and dress when there was another tap on the door and she quickly pulled on her skirt and blouse and went to open it. Hugo, still in his night attire and robe, pushed open the door, forcing himself into the room.

'No please, Mr Hugo,' she pleaded. 'Not again. Everyone is up – Mrs Brewer –'.

'Has gone downstairs, I've just seen her. Come

along Emily. Be a good girl like you were last night.' He had a lascivious gleam in his eyes as he pushed her towards the bed. 'I know it's early, but I can't wait.'

She didn't cry. She simply lay there, her body inert, her mind blank, distancing herself from what was happening as he grunted and groaned above her. It didn't take so long this time and as he rolled off her he complained, 'I'm whacked, I'm going back to bed. Send me some breakfast up about eleven. Oh, yes, and send it up to Mrs Purnell too.' He grinned and squeezed his hands around her breasts. 'My dear little wife, I mean, not my mother.'

She was nervous and afraid once they were back in Mrs Purnell's house and during the next few weeks she kept her bedroom door firmly locked. She slept little, for she was convinced that she heard Mr Hugo's step outside her door and several times the doorknob turned. He caught her alone a few times as she went about her duties and holding her fast whispered to her to unlock her door at night. She shook her head and she saw the anger on his face.

Deborah constantly demanded her attention until Mrs Purnell grew exasperated and complained to Hugo. 'Emily is *my* servant paid by me to attend me! You must find someone else for your wife. I am irritated beyond belief at hearing her calling, *Emily, Emily,* all over the house!'

Hugo sighed. 'Why don't we get *you* someone else and we'll have Emily? It's the only way to satisfy Deborah, she's so used to having her own way.' He tapped his fingers together and mused. 'And then Emily could come with us to Italy.' He grinned as Emily knocked and came into the room with a tray of coffee. 'You'd like that wouldn't you, Emily? To come to Italy with my wife and me?'

Emily turned pale and her mouth worked as she thought of a suitable reply. 'I'm not a very good traveller, sir. I'd rather stay here.'

'Would you?' His manner was abrupt and his voice sharp. 'Well, you're not in a position to choose. If I decide you should go to Italy, then go you will or be given notice.'

Mrs Purnell flushed. 'That will be all, Emily,' and turned to Hugo as Emily scurried from the room. 'Don't you dare threaten my servants! I pay the staff in this house. When I am dead and buried you will do as you like, but not until then! You will not take Emily with you! I need her here and the sooner you take your whining wife out of the country the better!'

Hugo had taken his new wife to visit his friends and introduced her to the gaming clubs which he frequented, but he soon grew tired of hearing her squeals of laughter as she became more and more excitable as she watched the card games and demanded to play; Hugo's friends, initially amused by her childish antics, would encourage her to dance or sing and plied her with wine, but then became bored with her and turned their backs, which made her even more confused and demanding. 'For God's sake, Purnell; take your wife home,' someone shouted one night when Deborah had shrieked and giggled over a game of crib. 'We can't concentrate when she makes that racket. Is she a halfwit or what?'

There was a sudden silence and Deborah turned around, her eyebrows raised and her mouth half open as she heard the insult. All eyes turned to Hugo, who was stretched out in an easy chair about to take a glass of wine from a serving girl. He took the glass and, reaching out, threw a coin down her neckline and moued a kiss. He took a sip of wine and, holding the glass high, carefully turned it this way and that, as if examining the clarity. 'As a matter of fact, old boy, yes she is.'

Deborah let out an ear-piercing shriek and flung herself at Hugo, spilling the wine down his shirt and over her dress. 'You are not allowed to say that! You're not, you're not! Papa won't allow it.'

Hugo roared with laughter as he extricated himself from Deborah's flailing hands and, grasping her tightly, coarsely remarked, 'That is of no significance whatever my dear. Your darling papa isn't here to stop me!'

'No, you can't come,' he said to her on his next visit to his club. 'You've not been good so you must stay at home with my mother.' He grinned and said maliciously, 'And if I hear you have misbehaved whilst I am out I shall take Emily instead next time.'

'But she is a servant,' Deborah gasped. 'You can't take her.'

He looked in the mirror as he fastened a silk stock around his neck. 'But she is a very pretty servant is she not, Deborah? Don't you think?'

She gazed blankly at him through the mirror. 'Is she prettier than me?'

'Oh much prettier. Quite beautiful. I'm very fond of Emily.'

Deborah stared at him with venom in her eyes, then turned her back and stalked to her room, banging the door behind her.

'Do not leave your wife with me!' Mrs Purnell stated flatly a week later. 'I cannot cope with her. My friends do not wish her to visit as she is too disruptive. Do please make arrangements to travel to Italy as soon as you can. I am an old woman, Hugo,' she pleaded. 'I need peace and quiet and my own friends around me. Not a demanding, wilful child.' She looked him in the eyes. 'Either that or you find a house of your own.'

Hugo sighed. 'All right, Mother. I'll take her away. I don't suppose you'll relent and let me take Emily with us?'

'No.' She was emphatic. 'You must find another maid. Besides, Deborah seems to be most vindictive towards Emily just now. I can't think why, when she was so fond of her before.'

Emily sat on her bed and wept after they had watched Hugo and his wife and their new maid drive away on their journey to Italy. Such relief. Such a burden lifted. No more worrying over Hugo trying to get in to her room, nor the pain of being the butt of Deborah's temper, for no matter how Emily tried to please her, it seemed she could do nothing right and it wasn't just Deborah's ill temper, Emily had felt the hard slap of her hand too.

It was now March and she prayed they would

stay away all of the summer, although she had overheard Hugo tell his mother that they wouldn't stay in Florence during the hottest part of the year, but would perhaps visit the Italian lakes before beginning their journey home.

Later in the day she walked down Whitefriargate towards the Market Place on an errand for Mrs Purnell. The day was cold, though bright; it brought roses to her cheeks and she suddenly felt a freedom which she hadn't felt in weeks.

'Good day, Emily.' She stopped and turned and looked up at the man in uniform who touched his hat.

'Mr Linton!' That same face which had appeared during Hugo Purnell's rape of her body, suddenly brought back the terrifying ordeal. Shame flooded over her and she felt the blood drain from her face and a sensation of nausea.

A small frown wrinkled his brow. 'Are you well?' he asked. 'Still with Mrs Purnell?'

'Yes,' she whispered, 'for the moment.'

'Ah, you're thinking of changing positions? I heard', he said, when she didn't immediately answer, 'that Hugo Purnell has recently married?'

'Yes, sir. Mrs Hugo Purnell was formerly Miss Deborah Francis.'

'And are the happy couple away?'

'Yes, sir. They left today for Italy.' Her voice became lower and flatter as misery overcame her. Could he tell that she was not the person she had been?

'I am leaving the area too,' he said. 'My final examinations are over and I have a commission to join my ship.' He swallowed and ran a finger inside his collar. 'I, erm, I shall be away for perhaps a year or possibly longer. I – I do hope that if you decide to leave the Purnells you will leave a forwarding address.' He looked down at his feet. 'It would be nice to meet you again for a chat, Emily.'

She felt incredibly sad. She had harboured no impractical intent towards him, their worlds were too far apart for that, but to be able to speak to him sometimes, to pass the time of day, would have been such a joy. 'It would not be possible, Mr Linton,' she said softly. 'Circumstances would not allow it.' She blinked her eyes as emotion swept over her. 'Good day to you, sir. I wish you well in your life.'

He touched his hat again as she started to move away, puzzlement in his eyes. 'And I you, Emily.' He caught hold of her arm. 'My grandmother taught me that anything in life is possible, that I should never think that it isn't.'

'I'm sure that she was very wise, sir.' Her voice showed that she was not convinced. She dipped her knee. 'Goodbye, Mr Linton.'

Chapter Fifteen

'Get a move on, Emily. What's the matter with you, girl?' Mrs Purnell was impatient as Emily fumbled with the laces on her mistress's stays and stammered out her apologies.

'Not so tight. Not so tight, I can't breathe. I'm not eighteen you know! I just want a nice shape about my waist, that's all.' Mrs Purnell was very plump, but she was still very fashion conscious and liked to wear the latest styles. 'You're putting on weight, Emily, your skirt is far too tight. You'll have to let it out.' She shook her head in admonishment. 'I can't afford to be buying you a new outfit. Not until next year at any rate.'

Emily flushed and didn't say that she had already released the seams on her skirt. She was aware of the thickening around her waist and the fullness of her breasts, and of the lethargy which stole over her from time to time and she was very worried. She looked at herself in the hall mirror when no-one else was about, turning this way and that, trying to detect by her shape, whether or not her worries were real or imaginary.

She had had a bout of sickness for a few weeks,

but then so had the kitchen staff and they had blamed it on some tainted meat. The weather had been warm throughout the spring and food had gone off much more quickly than was usual, and now at the beginning of summer the weather was even hotter and stickier, and it seemed that there was no air circulating in the narrow streets of the town, which were always crowded with people.

'Call for a cab,' Mrs Purnell said when her dressing was complete. 'You can ride with me to Mrs Marshall's and then walk back. I won't need you any more until this evening, so you might as well be useful here as wait around chatting to the Marshall servants.'

Which was a pity, thought Emily, for I would like to see Ginny and have a talk to her. She had no confidantes here at Mrs Purnell's house and she felt as if she needed a friend.

But Ginny was just about to go on an errand for Mrs Marshall when they arrived, and so she waited for Emily to settle her mistress and take instructions on what time to come back for her. 'Mrs Marshall is going to Scarborough in July,' she said as they stepped out together. 'I expect she'll be asking Mrs Purnell to go with her again.'

'Will you be going, Ginny?' Emily asked. 'I hope Mrs Purnell takes me. I'd love to breathe in some sea air. It's so hot and smelly here.'

Ginny agreed. The stench of the whale blubber and seed oil hung over the town. It clung to curtains and fabric and no-one could open windows or doors for fear of letting the odour into their houses. 'Mrs Marshall might take her housekeeper and one of the other maids this time. She gives everyone a turn.' She gave a wry smile. 'We are supposed to think of it as a privilege and a holiday.'

It was like a holiday for me, Emily thought, though I have never been on one to know. But it was the best time of my life. She smiled as she reminisced over dancing with Philip Linton at the Spa and the soft words that he had whispered.

They walked briskly from Albion Street, where Mrs Marshall lived, and as they crossed over the Junction Bridge towards Whitefriargate, avoiding the crush of wagons and carts which were being driven towards the Market Place, Emily suddenly felt dizzy and nauseous. 'I'm sorry, Ginny, I'll have to stop. I don't feel well.' She leant against a bollard and bent over. 'You go on.'

'No, I'll wait.' Ginny looked down anxiously. 'What's made you sick? Is it the stink? You should be used to it by now.'

'I don't know. Probably. No. It's not.' She looked at Ginny apprehensively.

'You've been caught! You're expecting!' Ginny's eyes flickered over her face. 'I didn't know you was courtin'.'

Emily shook her head and wiped the corner of her mouth with a square of hemmed cotton. 'I'm not,' she whispered.

Ginny stared at her, her face expressionless. 'You've been raped! Who by?'

'Hugo Purnell.' She could hardly bring herself to say his name.

'God rot him,' Ginny hissed. 'You know he'll

deny it. You'll be given notice just like 'other lass.'

'Which other lass?' Emily stared back at her. 'At Mrs Purnell's?' A vague memory stirred of Mrs Purnell telling her that the previous maid had to leave because she was in trouble.

'Ask Mrs Anderson.' Ginny put her arm about her. 'She knows.'

'I daren't,' Emily stammered. 'I'm afraid of telling her what's happened. If I'm given notice, what will I do? Where will I go? Who'll employ me?'

Ginny shook her head. 'No-one will employ you without a reference and especially not if you're pregnant. When did it happen?'

'In February,' she whispered. 'His wedding night.'

'Scum,' Ginny muttered between her teeth. 'Viper! But it's too late to do anything. This is a pretty pickle, Emily, and no mistake.'

Mrs Purnell joined Mrs Marshall in Scarborough for a month and took Emily with her, but somehow the resort had lost its charm. There was no Ginny to talk to because she had stayed behind in Hull, as she had suggested she might, and all Emily was required to do was accompany the two ladies when they took the air along the Esplanade, or carry their parcels home from their frequent shopping trips. Even the carriage drive up Oliver's Mount, the finest terrace in England from where could be seen the surrounding views of the ocean, castle and the hills of the Wolds, failed to delight her as it had done the previous year.

She avoided going near the pier in case she should meet Ben Thompson. She was in no mood for pleasantries or protestations of affection, and when out alone she walked swiftly with her eyes to the ground to avoid the glances of ardent young men.

''Sea air has done you good, Emily,' Mrs Anderson remarked when they returned to Hull. 'You were looking very peaky before you went away.'

'I feel much better, Mrs Anderson.' In truth Emily did feel much better in health. The lethargy had left her, as had the sickness, but inwardly she was very troubled and finally she decided that she would have to confide in Mrs Anderson when she announced that Mr Hugo and his wife would be returning from abroad in October.

''Mistress isn't too pleased about it,' said the housekeeper grimly. 'She hasn't said as much of course, but I can tell. I know her well enough to know when she's displeased. She's not looking forward to having 'young mistress back with her tantrums and sulks.'

'You don't look too happy about it either, Emily.' Cook must have noticed her pallor at the news. 'You'll be 'butt of her nonsense again, I expect.'

'She can't help it.' In spite of her fears, Emily rose to her young mistress's defence. 'It's not her fault. She has to be treated gently and kindly. It's when she gets excited that she becomes –'.

'Deranged!' Dolly hooted. 'She's definitely got a screw loose.'

'That's unkind,' Emily said hotly, 'and not respectful.'

'That's enough, Dolly.' Mrs Anderson was sharp.

'Now get about your work, and you come with me, Emily.'

'So tell me what's troubling you.' She had pointed up the stairs and followed Emily to her room, where they couldn't be overheard. 'If it's not 'young mistress returning home, then what is it?' She stared hard at her and Emily knew that the housekeeper had probably guessed the truth.

'It's Mr Hugo,' she whispered and hung her head. 'I'm afraid of him.'

'Has he seduced you?' The housekeeper was terse, her questions sharp. 'Or have you been willing?'

'He did. But I never gave him any reason to think –'. She swallowed and whispered, shocked to think Mrs Anderson would doubt her. 'It was after the party on 'night of his wedding. He'd been drinking and he forced his way into my room.' She started to sob as she relived the horrors. 'His mother was sleeping in 'next room. I think he'd given her a sleeping draught. He was horrible. Horrible! Then – then, the next morning he came back again.' She broke into uncontrollable sobbing. 'When we came back here I kept my door locked, just like you said I should, but he was always up here, trying the door.'

She blew her nose hard, but still the tears fell as she said, 'He's got me pregnant, Mrs Anderson. He's taken away my virtue. I'm worthless! I was always a good lass, honest to God I was. But now I'm nothing.'

Mrs Anderson sank down on Emily's bed. Above her on the wall was the tract of the Servant Girl's

Prayer. 'Scum of the earth,' she muttered.

'No! No!' Emily protested. 'It wasn't my fault.'

'Not you, girl. Him! Our master whose desires we must obey. Well, you've obeyed his desires all right and look where it's got you.' Her mouth tightened. 'You know that he'll deny it? He'll say that he's never touched you or else that you led him on.'

'It's not true.' Emily vehemently shook her head. 'I swear that it's not!'

But Mrs Anderson didn't seem to be listening. 'He might give you some money to keep you quiet, of course, especially now he's got a young wife,' she murmured. 'It won't take folks long to add up two and two to know when it happened.'

'You do believe me, then?' Emily felt a small measure of relief.

'Oh aye. It's not 'first time.' Mrs Anderson glanced around the small room. ''Other maid that got caught was my niece Jenny in this very room. Onny she was more than willing, young strumpet! She thought he'd look after her, like he said.' She gave a coarse laugh. 'He looked after her all right! Gave her some money, which she spent on fancy clothes and gin, and now she's next door, her and her bairn.'

'Next door?' Emily was puzzled. An elderly gentleman lived next door with his housekeeper and valet. 'As a maid?'

'In 'workhouse,' Mrs Anderson answered grimly, 'where you'll probably end up.'

They agreed that nothing would be said to Mrs Purnell just yet, or to the other servants, and hoped that they wouldn't notice Emily's increasing plumpness, which in the current fashion was regarded as very desirous. She looked well, a fine bloom touched her fair skin, and her blond hair shone when she let it down to brush it. Mrs Anderson took care to let her off arduous tasks and Emily found that the housekeeper's previous sharp manner hid a solicitude which had not formerly been apparent.

'They'll be home at the end of 'week during October,' Mrs Anderson announced. ''Mistress has had a letter. Get a fire lit in both bedrooms, Dolly, and Emily you'd better order some extra flowers from 'florist to put in Miss Deborah's room. Off you go,' she said meaningfully. 'Go now.'

Emily thankfully put on her cloak and went out. Mrs Anderson must have guessed that she would be upset by the sudden news and would need time to prepare herself. She glanced at the workhouse gate as she passed and shivered. She had seen many of the inmates coming out from within its gloomy walls. They all looked thin and ill, with scabby faces and shabby clothes, and she wanted to weep as she thought that same fate might await her.

I shall have a child to look after. A child I don't want. That I never asked for. I never expected this. She thought of her friend Jane, pregnant by Brown and wondered if they were married yet. She has her mother to help her, and her sisters. They'll be poor, but the child will be loved and cared for. I have no-one.

Her tears were still falling as she entered the

florist's shop. She had been in here only occasion-ally, as a regular order was sent to Mrs Purnell's every week. An assistant took the extra order and through the back of the shop Emily saw an older woman, who looked up from her desk and gazed at her, and whom she guessed was the owner. The perfume of the flowers drifted over her, the heavy perfume of roses, lilies and exotic flowers brought in from abroad and lingering beneath that the homely cottage-garden scent of sweet lavender and rosemary. She wiped away tears, which came so readily these days.

'Does the scent upset you?' the older woman called to her.

'Oh no.' Emily smiled through her tears. 'Not at all. It reminds me of where I used to live – in 'country. There were so many nice smells there.'

The woman nodded in agreement then bent her head, but glanced up again as Emily took her leave.

'They're here. They're here. Run up and tell 'mistress, Emily. 'Rest of you, tidy yourselves up while I open 'door.' Mrs Anderson barked out instructions three days later as the front door was hammered on with great force.

'You don't need to come and tell me,' Mrs Purnell said as Emily entered her room. 'I know well enough who gives orders to break down the door.' She seemed flustered yet pleased to welcome the return of her son. 'I do hope everything is going to be all right. Do you think the tour will have been good for my son's wife, Emily? Her health, you know? You knew her before.'

'I don't know, ma'am. I wasn't at Elmswell for very long and I don't remember Miss Deborah – Mrs Purnell, ever going away.'

'Hmm. Well, we'll have to wait and see, I suppose.' Mrs Purnell rose from her chair and went to greet her son and his wife and Emily followed behind and joined the line of servants who were waiting in the hall to greet them.

Hugo was tanned and handsome, but Deborah was pale and wan and trailed behind him. Behind her was the maid, perky and dark with a saucy look about her. Hugo bowed and kissed his mother and she then gave Deborah a light kiss on her cheek. He turned to greet the staff. 'Mrs Anderson.' He gave a slight nod of his head to the stony faced housekeeper. 'Cook, Dolly.' He moved on towards Emily. 'Emily.' A smile played around his mouth and she trembled as she dipped her knee. 'How very well you look, Emily.' He took Deborah's hand and drew her towards him. 'Say hello to Emily, my dear. Doesn't she look well?'

Deborah stared at Emily, her eyes were dull and her mouth worked, as if she was trying to say something but the words wouldn't come out.

'And you have all met Alice.' Hugo indicated the new maid. 'Alice has been a treasure, hasn't she, Debs? Knows exactly how to look after you?'

Alice smirked and then took hold of Deborah's arm. 'We'd better go up for a rest, ma'am. It's been a long journey.' She turned to Emily standing at the end of the line. 'Send up some broth and a little bread for Mrs Purnell, she needs to take some refreshment before her medication,' and she propelled her mistress up the stairs.

Hugo smiled. 'A treasure,' he repeated and escorted his mother to the drawing room. 'You wouldn't believe the difference Alice has made to Deborah.'

Mrs Purnell frowned. 'She looks a little flighty to me. And medication? What medication is Deborah taking?'

Hugo stretched himself out on a sofa and yawned. 'I found a fantastic doctor in Florence. Deborah had been making a fuss as usual, getting quite hysterical over nothing, and I spoke to one or two people about it and this fellow was recommended. He gave Deborah a few drops of his magical potion and it worked; mark you, she wouldn't take it at first, she had to be held down. But now she's as meek as a lamb. No trouble at all.'

His mother looked worried. 'But what is it? Is it addictive? I don't like the idea –'.

'I have his assurance that it is perfectly safe.' He got up from the sofa. 'If you will excuse me, Mother. I must get changed out of these clothes. Then I'm off to my club to see what's been going on in my absence.'

He arrived back home after midnight and strode softly up the stairs. He hesitated for a moment on the landing, then continued up to the next floor. He turned the knob on Emily's door. It turned and he smirked and entered. 'Emily,' he whispered, 'what a good girl. Are you pleased to see me back?'

The light by the bed was turned low and a hand reached out to turn it up and show Mrs Anderson sitting on the bed fully dressed. 'Emily isn't using this room any more, sir.' She stared at him with hatred in her eyes. 'You've ruined her, just as you ruined Jenny. You should be ashamed, sir.'

He strode across towards her and grabbing her by the collar hauled her off the bed. 'Don't you dare speak to me like that, you old hag, or you'll be sorry.' He wrenched at the neckline of her dress, tearing it. 'I could give you a taste of the same if I fancied to.' He sneered. 'It would be the first time, wouldn't it? The first time you had a man's hand on you?'

'Sir,' she gasped, 'Mr Hugo! Have some respect. I am a single elderly woman.'

He pushed her roughly back on to the bed. 'Then you hold your tongue or it'll be the worse for you.' He turned to go. 'And tell Emily I will be waiting for her.'

'Emily is pregnant,' she blurted out. 'You must leave her alone.'

He raised his eyebrows and laughed. 'Pregnant! And I suppose she's saying the bastard is mine?'

Mrs Anderson said nothing, just swallowed nervously and clutched her hands together.

'Give her a shilling and dismiss her,' he said curtly. 'It has nothing to do with me.'

Chapter Sixteen

Emily spent the night in Mrs Anderson's room, but she didn't sleep. She had been racked with pain in her back and she had achingly paced the floor, worrying over what Mr Hugo would say to Mrs Anderson when he discovered that they had exchanged rooms, for Emily had heard him creeping up the stairs towards her room.

Mrs Anderson tapped gently on the door at five o'clock, whispering to let her in. Her face looked grey and her eyes were heavy as if she hadn't slept either.

'He says I've to dismiss you. I'll have to speak to 'mistress.' She seemed frightened and confused.

Emily held her arms across her stomach. She felt sick. 'What am I to do, Mrs Anderson? I feel ill. Where can I go?'

The housekeeper shook her head. 'I can't help you. He's threatened me. I'll lose my position if I do any more and where would I get work at my age?'

'I'm sorry.' Emily started to cry, as once more the pain stabbed in her back and she drew in a deep breath. 'I don't want you to get into trouble on my account.'

Mrs Anderson's eyes narrowed. 'Have you started? Is 'babby coming?'

Emily's mouth grew round in dismay. 'I don't know. I've been awake all night.'

'Come upstairs.' Mrs Anderson gathered Emily's clothes together. 'Go back to your room. It might be a false alarm, but we can't take 'risk. You can't give birth here.'

She bundled Emily upstairs as quickly and quietly as possible. 'Stay here. I'll say you're poorly. Keep 'door locked and try not to make a noise.'

Emily lay back on her bed, but she was restless and the pain in her back gradually grew worse and moved round to the front, pulling and dragging at her. She sat up and stared at the window as sunlight started to filter through as the morning mist disappeared. 'I'm in labour,' she whispered. 'I'm going to give birth and there's no-one here to help me. What do I do? I might die!' She knew of no-one who had experienced childbirth. Granny Edwards had never spoken of it and Emily's only knowledge was observation and whispered conversation with her former school friends.

After a while the pain eased and she tiptoed to the door and opened it a crack and listened. She could hear voices down below. One was Hugo's and she thought the other was Mrs Purnell's. Then she heard the front door closing and the sound of a carriage pulling away.

Mrs Anderson scurried upstairs with a slice of bread and a pot of tea. Emily was glad of a hot drink, but couldn't eat. 'I think 'babby's coming, Mrs Anderson. I feel so strange.'

173

'God help us!' Mrs Anderson was distraught. 'I don't know what to do! I've never seen a babby born afore.'

They stared at each other. 'Neither have I,' Emily whispered. 'Only kittens and lambs. But it's a natural thing, Mrs Anderson, so I'll just have to get on with it. What did Mrs Purnell say?'

'I haven't told her.' Mrs Anderson shook her head. 'They've all gone out visiting. I thought I'd leave it till later. I didn't want to ruin her day.'

Emily sweated and groaned all day and Mrs Anderson came up at intervals, bringing her hot and cold drinks and an armful of old sheets which she asked her to put over the bed linen. 'Dolly's from a big family, shall I ask her what to do?' she asked, as Emily panted over the iron bedrail.

'No. Don't tell anybody. It's best that they don't know, then they can't get into trouble.'

Mrs Anderson took her drawstring purse from under her apron. 'Mr Hugo said I had to give you a shilling and dismiss you,' she said slowly, 'but you have some wages to come.' She tipped out some coins onto the table. ''Mistress might give you something, but on 'other hand she might not. She doesn't like this kind of thing.'

Emily gave a short sharp sound, somewhere between a laugh and a cry. 'I'm not very happy about it either,' she groaned. 'It's not something I planned. Not yet anyway.'

Mrs Anderson was getting more and more nervous. 'I'll have to go down. 'Family will be back soon and I don't know how long I can keep you up here without them in 'kitchen getting suspicious.'

Emily wiped the sweat from her brow. 'You go, Mrs Anderson. I'll be all right.'

But the housekeeper was no sooner gone than she was once more riven with pains, which came faster and faster. She paced the floor, she crouched, she knelt, trying to find some relief until at last she could no longer hold back her cries, and as she opened her mouth to scream, she gave birth and the cry faded. The infant slid from her body to lie still and lifeless between her thighs.

She was barely conscious of what happened next, only that it was a boy and there was something wrong. He was so tiny and his colour didn't look healthy. As if in a trance, she cut the cord which bound them together and picking him up, she wiped his mouth and nose and eyes of mucus with her fingers, and gently patted his back. There was no response so she carefully opened his small mouth and softly blew her own breath into him. She felt his chest for the sound of a heartbeat, but there was nothing. She had often in her childhood held a baby bird and felt the flutter of a tiny beating heart, but there was only stillness within this child's body. She leaned towards the drawer by her bed and taking a clean white shift from it she wrapped it around him and held him close.

'A shilling for your life,' she murmured as she gently rocked him, 'a life which didn't even begin.'

It grew darker as she lay with the child in her arms, but she didn't bother to light the lamp. She felt no pain now, only sorrow in her heart for this child which had come from her body. The child which she hadn't wanted but which she knew she would have come to love, even though the begetting of him had been so abhorrent to her.

She sat for a long time rocking the infant, her mind blank, not thinking of what the future might hold, until she heard the slam of the front door and she knew that the Purnells had returned. They would go to their rooms and change from their travelling attire into their supper dress. She would be missed, but she guessed that Mrs Anderson would make an excuse for her and send Dolly up to help Mrs Purnell to change, whilst the new maid Alice would assist Miss Deborah.

'Then they'll go downstairs,' she mused, 'and won't come up again until bedtime.' She looked down at the infant and touched his tiny cold hands. 'I shall have to leave you', she murmured, 'because I don't know where I'm going. I only know that I can't stay here.'

She placed the child on the bed and lit the lamp, then washed herself and tidied the room, taking the soiled sheets from the bed and heaping them in a corner where Mrs Anderson would attend to them. She took her own few possessions from the drawer and wrapped them in a bundle, then listened once more at the door. She heard Hugo's coarse laugh and a band of hatred tightened around her chest. Deborah's thin voice called out and the authoritative voice of her maid answered her. Their footsteps sounded on the stairs, followed by the pad of Mrs Purnell's feet as they all went down for supper.

There was no-one about as she slipped down the

stairs to Hugo's room. A lamp was turned low and a fire was burning brightly in the hearth and already the bedcover had been turned back for him. She moved one of the pillows and carefully placed the child on it, still wrapped in her shift. 'Sleep well, poor baby,' she whispered and bent to kiss his forehead. Then she made the sign of a cross on his brow. 'Heaven bless and keep you.'

She placed the shilling which she had taken from the few Mrs Anderson had given her and placed it on the pillow beside him, then rising up she glanced around the room and gave a sudden gasp. Above the fireplace and directly opposite the bed, where Hugo would see it as he lay between his sheets, was the portrait of the naked woman which he had forced Emily to look at, saying that it resembled her.

The portrait had been removed from his wife's room since their return from Italy and only Hugo could have moved it, for Emily knew that no-one else had had instructions to do so. As she stared at the portrait she felt a real fear. His desire for her then was unsated, his covetous appetite not yet satisfied. She trembled at the realization that his lechery still reached out towards her. She wanted to scream and shout in her own defence, but she could only remain silent. No-one would believe her. She was a fallen servant girl and he a gentleman. A babe lay dead, her own life altered beyond belief, and she wanted revenge.

She picked up the poker which lay in the hearth and plunged it into the coals as if she was plunging it into Hugo Purnell's heart. It sizzled and she turned it until the tip was red hot. She withdrew it and, holding it high, sank the burning end into the picture. The canvas curled and smoked, leaving a black circle. She gave a wild smile and her eyes gleamed. She lifted the poker and struck, again and again, striking the canvas and the gilt frame until it splintered and the image of the naked woman hung in shreds.

She backed away, awestruck at the damage she had done, and hastily threw the poker down, where it slowly burned a small hole in the carpet. Her heart beat with a violent intensity and she glanced fearfully around the room as if to see if anyone was watching. She put her hands to her mouth to stop herself crying out. What had she done? What would they say? They would know she was the one who had caused the damage. She gave a sudden laugh. They would also know whose child it was lying in Hugo's bed.

Quietly she opened the door and looked out into the corridor. There was no-one there. She crept back to her own room, trembling with fear and anger, her hands shaking as she gathered up her bundle. There were sounds of voices coming from the dining room and the smell of food drifted up from the kitchen as she crept downstairs, reminding her that she hadn't eaten all day. She crossed the hall and unlatched the door and heard Dolly's voice as she came up the kitchen stairs. She closed the door quietly behind her, went down the steps and into the dimly lit street.

The wind blew cold. A north-easterly wind which she remembered Sam used to say came from the steppes of Russia, though he had no idea what or where those steppes were. She pulled her cloak about her, gathering up its warmth and felt weak, physically and mentally. Take hold of yourself, Emily, she chastised herself. You're young. Your body is strong and healthy, it can withstand pain. She scurried on, not knowing quite where to go but heading towards the High Street, where she knew there would be plenty of people about and where she could hide if anyone should come looking for her.

She drew abreast of the King's Head Inn and stopped. There was warmth and the sound of people singing and the smell of food coming from its interior. It was an ancient inn built of brick and timber with overhanging mullioned windows and she stood in the doorway and looked in. She had never been in an inn before and she hesitated about doing so now, but she leant against the door jamb, feeling faint and dizzy.

'Well, is tha going in or coming out, my lovely lass?' a voice behind her called out and as she turned to answer, the sudden movement brought a curtain of blackness which engulfed her and she pitched forward in a crumpled heap on to the inn floor.

Chapter Seventeen

'Mrs Purnell, please! You must take your medication.'

'I will not and you can't make me.' Deborah stared obstinately at the maid, who was holding the bottle and spoon.

'I'll tell Mr Hugo,' Alice menaced. 'He'll make you take it. Like he did last time.'

A flicker of fear shadowed Deborah's face. She hated being held down. Last time it was the doctor and Hugo who had held her, whilst a nurse pinched her nose and poured the fluid down her throat. But she didn't think Hugo would do it when they were in his mother's house. Mrs Purnell, Deborah had discovered, didn't like a fuss over anything.

'Come along,' Alice wheedled, 'be a good girl.'

'Don't you dare talk to me like that!' Deborah shrieked. 'Just remember your place.'

'Beg pardon, ma'am.' The cynical look of disdain was lost on Deborah as her maid bobbed her knee in apology. The familiarity which Mr Hugo had shown towards Alice had assured the servant that she could do and say, within reason, anything she wanted in this household.

She approached Deborah again with the bottle tipped and the spoon at the ready. 'You don't want Mr Hugo to get cross, do you, ma'am?' She smiled as if at a child. 'Come along now.'

Deborah let her get close and then with a sudden swing of her arm she let fly, pushing the maid off-balance and spilling the syrupy liquid all over her. She ran towards the inner door which led to Hugo's room and pushing it open dashed inside and locked the door behind her. 'You take it if you have a mind to,' she shrieked through the door, 'because I won't. And I shall tell my papa about you.'

She heaved a small sigh of satisfaction. She hadn't won many battles since marrying Hugo. He seemed always to get the better of her and, although at first he had been kind and patient, whilst in Italy he had been increasingly bad tempered with her, making her take the horrid medicine as well as leaving her alone with Alice whilst he went out. And when she objected, he shouted at her and threatened that he would lock her up if she didn't behave.

She wrinkled her nose. There was a strange smell. Not the usual smell of pomade which Hugo used for his hair dressing, but an acrid smell of burning. She looked towards the fire. It was burning low and needed a stir. Where was the poker? She glanced around. Why was it on the carpet and not in the hearth? She picked up the poker and saw it had burned a hole in the carpet. She drew in a breath and threw it into the hearth.

Hugo might think she had done it. Then her eyes travelled upwards. The painting which Hugo admired so much was torn and burnt, and as she stared, Hugo, with Alice behind him, opened the bedroom door.

He too stared at the painting. 'Who's done this?' he demanded. 'Deborah?'

'No. No! It wasn't me, Hugo,' she stammered. 'The fire must have burnt it.'

He strode across the room and, taking hold of her by the shoulders, shook her. 'This is deliberate. If I thought you –!'

'No, sir. Miss Deborah was with me until a few minutes ago,' Alice interrupted, fearful that she would be blamed for not watching her mistress more closely.

'Then who –?' He glanced around the room. 'One of the maids?' His eyes lit on the bed, noticing the disarranged pillow and Alice too looked towards it. She gave a small cry and put her hands to her mouth.

Deborah ran towards the bed. 'There's a baby. Hugo! Oh, a tiny little baby.' She smiled and bent to pick it up. 'Is it for me?'

'Leave it,' he roared. 'Don't touch it.'

Alice drew near and peered at the baby. She screwed up her mouth. 'Stillborn by 'look of it, sir. Never drawn breath. I've seen 'em afore.'

'Fetch Mrs Anderson', he bellowed, 'straight away. And then both of you get out.'

Mrs Anderson, her face pale, clasped her hands tightly together as she entered the room. She had been to check on Emily only ten minutes earlier and found her room empty. She had been unable to go up before as her attention had been required by Mrs Purnell, and she had no idea whether or not Emily had given birth or where she had gone. In her ignorance she assumed that Emily had left to have the baby elsewhere. She gaped at the still form in the bed and then looked up at Mr Hugo.

'Well?' he demanded. 'Whose child is this? And what is it doing in my bed?'

She licked her lips and whispered. 'I don't know, sir.'

'You don't know!' He put his face close to hers. 'I think you do,' he hissed. 'It belongs to that little slut Emily, who's seeking to lay the blame on me.' He shook her by the arm. 'Isn't it?'

'I don't know, sir,' she trembled. 'She'd gone into labour it's true, but I don't know what happened or where she is. Her room's empty. She's gone!'

'Who has gone?' Mrs Purnell stood in the doorway, brought upstairs by the commotion. 'What is happening, Hugo!'

'That little drab whom you are so fond of, Mother. Emily. She has given birth to a bastard in our house and seeks to lay the blame at my door by leaving it in my bed!'

'Emily? But I would have known. Anyway, she wouldn't do such a dreadful thing. She's a good girl.' Mrs Purnell crossed the room to look in the bed and then recoiled. 'We must send for a doctor and a priest. It doesn't look healthy.'

'It's too late for that, Mother.' His eyes flashed from his mother to Mrs Anderson and then back again. 'I think that she was so ashamed of how far she has fallen that she has murdered the child.' His mouth twisted into a thin, hard line. 'We must send for the constable straight away.'

Emily came around to find herself lying in a chair by a fire and surrounded by a crowd of interested faces. 'Oh! Where am I? What happened?'

'You've just fainted, m' dear. And you're in 'King's Head, 'best inn in town.'

The woman who spoke was elderly, with a white apron over her dress and a pleated bonnet on her grey hair. 'Seems to me', she said, 'that you're in need of some victuals.'

'Yes,' Emily whispered. 'I am hungry. I haven't eaten all day. I – er, I've just come off 'York coach.'

The woman raised an eyebrow. 'Oh, aye? Running late is it?'

Emily flushed, caught out in her first lie.

'You don't need to tell me owt,' the landlady said. 'I keep my own counsel. What folk get up to is nowt to do wi' me.'

'Could you let me have a room for the night,' Emily ventured, 'and a little supper?'

'Aye, if you can pay,' she nodded. 'In advance!'

'I can pay. Could I see the room, please?'

The inn had many small rooms with smoky fires and the stairs were narrow and steep. As Emily wearily hauled herself up them she felt that she could sleep where she dropped. But she pulled back the sheets on the bed she was shown and saw that they were clean, and putting her hand on them felt that they were aired. 'Thank you,' she said when the woman told her the terms. 'If you could include a bowl of soup and a little chicken in 'price, I'll take it for tonight and tomorrow night.'

The landlady agreed, glad to have a quiet resident and money in her hand and when she brought up a bowl of steaming soup and a plate of cold chicken, Emily was sitting by the fire with her shawl around her and her stockinged feet in the hearth. She had let her hair down and was plaiting it in a single braid over her shoulder.

'Pretty hair,' said the landlady as she put down the tray, 'lovely colour,' then added, 'I'll send 'maid up with a warming pan, though as you already noticed, miss, I keep my beds well aired. But it's a cold night and if you've been travelling far –'. Though she had stated that she kept her counsel, she was obviously very curious about Emily. 'You're onny a young lass to be travelling alone at this hour of night. It's not safe. 'Town is full of footpads and ruffians!'

'I haven't much money,' Emily confessed. 'No-one would want anything that I have.'

'Don't be too sure about that,' the woman said darkly. 'Some villains would take 'boots off your feet and 'bonnet off your head if you weren't looking.'

With this dire warning she left her and after the maid had brought up the hot coals in the warming pan and run it about the bed, Emily undressed and climbed into bed and, with her hands clasped together, made a silent prayer for the dead child and another one for herself.

She slept for most of the next day, exhausted by

the trauma of the birth, though she roused herself to drink the hot chocolate which Mrs Thomas, the landlady, sent up for her. In the evening the maid knocked on the door to enquire if she would be down for supper. 'No, thank you,' she said, 'though if you would build up 'fire I'll take a little soup up here.' She dared not ask for more as she wanted to conserve what money she had.

She ate the soup and slept once more and the following morning woke refreshed in body though troubled in mind. She washed and dressed and went downstairs. Mrs Thomas greeted her and poured her a cup of coffee. 'Where are you off to this morning, m' dear?' she asked in idle curiosity.

'Beverley,' Emily answered swiftly. 'I have an aunt there.'

'Ah! Did you not think of getting off 'coach there the other night?'

'I – er, no. I had some business to attend to in Hull.' I am useless at lying, Emily thought. I have had so little practice at it.

'Well you've missed 'morning coach. Next one isn't until five o'clock. Unless you can get a carrier. That would be your best bet, save you hanging around all day. 'Course you're very welcome to stop here, but I'd have to charge you extra.'

'No, thank you. I'd best be off.' She gathered up her bundle. 'Thank you, you've been very kind.'

Mrs Thomas gazed at her. 'Here,' she said, 'have another cup and a slice o' toast. Can't have you travelling without summat inside you. You still look a bit peaky.'

Emily put down her bundle gratefully. 'I haven't been well,' she said, 'though I do feel much better after the rest.'

'Well, I hope your aunt takes care of you when you get to her,' Mrs Thomas said sagely. 'And then you'll be looking for work, I expect.'

'Oh yes,' Emily said eagerly. 'Do you know of anyone in the Beverley area who would want a maid?'

'Plenty of people of quality in Beverley would take a fine young lass like you; or else,' she added, almost as an afterthought, 'there's inns and publics if you haven't a reference.'

That's the difference, Emily pondered as she sipped her coffee at a table by the window, whilst Mrs Thomas busied herself with a duster. I won't be able to get a decent place and even if I did, sooner or later I would be found out. There would be somebody who would know Mrs Purnell, and how dreadful if I should meet her face to face.

The door from the kitchen flew open. 'Mrs Thomas!' The young maid who had brought up the coals and the chocolate was agog with excitement. 'You know that young woman that's been staying? Well, there's posters up in town wanting to know of her whereabouts –'. Her voice trailed away as she noticed Emily sitting by the window.

Mrs Thomas's eyes grew hard. 'How do you know it's 'same young woman?'

'It said she had long fair hair, Swedish or Norwegian type it said,' she whispered. 'It's her all right, there was a full description.'

'Nonsense.' Mrs Thomas was sharp. 'Why is she being looked for?'

The maid's eyes grew wide and her mouth grew slack. 'It said she's wanted for 'murder of a bairn.'

Emily dropped her cup, splashing the coffee over the table. 'No! It's not true.'

''Constables are coming.' The maid continued to stare at Emily. 'They're on their way.'

'Here?' Mrs Thomas let out a shriek. 'Coming here?'

The girl nodded, still with her eyes on Emily. 'When I saw 'poster I dashed to Blanket Row police station to tell 'em. I knew tha wouldn't want her stopping here. Not a murderer!'

'You stupid girl!' Mrs Thomas fetched a clout around the girl's head and as she ducked gave her another one. 'Fetching police here! This is a respectable establishment. We shall have all riff-raff of 'town here, wanting to know all about her.' She gave her a push. 'Get down to 'kitchen and don't say another word to anybody, do you hear?'

She picked up Emily's bundle and thrust it into her hands. 'Come on. Be quick. You can be off before they get here.' She hurried her towards the door. 'I'll not say owt if you don't.'

Emily could barely speak. 'I never did anything,' she gasped. 'In God's name I didn't.'

Mrs Thomas didn't answer, for as she opened the door, a constable and sergeant of the police force stood on the step.

'Emily Hawkins?' said the sergeant.

Emily nodded. She felt faint and black spots danced around her.

'We have to ask you to come with us, miss. It's alleged that you've committed 'sin of murder on a newborn child and wanton destruction of property.'

Chapter Eighteen

The servants were questioned by the police, but they knew nothing, not even that Emily was expecting a child. 'She kept it well hidden,' Dolly muttered, 'though of course she was a well-made lass so we wouldn't notice.' She was rather annoyed that she hadn't known. Mrs Anderson admitted that she had known but hadn't told Mrs Purnell, though she had intended to.

Hugo was closeted in the study with the police and it was he who had made the charge.

'She doesn't seem 'usual type, sir,' said the constable. 'I was the one who made 'arrest and she seemed quite innocent to me, not like some of 'harpies I see. And I don't know much about babbies, that's women's business, but it could have been born dead.'

'Ha! Don't be misled by her.' Hugo pointed a finger at him. 'She might look like an angel but believe me, had I not been happily married I might well have succumbed to her advances and she's not the sort to want children hanging around her skirts! And then there's the destruction of the painting,' he added. 'She is obviously vicious to do a thing like that.' He sighed. 'It was a particular favourite of my wife's.'

The constable raised his eyebrows. 'Really, sir.'

Hugo gave a small smile. 'Indeed. My wife is a lover of art. She is devastated by the loss.'

'Could I speak to your wife, sir? See if she can shed some light on what has happened?'

'I'm afraid not.' Hugo rose to his feet, summarily dismissing him. 'She is in delicate health and this dreadful event has upset her greatly. She has taken to her bed in some distress.'

'I'm sorry to hear that, sir. Then I'll wish you good day. You will, of course, be called as a witness at the hearing. But not yet.' He shook his head. 'These cases take weeks to come to court.' He hesitated. 'I suppose there's no-one who would stand surety for 'young woman? She'd not be a danger to anybody.'

Hugo drew in a breath of horror. 'Certainly not! Think of the effect on my wife and mother if they thought she was roaming the streets. No, keep her where she is. Let her repent on her sins at leisure.'

Mrs Purnell sat in her sitting room with the curtains closed and her smelling salts clutched to her bosom. She had thought long and hard on this terrible situation and had come to the only conclusion possible. But Hugo was her son and she must stand by him.

'Sit down, Hugo. I want to talk to you. I am very upset over all this business. Very upset indeed.'

'And so you might be, Mother,' he said smoothly. 'It's a dreadful affair. Of course we realize now why

Roger Francis wanted rid of her; she was obviously trouble right from the start.'

Mrs Purnell looked startled. 'Surely not. She was so young when she came, and so pretty,' she added regretfully. 'I can't think that it was so.' She gazed frankly at her son. 'I cannot contend with this upset, Hugo. It is an affront to my nerves. You know how I hate scandal! So I've made a decision. I'm not accusing you, don't think that I am, but there's something amiss here,' she raised her hand as he started to speak, 'and I don't really want to know what it is.'

He shuffled slightly and shrugged, but made no answer.

'I want you and Deborah to leave here: buy a house of your own where you can do as you like when you like.' She saw his expression change. He was going to argue with her, so she added swiftly, 'There will be the trial, the police will want to question you again, seeing as you and Deborah found the child and I don't want them in my house. I am old, Hugo,' she pleaded. 'I need a quiet life.' And neither do I want your wife trailing around after me wherever I go, she thought. Already there were hints from her friends that Deborah was not welcome.

'All the more reason why I should stay, Mother,' he wheedled. 'I can look after you.'

'I don't need looking after, Hugo,' she said sharply. 'I pay servants to look after me! I want my house to myself. You must buy a house for yourself and Deborah. Go to Hessle or Anlaby, those places are close enough to town for shopping or your clubs – and the air will be better for her.'

'This is my house too,' he said curtly. 'Father always said so.'

'Not until I die.' Her mouth set in a tight line. 'It was written into his will. It will come to you after I die. Not before!'

They stared at each other, locked in acrimony. 'I have made up my mind, Hugo,' she said firmly. 'I want you to leave this house and take your wife with you.'

The constable had put manacles on Emily's wrist as they left the inn and attached them to his own wrist. 'Please don't,' she pleaded. 'I won't run away.'

He looked down on her. He carried a truncheon and a rattle and seemed huge in his tall hat and navy swallow-tailed coat. 'We've heard that one before, haven't we Sergeant Harris?'

The sergeant looked concerned. He was dressed similarly to the constable, but had silver-plated buttons on his coat and wore white gloves and carried an umbrella. 'Sorry miss, but we have to.' He put a rope round her waist and twisted it around his hand. 'If we mislaid you, we should be in trouble with 'inspector. Don't worry,' he said. 'I'm sure it'll all be sorted out.'

She kept her head bent as she was marched down the thronging Market Place towards the police station in Blanket Row, hoping that she wouldn't be recognized by anyone and praying that this was some dreadful mistake, a nightmare from which she would soon awaken.

'Charge of murder of a newborn child,' said the

constable as they passed through the heavy gaol door, 'and wilful destruction of property.'

'No!' Emily gasped with muffled breath. 'No! It's not true. The baby was dead. He never drew breath. I tried to revive him.' She started to sob. 'Please. You must believe me. I'd never do such a wicked thing.'

The clerk at the desk didn't look up, but started to write laboriously in a large book. 'Name? Last address? Occupation?'

She gave them, choking and almost fainting with fear, then the clerk looked up and asked, 'Witnesses?'

'Mr Hugo Purnell and his wife; address Parliament Street, same as 'prisoner.' The sergeant looked at Emily with something like sympathy as he spoke. 'Occupation, gentleman.'

'She can't stop here,' the clerk continued writing. 'We're full up. Besides she needs to be secure on that charge. You'll have to tek her to Kingston Street gaol until 'magistrate's ready for her.'

Emily felt her heart beating faster in her chest as the name of the House of Correction was given. This was the place where villains, thieves and felons were taken to atone for their sins. They were put to the treadmill or made to crush whiting. Surely, surely, they couldn't mean to take her there?

The constable expressed annoyance at having to trail further across to the edge of the town to deposit Emily, but there was nothing for it; the police station was small, overcrowded and in-adequate for keeping prisoners for very long.

The House of Correction was built in an oval shape around a sunken area, with five prison buildings leading off from it. There were separate wards for male and female debtors, other cells were classed for various kinds of delinquency, and between the work buildings and the cells there were open yards containing water pumps. Overlooking the whole of the building the governor's house stood like a sentinel on duty.

Emily shook, hardly able to hold her hands still as they unfastened the handcuffs and, with the rope still around her, took her down a flight of stone steps and through into a long, dark, brick-built passageway barred at both ends by an iron gate. 'Nowt to do with us, miss,' said the sergeant almost apologetically, 'but a child's body has been found, there's a damaged picture, and a charge has been made against you.'

She said nothing. There seemed to be nothing to say. Who would believe her? Who would take her word against that of Hugo Purnell? A gentleman?

They led her down the passage, past locked doors, down another flight of steps, lit only by a flickering lamp high on the wall, and into another passageway, damp and fetid, which made her wrinkle her nose in disgust. A sickening stench of unwashed bodies met her as they urged her towards an iron gate which led into a large square cell divided into two, one of which held male and the other female prisoners. Some of the women rose from their seats on the floor as Emily and the constables entered and it seemed to her that they were like ghouls from hell with their dark, shadowed faces, matted hair and rough fingers which picked and pulled at her clothing.

'Get back!' Sergeant Harris roared at them. 'Go on. Get back, you old drabs!'

'Who's this then, Harris? Here's a pretty customer.' A dishevelled woman with clothes in rags and dirty hair leered at Emily. 'What 'you been up to, dearie?'

Emily stepped back in horror. Surely they wouldn't lock her up with people such as this?

'Put her in a single cell,' Harris advised. 'She'll be safer on her own than with this rabble.'

'Here! Who 'you calling rabble?' A voice echoed from the male cell.

'It's what I'm calling you, Briggs, 'cos that's what you are. Now just keep quiet.'

They unlocked another iron gate, which made a small cell against the outer wall and was open to the view of the larger one. There was a short bench against the wall, just long enough for a small person to lie on, though not comfortably, a rough blanket was folded upon it and a bucket placed underneath.

Emily turned to the guards horrorstruck. 'You're not leaving me here?'

'Best room in 'house,' the constable grinned. 'Unless you'd rather bed down with this lot!'

The female prisoners gathered about her cell, looking curiously at her through the bars. 'What's she in for?' asked one scrawny old woman, who like the others was dressed in rags. 'She's onny a bairn.'

'Been pinching stuff, I bet,' said another woman, who stood with her arms folded, watching. 'Can't trust these pretty lasses. If they're not on 'game, then they'll pinch 'clothes off your back.'

'You can talk, Meg,' a woman in the corner guffawed. 'If anybody knows about it, you do.'

'Hah!' The woman named Meg cavorted around the cell, her hand on her swaying hip. 'Saying I'm pretty, eh?'

'No, you ugly whore, I'm not,' the woman growled. 'Leave 'lass alone.'

'You'd better not meddle with her.' Benton locked the iron gate behind them. 'She's in for murder.'

There was a sudden silence as this news was imparted and the women moved back slightly. Emily gripped the barred gate. 'I didn't do anything,' she wept. 'They said I killed the baby, but I didn't. He never took a single breath.'

The man Briggs in the next cell shouted, 'It's a sin to kill. You'll rot in hell!'

'Leave her alone!' Meg and the old woman both shouted back in her defence. 'What do men know?'

The old woman put her face against the bars. 'Don't make no difference whether tha did it or not, dearie. If they say that tha did, then tha'll hang, like lass in next cage will, so start saying tha prayers now.'

Emily slid to the ground, too weak to summon the strength to lie on the bench. They were trying to frighten her. They couldn't mean that she would die for something she hadn't done? Then she thought of the damaged painting. That at least was true. She had deliberately taken the poker and burnt it. She must have been mad for a few minutes to do such a thing. Should she say that? Should she say that her sanity had vanished at the death of the child? But would they then lock her up with the insane?

She retched at the thought. She had heard such terrible things about those poor lost souls. No, she must tell the truth, as she had always done.

She shuffled onto the bench and lay down, pulling the blanket over her. But then she threw it off. It smelt mouldy, like over-ripe cheese and she thought wretchedly that others had lain beneath it, perhaps with dirty and verminous bodies. She huddled into herself beneath her cloak, closed her eyes and waited for someone, anyone, to come and rescue her.

The day dragged on and she had no means of knowing the time. It was dark, with only one small window at the top of the wall in the main cell, which she assumed would be at ground level as she had come down two flights of stairs, but the window was grimy and very little light came through it. Presently another warder came through with a lamp, which though shedding a little light gave off a noxious smell of dirty oil.

'Soon be suppertime.' One of the women came across to her. 'If tha doesn't want it, can I have it?'

She sat up, confused. 'What? Suppertime?' She must have dropped off to sleep. Why had no-one come to release her? 'No,' she said in answer. 'I must eat, I haven't eaten since breakfast.' She thought of the extra cup of coffee which the land-lady of the inn had pressed on her. If she had refused it, she would have escaped the clutches of the constables and been safely in Beverley now.

'Tha won't like it.' The woman, disappointment in her voice, turned away. 'Not what tha's been used to, I'll be bound. Nobody likes it when they first come in.'

Well, I shall eat it, whatever it is, Emily thought. I must keep up my strength. But when the bowl of greasy soup was handed to her through the metal flap on the gate, her stomach turned. 'Is there anything else?' she asked meekly.

The warder gave her a contemptuous glance. 'Want me to nip to Station Hotel? I'm sure they'll put on a little delicacy for you!'

Humiliated, she took it from him and then the piece of dry bread which he held in his hand. 'Thank you.' She raised her eyes to his, but he didn't seem to see her, there was merely indifference written on his face.

Meg came across to her. She was chewing on her bread with apparent enthusiasm. 'If ever you don't want your supper,' she whispered with her mouth open and full of bread and stained teeth, 'don't give it away. Sell it! You never know when you'll need a copper or two.' She leant towards the bars. 'If you've got money, it can buy another blanket or a bit o' meat. Or better still,' she added, 'get somebody to bring summat in.'

Emily stirred the cold soup with the tin spoon, but couldn't bring herself to taste it. Who could she ask to bring food in? The only people who knew she was in prison were the Purnells and their servants, and they were not likely to come. Would Mrs Anderson? No, she wouldn't dare. She would be too afraid of incurring Hugo Purnell's wrath and losing her position. There was nothing for it then. Tentatively, she raised her spoon to her lips and sipped. It tasted of cold, tainted grease. She dipped the bread into it and chewed. The bread was stale and she doubted there was any nourishment in it, but she finished it and felt a slight sense of gratification that her willpower had overcome her repugnance.

She barely slept that night, kept awake by the muttering, groans and snores of the other prisoners, and she thought she could hear the scurrying of mice or rats. For breakfast the next day she was given a slice of bread and a mug of lukewarm tea, and after she had eaten she sat on her bench staring out through the bars at the other inhabitants. At noon, a slice of tough meat of unknown origin, an undercooked potato and a mug of water were given and at supper a bowl of soup, the same flavour as the night before.

Each mealtime gave her the measure of the days; six days passed and no-one had been to tell her what was to happen to her. She had questioned the warders, but they merely shrugged. The only person who showed any sympathy was the sergeant who had arrested her, who, when he brought in other prisoners came to speak to her and advised her to be patient, that it could be some time before she was called before the magistrate.

'Have you no family you could write to?' he asked. 'Nobody who could speak for you or stand surety?'

She shook her head despondently and he went

away. Only Sam, she thought, and poor Sam couldn't do anything. Perhaps Mr Francis might, she pondered, if only I could get in touch with him. But who would post my letter?

The following day she heard her name being called down the corridor. 'Emily Hawkins! Here's a visitor for you.' She rushed to the bars. Who could it be? Her heart pounded and she felt sick with anticipation. She smoothed her hair and her dress and felt that she had never been so unclean. One small bowl of water was all they were given each morning for washing and she had to complete her toilet in view of everyone else. The other prisoners, she noticed, didn't bother to wash.

'Ginny!' Emily burst into tears at the sight of her friend. 'Oh, Ginny, I'm so glad to see you.'

Ginny clasped her hands through the bars. 'Emily! I only heard 'other day. I met Dolly in Whitefriargate and she was bursting to tell somebody. She said it had been in 'newspaper, though of course I didn't see it. And then Mrs Marshall asked me what I'd heard. Mrs Purnell's not been seen, seemingly she's really upset and has taken to her bed.'

Emily wiped her tears. In the newspaper! What humiliation. Whatever would they say about her? 'It's not true, Ginny, I didn't kill that poor baby.'

Ginny patted her hand. 'I know that,' she said gently. 'If you were going to kill it you'd have done summat afore. But what about 'picture? Dolly said you'd smashed a picture with a poker.'

Emily nodded and tears came to her eyes again. 'I did,' she snuffled. 'I was so angry with Hugo

Purnell and how he had treated me when I saw that dreadful picture staring at me and reminding me of what had happened, I couldn't help myself.'

'Listen,' Ginny said urgently, 'I can't stop long. I'm on an errand for Mrs Marshall and I'll be missed. I've had to give 'warder sixpence to let me in, so tell me quick is there anything I can bring in next time?'

Emily was so grateful that Ginny would consider coming back to this dreadful place that she started to cry again, but she stemmed her tears and said, 'I'll give you sixpence for next time, Ginny, and could you try to get me a blanket? It's so cold in here, especially at night.'

'And what about food?' Ginny, ever practical, asked. 'Shall I bring you a bit of dinner? But I don't know when it will be. It'll depend when I can get out without being missed.'

The warder appeared at the gate. 'Time's up, miss.'

Emily clung to Ginny's hand. 'Ginny! Can you write a letter?'

'Aye,' she said. 'I can, though I haven't a good hand.'

'Write to Mr Francis for me, at Elmswell Manor in Holderness.' She glanced at the warder impatiently rattling his keys and spoke urgently, 'Tell him what's happened and tell him I'm innocent! And tell him – tell him that, if he has any fondness for Miss Deborah, to come and take her home.'

Chapter Nineteen

Ginny came back three days later with a clean blanket and a dish of cold chicken and beef. 'Mrs Anderson sent 'blanket,' she said. 'I went and asked her, I knew she could get one without it being missed better than I could. It's an old one,' she added. 'It was going to be cut up anyway.'

Emily took it gratefully and wrapped it around her shoulders, then ravenously tucked into the cold meat.

'I sent 'letter to Mr Francis like you said,' Ginny spoke softly, 'but don't bank on it too much, Emily. He might not want to be involved with you – you know, because of his daughter.'

'Oh, yes. Of course,' Emily was downcast. If Mr Francis failed her then there was no-one else who could help. She put down the plate, her appetite gone. 'Ginny! The women in here say I could hang. There's a woman next door,' she pointed to the cell next to hers and her hand trembled, 'she's going to York Assizes to be tried for murder and they say she'll hang.'

Ginny turned pale and she took hold of the bars of Emily's cell to steady herself. 'But you're innocent, Emily! 'Bairn was stillborn. They won't hang you for damaging a picture, will they?'

'I don't know.' Emily started to tremble. 'If it was worth a lot of money, perhaps they will.'

After Ginny had gone, she picked at the remains of the meat and then lay down again on the bench. The days were so long, nothing to do but gaze into space or listen to the ramblings of the other inmates. Two of the old women had gone to court that morning, charged with drunkenness. They had grumbled at being turned out in the cold weather. 'See thee again, dearie,' one of them had called to Emily. 'I expect tha'll still be here when I come back next time.'

Emily had stared after them. Surely they wouldn't come back to this dreadful place? Surely they would try to curb their excesses and stay away? Or, she pondered, perhaps they have little else to comfort them; perhaps this was the only roof which gave them shelter.

Meg sauntered over to her cell. 'Did you eat all o' that chicken?'

'Yes,' Emily whispered. She wasn't in the mood for talking, and besides, Meg had a most disagreeable odour, her hands and fingernails were filthy and her thick hair was tangled and unkempt.

'That's a pity. I was going to ask if you'd sell me a slice.'

'Sell it?' Emily was astonished. Where would she get the money from to buy food?

Meg grinned. 'Think I don't know how to get money? I've been earning money since I was thirteen.' She picked at her teeth. 'Providing

you're not too particular you can allus mek money
– even in here.'

Emily turned her back in disgust and faced the
wall. She was ready to die. Death was preferable to
staying here with these revolting and offensive
people.

'Listen!' Meg, unoffended by Emily's attitude,
claimed her attention again. 'Listen to 'Lark.'

Emily turned over again. 'What? What do you
mean?'

'Can't you hear her? We call her 'little Lark.' She
gave a guttural laugh. 'Not that I've ever heard
one.'

Emily sat up and leant on one elbow to listen.
How was it possible to hear birdsong so deep inside
these grim walls? Besides, she hadn't heard a lark
since coming to live in Hull. The lark was a country
bird.

Meg wandered over to the gate which closed
them in from the passage. She stood leaning
against it, her head held up and her eyes closed as
if concentrating. Emily looked at her. With her face
in repose and her neck stretched, she looked
younger than she had originally thought her.
Once, perhaps, she had been a fine-looking
woman, she mused, but life had made her ugly.
Emily looked round at the other prisoners, they
were all silent, some picking at their sores or
scratching their heads, but all were silent.

Then Emily heard the sound that they were all
listening for. From somewhere above them in one
of the far cells, came a voice, a voice so pure and
sweet that it seemed inappropriate in this grim

place. The voice raised in song was poignant and sensitive, it soared indeed like a bird on the wing. It conjured to Emily a scene of open countryside, sweet-smelling herbs and blossom, warm sun and gentle rain, and as she wiped a tear from her cheek, she saw that others were doing the same.

'Who is she?' she whispered to Meg as the song-bird finished. 'Why is she in here?'

Meg shrugged and shook her head. 'They say she killed her parents. They also say she's a lunatic.' She raised a thumb towards the end of the passage-way. 'Some of 'em are locked up in gaol 'cos there's nowhere else for them to go.' She sat cross-legged on the floor next to Emily's cell, her ragged skirts showing her bare knees and dirty ankles, and put her head in her hands. 'I onny know when I hear her sing I want to die and go to heaven.'

They were disturbed during the early hours of the next morning by the sound of raised voices, the rattling of keys and the gate being opened. A woman was pushed unceremoniously inside the main female cell. 'I'll have you for this,' she shouted at the warder. 'Just see if I don't.'

'Hello!' Meg got to her feet and surveyed the woman. 'Well, well, well! If it isn't Queen of 'Night! Fancy meeting up wi' you again.'

Emily, half-asleep, peered through the bars at the newcomer. Then she sat up and took more notice. The woman was dressed in a dark red gown edged with black. An expensive cloak was draped about her shoulders, she wore a feathered hat on her head and a very haughty expression on her face. Surely there was some mistake, Emily thought.

Why would a well-dressed woman like this be bundled into a cell?

The woman looked Meg up and down and then turned her back on her and stared across at Emily.

'Hey,' said Meg, 'aren't you going to say hello to your old pal? Sisters!' she grinned.

'Sisters! What are you talking about? You're no sister of mine.' Her voice, though rasping, was not hard and guttural as Meg's was. 'I have no idea who you are.'

'Come off it, Queenie. You know what I mean. Sisters of 'same trade. And you know who I am right enough. Turned me away from your doorstep once. Said I was pinching your trade!'

Queenie's lip flickered and she drew herself up as tall as she could, which wasn't far as she was short and plump. 'I don't know what you are talking about. I run a respectable lodging house.'

Emily stood by the bars listening. Whatever could Meg be talking about? She had a feeling that she was being offensive to this lady.

Meg circled the woman. 'Oh, we know that, Queenie! We know what happens in your house. Not quite one of 'best houses though, is it? Sort of half-way to 'bottom!'

Queenie put her head up and sneered. 'Not down in 'gutter though, like some we know.'

Meg launched herself at Queenie with such force that they both fell over. Queenie's hat fell off and one of the other women rushed in and took it to her corner, where she promptly sat on it. The two women punched and scratched and kicked and uttered oaths and blasphemy that Emily had never heard before, and she looked on with her eyes wide and her hands clasped to her mouth whilst the other inmates cheered and shouted and egged them on.

'What's going on?' The voice of the warder bellowed as he sauntered idly down the corridor, swinging his keys. 'I knew there'd be trouble putting them two together.' He watched them through the bars as if enjoying the spectacle of the two women rolling around the floor. Meg was holding Queenie by her hair and pulling for all she was worth, whilst Queenie dug her fingernails into Meg's face.

Emily turned away. It was horrible. The women's legs were showing almost up to their thighs, their bodices were ripped and the men in the adjoining cells were shouting obscene suggestions at them. 'Aye,' Meg shouted back at them, 'if tha can pay – which I doubt.'

The warder blew on a whistle and another warder appeared. They turned the key in the lock and entered. 'Right, come on. Break it up!' They hauled the women apart. 'Put Meg in one of 'other cells,' said one warder to the other. 'She'll have to double up with 'murderess. No, not that one, she'll be off in 'morning. This one.' He pointed to Emily. 'She's quiet enough. She'll not be a bother.'

He unlocked Emily's cell gate and pushed Meg inside as she hurled abuse at her rival. 'Queen of 'Night!' she hissed. 'Devil's Daughter, more like!'

'Hah!' Queenie laughed and shouted back, shaking her fist. 'We'll see who's out first.'

Meg sat down on the bench next to Emily, breathing hard. 'Look at that,' she muttered and surveyed her bare arm, which had several long red scratches on it. 'Look what that bitch did!'

'Shall I bathe it for you?' Emily offered. 'I've still got some water and it's fairly clean.'

Meg stared suspiciously. 'What? What do you mean?'

'Bathe your arm. In case there's any dirt from her fingernails.'

Meg put her head back and laughed. 'By, you're a right one! Dirt in her fingernails!' She roared again as she looked at Emily's solemn face. 'I don't know what you're doing in here! Listen,' she said, becoming serious and putting her head close to Emily's, 'she's got more than dirt under her fingernails! She's got vice, debauchery and she's got murder for a start, and plain water'll not wash that out. They might call me immoral and throw me in here now and again, but it's my living. But I'm not depraved and I've never hurt anybody in my life. I give 'em what they want and nowt more.'

'I see, I think.' Emily was confused. 'But if she's murdered someone, why hasn't she been tried?'

'I'm not saying she did it with her own hands.' Meg stared out into the other cell. 'But I had a friend who went to work for her. She was fourteen, same as I was. They fished her out of 'Humber a month later. She wouldn't do what they wanted, so they got rid of her.'

Emily felt sick. 'How do you know?' she whispered.

Meg gave a small smile. 'Huh. I just do. Folk in my line o' work talk to each other. We know what goes on in this town.'

The next morning, just after their bowl of gruel, which Queenie disdainfully refused, a warder came and unlocked the gate. 'Come on then, Queenie, off you go home. Your friends have paid up as usual.'

She brushed herself down and glanced contemptuously at the crowd of prisoners watching her. 'Somebody has stolen my hat. But keep it,' she mocked. 'It's worth nothing! Just a frippery that I bought to amuse myself. I'll get another.'

She looked the warder up and down. 'And I'll thank you not to be so familiar. My name is Mrs Plaxton.'

'Poxy Plaxton,' one of the men called mockingly. 'I'm glad I can't afford any of thy wenches.'

She walked out of the cell, swirling her cloak about her and waving one hand in farewell.

'How is it she's gone out?' Emily was at a loss to understand.

'One of her gentlemen will have paid to get her out,' Meg pulled a derisive face. 'And 'bitch won't come to trial 'cos half of 'magistrates in 'town are her clients.'

Early the next morning the prisoners roused themselves and gathered about, whispering to one another. Some of them were nervously watching the gate as if waiting for someone. Then someone whispered, 'Here's 'priest coming. It'll be today then!'

A black-garbed priest was let into the cell next to

Emily's by two of the warders, who then positioned themselves outside.

'What's happening?' Emily called softly to Meg, who was standing by the bars watching.

''Lass in 'cell next door. She's going to York Assizes this morning. She killed her husband. She's Irish Catholic and 'priest's here to hear her confession.'

Emily felt a great blackness coming over her and sank to the floor in a faint; when she came to, the prisoner, the priest and the warders had gone and Meg was on her own side of the cell looking through the bars at her.

'She went quietly,' she said. 'I don't think she believes it's happening.' She pursed her lips. 'Don't know what'll become of her bairns 'cos if they don't top her, they'll transport her.'

Emily sat huddled in her blanket all the morning. Could this happen to me? Can my life be snuffed out like a candle flame when I haven't yet begun to live? She looked round at the other prisoners, they seemed to have already forgotten about the young woman and were concentrating now on their own discomforts.

They were quite often disturbed by visitors coming to the gate to peer in at them. People who had imbibed too well, who thought it would be a jape to bribe the gaolers to let come and look at the dunghill degradation into which other, lesser mortals than they could fall. They peered with hungry fascination into the cells, the women to gasp from behind their handkerchiefs and the men to leer and sometimes jest.

The prisoners, ever mindful that they could make money, would whine and put out their begging hands. 'Not for me, for my poor bairns,' the women would cry, whilst the men would grasp the women visitors' wrists with their horny, rough hands, and tell of the wife and children they had left starving at home. Sometimes someone would fling a coin and there would be a general scramble to retrieve it, but at other times someone would offer a coin and then snatch it back with a loud laugh and return it to their purse. Then a torrent of abuse was hurled at them and tales of what awaited them in the Devil's world when they got there.

Emily crouched as far back in her cell as she could when these visitors came. She couldn't bear the shame, couldn't bear the thought of being the object of ridicule or the laughing stock of these people come to gloat. I have no hope, she thought, locked in her cave of despair. I am as doomed as that poor woman in the next cell whose face I never saw.

She was lying facing the wall when she heard the rattle of the gate and her name being called. 'Emily Hawkins! Rise up.' She scrambled to her feet as the warder unlocked her cell.

'What? Where am I going?' Fear hit her. 'Am I going to court?'

'No.' The warder had little to say. 'You're being moved.'

'But why?' She started to cry. Was this the start of procedure which would lead to the hangman?

'Where 'you tekking her?' Meg stood between

the warder and the gate. 'Come on, where's she going?'

'Nowt to do wi' you.'

Meg sidled up to him. 'Aw, come on. You can tell me!'

The warder hesitated, then gave a small smile. 'It'll be a favour, Meg.'

She nodded. 'Just tell us where you're tekking her.'

'She's being put in one of 'other cells. Comfort of home in there,' he added caustically.

Meg moved back. 'You've got a friend after all then, Em! You'll be too good for 'likes of us when you get up there.'

Emily stared. She was frightened. She didn't believe them. They were going to hang her without a trial. 'No,' she shrieked. 'I won't go! Let me stay here.' Somehow she had become accustomed to these outcasts of society, familiar with their disgusting habits, their scratching and swearing, their fighting and brazen shamelessness, born she was now quite sure, out of hopelessness and misery.

Meg grinned. 'She wants to stay wi' her pals, don't you, Em? You'll miss us, won't you?'

Emily looked over her shoulder as she was dragged away. 'Yes,' she whispered, 'I will.' But Meg had already turned her back and was walking away.

Chapter Twenty

'Who sent me in here?' She was bundled with her belongings into one of the cells in the passageway, which, although it was open to view through the barred door, was slightly larger than the small cell she had just occupied.

'Don't know, but I shouldn't complain if I were you,' said the warder. 'There's not many have this luxury.'

It's hardly luxury, she thought, looking around at the damp, streaming walls and the straw mattress on the bench, but it had a grate with a low fire burning and it had a single wooden chair and on a shelf a stub of candle, and she was grateful for that at least to her unknown benefactor. She was brought some soup, slightly warmer and not quite so greasy as she had eaten previously and she sat by the fire and felt a glimmer of hope where there had been none before.

It must be Mr Francis, she pondered. No-one else would do this. Towards the end of the afternoon, just as she had lit the candle from the dying remains of the fire, she heard the sound of footsteps coming down the stone passageway; the heavy tread of the warder's boots and lighter steps such as a woman might make. She didn't look up, but sat staring at a puff of smoke which tongued around the last sliver of wood and curled its way into the room.

The iron key rattled in the lock and startled she jumped up. A woman was entering and the warder was locking the gate behind her. She had her face covered by the hood of her cloak and in the gloom Emily couldn't see whether she was young or old.

'Have you come to share my cell?' Emily asked softly. 'I thought I was to be alone, but I shall be very glad to have some company in this dreadful place.'

'I can only give you my company for an hour,' the woman whispered. 'I have been asked to come and see you.' She shuddered and turned her head to glance around her surroundings. 'And in truth, I don't think I could bear to stay longer between these walls.'

'Who are you? Who has sent you? Please, won't you sit down?'

The woman removed a basket from beneath her cloak and sat gingerly on the chair, then quickly got up again and called the warder who was standing outside. 'Send more wood for the fire,' she demanded. 'And more light.'

The warder, to Emily's astonishment, hurried away, to return a few minutes later with a bundle of twigs and a lantern. The woman nodded, but didn't thank him, and he again locked the gate and waited outside.

'Thank you,' Emily said gratefully. 'I don't know

who you are, but I thank you from the bottom of my heart.'

'It's not me you should thank, but Mr Francis,' the woman said softly and removed her hood to reveal, even though the cell was filled with dark shadows, a neat head of fair hair stranded with silver and coiled into a thick chignon at her neck. Not a young woman but a middle-aged one with fine features and large eyes.

'I knew it,' Emily breathed. 'I knew if I appealed to him he would help me. I am so grateful,' she began again, overcome with emotion.

The woman hushed her. 'He would have enquired about you even without your letter,' she said, keeping her voice low so that the warder wouldn't hear. 'He read of the case in the newspaper and was of course very concerned, especially', she added, 'as his daughter was involved.'

'Oh, but she wasn't,' Emily stressed. 'It was Hugo Purnell, not Miss Deborah – I mean Mrs Purnell, as she now is. It had nothing to do with her.'

'But –'. The woman sounded puzzled, 'I understood that you damaged one of her pictures. That is what the police are saying.'

'No,' Emily cried. 'Mr Hugo said he had bought the picture for her, but it wasn't true.' She put her head in her hands and started to sob. 'It wasn't the kind of picture a gentleman would buy for his wife! He – he bought it for himself.'

'I see,' the woman said quietly. 'And did it offend you? Is that why you damaged it?'

Emily nodded and wiped her eyes with her shawl. 'Yes,' she whispered. 'He told me that the woman in it reminded him of me. She was naked!' she breathed, hardly daring to speak of it. 'I was so ashamed.'

The woman took a deep breath. 'And the child you bore? It was Hugo Purnell's?'

Emily nodded again, unable to say more, yet feeling such relief that she had told this stranger.

'He will deny it in court, you know that? Even though eventually he will boast to his friends of it.'

Emily looked up. 'Will Mr Francis be able to help me? I shall understand if he can't come himself because of Miss Deborah, but will you be able to see him and tell him? Are you a friend of Mr and Mrs Francis?'

The woman hesitated. 'Yes – of Mr Francis. We have known each other for many years, since we were very young. Not Mrs Francis. We have only met once.'

Emily was puzzled and wondered how she could be a friend of Mr Francis and yet not of his wife; perhaps not of their circle, she thought. She had a pleasant voice and manners, yet did not have the upper-class tone that Mrs Francis had, and Emily knew well enough that Mrs Francis was a stickler for propriety and people knowing their proper place.

'May I know your name?' she said shyly. 'When I think of your kindness in coming here, I would like to have your name in my thoughts.'

'My name is Mary,' she smiled and Emily thought how lovely she was, how her face glowed when she smiled.

'Is that what I may call you?' she asked. 'Would it not be impertinent? Don't you have a married name you would prefer me to use?'

Mary looked sad for a moment and gazed into the flames of the fire before saying softly, 'Mary Edwards is my name, Emily, and I am not a married woman, although I am known as Mrs Edwards in my business.'

'Oh,' Emily said eagerly, 'I have relatives called Edwards; Hannah Edwards, though she's dead now, and her grandson is Sam Edwards.'

'Yes, I know.' Mary looked her full in the face and there was grief written there. 'Samuel is my son.'

There was silence between them. Mary Edwards sat with her hands folded in her lap as she waited for Emily to absorb the knowledge she had given her. Then Emily whispered, 'Was it shame that drove you away? I felt shame when I gave birth. I knew I would be considered impure, a fallen woman, even though it wasn't my fault.'

Mary shook her head. 'No. I felt no shame at giving birth to a child whose father I loved and who loved me. No, it went much deeper than that. I knew that if I left, both my son and his father would have a better life without me.'

'But no-one knows who is Sam's father!'

'No,' Mary said. 'They don't. Not even my mother knew, though sometimes I wondered how she didn't guess.'

'Sam is a good man,' Emily explained tenderly, 'but he needs to be looked after. Mr Francis has placed him with a family on a farm in Holderness and they are taking care of him.'

'Yes,' Mary smiled. 'I know. I know everything about him. How he has grown from childhood into manhood. What work he does, what his pleasures are. I even know about you from the time you went to live with my mother.'

Emily's own problems faded into the background as she listened, astonished at this revelation.

'Your father', said Mary, 'was my cousin. We were very close when we were young. That's why you were sent to my mother when he became so ill. He and your mother knew that you would be well cared for, they knew how she had cared for Samuel.'

'But your mother would have stood by you. Why didn't you stay with her?'

'I came to see you, Emily, and attend to your needs,' Mary admonished gently. 'What happened to me is in the past. We must look to your future now.'

Emily, brought back to the present, looked at her with a frightened expression. 'I don't think I have one,' she whispered. 'I can't see further than the hangman.'

'Hush, hush. Don't speak so,' Mary chided. 'We must think of what is the best thing to do. Is there anyone who will speak on your behalf?'

'No-one,' she said. 'I have no family. Only Sam,' she added, 'and he can't help me. I have no influential friends. There's only Mr Francis and he knew me only for a short time.'

'He will do what he can,' Mary assured her, 'but it is a little difficult for him. His wife –'. She hesitated. 'His wife will object if she finds out. Because of your connection with me,' she added.

'I don't understand,' Emily began. 'Your connection with me? Why should she object?'

'We are related, Emily. I explained that your father was my cousin!' She took a deep breath. 'And Roger Francis is Samuel's father.'

The hour of her visit passed quickly as she related the story of how she and Roger Francis had fallen in love when she was a servant girl and he the son of the house where she worked. She emptied her basket of the things she had brought for Emily. A warm shawl. Soap and towel, a new hairbrush and cotton handkerchiefs. A small tin containing sweet-cake, and some fruit, which she pressed her to eat for its goodness. Then she brought out a small posy of sweet-smelling flowers. 'Not practical, I know,' she smiled, 'but I thought they might cheer you.'

Emily pressed her nose into the fragrance, then she looked up at her. 'I remember you! I've seen you in the florist's shop!'

Mary nodded. 'It's my shop. Roger Francis bought it for me over twenty years ago. But', she said proudly, 'I paid him back every penny, even though he didn't want me to. I wanted to be beholden to no-one. I didn't want anyone to say that I was a kept woman.'

'And – and –'. Emily was hesitant, not wanting to pry. 'Do you love him still?'

'Oh, yes.' There was a radiance about her as she answered and once more Emily thought how lovely she was and that there was little wonder that Mr Francis had fallen in love with her. 'More than ever.'

'And he? Does he still –?'

Mary lowered her eyes and Emily felt she had intruded, that she shouldn't have been so impertinent as to ask the question, but then Mary looked up and laughed. 'Yes. I'm happy to say that he does.'

After she had gone, Emily lay on the mattress with her new shawl wrapped around her; it smelt of flowers and dispersed the odour of damp walls and mildew which permeated the building. She thought of all Mary had told her and of what she had not. And piece by piece, bits of the puzzle dropped into place. Remarks made by Mrs Castle, the cook at Elmswell Manor, who had said the master had made a mistake in bringing Emily there. 'She had known,' Emily murmured to herself. 'She had been there a long time. And she had kept the secret all those years.'

A memory of Mrs Francis came to mind. Of the day when Deborah had let down Emily's hair so that it streamed around her shoulders. Mrs Francis had been startled when she saw her, she remembered, and had asked, 'not her daughter', and Mr Francis had been angry and yet defensive as he denied it.

I must have reminded her of Mary, she thought. I must have a look of her, the same-shaped face, the same blond hair. And Mr Francis too used to look at me as if he was seeing someone else. She thought of the love that he and Mary still shared, in spite of the differences between them and, inexplicably, Philip Linton and his whispered words to her at Scarborough, came to mind. It is possible then, she mused sleepily, to love someone of a different class! And I didn't think that it was.

She slept better that night; she had not been given any further hope, yet now she felt that she wasn't alone. And I have a kinswoman. Someone I didn't realize existed; and I feel that she would care about what happened to me.

Three days later she had another visitor. A man, who said he was a lawyer and had come to consider her case. 'Mrs Edwards has asked me to represent you,' he explained. He was a large man in black clothing who seemed to fill the whole of the cell. 'She speaks highly of you and, although it is a very serious charge against you, there could be miti-gating circumstances.' He looked solemnly at her over a pair of round spectacles as if weighing up her character and explained the procedure of the hearing at the magistrates' court, when it would be decided whether or not she should stand trial at the Assizes. 'Well, Miss Hawkins, we will try. We will cheat the hangman if we can.'

Roger Francis mounted the steps of Mrs Purnell's house, rang the bell and waited to be admitted to Mrs Purnell's presence. 'Forgive me for calling without an appointment, Mrs Purnell,' he said, on being shown through to her sitting room, 'but I was in Hull on business and had a desire to see my daughter. I haven't heard from her for some time, nor has she been on a visit.' He smiled thinly. 'She is obviously too busy with the delights of town to think of her Papa.'

'No, I don't think so, Mr Francis. She doesn't go out much just now.' Mrs Purnell felt slightly guilty that she didn't take Deborah with her on her own social visits, but she was such a trial. 'I, er – I think she is not too well at the moment. This dreadful business', she waved her hand vaguely, 'has upset her – has upset us all. I have only just started to go out again myself and then only to friends whom I know won't expect me to discuss it.'

'Of course,' he nodded. 'But Deborah wasn't actually involved in the disturbance which occurred, I trust?'

Mrs Purnell looked perplexed. 'Well, she was there when they found the child.' She sighed. 'Such a tiny baby. I have never seen one so small.'

'But it was your son who involved the police?' he persisted. 'Over his damaged picture?'

'Well, yes,' she admitted. 'Had it been left to me, I would never have involved them. I hate this kind of upset, Mr Francis, I really do.'

He sympathized. 'I quite agree. There would have been no need for this adverse publicity to sully your name, no newspaper articles for the public to gloat over.'

'Indeed.' She wiped away a sudden tear. 'I'm so pleased that you understand, Mr Francis.'

'Well, of course, it affects me also, Mrs Purnell, because of my daughter. We have never had any public scandal; as you know, we keep our problems at home where they belong. However,' he went on, 'because of this upset, I have come to ask you if it would be a good idea if I took Deborah home to Holderness until the hearing is over? That is, if she would like to come and if her husband agrees.'

'Oh, what an excellent thought.' Mrs Purnell was

most enthusiastic. 'And you know that they are in the process of buying a house of their own? It will give Hugo a chance to organize things in Deborah's absence and have everything ready for her return.'

'I didn't know they were thinking of moving,' he said, rather startled. 'Will Deborah be cared for? Have arrangements been made for a good house-keeper and someone to attend her? She has had you to guide her since her marriage, Mrs Purnell. She has no knowledge of running a household herself.'

Mrs Purnell clasped her hands in front of her. 'That is true,' she murmured. 'But I'm sure –'. She hesitated. 'I'm sure that Hugo will attend to those arrangements. Deborah has her personal maid, of course.' She gave another sigh. 'But I rather feel that she doesn't care for the girl very much. Oh, dear. I do wish that we still had Emily. She was such a treasure until she fell from grace.'

She rang the bell and asked that Deborah should come down, that her father was here to see her, and a moment later they heard her running footsteps as she clattered down the stairs and crashed into the room.

'Oh, Papa! Papa, I'm so pleased to see you.' She put her arms around him and hugged him. 'Why did you not write to your little Deborah? I have missed you so much.'

He kissed the top of her head. 'But I have written to you.' He smiled, but was concerned at her appearance, at how thin she was and so pale. 'Several times.'

'Why, Miss Deborah, you know that your father has written to you. Don't you remember?' The maid Alice stood in the doorway.

Deborah froze her with a look. 'No-one asked you,' she said rudely. 'Go away. I will send for you if I need you.'

Alice swallowed. 'It's time for your medication, ma'am. You mustn't miss a dose.'

'What medication is that?' Roger Francis enquired anxiously. 'Have you been ill, my dear?'

Deborah shook her head. 'I don't think so, Papa.'

'When we were in Italy, sir,' Alice explained nervously, ''Mistress was feverish and an Italian physician prescribed some medication.'

'And you are still taking it?' he asked in consternation. 'I think you should see an English doctor and ask his opinion.'

'That will be all, Alice,' Mrs Purnell interrupted. 'Miss Deborah can take it later if necessary. Leave us now.'

Deborah sat on a stool at her father's feet and clasped his knees. 'How is Mama?' she asked. 'And my dear Mrs Brewer? Do they miss me?'

'Indeed they do,' he said. 'The house is very quiet without you.'

Mrs Purnell silently sighed and raised her eyebrows, but made no comment. What she would give for a quiet house again!

'I wondered if you would like to come back to Holderness for a short while?' he said. 'For a holiday! The weather is very sharp and crisp, but the roads are still good.'

Deborah jumped to her feet. 'Oh, yes please, Papa, I would like that very much.' She headed for the door. 'I shall go and tell Alice to pack.' Then she hesitated, a frown on her forehead. 'She doesn't have to come, does she? I shall have Betty Brewer to attend me.'

'Wait, wait,' he laughed. 'We must first of all ask your husband if he agrees. He might not want to be without you.'

Her face changed colour and expression, she became even paler and lost her animation. 'He won't mind,' she whispered. 'He never minds being without me. I stay with Alice.'

He felt curiously disturbed. She was frightened, he was sure of it. There was something wrong.

'Hugo won't mind,' Mrs Purnell said heartily, 'and it won't be for long. Perhaps until your new house is ready.'

Deborah stared at her. 'My new house? What new house?'

'You know, my dear.' Mrs Purnell gazed back at her. 'You and Hugo are to have a house of your own instead of living here with me.'

Deborah came slowly back into the room. 'No-one told me,' she whispered. 'Why didn't they?'

'But Hugo must have discussed it with you, Deborah. And besides, he took you to look at several houses!' Mrs Purnell's many chins wobbled as she patiently explained.

Deborah shook her head. 'No. We went for a carriage drive and Hugo and his friends went inside some houses. But I didn't. I stayed in the carriage with Alice.'

They heard the front door open and a murmur of voices and Deborah moved closer to her father. 'There's Hugo now,' said Mrs Purnell. 'You can ask him yourself if you may go, Deborah.'

As Hugo Purnell entered the room, Roger Francis noticed behind him, in the hallway, the hovering figure of the maid Alice and he assumed, he knew not why, that she had been waiting for her master to return. Hugo strode across to greet him. 'How do you do, sir! How nice of you to visit us. Don't you think that Deborah is looking well?' He took hold of his wife's hand and squeezed it affectionately. 'She was not at all well, you know, when we were in Italy. She is not a good traveller, I fear, are you, my love?'

Deborah stared at her husband and shook her head.

'I understand she has been taking some kind of medication? From a foreign doctor?' Roger Francis's tone of voice implied that foreign medicine was not equal to that of English.

'Excellent fellow!' Hugo rubbed his hands together and leant towards him. 'Highly recommended. I have his address if you would like it. Deborah has come on in leaps and bounds since she saw him, haven't you, Debs?'

His eyes stared mesmerically at Deborah and she wet her lips and nodded, her eyes not leaving his.

'I called', said Roger Francis, 'to ask if Deborah would like a visit home, to her old home, that is. Her mother would like to see her and I thought that –'.

'What! Leave me?' Hugo's face drooped. 'Out

of the question, I'm afraid. Whatever would I do without her? Besides, I'm buying her a new house! We went to see one in Hessle the other day and decided that would be just the thing. Good air – river breezes.' He patted Deborah's cheek. 'Deborah has to choose curtains and carpets and furniture before we can move in, haven't you?'

Her face became a little brighter, but still she was confused. 'If you say so, Hugo.'

'I do say so,' he smiled. 'And then –', his voice dropped as he turned to his father-in-law, 'we have this other nasty business coming up soon. I'm afraid that Deborah will be wanted as a witness at the hearing.'

Chapter Twenty-One

The weather suddenly became colder and down in the depths of the gaol the inmates shivered. Their toes and fingers turned blue, for few of them wore stockings or shoes and their food, barely warm when sent down to them, was usually covered in a skin of cold fat by the time it reached them.

Emily shivered by her small fire, which was always lit when the warders, in expectation of a gratuity, thought she expected visitors. At other times, they forgot to bring her wood to light it, even though she asked them several times. Mary came one day and had snow on her boots and she exclaimed at how cold it was in the cell.

'Do you know what day it is, Emily?' She put down her basket, which seemed fuller and heavier than usual.

'I've lost track of time,' Emily said wearily. 'I seem to have spent the whole of my life in this place.'

'It's Christmas Day,' she said. 'Didn't you hear the bells ringing?'

Emily shook her head. 'Christmas Day! Have I been here so long?' She started to weep. 'If only the hearing would start. I feel as if I have been forgotten.'

'Not forgotten, Emily,' Mary said, a shade reproachfully. 'Your friends think of you constantly.'

'I'm sorry,' she snuffled. 'I didn't mean you, Mary, or Mr Francis. You have been so good to me. I meant the authorities. Why don't they bring me to court and let me know the worst?'

'Mr Hibbert says the magistrates' hearing will be after the Christmas recess. So not long now,' she added, trying unsuccessfully to bring cheer to Emily. She started to unpack her basket. 'I've brought slices of goose, straight from the oven, and stuffing, roast potatoes and parsnips. I told the cabby to drive as fast as he could so that it wouldn't go cold before we ate it.'

Emily stared at her. 'Do you mean that you are going to stay and eat here?' she asked in amazement. 'But you must go home! If it's Christmas, you must have friends who want you with them. You can't spend Christmas here!'

'I can and I will,' she said, unwrapping plates and parcels. 'I do often spend Christmas with friends, but sometimes I spend the day alone, because that is how I like it – when I can't be with the one I want to be with. But this Christmas I want to spend with you and we shall pretend we are somewhere else. Where shall we be, Emily?'

Emily wiped away her tears. 'Tell me about your little house behind the shop. That's where I should like to be, so that I can smell the perfume of flowers drifting through.'

So in the cramped and cold cell as they ate their Christmas dinner, Mary told of her cosy house behind the flower shop with the heavy curtains to keep out the draughts and the bright cushions on the chairs and the rug in front of the fire, and Emily imagined that she was there and not incarcerated in a damp prison cell awaiting trial for murder.

'You must have missed Sam very much when you first went away,' Emily said. 'How could you bear it? I felt sad for my poor dead baby, even though I hadn't known him. But I cradled him in my arms and knew that I would have loved him.'

Mary was silent for a moment, then said softly, 'I have missed him every day of his life, though I'm sure he doesn't think about me. He won't even remember me. But', she sighed, 'I had to go. Roger was promised to someone else and his father told him he would disinherit him if he married me. I couldn't let that happen, he loves that place, that land, and I knew that he would always look after Samuel and my mother, which he couldn't have done if I'd stayed. It would have been such a scandal if people had found out. But', she said, 'if we had known what unhappiness lay in front of him, then perhaps we would have taken a chance and stayed together.'

'Unhappiness?' Emily queried. 'You mean because he didn't love his wife?'

'Not just that. You realize that Samuel is a – little slow?'

'Yes,' she said. 'Granny Edwards always said he wasn't right sharp. But he's clever in other ways,' she added defensively. 'He knows how to fish and trap.'

Mary smiled. 'I'm sure he does. Not like his step-brother and step-sister. Theirs is a more serious situation.'

Emily put her hands to her mouth. It hadn't occurred to her that Sam was related to Deborah Purnell and her brother. 'Oh,' she murmured. 'They say that the poor boy is insane. He's in an asylum. And Miss Deborah, she's, well – she's a little excitable!'

'Yes. Roger didn't know that derangement ran in his family. His father knew, for he had had another child before Roger, but he chose not to tell him. Not until it was too late. My Samuel was lucky,' she spoke softly and slipped into her native Holderness tongue, 'not like them other poor bairns.'

As they finished a portion of Christmas pudding and put away the dirty dishes into the basket, they heard footsteps coming down the passageway and Ginny appeared at the gate, clutching a basket. 'Oh, Emily,' she peered at her through the bars, 'I've been that worried about you.' The warder unlocked the gate and let her in and Emily intro-duced her to Mary, saying only that Mary used to know her father.

'I haven't been able to come before,' Ginny said. 'Mrs Marshall heard that I'd been visiting you, I don't know how, one of 'other maids I expect. Anyhow she said I hadn't to come again. She said she didn't want anyone from her house becoming involved. But then after dinner today I appealed to her and asked if I could bring you some victuals that were left over. They'll only be wasted, I said, and it is Christmas and Emily is half-starved in that place. So she said I could and that I had to report back to her and tell of what went on in these places.

'Old cow!' she said bitterly. 'Her and her cronies, they can't wait for you to come to court.'

'Well, it seems they won't have to wait long.' Emily's meal suddenly turned sour as she thought of what was to come, then she said, 'Ginny! As I've eaten well today, dare you ask 'warder to take you down to the other cell, where I was before? There's a woman there called Meg, she doesn't get any visitors and I know she won't have any extra food, so she'll be glad of mine. Will you do that for me?'

'But Emily,' Ginny objected, 'it'll keep. It's cold turkey leg and a bit of ham. Tomorrow you might be glad of it!'

'Tomorrow I'll think of how Meg would have been glad of it. She was kind to me in her own way, Ginny. I'd like her to have it.'

Ginny bent over and kissed her. 'You don't deserve to be in here, Emily. God must have been looking 'other way when all this happened. I hope Hugo Purnell rots in hell.'

The following weeks leading up to the court hearing passed very slowly. It was so cold. The wind whistled down the passageway and the damp walls had a thin layer of ice on them. Mary brought in extra blankets and a warm bonnet for Emily, and when Mr Hibbert the lawyer came to see her, his greatcoat buttoned up to his chin and a warm scarf over his ears, his voice echoed through the gaol as he complained of the cold, and he never stayed long.

Then one day Mary brought her a new skirt and woollen shirt and said she would take Emily's clothes home to wash. 'It won't be long now, Emily,' she said gently, 'and we must have you looking presentable.'

'How do I look?' she asked.

'Pale and thinner,' she said, 'but that is hardly surprising. But', she stroked her cheek, 'still beautiful.'

Emily knew that she didn't speak the truth. She knew from the way her skirt twisted around and her shirt hung on her that she was very much thinner. She felt dirty, even though she washed every day in a bowl of cold water. And when she looked down at her hands they seemed to be ingrained with grime, for everything she touched in the cell was flecked with soot and the dirt of many years.

A few days later she was surprised to hear Meg's voice as she was led past her door. 'Cheerio, my lovely,' Meg called. 'I'm off out again. I've served my time.' She grabbed the bars to Emily's cell and peered in. 'I'll not forget you and what you did for me,' she whispered. 'Saved my miserable life you did.' There were tears in her eyes. 'I didn't think there was any kindness left in 'world, but I was mistook.' She swallowed hard and shook off the warder's hand as he tried to move her on. 'It wasn't just 'food that you sent,' she said, 'it was 'thought that somebody was thinking o' me. God bless you. You'll get what you deserve one day.'

Emily thought of her words as two constables

came the next day to take her to the magistrates' court. Once again handcuffs were put on her and a rope was tied around her waist. Only this time she didn't walk, she was bundled into an open wagon with other prisoners, ready to be driven through the thronging streets of the town to the court-house.

The sharp bitter wind caught her breath and she screwed up her eyes against the brightness of the morning, used as she was to the gloom of her cell, and she thought she would never again know such shame, as the crowds and market traders shouted abuse at the prisoners as they were driven past them. Someone threw a rotten apple and the wagon was followed by jeering children and laughing youths. Emily was shackled by the rope around her waist to a painted whore with dyed red hair, who shouted obscenities at the onlookers and made indecent signs with her fingers. Next to her was a thief with a scarred and evil-looking face and on Emily's other side was a ragged young boy who cried constantly for his mother. If she could have sunk to her knees in prayer she would have, but the prisoners were packed so tightly together that they were kept upright by the press of each other's bodies.

Still shackled, she was put in another basement cell at the courthouse. 'Will it be today?' she whispered to one of the guards. 'Will the hearing be today?' But he was busy coping with the louder complaints of other hardier prisoners and didn't hear her.

'You'll have to shout up if you want to be heard,

dearie.' The whore leered at her. 'Nobody listens otherwise. What you up for?'

Emily couldn't say the word. It wasn't true. She hadn't murdered the baby. 'I'm accused of – killing a newborn baby.'

'And they caught you?' the woman said as if amazed. 'By, there's many a woman should be here then! Who can afford to bring a bairn into 'world? Who'd want to anyway?'

'But I didn't!' Emily was shocked. 'And it would be a sin if I had! A child has a right to life.'

The whore laughed. 'You're a little innocent aren't you? Don't know much about 'world that's for sure!'

'I know more now than I did,' she murmured miserably. 'More than I ever thought I would.'

'Some man's brought you down, I bet. Did he promise to marry you?' The woman scratched vigorously at her body.

Emily shook her head. She wouldn't discuss it, especially not with such a woman as this.

'Took you then?' the woman persisted. 'And then left you to carry 'burden? I know all about that,' she snarled. 'See it every bleeding day that dawns. Two-legged scorpions! Lechers! Destroyers of women!' She cursed and ranted, then pointed a dirty finger at Emily so that she cringed away, 'Tek my advice. Name him! Let his family and friends see him for 'thief that he is for tekking your virtue!'

'Emily Hawkins! Emily Hawkins! Come forward.' She jumped as she heard her name being called. This was it, then. The time had come. Frightened and trembling, she was led up stone steps, down a long gloomy corridor which was thronging with clerks carrying piles of parchment, young bewigged counsellors lounging idly against the walls and constables with prisoners shackled to them waiting impatiently for their turn to be called, and through heavy wooden doors into the courtroom.

She was only vaguely aware of the silence which descended on the room as she entered. A few murmurings and tut-tuttings as she was led toward a partially enclosed wooden dock where she was brusquely told to stand. One constable remained fastened to her by handcuffs and two more stood behind her. She turned her head. To the side of her, sitting on a long bench, was one of the constables who had arrested her. She saw Mr Hibbert dressed in his court robes and another ferret-faced man who sniffed down his long nose and shuffled his papers and scratched at his wig.

In the main area of the courtroom there was a great press of people, strangers to her; but no, there was Ginny, who gave her an encouraging nod. There was Mrs Anderson too, sitting next to her; she didn't acknowledge Emily but sat with her head down and her mouth in a thin line. Behind her was a young woman wrapped in a thin shawl with a mewling child on her lap and Emily wondered if it was Mrs Anderson's niece who had also fallen to Hugo Purnell's advances.

She lifted her eyes to the balcony above. There was Mrs Marshall with a handkerchief to her nose, the feathers in her hat bobbing as she chatted to other well-dressed ladies of society sitting beside her. There was no sign of Mrs Purnell, but Emily's eyes filled with tears as she saw Mary Edwards in a long grey cloak with a hood over her head, taking her seat.

After the silence which had greeted her, there rose a hubbub of noise and laughter as if the audience were waiting to be entertained at a theatre show, but this died away again as the doors once more swung open and all eyes swivelled to see Hugo Purnell with his wife by his side being escorted in.

Emily drew in her breath. Why did he have to bring Miss Deborah? She didn't look well. She was pale and trembling and stumbled as she took her place besides the long-nosed man, who, Emily now surmised, must be their lawyer.

'All rise!' called the clerk to the court and Emily's eyes were transfixed on the bewigged and black-robed justice who entered and took his seat at the bench. She looked on his face for a sign of warmth and human compassion, but saw only an austere and authoritarian resolve. This man then was to judge her. This man with the forbidding frown on his forehead would decide on her future, whether she should live or die.

Chapter Twenty-Two

Sergeant Harris, who had arrested her and who had also been sent for by Hugo Purnell, was the first to give evidence. It was his opinion, he said, that the child was stillborn.

'Have you seen a stillborn child before?' asked Mr Sneepe, Hugo Purnell's lawyer.

'No sir, I haven't,' the sergeant admitted, 'but I've seen children who've been murdered, and I know this one wasn't.'

'But you have never seen a stillborn child,' the counsel persisted. 'Therefore you couldn't be sure.'

'No, sir.'

'And you saw the damaged painting? Did you assess whether the damage was deliberate or accidental?'

'It appeared to be deliberate, sir.'

Hugo Purnell was called next to give evidence on finding the dead child and the damaged painting.

'What was your reaction, Mr Purnell, when you came across this poor dead child?' Mr Sneepe rubbed his hands round and round in an unctuous manner.

'I was shocked,' Hugo said smoothly, 'and horrified', he added, 'that such a thing should happen in my home. I tried to keep the discovery from my wife –', he spread his hands wide 'but too late, she had seen both the child and the burnt painting.'

'And did you know whose child it was?'

He shook his head. 'Not until I was told by my mother's housekeeper that one of the maids had become pregnant and that it was probably hers.'

Mr Hibbert stood up to question him. 'Did you call a doctor to attend the child?'

'I did not.' Hugo stared defiantly at him. 'I could see the child was dead, therefore I called the police. I understand a doctor was in attendance later to examine the child.'

'Do you have any idea why the child should be left on your bed? Was there an implication that the prisoner, Emily Hawkins, might have been suggesting that it was your child?'

Hugo indicated towards his wife in the court. 'I am a newly married man. Is it likely that I would dally with a young maid?'

There was a sudden guffaw from the balcony, where some of Hugo's friends had gathered. He stared stony-faced up at them. 'There has never been any such suggestion. Nor is there any reason why there should be.'

The doctor who had examined the child's body was a thin, nervous young man who answered in a low and hesitant voice when asked his opinion on the child's death. 'It was probably a premature birth,' he said, 'and therefore the child was unlikely to survive.'

There was a great sigh as if of relief from the main body of the court and the justice frowned impatiently. 'In your opinion, doctor,' he asked, 'would this child have survived with medical care?'

'It is possible, though unlikely,' he answered slowly, 'and it would depend on the mother's state of health and the conditions at its birth.'

'You mean if the mother had had medical attention?'

The doctor agreed and started to say something to the effect that many mothers were not able to afford a doctor, but the magistrate cut him short.

When Emily was called she could barely stand and had to hold the side of the dock for support. She answered to her name and agreed that she had been in Mrs Purnell's employ.

'You gave birth to an illegitimate child. Is that correct?' Mr Sneepe asked.

'Yes, sir,' she whispered.

'Was this your first child?'

She gasped. 'Yes, sir.'

'When discovering that you were with child, did you consult a doctor?'

'No, sir.'

'Why not, if this was your first child?'

'I was too afraid.'

'Afraid or ashamed?' He peered at her through narrowed eyes.

'Both, sir.' Emily kept her eyes to the floor.

'Do you have any marriage prospects?'

She agreed that she hadn't.

'So you took this newborn child to your employer's bedroom, where you laid him on the bed. You took the poker from the fire and burnt the picture on the wall?'

'Yes, I did, sir.'

There was a murmuring throughout the court as this damning evidence was given.

'Why did you damage the picture?'

'I was angry, sir, and upset.'

'Angry and upset? You were upset that you had given birth and had no marriage prospects! You had made no provision for the birth of a child, no clothing or lying-in sheets. If you were angry and upset enough to damage the picture, could it be that you were also angry enough not to try and resuscitate the child?'

Emily stared at him. How could he say such a thing? 'The baby was dead, sir,' she whispered. 'He never drew breath. I tried to make him live,' a tear ran down her cheek, 'but he wouldn't.'

Mr Hibbert stood up. 'Were you a virgin when you went to work at the Purnells' household, Miss Hawkins?'

Emily's cheeks burned and she hung her head. 'I was, sir.'

'And do you know the name of the child's father?'

There was another gasp from the court and the people in the balcony jostled and hung over each other in anticipation of a revelation.

She was silent for a moment, then spoke so quietly that the magistrate leaned forward and said, 'Speak up! I can't hear you.'

She looked at him and Mr Hibbert, and then looked around the courtroom and caught sight of

Deborah Purnell's white face. If she should tell that it was Hugo who had seduced her and made her pregnant, how would the Francises ever hold up their heads again? They had successfully kept from the world that they had insanity in their family and that Roger Francis had a mistress. Would they become a laughing stock if the world knew that their daughter had married a libertine, a seducer of innocence?

'I do know, sir.'

'And are you prepared to say who this man is?'

'No, sir. I am not.'

Mr Hibbert clasped his hands to his head; there was a great hubbub around the court and the justice banged with his gavel on the desk and ordered quiet or he would clear the court. Then he leaned forward and spoke to Emily. 'Why not?'

'There would be no point, sir. The baby is dead. If I name his father, it won't bring 'poor baby back. I didn't kill him, sir,' she pleaded, 'but I did damage 'painting and I'm sorry about that. I'd willingly pay for it if I had the money.'

'But that isn't good enough,' the magistrate barked. 'We can't have people damaging other people's property and then just saying they're sorry for it! And it seems to me, young woman, that either the unfortunate child's father wouldn't marry you, or else you are seeking to protect him and endeavouring to place the blame elsewhere! You had made no provision for the child, no clothing for it was found when your room was searched. By your own admission you abandoned the child and damaged the property of Mr Purnell, who had shown much kindness in employing you.'

He glanced around the court. 'Who knows the working of a woman's mind? I'm sure that I don't, not without further questioning at any rate.'

There was another loud burst of conversation and again the justice banged his gavel and ordered quiet. Emily stood perfectly still. She felt that she was frozen to the boards of the dock as she heard him utter the words that other evidence must be heard and that in his opinion the death of the child was caused by neglect; that the prisoner had caused wilful destruction of property and that she should be committed for further trial at York Assizes.

There was a great shout from the courtroom, waking Emily from her trance. It was Meg, her face red and angry and contorted. 'No,' she screamed. 'She's innocent. You've onny to look at her to know that!'

'Throw that woman out of court!' The magistrate jumped to his feet and waved his arms. 'This is a court of law!'

'No it's not!' Meg shouted back. 'This is men's law! You know who's to blame here. Everybody knows, onny she's too scared to name him. How many dead bairns have you fathered?' She pointed angrily at the magistrate and shook off the constable who came rushing to escort her out. 'I've seen you down at Queenie's, and I've seen him as well,' she yelled, pointing at Hugo Purnell, and there was uproar in the courtroom as she was dragged, shouting and kicking out of the court.

'Charge her!' the justice called after them. He

had a bright red flush on each cheek. 'Charge her with disrupting court proceedings.' He straightened his wig and adjusted the stock around his neck and sat down. 'Emily Hawkins,' he said, picking up his pen, 'I hereby issue a warrant for your committal at the next York Assizes.'

Mary Edwards went back to her shop; she dismissed her assistant for the afternoon, closed the door and put up a closed sign. She went into her living room at the back of the shop, threw some wood on the fire and sank despondently into an easy chair.

She sat for perhaps half an hour, then was disturbed by a gentle tapping on the rear door. 'Who's there?'

'Who else?' came the reply and she unbolted the door to let in Roger Francis, his face pale and his eyes heavy.

'Oh, my dear,' he said, holding her close, 'what a dreadful business. I never thought it would come to this.'

She started to weep softly, tears which she had held back all afternoon. 'I feel as if I have lost a daughter,' she cried.

'Yes,' he murmured into her hair. 'She could almost have been yours. The same gentle manner, the same hair, the same lovely face.'

She gave a sudden tearful laugh which was almost a sob. 'As I once was, Roger!'

'No.' He kissed her tenderly. 'As you are still.'

He led her to the chair by the fire and sitting down drew her on to his knee. 'We cannot let this pass.'

'But what can be done? It seems so hopeless.'

He passed a hand across his eyes and she exclaimed at how tired he looked. 'I haven't slept,' he said. 'I've been tossing and turning all night, worrying about the hearing and what it might mean. I left home at dawn and have been hanging around at one of the inns all day, waiting for the news. And now the news is bad. Very bad!'

'There must be something –', she said. 'The doctor's evidence!'

'Yes, he wasn't questioned enough from what I hear.' He was silent for a while and they both just sat stroking hands.

'Very well,' he said finally. 'I have dallied long enough. A decision has been made. There has been injustice perpetrated on a young, innocent girl.'

She nodded, keeping her eyes on his face. 'You must do what you think is right,' she said softly, stroking his cheek. 'Will you return home tonight, or will you stay?'

He put his head against hers. 'I would like to stay, if I may. You know that there is no comfort at home. My life is a sham, Mary. My wife doesn't care a button for me and my daughter's life is ruined.' He put his lips to her cheek and kissed her. 'And I am so lonely without you.'

Chapter Twenty-Three

Philip Linton strode eagerly down Whitefriargate towards Parliament Street and the Purnells' home. It doesn't matter one jot that she is a servant girl, he argued with himself. My grandmother was even less than that. She said that she had lived in the meanest streets of Hull when she was a girl. He only half-believed the tales which his father's mother had told him when he was young. She was an imaginative storyteller, weaving stories of river life and sailing ships and smuggling, and he never knew if what she said was true or not.

But no matter, he deliberated. I have thought of no-one else but Emily whilst I've been away and I must see her again. He remembered that she had said she might be looking for another position and leaving the Purnells' employ. The other servants will know where she is. I will ask if I find she has gone, but I will make an excuse for calling on Mrs Purnell and of congratulating Hugo on his marriage.

He was almost at Parliament Street when a young woman going in the opposite direction suddenly stopped and glanced his way. There was something familiar about her, yet he couldn't quite put a finger on how he knew her. By her plain dress, she was a servant.

'Sir.' The voice was hesitant. 'Beggin' your pardon, Mr Linton.'

He turned and looked at the young woman. Yes, he did know her from somewhere. 'Good afternoon,' he said pleasantly, 'I regret I cannot remember where we have met before!'

'I don't expect you to remember, sir, but it was at Scarborough two summers ago. I was with Emily, Mrs Purnell's maid.'

His face broke into a grin. What luck! She would know where Emily was. 'Of course! Ginny,' he said, 'at the Spa. They were playing *The Magic Flute*.'

Ginny nodded. 'Possibly, sir, I don't know. Mr Linton,' she hesitated, 'this is most improper of me and I hope you won't take offence, but I'm quite desperate.'

His hand slid to his pocket. 'No, sir,' she refused. 'Not for money! I work for Mrs Marshall still. Mr Linton, you do remember Emily, don't you? You danced with her outside the Spa.'

'I did and I do remember her, very well indeed.' I haven't been able to forget her, he mused. I don't think I ever will.

'Well, sir, she's in terrible trouble and it's her I'm desperate about.'

'Trouble?' His spirits dipped as he thought of the sort of trouble a young maid could get into. 'What kind of trouble? Has she lost her position with the Purnells?'

'Yes, sir. She has. But that's not 'worst of it. She's

in York gaol waiting to come to trial.'

He felt as if he had been dealt a hammer blow. His mouth became dry and he blurted out, 'On what charge? What is she accused of?'

'Murder of a newborn child and destruction of a painting, sir. But it's not true. Emily wouldn't do that! Can you help, Mr Linton? Do you have any influence?' Ginny's normally placid features started to crumple. 'It wasn't her fault! It was 'fault of another.'

His voice came out in a croak. 'I was just on my way to the Purnells. Do they know of this?' Ginny suddenly backed away. 'I beg your pardon, sir. I didn't realize you were a friend of the Purnells. I'm sorry to have troubled you.'

'No. Wait.' He delayed her. 'Are the Purnells involved in this? Have they accused her of something? I've been away on a voyage, I don't know any of the news from Hull.'

'Yes, sir,' she said reluctantly. 'Mr Hugo Purnell is, at any rate.'

His face tightened. He might have known that blackguard would be concerned. 'Ginny! We can't talk here in the middle of the street. Walk with me a little, there's a coffee shop not far from here.'

'I can't, sir, not now. I'm on an errand. I could meet you tomorrow about the same time. Sampson's coffee shop at two o'clock?'

He agreed and then wandered around the town, deliberating whether or not to call at the Purnells after all. Finally he decided that he would and climbing the steps to their home he rang the bell.

'I'll ask, sir, if Mrs Purnell is receiving visitors.

She hasn't been well,' the maid told him.

'I'm not well!' Mrs Purnell complained as he was taken through to her. 'But I'm glad to see you, Philip. Hardly anyone calls these days. This dreadful business, you know.'

He remarked that she didn't look in good health and how sorry he was if she was having some difficulties.

'Difficulties!' she exclaimed. 'A nightmare more like! And still not over. The case has gone to York.' She leant forward earnestly. 'It never should have, in my opinion, but no-one asked me!'

'I've been away, Mrs Purnell. I know nothing of what has been happening in Hull.'

She looked aghast. 'Then I can't tell you. I can't bring myself to discuss it. Oh, I know my friends tittle-tattle about it, but after the Assizes it will not be worth a straw to them and *my* life will be a shambles.' She pressed a handkerchief to her eyes. 'And as for that poor girl – what will her life be worth? Who will have her after this?'

He was beginning to feel agitated. Why didn't the woman come out with it instead of babbling on? 'The girl?' he pressed. 'Which girl would that be?'

'Why Emily, of course! And you know, don't you, that Hugo has bought a house in Hessle? Well, I didn't want the police here bothering me with their questions, so I told him he must go; and besides I couldn't abide his wife here any longer. Oh, I know it's not her fault that she's simple minded, poor thing, but Hugo knew, and he should never have married her. I told him so at the very beginning, but would he listen to me? Oh dear, no. I'm just his mother!'

He came out of the house, his head in a whirl. Was the woman in her right senses? Had she really confirmed what Ginny had told him, that Emily had had a child and had destroyed a painting belonging to Hugo and had been put in prison, pending a trial?

He staggered into the nearest hostelry and ordered a brandy, drank it down and then ordered another, which he held in his hands and gazed at, before gulping that down too.

An elderly man sat down at his table and nodded at him. 'Been far?' he asked.

'Portugal,' he answered vaguely.

'I was a seaman,' the man said, 'till I lost these.' He held up his right hand. Three fingers were missing. 'Got 'frost,' he said. 'Trapped in Arctic we was. Finished me off for good. I lost two toes as well.' He stared gloomily down at his feet. 'All I'm good for now is listening to gossip.'

'Gossip? Would you have heard of the trial of the young servant girl, Emily Hawkins?' He stared hard at the man. 'I think I might have known her.'

'Why, aye. I went to court! It helps to pass 'time, you know. She was a little beauty. But if I was you, sir, I wouldn't confess that I knew her. She hasn't named 'father of 'child.' He gazed back at Philip. 'She said she wouldn't, but as 'magistrate said, who knows 'workings of a woman's mind? She might have her own reasons for not naming him, though what good it'll do her in York gaol I can't think! He's a scoundrel anyway, leaving her to suffer like that.' He shook his head. 'She had 'face of an angel and looked like an innocent to me.'

Philip didn't go to bed that night and his emotions were torn between anger that Emily was no longer unblemished, doubts as to whether she might have willingly succumbed to another man's passion, and frustration that when he was about to declare himself he should find that she was out of reach. But why was she in gaol? Surely Hugo Purnell didn't want that! He must have known the penalties for wilful damage, why did he not just dismiss her? And why – he paced the floor – why would Emily, of all people, damage a painting? It just didn't make sense.

He finally went to bed and fell asleep at six in the morning, and awoke again at midday, washed and changed and told his landlady not to prepare any food for him, and went out to meet Ginny. He was early at the coffee shop and sat consuming several cups of coffee and toast, and with relief stood up to greet her as she came in.

She looked around nervously. 'I can't stop long, sir, and I hope nobody sees me.'

'Just tell me what happened, Ginny. I have heard such stories that I can't believe.'

She looked at him frankly. 'You must excuse my language, Mr Linton, but there's no other way of describing what happened to Emily.' A flush touched her cheeks and he saw that it was embarrassing for her.

'You may tell me, Ginny. I'm not going to be shocked.'

But he was. Shocked to the core as she told him that Emily had been raped by Hugo Purnell on his wedding night. He felt the blood drain from his face and he banged his fist on the table, disturbing the other customers, as she told what Emily had told her, that she had given birth alone with no-one to help her and that the child was stillborn. 'She said that she was so angry when she went into Mr Purnell's room and saw the painting still there, and it was as if he was laughing at her, that she picked up the poker and destroyed it.'

'It's a pity that it wasn't Hugo Purnell taking the blows,' he seethed.

'I'm only telling you, sir, because I don't know who to turn to – and when I saw you in 'street yesterday –'. She took a deep breath as if to check her emotion. 'I've met your parents, Mr Linton, and it's well known that they are honourable people – and I thought that perhaps –', she looked confused as if she didn't really know what she thought '– I thought that perhaps there was a chance that you might know of someone that might help her. I'm afraid that she won't survive gaol, sir. She's a gentle girl.'

'Indeed she is,' he murmured as he thought desperately for a solution. 'She has no family, I take it? No-one to speak for her?'

She shook her head and then gave a little smile. 'Someone did speak for her after 'hearing; a woman – a woman of ill repute. She shouted at 'magistrate that Emily was innocent and then she was dragged off to 'cells herself. I don't know how she knew Emily, unless they met in 'House of Correction.' She nodded as a look of revulsion passed over his face. 'That's where she was held, sir, with whores and thieves.'

He promised to do what he could. He couldn't say to Ginny that he was totally devastated, nor could he have explained his own feelings of protection, which were surging towards Emily, and those of anger against Hugo Purnell. I could kill him with my bare hands, he inwardly raged. How could he do this to a young girl and not give help when she needed it?

He had not yet obtained orders for another ship, and after his intentions of seeking out Emily, he had planned to visit his parents and sisters. Now those plans were abandoned and he turned his energies to finding out where Emily was and where the trial would be.

'She'll have gone to York already, sir,' said the clerk at the magistrates' office when he enquired. 'That batch of prisoners went a week ago. You'll have to enquire in York for 'dates of Assizes.'

He boarded the coach to York the next morning and as he was jostled and bumped along the road, he gazed out at the gentle rolling hills of the Wolds in the distance, and thought of his parents up there in their fine old house, who didn't even know he was back in England. I must write, he pondered, and tell them that urgent business has delayed me. They will wonder what it is, for if it was naval business then they know I would say so. Mother will guess that there is a woman involved. She is so very astute I can keep little from her. But of this I cannot tell them.

The revelation exploded in his mind, bringing everything into focus. I cannot tell them that Emily, whom I love, is languishing in York gaol on a charge of murder.

Chapter Twenty-Four

Emily blotted out the days spent in the cell below the town hall and the horrendous journey by coach from Hull to York. She had refused to believe that this nightmare was happening to her as, shackled by the ankles and wrists, she rode beside other prisoners on top of the coach with the rain hissing down, whilst the guards, all but one, sat inside. The one guard who rode outside was surly and harsh and had pushed them brutally on top of the coach beside the coachman, and then shackled them all together.

She spoke to no-one as she was led down to the cells in York gaol and waited for the nightmare to end. She had no visitors for four days and then Mr Hibbert appeared.

'Miss Hawkins, will you agree to say who is the father of the child? It may appear better for you if we know who he is and so give a reason for you damaging the property?'

'There would be no point,' she said dully. 'He would deny it.'

'Are you protecting someone?' he asked gently. 'It's no good, you know, it will be the worse for you if you don't tell. If you had good reason for doing this –'.

'I damaged the picture,' she said. 'I did it wilfully and I must take my punishment.'

'But, my dear child,' he pointed out, 'you don't know how hard your punishment may be.'

She raised her head and looked at him. 'I am prepared for death. Any other punishment cannot be worse.'

He shook his head. 'Believe me, Emily, it can. Death is not a punishment, in some cases it is a blessed relief. Think about what I say. Name the man!'

Three days later he came again to tell her that the trial would be the next day and to ask her if she had changed her mind. But her mind was dull and she had no thoughts in her head but to get the trial over; it was as if she was walking down a long dark corridor; there was no light or window, but only a black door at the end of it.

She had no idea of the pomp and ceremony that preceded the sitting of the Assizes, no conception of the procession of learned judges and dignitaries as they proceeded to court down the ancient streets of York and only knew as she was led upstairs to the courtroom, still manacled by the wrists but with her ankles free, that today was her Judgement Day.

She answered mechanically to her name and former occupation and said that she understood the charge against her, except that she didn't, not really, she was simply waiting to wake up. She saw, yet didn't see, the crowded courtroom and thought she must be hallucinating when she saw Roger

Francis and over by the door a man in naval uniform who looked like Philip Linton. She turned her head away when she saw Hugo Purnell take his seat, and Deborah Purnell looking thinner and paler than ever.

The judge at the bench was conferring with Mr Hibbert and the prosecuting counsel and nodding his head in agreement. She saw Mr Hibbert point over his shoulder towards the witnesses and again the judge nodded his head and the prosecuting counsel looking displeased moved away and consulted Hugo Purnell.

'It has come to my notice', said the judge, 'that there may be mitigating circumstances in this case. It is not for me to judge my fellow justices, but it appears that this case could have been tried at the Hull court rather than being brought to the Assizes.'

He looked solemnly at Emily. 'I have new evidence here from a separate witness; a gentleman of good standing, who is prepared to swear on oath that you were previously of good character and that Mr Hugo Purnell, who brought the case, may not be a reliable witness.'

Hugo Purnell rose to his feet. 'How dare you!' he spat out. 'How dare you sully my name!'

'Sit down, Mr Purnell! Do not speak unless requested to do so.'

Hugo, his face burning, sank down onto his seat and glared at the judge, who continued speaking.

'I have therefore taken into account the testimony of the police sergeant and the doctor, who has been questioned further, and decided that in the case of the child born to you, there is no case to answer. That the child was indeed stillborn and did not die because of your neglect.'

Emily lifted her head. Was there then some hope after all? She glanced around the courtroom seeking confirmation and saw Mary Edwards with a look of hopeful anticipation on her face, and she turned again to the judge.

'However,' he continued, 'you have stepped out of the bounds of respectability by conceiving a child out of wedlock, and in causing the wilful destruction of the property of Mr Purnell it is apparent to me that you are about to fall into a well of evil and on this you must be judged.'

The questions seemed to go on all day. They had a break at midday, when Emily was given water and offered soup, which she refused, and was then brought back into court again.

Again she was questioned, first by the prosecuting counsel, who emphasized the value of the painting and then by Mr Hibbert, who asked her if she had been offended by the painting.

'Yes,' she whispered. 'I was.'

'And this painting belonged to Hugo Purnell, did it?'

She hesitated. 'Mr Purnell bought it in Italy,' she said. 'It was a wedding present I think.'

'Did you think a painting of a nude woman was an unusual present for a man to give his wife?' Mr Hibbert persisted.

'Yes,' she whispered again.

'And where did Mrs Purnell hang this picture?' Mr Hibbert smiled and looked around the court.

259

'It was in Mr Purnell's room,' she said.

She was very tired. She had not eaten properly for days, she felt faint with hunger and the room seemed to swim before her. The figures of the judge and his clerk fused together giving two heads and one body, but only one mouth, out of which came language she couldn't understand. The constables of the court, the men of the jury and the members of the public melted together, then coagulated into grinning gargoyles which floated around the room, even touching the high ceiling, then splintered into fragments of arms, legs and heads which hurled themselves towards her.

'Prisoner at the bar. Do you understand what I am saying?'

She gazed absently at the judge and became aware of the jury standing still in their box, and members of the public muttering to each other. Mary Edwards had both hands pressed to her face. Emily shook her head. 'No, sir.'

'The jury have agreed on their verdict and you have been found guilty of wilful damage to the property of Mr Hugo Purnell, and although I understand that the circumstances at the time were trying for you – and I have taken this into account – it is nevertheless a major offence. I accept that the damage was done in a moment of anger, perhaps you were slightly deranged after the trauma of the birth, but nevertheless it was a destruction of property. You are only a young woman and could have a full life before you, providing you are put on the right path. I have decided therefore that rather than commit you to a prison term, I hereby sentence you to three years' transportation.'

She could hear a woman screaming. The sound was echoing in her ears. She was held tightly by both arms by two constables. 'Be quiet,' one of them hissed. 'You've been lucky. It could have been seven.'

The screaming went on and on and only stopped when the other constable put his hand over her mouth. 'All rise,' said the judge's constable and the court rose as the judge left the bench and departed; but Emily couldn't hold herself up, her legs were like water and she swayed between the two policemen.

'It's a mistake,' she gasped. 'What does it mean?'

'It means, little lady, that you're off for a sail to Botany Bay,' one said as they half-carried, half-dragged her back down to the cells. 'That'll teach you to be a good lass in future.' He grinned. 'Not much chance of that though, not where you're going.'

But I am a good lass, she ached inside. My da said I was, and so did Granny Edwards. What happened? How have I come to this? What wickedness did I do? The enormity of the sentence struck her and she sank to the floor on her knees. Would she ever come back? Would she even get there? Botany Bay was on the other side of the world! She wept and wept until she was exhausted and was lying with her head on the cold hard floor when the guard nudged her with his foot. It was dark and he hovered over her like an enormous shadow. 'A visitor for you.'

It was Mary and she was as consumed with grief

as Emily was herself. She put her hands through the bars to hold her. 'I never thought they would do this. Never, never, never.' Tears ran unchecked down her face. 'Will I ever see you again, Emily?'

Emily took a deep breath. 'Yes,' she said. 'I will come back. I don't know how, but I will and I'll have my revenge. Hugo Purnell has brought me down into this hell and I'll pay him back.'

Her voice was bitter and Mary, taken aback at her outburst said, 'But why didn't you name him as the man who raped you? It had to come from you, Emily! Roger spoke to the counsel and told him of the circumstances, he even told him that Hugo Purnell had married Deborah under false pretences and that he was an unreliable witness! That's why Purnell wasn't called to the stand.'

'It was because of Miss Deborah and Mr Francis,' Emily whispered. 'She looks so ill. I didn't want to cause her any more distress, nor Mr Francis.'

'Oh, Emily! Whatever will we do?'

'Nothing,' she answered wearily. 'We can do nothing. I'm just glad that it's all over.'

Philip waited until the courtroom had almost cleared then stumbled out of the doors. He sank down on to the nearest seat in the entrance hall and put his head in his hands. Transportation! I can't believe they can do this to her. Not for such an offence and under such circumstances! Criminals are transported, not innocent young women who have no badness in them. Why didn't she speak? Why didn't she tell of Purnell? Was it shame? Humiliation? Fear? Anger brought tears to his eyes and he pulled out a handkerchief to blow his nose. I'll kill him!

The courtroom doors swung open again and a woman dressed in a grey cloak and bonnet came out. She hesitated, looking round at the people milling about as if searching for someone, then catching sight of a man waiting in one of the alcoves, she walked across to him. What interest do they have? Philip wondered. Do they know Emily? They didn't look the kind of people who were there just for a day's entertainment as some of the public were. He was a gentleman by his dress.

He watched as they spoke, then the woman went across to a constable, spoke to him, then followed him down a corridor.

There's Purnell! Philip rose to his feet. Anger enveloped him and he clenched his fists. If he punched him now in the law courts would he be arrested? Yes, probably, he pondered. Far better to catch him leaving his club and lure him into some alleyway. He watched as Purnell's wife gave a sudden half-smile of recognition and started as if to move across to the gentleman at the other side of the hall, but Purnell caught her arm and held her back, then giving a barely imperceptible nod of his head to the man, he led her away.

'Sir.' Philip approached the man, who was sitting on a bench with his hand over his forehead. 'I beg your pardon for intruding, but did I not see you in court during the trial of Emily Hawkins?'

Roger Francis stood up. 'You did, sir.'

'My name is Philip Linton. May I ask if you have a particular interest in this case?' He saw a stiffening of the man's demeanour as he asked the question and hastened to add, 'I ask not out of idle curiosity but simply because I have had the honour of meeting the young lady.'

'The honour!' Roger Francis's face showed anguish. 'There are few gentlemen who would deign to admit knowing her after such words of derision from the judge and the verdict he has given.' He swallowed hard and rubbed his hand on his chest. 'Do you mind if we sit down? I don't feel well.'

They sat side by side on the bench and Philip said hesitantly, 'I am at a loss to know why the punishment is so harsh; from what I have heard Emily has been ill done by.'

Roger Francis spoke harshly. 'The punishment, Mr Linton, is designed not for the transgressor's good, but for the country's good. The system of transportation is designed to rid England of its mainly male criminal class – and the women, forgive me if I am blunt, are sent mainly as fodder for the men.'

Philip cringed. He had heard that most of the women who were sent for transportation were whores and thieves and as such were treated with contempt by law-abiding citizens, but the idea of them being sent out purely for men's pleasure was totally abhorrent to him.

'You heard the judge,' Francis went on. 'Emily has given birth to a child out of wedlock and although he has been informed of the circumstances, he, like so many men of his class, is still of the opinion that she is to blame rather than the man who dishonoured her.'

'Sir, may I know your name and your concern with Emily?' Philip asked in a low voice. 'I would like to know if I have an ally in overturning this decision.'

Roger Francis looked at him with interest. 'Roger Francis. I have known Emily's family for some considerable time and she is also a relative of – of a friend of my family; Mrs Edwards. That is why I am waiting, Mrs Edwards has just requested that she be allowed to visit Emily.'

'Oh! I understood that Emily had no family! I was mistakenly informed?'

'No, perhaps not. Mrs Edwards has only recently discovered Emily. Emily's father was Mrs Edwards's cousin, but Emily was not aware of the relationship until a few weeks ago.'

They spoke together for another fifteen minutes and discovered that Roger Francis knew of Philip's family, so giving a better footing for their discussion when Francis questioned Philip's interest in Emily.

'I have met her only a few times,' Philip flushed, 'but I was impressed by her charm. I was on my way to seek her out when I was approached by a friend of Emily's, who told me the whole sad story.'

'Why did this friend approach you, Mr Linton?' Roger Francis asked curiously. 'Did she know you?'

'Of me!' He smiled. 'There are some servants who know more than their masters and mistresses and Ginny appears to be one of those.' He grew serious. 'But it was mere coincidence that we met and I rather feel that she was clutching at straws. She could think of no-one who could help Emily.'

'So she is a true friend?' Roger murmured, then, looking up, he rose as Mary Edwards approached. 'What news, my dear? How is she taking it?'

'Badly.' Mary's eyes were red rimmed with weeping. 'She is so very bitter and it is not in her nature to be so. And the news is that she will be moved tomorrow down to the Thames. There will be transport ready in the morning to take the prisoners.' She stifled a sob, yet could barely speak for her emotion. 'And Emily will be one of them.'

Chapter Twenty-Five

Emily boarded the coach outside York Castle gaol with some difficulty. Her ankles were ironed as before and she was manacled to another woman by her right hand and a girl of perhaps fourteen by the left.

The girl sobbed and screamed and refused to climb on board and Emily was pulled by the woman climbing aboard and dragged back by the girl, who fell to the floor in her distress, pulling Emily and the other woman on top of her. Emily felt that her arms had been wrenched out of their sockets as she struggled to get to her feet. The guard rushed over to them and verbally abused them all, roughly pulling the girl by her bodice and thrusting her with Emily and the other woman into the coach.

He grabbed the handcuffs holding them and released the girl from them, then clasped her hands behind her back and manacled her wrists. 'Out,' he ordered. 'Get up on 'top. You two stop here.'

'Swine!' the woman muttered. 'I know his ma, she's no better than she should be.'

Emily turned away, the morning was dark and

dismal with a light rain falling and she watched with glazed eyes, through the coach window, as other prisoners, men and women, perhaps fifteen or twenty in all, came out of the prison yard and towards the waiting coaches and wagons. If I can travel inside it will be preferable to being on top, she pondered, remembering the journey from Hull to York. I believe London is a very long way.

Another guard looked inside. 'Who've we got here then? Hello, Molly. Got you at last, have they?' He grinned and winked. 'Nice little sail for you to Sydney Cove! Weather's good, so I hear, and plenty of husbands to choose from. I could almost wish I was going with you.'

The woman leaned back against the seat and gazed at him from beneath wrinkled and heavy eyelids. 'Why don't you, then? Take a free passage.'

'No thanks,' he said. 'Too many villains down there. Besides, my missus wouldn't go.'

'Leave her behind then,' she said idly. 'I'd see you all right. Go on,' she urged, leaning towards him, 'there's plenty o' land going cheap, plenty o' women – even cheaper.' She laughed coarsely.

He shook his head. 'I live in prison already. Why swap it for another one?'

The woman sniffed. 'You've no backbone. I'll be glad to be gone from this land.'

'Watch yourself, Molly,' he said gruffly. 'Watch that tongue o' yourn or it'll get you into trouble like it's done before. They might not give women the lash any more, but they have other ways of punishing them.'

He turned away and they were left alone for a few

moments. 'What did he mean', Emily asked in a trembling voice, 'about other punishments?'

The woman stared at her. 'They used to give women the lash, not as many strokes as the men, but enough to mark 'em. Now they're not supposed to, though I've heard some do.' She gave a sly sneer. 'I don't suppose you've had a strap on your white skin?'

Emily shook her head. She was starting to shake.

'They'll all be after you then, won't they? Officers, seamen, guards!' She jerked Emily closer to her and whispered. 'Stick by me, I'll pick somebody out for you. We'll find you an officer on board ship. Treat him right and we'll both do well. How about it?'

Emily fell forward, retching and retching as the woman's words brought Hugo Purnell to her mind. How would she ever rid herself of his memory?

'You sickening for summat?' the woman asked. 'I don't want you travelling next to me if you are!'

Emily wiped her mouth and looked into the woman's face. She was pockmarked, with a grey unhealthy skin. What sickness could I give her that she hasn't had already? She suddenly started to laugh. An hysterical, shrieking laugh as she thought terrifyingly of what was in front of her. She was to rub shoulders and share her life with whores, thieves and murderers. How would she survive?

Another guard came rushing forward as he heard the commotion and dragged them both out. 'She's mad,' the woman declared. 'Don't put her next to me!'

Their handcuffs were released and Emily was

pushed up on the front of the coach and the woman on the rear, the other prisoners were brought on board, the driver climbed up and with a crack of his whip they jerked forward. They were off, out of the city of York on the two-day journey to London.

They stopped for an hour that night whilst the horses were changed and were allowed to walk around the yard of an inn to stretch themselves, but their ankle chains and manacles were not removed and Emily kept her face hidden as customers came to the inn door to peer curiously at them. When she climbed back on board she was shaking with cold and hunger, for they had been given only a chunk of bread and water at midday, and only been allowed to step down to relieve themselves. As dawn broke the next morning only the fact that she was shackled to the other prisoners held her to her seat, for otherwise she would have fallen with fatigue, off the coach and beneath the horses' hooves.

No-one spoke as at midday, once more, they stopped and were given bread and water and a piece of cheese and staggered in a disordered circle in order to exercise. As the coaches and wagons entered the city of London the prisoners were subdued, meek and hungry and looked with dull eyes at the capital city, which would be their final destination point for their departure to another shore.

They followed their captors meekly into the gaol which was to hold them and sank wearily on to their straw mattresses, not minding the fleas or livestock which invaded them, but only glad to rest their weary bodies on solid ground and not feel the jarring, jolting movement of the coach or wagon below them.

Male prisoners sentenced to transportation were held in Pentonville prison and served a third of their allotted span incarcerated there; then they were given hard labour in the naval dockyards before sailing to finish their sentences in Australia. Most knew that they would never return, unless they could work their passage home; some had no intention of returning to the land which had abandoned them and appealed to the authorities to allow their wives and families to follow them.

Some of the women prisoners already held in gaol when Emily arrived had been there for weeks waiting for their transportation ship to arrive and their tempers were ugly. They abused the guards with foul language or else promised all kinds of favours if they were given special treatment. 'Tomorrow, tomorrow, you keep on saying,' one woman shouted through the bars. 'Yet we've been locked up for weeks in this stinking hole!' Some of the others rushed to the bars and rattled and banged on them, whilst other quieter, frightened prisoners, such as Emily, cowered against the walls, trying to make themselves invisible. But the rebellion was to no avail and those who complained too loudly and for too long were shackled to the walls of their cells.

Emily felt ill, dirty and depressed. Mary Edwards had promised that she and Mr Francis would appeal on her behalf against the sentence, but Emily had now given up all hope. There would be no release, she was convinced. Only Hugo Purnell could appeal to the authorities in mitigation for her crime, and he would not, of that she was certain, and she would not appeal to him, not ever. Her hatred of him, which was growing like a cancer inside her, was total.

Two hundred women prisoners were mustered together the next morning and once more ironed by their ankles and chained in groups of six. They had been brought to the capital from all over the country, from towns and from country villages. Some of the women cried for their children, a number of them dropped to their knees and prayed, whilst others cursed and ranted at God, the queen and their captors.

'Right you are, ladies,' called one of the guards. 'This is what you've been waiting for. You're off on a little sea voyage. Hope you've said goodbye to your next of kin, 'cos if you haven't it's too late now. You're outward bound in a week.'

Emily shook in every limb as she waited. She could not hold her body still. This is the end of the life I have known, she wept. There is no-one to save me now. And, as once before she had stood on the river bank and said goodbye to Sam, to Granny Edwards and her childhood as she had set off into adulthood, she said a silent goodbye now. To Mary Edwards, to Roger Francis, to Sam and the friends she had made in service, and Philip Linton, she sighed, who once danced with me and made me happy.

I'm so glad that he doesn't know of this. I would be so ashamed if he should hear of my downfall and think ill of me. She spared a thought for Deborah Purnell and even in her own anguish she felt a stab of sorrow for her and the life she would lead with her husband. Poor, poor lady, she considered, I would rather be as I am now, than be as she is and married to him.

They walked in file towards the river, down narrow, unlit cobbled streets with ancient, decrepit courts and alleys leading off them, where people came out of their decaying ramshackle houses and silently watched them pass. The sun came up as they travelled, but the sunlight only served to emphasize the poverty and degradation of the area, where barefoot, ragged children played in the filth-choked gutters.

They passed the dockyards and saw the shackled, labouring felons, who looked up as the procession went by. The river was busy with traffic, with coal barges, dredgers and cargo ships, whilst on the muddy banks scavengers and mudlarks searched amongst the stinking sewage for their fortune. They saw the infamous old hulks, where once the First and Second Fleet of prisoners had been packed in the dark in dank and dirty holds, without light or air before being sent to the other side of the world, and which were still used when the prisons were full.

This is wrong! Emily suddenly rebelled. Why should people be sent into exile for crimes of poverty? During the night, unable to sleep, she had listened to muttered conversations, of complaints and weeping, and recognized that not all the prisoners were hardened criminals, but that some had stolen to feed their children or pay their rent. Her gaze drew across the river. A five-masted barque rode at anchor, seamen swarmed high out on the yards overhauling the rigging, whilst below, carpenters hammered and sawed and caulked the decks, and in the surging water three ships' lighters packed with provisions, barrels of water, chickens, sheep, pigs, goats and their kids were being rowed towards it.

The prisoners waited all the morning, shivering in the cold river air and watching the activities of officers and men as they travelled between ship and shore, until finally the lighters were empty and the guards were given orders to move the women forward to be taken on board.

I'd like to sail on a ship. Her own childish voice came back to her in memory. I used to watch the ships sail down the Humber and wonder where they were going. But I haven't seen such a ship as this. This was a stalwart vessel designed to sail under its own power of canvas on the great oceans of the world. This ship, she thought, could ride the huge seas and capture the winds of any storm in its square sails and make them fly; and in spite of her fear she felt a tremble of excitement as she was rowed towards it.

Their hands were freed, but the chains were kept on their ankles as the lighter bobbed alongside the ship. 'Right,' called a soldier, who had a rifle by his side. 'Climb aboard.'

'Bear a hand, mate,' one of the seamen called to him. 'They'll not make it up jack ladder on their own!'

The lighter dipped and bobbed as the women tried to get a foothold on the rope ladder. The anklets were just wide enough for them to lift one foot above the other to gain the step, but the boat swayed so much that most were afraid of falling into the water. Though their lives were meaningless, yet still they clung to them as firmly as they clung to the rope which kept them between life and death.

The soldier handed his rifle to one of the seamen and stood by to put a hand against the women's backs as they struggled to reach the ladder from the plunging boat. He grinned at their efforts and leeringly peered up their ragged skirts as they climbed up towards the deck.

'Get your hands off me!' Emily pushed him away as he put his hands on her buttocks to push her up. 'I can manage.'

She felt the ladder shake and looked up. An old woman had gone before her and was hesitating half-way up. Emily had noticed her on the journey from the gaol. She had barely been able to walk; her shuffling feet were bare and festering and her back was bent and she moaned constantly.

'Come on, Mother!' the soldier shouted. 'Get a move on.'

The woman appeared not to have heard him, but had half-turned and was staring down into the water. Suddenly she looked up into the sky. 'God help me,' she cried pitifully and letting go of the ladder she flung herself off and into the swirling water below.

Emily clung on as the ladder shook and with terrified eyes looked down. The women in the lighter shrieked and cried, 'Get her out. Get her out. Save her, for God's sake!'

The seamen pulled on the oars to where she had fallen in and Emily was left stranded, clinging to the side of the ship, with nothing below her but the deep water which had just swallowed up the old woman. She looked up, the seamen on board had rushed to the side on hearing the shrill cries.

'Man overboard,' someone shouted. 'Fetch a grapnel.'

Emily started to climb, her heart raced and she dared not look down and somehow she reached the deck, where she was hauled aboard. She looked over the side. They were searching in the water with a grappling hook, but the woman had gone. Weighted down by her chains and her misery she appeared just once before the waters gathered her in and closed over her.

'Get this lot below.' A harsh command was shouted and Emily was bundled with others already waiting on deck, towards a companionway. She stumbled down steep ladders below decks, almost falling on top of the other women as the press of prisoners came up behind her, below again to a lower deck until they came to a halt between decks, where, bent double, for they could not stand upright, they were told to stay. A grated barricade spiked with iron confronted them and wooden hatches above let in only a dim light. The air was foul and damp and as, in silence, they gazed at their surroundings the door was clanged shut behind them and they were left in darkness.

Chapter Twenty-Six

Time had ticked by as Philip discussed with Roger Francis and Mrs Edwards the chances of obtaining a reprieve for Emily. He had travelled back with them from York to Hull, which was the original point of Emily's arrest, and talked to the magistrates' clerk, who had given him little hope unless the complainant agreed to withdraw charges. But Hugo Purnell had disappeared. He was not at his own home in Hessle or at his mother's house and she did not know of his whereabouts.

'I haven't seen him since he went to York for the trial,' Mrs Purnell complained at Philip's enquiry. 'He'll be angry about the report in the newspapers, I expect. It said', she lowered her voice, 'that he wasn't a reliable witness. What shame! I can't believe anyone would say that of my son!'

'I shall go to London,' Philip told Roger Francis and Mrs Edwards when they met in her home behind the flower shop. 'I will ask at the Home Office what must be done to rectify this injustice. And if you could continue to look for Purnell, sir?'

'I will.' Roger Francis looked strained. 'I am anxious also about my daughter. Emily warned me, and I fear for Deborah's condition if she is not cared for.'

Philip looked from one to another. 'I don't understand. Your daughter surely isn't under any threat from her husband?'

'Mr Francis's daughter has a delicate constitution,' Mary Edwards explained. 'She might well suffer under the strain of all the past events. She needs care, and Hugo Purnell seems to be incapable of providing it.'

As Philip settled himself in the railway carriage to take him on the first leg of his journey to London, he pondered on how Hugo Purnell had come to meet and marry Roger Francis's daughter, and how surprising it was that he had taken on the responsibility of a delicate wife, when, he reflected, it seemed out of character for the fellow. It could only be money, he decided, no other reason. And as he ruminated on this and then on Emily, he remembered that he never had received the money which Hugo owed him, which Mrs Purnell had endeavoured to pay and which was stolen from Emily. So the blackguard still owes me!

A blank wall of bureaucracy confronted him when he enquired about the petition of reprieve. He was sent from one office to half a dozen others, from one clerk to six more and in each case was given a sheaf of papers, each with dozens of questions requiring intricate answers. Finally, one clerk, more helpful than the others, suggested, 'Why don't we look at the prison lists, sir?' He had observed Philip's naval uniform. 'If we could find out where the prisoner is held, perhaps you could delay her departure.'

They poured over the Assize agenda books of female convicts tried at the county courts, until finally, the clerk, with his practised eye exclaimed, 'Hah! Here we are. Emily Hawkins of York, committed for trial on charge of neglect of newborn child. Charges withdrawn. Wilful damage to property. Sentenced to three years' transportation. Would that be the lady, sir?' His friendly gaze had withered somewhat as he read out the details.

'Yes. Yes! Does it say where she is?'

'The *Flying Swan*.' The clerk snapped the book closed. 'I fear you are too late, sir. I saw the ship only yesterday. The convicts are boarded. She's ready to sail.'

Philip gazed vacantly at the clerk. So there is no time to ask for a reprieve! What shall I do? What can I do? And as he walked out into the damp overcast afternoon, he realized that there was only one thing that he could do if he wanted to save Emily, and that was to try and obtain orders to sail with the *Flying Swan*.

'I really need the experience, sir.' Philip pleaded with his father's old friend and shipmate, Commander Allen. 'I've served on paddle and propeller, but old wooden ships like the *Flying Swan* will soon be obsolete. I'd like to think that I had once sailed with only the power of sail.'

'I quite agree,' Commander Allen said heartily. 'Your father and I know that sailing a square rigger is the very best kind of life, but there are other ships. You surely don't want to sail in such an old tub with a holdful of convicts? And to Australia of all places!'

'Yes, sir, I'd like to see Australia.' He was clutching at straws. He had to get a position on the ship now that he had discovered that Emily was on board. 'It's an up-and-coming country, so I hear.'

'Pah!' The commander leaned back in his chair. 'The place is full of thieves and murderers! They're not even wanted when they arrive.'

'But there are the emigrants, sir.' Philip insisted. 'People are going in their thousands.'

'Yes, but what sort of people are they?' Commander Allen shook his head. 'Not our kind. They're poor farmers, labourers, folk without any hope or money, they'll not do any better in that empty land than they've done here.'

Philip's spirits sank. He didn't know who else to appeal to. Commander Allen was the last person of influence that he knew.

'Still,' Commander Allen sighed, 'if you're determined.' He picked up a pen and reached for a sheet of paper. 'Go and see Captain Martin, he's in command. But don't set your hopes on it. She sails in a couple of days, so he might well have a full complement of men. Give him my regards.'

Philip beamed, thanked him and took his letter of introduction. At last! One more hurdle to get over, and there had been so many.

He finally found Captain Martin in an inn near the dockside, and presented his letter of introduction from Commander Allen. He read it with a frown above his nose. 'Well, Mr Linton,' he said, looking up, 'your credentials are excellent as are your references, but I'm fully manned. If you'd been here a week ago when I was desperately short of manpower!' He was a small man with an anxious face and fading red hair. 'Nobody wants to sail a convict ship any more, they're nothing but trouble even when we reach Australia. I've had to promise every man a bonus if we make good time. We're easting down, non-stop via the Canaries, Rio, and downwind to the Cape. Three months! Three and a half at the most.'

Philip's face must have showed his disappointment, for the captain added, 'Why this ship?'

'I've heard so much about her, sir,' he lied. 'And I wanted to sail under canvas only.'

'Did you, by jove! What a pity.' He pursed his lips. 'Good navigator are you?'

'Yes, sir.' His hopes rose. 'I completed my examinations at Trinity House some time ago.'

'Mm. Well, it still don't make a difference,' Captain Martin said. 'I haven't a place for you. Pity you're not a sawbones. If you had been I could have made use of you!'

Philip shook his head. 'I'm not a medical man, sir, and I don't have a warrant as such, but I've completed courses on treatment of accidents on board ship, bandaging, medication and so on, and I've read up on naval hygiene, seamen's maladies, cases of typhus and the treatment required and so on.'

'Have you?' Captain Martin rubbed his chin thoughtfully. 'Hmm. I don't suppose you would consider – no, of course you wouldn't, you have a fine career ahead of you.'

'What, sir?' he asked eagerly. 'What had you in mind?'

Captain Martin looked around. The inn was full of seagoing men, eating and drinking. He leaned forward and lowered his voice. 'I've got a surgeon-superintendent. Excellent fellow. The very best.'

He paused and Philip fervently wished he wouldn't dither so much but just speak what was on his mind.

'Except for one thing.' He put his mouth close to Philip's ear. 'He's a drunk! Can't hold his liquor.'

Philip waited. What was he going to suggest?

'I couldn't get anyone else and I can't sail without a surgeon, so I had to take him. Now, you may not agree of course, and the rate of pay wouldn't cover a lieutenant's rank – more like a midshipman, but it would help me tremendously if you could come on board as his mate. Keep him off the rum, you know, and help with general duties in the sick berth. There's always sickness on a convict ship. Poor beggars are half-dead before they're brought aboard.'

'I'll do it, sir. Be glad to.' Relief rushed over him. 'It er, it will be a great experience for me.'

'Hm!' Captain Martin eyed him candidly. 'It will certainly be that. But you might wish that you had done otherwise at the end of it. This will be a tricky run. We've got females on board as well as men and that always means trouble, and mark my words, none of them'll be wanted when we reach Sydney. We'll be lucky if we're not turned back. But still, come along, Mr Linton.' He rose from the table.

'Let's get your orders sorted out before you change your mind.'

Later as he stowed his gear in the cabin he began to rationalize his actions. He must be completely mad! This was such a very old ship, though she was sound. She had been fully inspected by the Navy Board in order to take the convicts, and the contractor had honoured his obligation to provide ample provisions. Philip's cabin, one of five on the main deck plus the master's cabin, was no more than six feet in length and, as in other ships in which he had sailed, had such a low ceiling that he was unable to stand upright. He was provided with a small desk and a wooden chair and a hammock was slung alongside a storage cupboard.

He fastened his father's old sea box to the leather strap which was attached to the deck planking and wondered how his parents would react to the brief letter he had sent them to say he was sailing for Australia. He took off his coat and hung it on one of the hooks behind the door, stowed the hammock to the wall and sat down on the chair. Well, he thought. Here I am. I made my decision for better or worse and I may not even see Emily! Two hundred female convicts on board, what chance do I have of talking to her and will she want to see me or talk to me?

He stacked his books on the shelf above the desk, then took his spare clothing and stowed it in the cupboard and went out on deck to meet his fellow officers.

The upper deck was strewn with blocks, tackles, chains and rope as the able seamen made their last overhaul before leaving port. Philip strode over it, knowing that in just a few hours all would be in place and ready for use. Above on the yards and ratlines young seamen and boys crowded like swallows waiting for the call, as they checked the rigging and checked again.

A small boat was being rowed towards the ship and he could hear the sound of singing from its one and only passenger. He leaned over the bulwark and watched as the bowman raised his oars vertically, shipped them and steadied the vessel to enable the passenger to climb the jack ladder. He was dressed in an officer's uniform and carried his hat between his teeth. Philip put out a hand to help him aboard and breathing heavily he fell onto the deck.

'Thank you good sir, much obliged.' His words were slurred and thick, and Philip guessed that here was the surgeon he was to work under, Mr Clavell.

'I thought I was adrift.' Mr Clavell clambered to his feet and raised his arm in a salute to the seaman below as he shoved off clear of the ship. 'If that young fella hadn't reminded me which ship I was supposed to be on – I couldn't remember.' He gave a small belch. 'I knew it was *Flying* something or other with convicts on board.' He gazed glassily around. 'This is it, I suppose?'

'Yes, sir.' Philip grinned. 'The *Flying Swan*. Captain Martin is master.'

Mr Clavell sighed. 'Ah! And you are?'

'Lieutenant Linton, sir. I'm to be your mate.'

'My mate? Nobody said I was to have a mate! Jolly

good. Glad to meet you. I'm sure we'll get on.' He returned a wobbly salute. 'Tell you the truth,' he lowered his voice and put a hand on Philip's shoulder, 'tell you the truth, Mr Minton –'.

'Linton, sir!'

'Yes. Well –! Oh yes. Tell you the truth, I'm three sheets to the wind and I really must have a zizz. Do you happen to know where my cot is?'

Philip found the surgeon's cabin, which was next to his own and thought it fortunate that Mr Clavell's cot was a wooden one and fixed to the wall of his cabin, as he doubted if he would have been able to get him into a swinging hammock like his own. He took off the surgeon's coat and removed his boots and placed them neatly where he wouldn't fall over them and then went in search of the captain to report that the surgeon was on board.

'Was he drunk, Mr Linton?' the master asked.

'Half seas over sir,' Philip admitted. 'He's sleeping it off.'

'Just as well we don't need him! Well, Mr Linton, you must have a good reason for setting sail in such a hurry, but I'm glad to have you aboard. Are you escaping some young woman?'

'No, sir.' It wouldn't do, he thought, to tell Captain Martin the real reason for being on board the *Flying Swan*. 'Not escaping from – but searching for.'

Captain Martin looked taken aback. 'In Australia? Are there not ladies aplenty ashore in England?'

Philip agreed. 'I'm sure there are, sir, but not to

my fancy.' He hesitated, then asked, 'Are all the convicts on board, sir?'

'All below, 'tween decks.' He looked grim. 'They're going to be uncomfortable for a day or two but I daren't let them out until we're well at sea. Some of them might try to jump overboard if they see the homeland disappearing.'

'Are they all well, sir?'

He shrugged. 'As well as can be expected after being in gaol. Some of them are troublemakers so I've been told, the women as well as the men, but there's no sickness that I know of.'

The captain moved away, then turned back. 'Don't be tempted by the women, Mr Linton. I know that officers have the pick of 'em, but it's not wise, they'll pass on the clap sure as eggs is eggs.'

'They're surely not all whores, sir?' Philip said quietly.

Captain Martin shrugged. 'Perhaps not, but I wouldn't take a chance. But no time for this, Mr Linton. We're outward bound on the morning tide.'

'All hands to quarters!' A drumbeat sounded.

'Aye, aye, sir.'

'Away aloft!'

'Aye, aye, sir.'

'Ease away. Let go the brails. Handsomely does it!'

Philip stood on the quarterdeck as orders were given. This wasn't his watch. His orders were to keep an eye on the surgeon, though he had been given the dog watch also; but as he felt the timbers move beneath his feet and heard the creak of the canvas as the sails were trimmed, and with a fair wind sighing, he became part of the whole as officers and crew obeyed their instructions implicitly and the great ship slipped her moorings and slid gently out of harbour, down the Thames and towards the open sea.

Chapter Twenty-Seven

As Emily's eyes became accustomed to the darkness and made out the state of their captivity, she was overcome with misery, despair and self-pity and only wanted to sink to the floor and die. I have no reason to live. No-one to live for. Why should I make any effort to prolong my life? If there was just someone, someone who could hold my hand, bring a word of comfort or even take a crumb of comfort from me, though I would find it an effort to give it, I just might find a reason for my existence.

She elbowed her way through the crush of women to where bunks were placed on either side of the deck, all the way to the bows. Here was where they would sleep, with their ankles still ironed to add to their discomfort. A grated barricade spiked with iron had been built across the ship at the steerage bulkhead and though there was only gloom, she was sure she could see eyes watching them and hear the whisper of voices. At the other end was another barricade, behind which were the male convicts, or the government men as they were called by the gaolers. They had cheered the women as they'd arrived and some were making lewd suggestions. There is no privacy, she grieved, and looked around for a place where she wouldn't be seen and found a top bunk close to a hatch, where she hoped for a little air.

The door opened again and another dozen women were herded into the already crowded space. 'Get your hands off me, cur!' A woman's voice hurled a stream of expletives at the sentry who had thrust her down the companionway, and cast a slur on his birth, his mother, his father and his grandparents. The cursing was so rich and strong and explanatory that in spite of her misery, Emily couldn't help but smile. If only I could be so brave, she thought. If only I could be so fearless instead of weak and afraid.

The woman pushed her way through the crowd of women, some of whom were milling around in confusion, whilst others had simply sat down on the deck planking, weeping and crying. 'No use wailing,' she shouted at them. 'It won't do you a ha'porth o' good. You've got to stand up to 'em, otherwise 'beggers'll grind you down.'

Emily sat forward. I know that voice. But from where? It was a northern voice, not one of the strange mixtures she had heard in the London gaol, not southern or Cornish or middle England, but an accent that was familiar. 'Meg!' she breathed. 'Can it be?'

'Meg!' she called out, an edge of hysteria in her voice. 'Meg! Is it you?'

The woman stopped her grumbling. 'Who knows me by me name?' She moved towards Emily's corner, peering into the gloom and demanded, 'Who knows me?'

Emily stood up. 'It's me,' she said, with tears gathering in her eyes. 'Emily Hawkins.'

Meg came slowly towards her. 'Emily? Em from Hull?'

'Yes.' Tears streamed down Emily's face. 'From Kingston Street gaol.'

Meg stood in front of her. 'Little Emily? They never sent you here, after all?' She shook her head. 'There's no justice in this land.'

'Meg!' Emily's voice trembled. 'I'm so sorry that you are here in this terrible place, but I'm so glad, so very glad to see you.'

A tear coursed down Meg's face, but she dashed it away and said softly, 'And I'm so happy to see you again, Em. So very happy.' She put out her arms and Emily did likewise and they hugged and cried and wept together.

They sat on the bunk and whispered in the darkness and Emily asked how Meg had come to be here. 'Not whoring,' Meg said bluntly. 'They can't get you for that. No, it was because I slandered 'magistrate. You remember, Em, at your hearing?'

Emily gasped. Surely Meg hadn't been transported because of her?

'I said I'd seen him at Queenie's, which I had. He's a visiting magistrate,' she explained, 'not a regular one from Hull, and every time he comes he goes to Queenie's. I suppose he thinks his wife won't find out if he plays away from home. I've seen 'other bloke there as well,' she added. 'That one who brought 'case.'

'Hugo Purnell,' Emily said, his name bitter on her tongue.

'Aye, him. Well, when they took me down to 'cells after I'd yelled at him, I was accused of slander and they locked me up again. And while I was waiting in gaol for 'next hearing, 'police were sent to 'house where I lodge and found some stolen stuff. I swear to God I never took it, Em, but they said I did. It was silver and such and what would I do with owt like that? Anyway, I was sent to York, like you was, and must have followed you here. Though I never knew. I thought you'd got off 'charge! Somebody said that you had, but I can't read 'newspaper and nobody else I know can either.'

'They dropped 'charge about the baby,' Emily said, 'but I was charged on 'damage to the painting, which I admitted, and sentenced to three years' transportation.'

Meg smiled a grim smile. 'You know why, don't you?'

Emily nodded. 'The gaols are full in England.'

'Hah! Don't you believe it! And it's not because of what you did. It's because they need young lasses out in 'colonies! There's so many men out there, they need 'women to keep 'em quiet. They're going to fill 'country wi' troublemakers, give 'em a wife and hope they'll breed and stop there.'

'I can't believe what you're saying! They wouldn't do such a thing!' Emily was horrified.

'You don't really think that you'll be allowed back, do you?' Meg's voice was cynical. 'How would you get back? Who'd pay your passage?

'Government's not going to, not when they've taken trouble to send you out! Men can get back if they've a mind to, they can work their passage on board ship. I know one who did, but 'women –'. She shook her head. 'Don't even think about it, Emily. If you survive 'journey, then you're there for good. Don't gather up any hopes. We'll not be coming back!'

An officer came with a guard to instruct them on procedure. He told them to form groups of six and the six were to share each bunk. They were each given a straw mattress, a blanket and a thin pillow, a wooden bowl and spoon. One woman from each group would be elected matron and organize the collection and distribution of food. 'Think yourselves lucky that conditions have changed for the better,' he shouted at them. 'You wouldn't have had such comforts a few years ago.'

He said they would be given a kettle to share with three other groups so that they could make a drink and once they were under sail they would be allowed on deck and allowed to wash and be given clean clothing. Some of the women were wearing little more than rags and they shivered in the cold. Emily still had her cloak, but she feared she would lose it before the voyage was over. It was dirty and torn at the hem, but it was warm and she wrapped it around herself and Meg when they slept.

'God bless you, Em,' Meg murmured. 'You're such a comfort to me.'

'I? No, it's you that comforts me.' Emily pondered on when she had first met Meg and had been so disgusted by her manners and appearance. 'I didn't want to live before you came on board, Meg. Now I know that I can go on. You're so brave.'

Meg started to weep at her words. 'I'm not brave. I'm terrified! And I've never in my life had anyone who cared about what became of me. Not my ma or my da, whoever he was, not till that day when you sent your Christmas dinner to me. You could have kept it, but you didn't. You thought of me and nobody has ever done that afore. I'll never forget that. Never till my dying day!'

Meg was elected the leader of their group. The decision was unanimous as she was the one who dared to ask for what was required. She was given an extra blanket for one member of their group, an elderly woman who shivered with the cold and who, the others whispered, would never reach her destination.

They had no conception of time during the period they spent in port as no light came through the hatches, but one day as Emily lay sleepless on the bunk, she suddenly felt a different movement, not the gentle rocking she had become accustomed to but a deeper plunging and rolling and she heard too the sound of commands being given, of voices answering and the rushing tread of feet above them. 'Meg,' she whispered urgently, 'I think we're moving. We are! We're under sail!'

'God help us!' Meg leant on one elbow. 'I'm that scared, Emily.'

Other women were sitting up too, looking from one to another in their anxiety. Some were praying, others were crying and soon the noise they made grew louder as their fear spread to each other.

'Quiet!' A sentry opened the door; he had a rifle in his hand. 'Less noise down there.'

'Are we sailing?' Meg scurried across to him. 'Tell us what's happening, for God's sake.'

'Aye, we're sailing all right. Breathe in your last breath of English air!'

'What? Down here?' Meg said defiantly. 'There's been no air down here since we came on board! Open 'hatches for us! Go on, we can't get a breath.'

'Can't.' He started to close the door. 'Orders. You'll come up when we're clear of England.'

'Clear of England! I can't wait!' Meg muttered and turned away. Then she caught sight of a male convict staring at her through the barricade. 'Who you looking at?' she demanded and thrust her face towards him. 'Haven't you seen a woman afore?'

'Not for a long time,' he answered quietly. 'You'd be well advised not to cause trouble for yoursen.'

'Trouble!' she muttered. 'I was born to it, mister.' The ship gave a sudden lurch and she grabbed hold of the barricade to stop herself falling. The man laughed and she scowled at him and shook her fist. 'Bleeding government men. Pimps and thieves!'

'Aye, that's us, missus.' He stared at her through the bars, a look of resignation on his face. 'No good for owt.' He suddenly started to sing, his voice cracked and distorted as if in pain.

'Old England don't want us
and nor does our queen
We're thieves and we're murderers

not fit to be seen
So we're off to Australia
in a tall ship so grand
For England don't want us
in her fair pleasant land.'

His face worked as if in emotion and he wiped his nose on his sleeve. Meg fell silent. 'Sorry,' she muttered. 'I didn't mean owt.'

The other men took up the words and started to sing too, loudly and boisterously as if to hide their feelings, though there were some who couldn't sing for weeping.

'First time I've ever said sorry to a fella in my life.' Meg climbed back onto the bunk next to Emily. 'It's you, Em.' She gave a lopsided grin, but her voice was choked. 'You're mekking me soft.'

'They're maybe not all wicked,' Emily said quietly. 'And they'll all be leaving somebody behind. A mother, wife or children maybe.'

'Aye.' Meg lay down on the bunk again. 'That chap yonder. He didn't sound as if he came from these parts, London I mean. No, he sounded more like from our way.' She gave a deep sigh. 'I've probably met him at some time. There's few that I haven't.'

For two days they were tossed and thrown about as the ship ran into deep water. Many of the women were sick and the stench became unbearable. Meg and some of the other matrons hammered on the door and pleaded with the sentry to open the door or hatches to let in some air, but their request was refused. Finally on the third day, when most lay in a sick stupor, the hatches rattled and were drawn to one side and a dim light came through the bars from the deck above. The door opened and an officer and two guards appeared.

'Fifty women, ten at a time, can come up,' said the officer. 'I want no trouble. If you give any you'll come straight down again and be given only bread and water for a week.'

'Well, we wouldn't want to miss out on our little luxuries, now would we?' Meg began, but was hushed by Emily and the other women as they queued to take their turn to go up on deck. But it took so long. As each woman reached the upper deck she was given a number which corresponded with her name on a list, and this number was pinned to her clothing. They were allowed up on deck for half an hour and then brought below again to give the others a turn.

Emily and Meg were in the last fifty to get their numbers and go on to the quarterdeck and by now the evening dusk was gathering. The sky was suffused with red and yellow and the sea reflected the colours, and it seemed as if the ocean was on fire. There was not a sign of land, not a shadow to show where they had come from; they were completely surrounded by water.

'It's so beautiful,' Emily whispered, 'but so vast.' She stared around her at the mighty wastes of sea and then up into the sky. 'We are like nothing out here.' She gazed up at the masts and the rigging and the great white sails billowing and felt the power of the ship beneath her. 'The *Flying Swan*,' she murmured, 'she's well named.'

'You down there,' a voice called out from the forecastle, 'keep moving. You've all been complaining of being cramped below, so start walking! Come on, jump to it. Round and round. Round and round!'

'Do you think he's ever tried walking with irons on?' Meg said fiercely. 'Son of a bitch, standing there giving orders!'

'Hush! Maybe they'll let us take them off in a day or two when they think they can trust us.' Emily was fearful of trouble. 'At least we're up on deck and can breathe at last.'

At sunrise the next morning the door was opened and they were allowed on deck, two hundred women and one hundred men, but they were carefully segregated and all kept on their irons, the women in their ankle bracelets and the men fettered in heavy ankle irons which had a chain attached to an iron band circling their waists, allowing them only to shuffle. They had to bring up their bedding to air and then stow into lockers, then a working party was organized and sent down to scrape and clean and disinfect their quarters.

The old woman who shared their bunk had to be helped up the companionway, her legs were so stiff she could barely put one foot in front of the other. 'Leave me,' she kept repeating, 'I only want to die.'

But the other women forced her on, one on each side of her and one behind until they got her on deck, where she lay down as if the effort had been too much for her.

'She needs a doctor,' Emily said and turned to a seaman passing by. 'Can you get a doctor?' But he ignored her as if she wasn't there and walked on.

Though they were glad to be out of the dark interior, it was cold on deck, the wind was sharp and cut through them like a knife. A group of midshipmen came with a pile of clothing for them. 'Here you are, sort it out between yourselves. Find something to fit and change when you get below. Then leave your own clothes in a pile to be removed later.'

Emily looked with dismay at the heap of rough clothing. There were skirts and shirts and jackets, but all made from coarse material, serge or hemp, not wool as she was wearing now. Worsted stockings and shoes were piled into a heap and there were shawls too, grey and thin and some of the women who were without warm clothing fell on to them eagerly, snatching them from each other's hands.

Buckets of sea water were hauled over the side of the ship and the women rinsed their hands and faces, trying to rid themselves of the stench which pervaded them all. 'I'm full o' fleas,' Meg complained, scratching herself. 'I've never had as many as this in my life.'

'The sea water will get rid of them,' Emily said hopefully as she swilled herself, then shrieked in horror as she saw her own skirt was crawling with the creatures. She tore off her skirt, not minding that she was in public and grabbed a twill one from the pile which was left. It was scratchy but clean and she plunged her own skirt into a bucket of sea water which was standing near.

The day passed slowly and monotonously, broken only by the serving of breakfast and dinner rations which the matrons and mess captains collected and shared out amongst their group. The rest of the time they either sat or shuffled around the narrow deck and waited for the day to end.

Emily and Meg collected clothing for the old woman and helped her down below again. The fresh air had done nothing to alleviate her discomfort and she refused her food when it came at suppertime, but lay on the bunk and closed her eyes. They shared out her food between the five of them, the dishes were cleared and washed in a bucket of sea water and put away, and though it was not yet night, the hatches were closed and the door banged shut.

'The end of a perfect day,' Meg muttered. ''Night, Em.'

'Goodnight, Meg.' Emily lay down beside her. The smoke from the fumigation still lingered and invaded her nostrils and stung her eyes. She was cold, the sea air had been exhilarating but biting. Her cloak had been taken from her and she felt she would never be warm again. They say it's warm in Australia, she pondered. How long before we are there? Three months, some have said. Others say six. She sighed. It will seem like a lifetime.

Chapter Twenty-Eight

Philip had peered through the barricade into the women's prison. 'They need air,' he'd said to Lieutenant Boyle. 'The rules are that they must have adequate ventilation.'

'They'll get it when we're under sail, not before.' Lieutenant Boyle was a red-faced, portly man only a few years older than Philip, but his rise had been swift. He had connections. He was also aggressive and domineering and few people stood in his way. If they did, he trampled firmly on them until they moved. He now had the position of first mate, second in command under Captain Martin. 'If I had my way,' he muttered as he turned away, 'they'd stay below until we reach Sydney.'

Philip had looked searchingly amongst the women, though it was difficult to see their faces in the gloomy interior. I can't see her! Oh, God. What if she isn't here! But she has to be, I saw her name on the list.

He turned away and tried to attend to his duties. The surgeon had been given a small ward for the sick. Enough room only for two bunks and a long table for surgery. Philip's task now was to awaken the surgeon and try to make him sober. He shook him. 'Sir, the prisoners need attention. Their conditions are appalling.'

Clavell opened his eyes. 'Well, of course they are! What do you expect? They're convicts! They don't get feather beds. Wake me up when we're under sail.' He closed one eye and peered up at Philip with the other. 'Then we'll sort it out.'

Clavell was stone-cold sober three days later and stood on deck with Philip and Lieutenant Boyle observing the prisoners. 'The women's shackles can come off. They won't be any trouble,' he stated. 'But keep the men in theirs for a bit longer.'

Lieutenant Boyle objected. 'They're more docile when they're ironed. They'll torment the men if they're free.'

Clavell glared at him. 'The prisoners are my responsibility, Mr Boyle. They are women with women's functions. Take the irons off!'

A great cheer went up when the first irons were unfastened and a cry of 'God bless you, sir,' wafted towards them. 'You see, Mr Boyle,' Clavell smiled, 'a little good will goes a long way! Are they getting their daily dose of lime juice and their full ration of meat?'

Boyle in a surly manner conceded that they were getting what they were entitled to. 'No more and no less.'

Clavell nodded. 'Make sure the accommodation is swabbed and disinfected every day, that's the way to keep disease down. Now, Mr Linton, do we have any sick?'

'None has been reported, sir.' Philip was still

searching the deck for a sign of Emily.

'Good. We can start with a clean slate.'

'Looking for somebody, Mr Linton?' Boyle murmured after Clavell had gone below. 'Fancy a little romp? There are one or two that I wouldn't mind trying out. There's a dark-haired filly and a blonde one. Look over there to the right. When they're cleaned up a bit they might be safe to use.'

Philip turned and stared at him. 'It's against captain's orders,' he said quietly.

'Phew!' Boyle blew a derogatory laugh. 'Think he doesn't know when it goes on? Everybody has one – or two. It helps to pass the time on this damned run.' He stared down towards the quarterdeck. 'Yes,' he said softly. 'The blonde one. That's the one for me.'

Philip glanced towards where Boyle was looking and drew in a sharp breath. It was Emily! She had swilled her face in a bucket of water and had tossed her hair back so that it was blowing in the wind. Then she lifted her arms behind her neck and coiled the thick hair into a bun.

'What do you think, Mr Linton?' Boyle smiled thinly. 'Shall we fight for her?'

Philip wanted to punch him on his nose, but held his temper. 'I think we should find out a little more about her first,' he said. 'You can't be too careful, Mr Boyle. You wouldn't want to catch anything nasty to take home to your wife, would you?'

Boyle glared at him. 'I'm always careful. Besides, I won't be home for another twelve months. What's a man supposed to do?'

Philip turned away. 'Excuse me, Mr Boyle. I have

duties to attend to.' He had to think fast. He had to get to Emily before Boyle did.

'Meg,' Emily whispered early one morning, 'Meg, I think the old woman is dead!' She had leaned across to check on her several times during the night. The ship had tossed and rolled and many of the women had cried out, but the old woman had made no sound, but just lay there unmoving.

'Oh, damn,' Meg muttered. 'Now we'll lose her rations! Are you sure?' She turned to her silent neighbour and put her fingers to her neck, then bent her head and put it against the woman's chest. 'I can't hear anything. I think you're right. What'll we do?'

'We'll have to call 'sentry.' Emily made to slip off the bunk to the floor, but Meg stayed her.

'Wait a minute,' she whispered and woke the other women who shared the bunk and beckoned them to move closer. 'Listen. We don't have enough to eat, do we?'

The others shook their heads.

'And now we're going to lose 'old woman's rations which we've been sharing for 'last few days.' She glanced around to make sure that no-one else was listening. 'Well, I propose that we leave her where she is for another couple o' days, till, you know, till we've got to move her.'

'What are you saying?' Emily burst out in a hoarse whisper. 'You mean leave her next to us? But she's dead!'

'Shh! But nobody knows she's dead,' Meg insisted. 'Nobody even knows she's here. We don't even know 'poor old lass's name.'

They all stared down at the old woman's body, still clad in her iron anklets, for she hadn't been able to get to the upper deck again to have them removed.

'But, won't she —?' One of the other women wrinkled her nose. 'You know —!'

Meg shook her head. 'No! Not for a bit anyway. We could get today's food and maybe tomorrow morning's anyway. We might have to have her moved after that.'

Emily put her head in her hands. What had they come to when they stole from the dead? Yet she was hungry. There wasn't enough food to satisfy them, the rations were small and inadequate.

'Are we agreed then?' Meg looked at them all for confirmation. 'I'll be 'one to get 'stick anyway if we get found out, seeing as I'm 'one who goes to collect 'food.'

So it was agreed, though reluctantly, and Meg went to fetch the rations for six in the usual way. But Emily found she had lost her appetite, she couldn't eat with the old woman lying there and she certainly couldn't sleep, though Meg seemed to have no bother at all and snored in her usual manner as she lay next to the old woman's corpse.

The next morning they agreed that she would have to be moved. There was no air and the stench of two hundred females and one hundred males trapped below decks was strong enough, without the added odour of a dead one.

'I'll fetch breakfast first,' Meg decided. 'Then I'll call 'guard.'

*   *   *

'Good God!' Mr Clavell held his handkerchief to his nose. 'Where has she been?'

Philip put his hand over his mouth. 'Down below, sir. The guard said the women swore they hadn't realized she was dead!'

Clavell shook his head. 'They've been sharing her food rations, that's why she hasn't been brought up. Prepare her for burial, Mr Linton. Let's get the poor soul to her rest.'

The women watched as the shroud slid down the platform to be swallowed up by the waters. No ceremony, but a simple prayer to send her on to the next journey. 'We know nothing about her,' Emily said quietly. 'Not her name or if she had a family or why she was being transported. It's not right,' she protested. 'It was a life, God given.'

Meg nodded. 'And God taken away, Em. Come on.' She took her arm. 'Let's take a stroll.' The weather had become warmer as they sailed towards the Canaries, though the Atlantic breezes were strong and blustery. They perambulated around the deck, then stood to watch the young boys clambering up on the yards, adjusting the rigging. The seamen were more friendly than the soldiers and some of them stopped briefly to exchange banter, but always moved off swiftly when an officer appeared. 'There's a couple of officers watching you, Em,' Meg remarked casually. 'Better watch out.'

Emily glanced around. 'Who? You're imagining things!'

'No, I'm not,' she insisted. 'One's that swine who

told us to keep moving when we first came up on deck, you remember? I haven't seen 'other one afore.'

Emily screwed her eyes up against the brightness. She saw two officers by the bow, but couldn't see their faces. She gave a grim laugh. 'We're not strolling at 'Scarborough Spa, Meg! We're convicts on a ship bound for Australia. They're probably worrying that we're planning a mutiny!'

'Wish we could,' Meg muttered. 'I'd be first to volunteer.'

As the days progressed, though the time lay heavy and monotonous, a routine of sorts came into being. The women took turns with the men at swabbing and stoning the decks and they were able to wash their clothes, although the stench of disinfectant never left them. Sometimes some of the women disappeared for a few hours, re-appearing later looking pleased with themselves and remarkably not as hungry as they had been. Meg knew where they had been, though she doubted if Emily had even noticed. *If I could get fixed up with somebody we could both eat,* she thought. *Me and Em.* She had seen money changing hands when the food was brought round and some ate better than others. *It wouldn't matter to me as long as they paid up.* But she knew that she wouldn't attract anyone but the lowest seaman, and she doubted that they had money to spare.

Then one night after they had been locked up for several hours the door opened and the sentry called out, 'Emily Hawkins! Come for'ard.'

Meg looked towards the door and then down at Emily, who was sleeping. She got down from the bunk and made her way to the sentry. 'Who wants her?'

'One of the officers; sent for her specially.'

'Which officer?' Meg persisted.

'What's it to do with you?' He opened his mouth to call again, but she forestalled him.

'It's not that pig that's allus lording it over everybody? 'One with a mouth like a sewer?'

'No, not him,' he grinned. 'It's surgeon's mate.'

'Surgeon's mate?' He might do, she pondered. 'All right, tek me to him.'

'You? You're the one he sent for?'

She nodded. 'Aye. Emily Hawkins. That's me.'

'By, he must be desperate,' he said disparagingly as he let her out and locked the door behind them. 'No offence, like, but I'd have thought he'd have had better taste.'

'Thanks,' she said, unoffended. 'If I can do owt for you sometime, let me know.'

Philip took three paces forward and three back, and again three forward and three back, that was as far as he could stride in his cabin, and he was nervous. What would she say when she saw him? Would she be overcome with shame or joy? Would she rail at him for finding her in such a base condition? Would she ask why he was here and would he tell her? He tried out different stories in his head. He would pretend that it was mere coincidence and that he had been so surprised when he had discovered her on deck. Or that he had been checking the list of names after the old woman had died and couldn't believe it when he had seen her name on the list.

He took off his coat and put it over the back of his chair, then jumped at the knock on the door and sat down at his desk with his back to the door. 'Come in,' he said huskily and, after tapping down some papers, he slowly turned around.

He stared with his mouth apart. 'Who are you?'

Meg licked her lips. 'Emily Hawkins, sir.'

He put his hand to his brow. There must be someone else with the same name! But I would have noticed on the list. He took a deep breath and stood up. 'I think not.'

'Well, no sir.' She gave a nervous laugh. 'I'm not.'

He had seen the woman before. He recognized her as the woman walking with Emily on the deck, but he hadn't seen her properly. Now that he did, he knew what she was and what she had probably always been. Why had she befriended Emily? He saw the boldness in her face, but something else also. An appeal! But why?

'Fact is, sir, Emily Hawkins is not available, but I am. Emily shouldn't be here, it was an injustice and she's an innocent, both of her crime and in her womanhood.' She kept her eyes fixed on him. 'I'm appealing to your better nature, sir. Leave Emily alone, she can't give you what you want. But I can.' She glanced around the cabin. The hammock swung as the ship dipped and rolled. 'You can shut your eyes, sir. You don't have to look at me.'

'You'd do that for her?' he asked softly.

'Aye, and more. She's a good lass and deserves better than life's handing out to her.'

He smiled. He had never realized how wrong he could be in assessing someone's character. 'What's your name?'

'Meg, sir. You don't need to know more 'n that.'

'Well, Meg,' he sat down on the chair, 'you're obviously a good friend of Emily's so I can tell you that it wasn't my design to force my attentions on her. I was –'. He hesitated. 'I am – merely bringing her news of someone she was acquainted with. Someone from the town of Hull.'

'From Hull, sir!' Meg's face lit up. 'Do you know that town?'

He nodded. 'I do. I was at school there.'

'Don't tell me!' She waved a finger at him. 'Trinity House, I'll be bound.'

He agreed and she rushed on. 'I never thought – never ever thought I'd meet up with anybody again who knew my home town.'

'Meg! I'd be obliged if you wouldn't tell Emily about me. I want to tell her myself. I'm not sure how she will take it, seeing me here.'

'You mean that you know her?' Meg frowned suspiciously. 'How?'

'I'd rather not say. If Emily wants to tell you, then she can.' He stood up again. 'Now, will you ask the sentry to bring up the real Emily Hawkins?'

Chapter Twenty-Nine

'Why am I wanted, do you think?' Emily was nervous. 'Have I done something wrong?'

'No,' Meg assured her as she woke her and whispered that she was wanted above by the surgeon's mate. 'He's probably just checking everybody's health.'

'Now? When we've been battened down for the night?'

'Just go!' Meg insisted. 'It'll be all right, I promise.'

Emily followed the guard, who on reaching the door of the cabin, winked at her. 'He must have quite an appetite, young surgeon, though his second course looks more palatable than his first.'

She stared at him. What was he talking about? He didn't mean –! She was suddenly very afraid. What was it the woman in York gaol had said about the officers wanting me? That she would pick someone out for me so that they could both eat! She felt sick and faint and she stumbled. Her legs were shaky as if they were fettered even though the irons had been taken off. The sentry glanced curiously at her and then knocked on the cabin door. A voice called to come in and he pushed her inside.

She kept her head lowered and didn't look up until her name was spoken. 'Emily.'

It was said so softly that it was as if she imagined it. She lifted her head and took a short, sharp breath. 'Mr Linton!' The cabin though well lit by a lamp seemed to grow dim, there were stars swirling dizzily around her and she felt herself sway.

'Come and sit down.' He took her arm and propelled her gently to the chair by the desk. 'Would you like some water?' he asked quietly. 'Or a little brandy?'

'Water,' she gasped, 'please.'

He busied himself pouring the water from a jug into a glass whilst she tried to make sense of the situation. Why was Philip Linton on board this ship? But of course, he could go anywhere, he was a naval officer. But how strange, of all the ships in England, he should be on this one. A terrible shame washed over her. *He must know all about me, it will be written down somewhere.*

She sipped the water and he perched on the corner of his desk. 'I won't say how glad I am to see you, Emily,' he gave a small smile, 'but nevertheless, I am. But I'm also so sorry to see you in this predicament.'

She nodded, too overcome to say anything.

'I had heard of your trial,' he explained. 'I saw your friend, Ginny, when I was in Hull and she told me of it.'

'I suppose everyone was gossiping about it?' she said bitterly. 'My name would be on everyone's tongue.'

'Not everyone thinks ill of you, Emily.' His voice was soft. 'Your friends don't.'

'Friends?' Her voice was cynical. 'What friends have I? My friends are here on board ship and no-one would think well of them!'

'Try not to be bitter, Emily,' he pleaded. 'We are doing what we can to help you.'

Her eyes opened wide. 'We? Who are we?'

'Roger Francis. Your relative, Mary Edwards.'

She gasped. 'You've met them? When? Where?'

'In York,' he said briefly. 'They are still petitioning for your reprieve.'

She shook her head. 'It's too late for that. Don't they realize that I'm on a convict ship and I won't be coming back?'

He leaned forward and took hold of her hand. 'Don't say that, Emily. Don't give up hope.'

She looked down at his hand on hers, but made no attempt to move it. 'The other women on board say that we are sent out to Botany Bay, not for our crimes, but to please the men who are there.' She lifted her eyes to his and said candidly, 'If I find that is true when we get there, then I shall take my own life.'

He was appalled. How crushed and wretched she must be to consider such an act! And yet it came to him with such passionate certainty that she was still so pure in mind that the terror of death was preferable to the disgrace of becoming defiled.

'Emily, I have an idea to make you more comfortable whilst you are on the ship.'

She looked at him suspiciously and withdrew her hand from his. Was he, after all, like other men and not the hero she had dreamed him to be? She had seen other women going off with seamen and officers, was he going to offer her some inducement to do the same?

He flushed slightly. 'Some of the officers on board take the women as – er – friends, and look after them. It is not strictly allowed, but it happens. I – I do not agree with it, personally, but I am saying to you that in order for you to be more comfortable –'.

'What are you trying to say, Mr Linton?' Her voice was icy. So he was like other men. She felt a cold chill around her heart. She was so disappointed. He had seemed so honourable.

'I – I'm not suggesting anything improper, Emily,' he pleaded. 'But – but we would have to pretend that you were coming here for something more than a friendly chat.'

She softened slightly, but still harboured doubts. 'What then?'

'You could come, perhaps a few times a week.' He glanced around the small cabin. 'You could sleep in the hammock and rest easier than down below. I won't trouble you, you have my word. But I would have to put the word about so that the others will keep away.'

'The others? What others?'

'Well, one other who has watched you. He intends to invite you to his cabin.' His mouth tightened. 'He is a reprobate, like another we both know.'

Her face paled. 'Like Hugo Purnell? You know what happened?'

'Yes,' he said simply. 'I do. Ginny told me.' But it makes not a scrap of difference, he thought as he watched her. You are still so innocent, and so lovely in spite of your tangled hair and your prison clothes.

'Then you know that I have been ill-used by one man, Mr Linton,' she said bluntly. 'My life is in ruins because of him. How can I trust another?'

Because I love you, he wanted to say. Because I am travelling to the other side of the world to be with you, to protect you and if possible to bring you back. But he simply said, 'It will be difficult for you, I realize, but you have my word. That is all I can offer.'

She got up from the chair. 'I have no reason not to trust you, Mr Linton. You have always behaved very properly towards me. Forgive me if I have behaved rudely towards you, but I have been under a great deal of strain.' She paused. 'I'll come. Will you send for me?'

'Come tomorrow evening. I'll tell the duty guard. And Emily,' he hesitated slightly, then reaching towards the chair, put his hand into his coat pocket, 'this will seem distasteful to you, but I must give you something for coming.'

He handed her a coin and she looked down at it in her hand. 'Use it to buy extra food, then the other women will think they know why you come.'

He escorted her out of the cabin and through the dining hall, where some officers were sitting at a long polished table. There were pewter tankards and china dinner plates in front of them, for they were at their supper, but they turned to watch

Emily as she passed. They went down the companionway to the lower decks and passed other women returning from rendezvous. She shivered. I will now have a reputation for being immoral. But does it matter when I know differently? He is a good man, I'm sure of it, but the other women won't believe that. Will Meg? Should I tell her?

Meg was awake and waiting for her. 'Well,' she asked. 'What did he want? Summat, I'll bet!'

'You wouldn't believe me if I told you, Meg! It's the most extraordinary thing.' She told her in whispers that she had met Mr Linton before and that he had met her only relative who was still trying for a reprieve. 'I told him that it was impossible, but he said I mustn't give up hope. But of course I have. Is it possible, do you think, that anything can change?'

Meg shook her head. 'I doubt it. Not for 'better anyway. But he seems a decent enough young fella –.'

'How do you know that?' Emily said, surprised. 'Have you met him?'

'Er – no! But I've seen him, haven't I? That day up on 'deck and I can generally tell. There's not much I don't know about men just by looking at 'em.' She bent her head towards Emily and gazing intently at her, whispered, 'So what did he really want? And did he pay for it?'

Emily opened her palm and showed the coin. 'We can buy extra food tomorrow, Meg.'

Meg sighed and shook her head. 'As I thought,' she murmured. 'As I thought!'

The time Emily spent in the cabin became her

oasis, a refuge from the stench of the convict accommodation and the foul air which they all breathed. As they passed the islands of the Canaries, the weather became hotter and the lower decks became unbearable. She swung sleepily and contentedly in the hammock and watched from half-closed eyes as Philip Linton worked at his desk, sometimes with his shirtsleeves rolled up and his shirt neck open. Occasionally other officers or seamen would knock on his door and glance at her through the doorway as they spoke to him.

She slept nearly all night on one visit and opened her eyes to find him standing looking down at her. 'Wake up, Emily,' he said softly, 'it's time for you to go,' and he walked her back as dawn was breaking and the stars were disappearing into the heavens.

The other women in her bunk were envious and they discussed the handsome young lieutenant as they shared the extra food which her money bought. Only Meg was grumpy and short-tempered with her, but Emily put this down to the intense oppressive heat which was building up. Storms were brewing too and when they hit the prisoners were confined below, the air scuttles were closed and the hatches firmly fastened. The atmosphere was putrid and many of the women fainted from lack of air. The male convicts rebelled at being kept down and some were manacled to their bunks to avoid trouble.

'Sir,' Philip looked up from bandaging a seaman's hand as Mr Clavell came into the sick room, 'could the women stay on deck at night? It's a hell hole down below. The bilges are stinking and we're going to have a crop of illness if we're not careful.'

Clavell nodded. 'I was thinking the same thing, Mr Linton. I'll go and speak to the captain now.' He was quite sober, though he had had a drink and Philip hoped that he hadn't guessed that he had watered down his rum.

He came back ten minutes later. 'The captain's sick. I've ordered him to his bunk, and yes, he says the women can stay on deck until midnight. The men are not going to like it, it's just as bad for them, but captain says we can't have both out together, not at night.' He pursed his lips. 'Can't say I blame him for that, the men are getting restless.'

'There'll be more air circulating below once the women are on top.' Philip was sweating, beads of moisture were gathered on his top lip. Poor devils down below, he thought, though it would be easier for them now that their anklets had been removed. 'And perhaps their water ration can be increased?'

So the women were allowed to stay on deck and they lay on the planking and still sweated as the ship coursed on towards the equator and the male convicts grumbled and complained when they were brought back down at midnight.

Captain Martin became feverish and couldn't stand and Lieutenant Boyle took over command. This caused Philip some annoyance as the officer had been particularly disagreeable towards him on discovering that Emily was visiting his cabin. 'Found out if she's clean, Linton?' he'd sneered. 'That's what you were worried about, isn't it? Bothered about whether she's had the clap!'

Now that the captain was out of commission, Boyle, though he was a good seaman, took great pleasure in issuing fresh orders contrary to those of Captain Martin. 'Get the women down below,' he barked one evening. 'We'll have no mollycoddling whilst I'm in charge.'

The women shouted and screamed as they were pushed below and the men too objected on their behalf. 'Let them up, sir, they'll do no harm,' a voice called from the men's side.

'Who's that?' Boyle pushed his way through the sentries and confronted the convicts through the barricade. 'Who is it who's objecting?'

There was a sudden silence, then a voice said, 'I am.' A man pushed his way forward. 'It's like hell down here. Let 'women come up.'

'Aye, let them up.' A chorus of male voices shouted in support.

'Iron that man and fasten him to his bunk. I'll have no insubordination.' Boyle started to climb the companion ladder, but a great shout of anger stopped him. 'Any trouble', he hissed, 'and I'll confine you all below for the next week.'

The shouting stopped but an agitated murmuring continued until the door was clanged shut and they were left to sweat. Meg picked her way through the mass of women who had stretched out on the planking rather be confined to their bunks, which they had to share with other sweating bodies.

'Sorry, lads.' She peered through the barricade. 'It was a good try. Who's 'chap who's been ironed?'

'John Johnson,' the voice shouted. 'Who are you?'

'Meg,' she called back. 'Thanks anyway.'

Two seamen had also got the fever and after Philip had attended them he went up on deck and was surprised to find that the women were not there. He went below decks and came to the door of their accommodation, where he found three armed guards instead of one and the same at the male convicts' door. One of the guards barred his way. 'None of the women are allowed up tonight, sir.' Beads of sweat stood out on his forehead and his lips were dry and cracked.

'On whose orders?'

'Lieutenant Boyle's, sir. They're to stay below until the morning. That's all of 'em, sir,' he added meaningfully. He was the guard who had first escorted Emily to Philip's cabin. 'It's hard luck on 'em, sir. There's a pregnant woman down there, and a couple of old 'uns who might not last the night.'

Philip turned away, seething with anger. Who did Boyle think he was, playing God with people's lives? These people might be criminals, but they were entitled to some compassion. He made his way back to the sick berth, intent on searching out the surgeon. Clavell alone could oppose Boyle in this matter. But he wasn't in the sick berth or in his cabin, nor was he in the captain's cabin when he looked in. He eventually found him on deck curled up at the feet of the helmsman, snoring loudly with a bottle tucked under his arm.

'You'll not rouse him tonight, Mr Linton.' The helmsman kept his eyes straight ahead. 'He's gunnels under. Best put him to bed.'

Philip called a midshipman to help him and together they hauled Clavell into his bunk. He opened one eye as Philip tried to take the bottle from him and clung to it with both hands. 'It's empty, sir,' Philip said. 'Not a drop left.'

'Hah! Plenty more where that came from,' Clavell slurred, and peered at Philip. 'And don't think you'll find them, 'cos you won't.' His mouth dropped open and he snored with abandon.

'It's my decision, Linton,' Boyle said lazily when Philip questioned him about the women being kept below. 'You haven't the authority and Clavell is as drunk as a lord, so there's nothing he can do either. They can all come up in the morning. We'll be crossing the Line at noon and we'll have a bit of fun with them then, eh?' He gave a cynical grin. 'Sorry if I've spoiled your love games, Linton, but I'm sure she'll be all the more eager after being deprived of your company for a night or two.'

Philip turned away. If he assaulted a superior officer, the punishment would be severe. He would lose his position and be stripped of his rank and probably put in irons, but he badly wanted to take the man by the throat and throttle him.

When the prisoners came up the next morning, one of the older women had died and the other was very sick. The pregnant woman had started in labour. 'Get her into the sick berth,' Philip ordered one of the guards, 'and then bring the sick woman on deck.' He went to report the death of the woman to Boyle.

'Another death, Mr Linton?' Boyle said. 'It's not going to look very good for your reputation, is it?'

'The reason why will be logged, Mr Boyle,' Philip replied sharply. 'She probably died because of lack of air.'

Boyle sneered. 'But you don't know that, do you? You're not a medical man! Which makes me wonder just why you are here, serving as a surgeon's mate? The sort of job that any apothecary's apprentice could do! Blotted your copybook somewhere?'

Before Philip could reply they were called away by the shrill pipe of the bosun's whistle. 'Approaching the Line, sir,' the bosun's mate hailed.

All hands on deck, called the pipes.

'Heave to,' Boyle commanded. 'Away aloft. Bring her up, but gently.'

The helmsmen steadied the course and the seamen and officers met each command instantly. The sails were trimmed and the great ship was brought up with her head to the wind, where she rode gently in the blue green waters, like the swan whose name she had been given.

Chapter Thirty

King Neptune came on board. He appeared from the lower deck with seaweed in his hair and beard, a tinsel crown on his head and a wooden trident in his hand. By his side were mermen, their seamen's clothes draped in weeds and clutching the laughing young midshipmen who had not yet crossed the equator. The convicts gathered around prepared for the fun. A tot of rum was handed round to everyone, seamen and convicts alike.

'Have they taken that fella Johnson out of his irons?' Meg asked one of the guards. 'Is he on deck?'

'Aye.' He nodded and pointed to a fair, bearded man standing at the edge of the crowd. 'We've to keep an eye on him. Boyle's got him marked down as a troublemaker.'

'Who?' Emily asked. 'Is he the one who argued with Boyle?' She wiped her face with her sleeve. There was no respite from the heat. Many of the women were ignoring the ceremony and were hanging over the bulwarks trying to catch a breeze. Some of them were blistering from the sun.

Meg nodded, then laughed as Neptune's

mermen lathered a young officer with soap and tar and feathers and handed him to Neptune, who shaved him with a large wooden razor, cut his hair and dunked him into a tub of seawater. Boyle handed Neptune and the officer a tot of rum. 'Next,' he cried and gathered up another young midshipman, for whom the same procedure followed, then came other seamen and officers who hadn't crossed the Line before and again tots of rum were handed over.

'Now the prisoners,' Boyle called. 'We'll have to have volunteers, there isn't time for all of you. You,' he pointed to one convict, 'and you,' he pointed to John Johnson. 'Only this time, your Majesty,' he addressed Neptune, 'we'll have it done properly. Over the side!'

The two convicts looked at each other and so did some of the seamen. 'The man's a sadist,' Emily heard one of the guards say.

The two men were lathered with tar and soap over their heads and neck, the tar was sticky with the heat and they put their heads down to keep it from their eyes. 'Fetch the rope,' Boyle grinned and Neptune objected. 'It's not safe, sir.'

'Perfectly safe,' Boyle said as he hitched the rope over Johnson's shoulders and around his waist. Johnson started to struggle. 'Keep still,' Boyle said, 'or I might forget to pull you up.'

He ordered two seamen to stand him on the bulwark and another two to hold the rope and with a great shove he pushed him overboard. Everyone leaned over to watch as Johnson rose up spluttering and cursing. There was some laughter but not much, as he was hauled aboard. 'And again,' Boyle called, 'three times is the norm.'

Johnson struggled. 'I'll kill you, you bastard,' he shouted.

'Or sometimes it's six,' Boyle answered cheerfully.

'Stop it!' Meg hurled herself at the officer. 'Stop it! What gives you the right to do this?'

Boyle held her at arm's length and a guard rushed over with his rifle at the ready. 'I have the right to do what ever I want with you scum,' he snarled. 'Bring him aboard,' he ordered the seamen who were holding Johnson. 'We'll have the little lady instead.'

Meg lashed out and the women screamed and the men shouted, but the guards had their orders and Meg was held with her arms behind her back and marched towards Neptune, who though almost drunk, was sobering very quickly. 'I don't usually perform on the women, sir.'

'Well if you won't, I will.' Boyle rolled up his coat sleeves and pulled Meg roughly towards him and the tub of tar.

Emily stood horrified as she watched Meg's hair and face being tarred and then feathered with seagull feathers, but she swore and lashed out with hands and feet as Boyle struggled to hold her. 'No,' Emily shouted and the other convicts joined in the cry. 'Stop, stop,' and she hurled herself towards Boyle, beating him with her fists.

'Stop!' Johnson broke free from the seamen and he too tore towards Boyle with his fists flying.

Philip had watched the ceremony of the

324

midshipmen and then hurried back to the sick berth. The pregnant woman was in a lot of pain and he didn't know what to do. He had never witnessed childbirth, he didn't know anything about it and wasn't keen to find out. He only knew that the woman was frail and sick and he questioned her as to when she might expect the child. 'I was six months' gone when I came on board, sir,' she said. 'So it could be any time. It's my third. I know what happens.'

'I'm glad you do', he said, 'because I don't. Will you be all right whilst I go and fetch the surgeon?'

He hurried away and prayed that Clavell was sober and heard the shouts coming from the upper deck. I'm missing all the fun, he thought, but perhaps it's just as well as I haven't crossed the Line.

He managed to rouse Clavell and poured him a glass of water, which he spat out. 'Don't ever give me that again, Mr Linton,' he objected. 'Pour me a tot of rum and I'll be as right as ninepence.'

He drank it straight down and stood up. 'There, what did I tell you?' He looked around with bleary eyes. 'Are we at anchor or am I less drunk than I thought I was?'

'We're crossing the Line, sir. The ceremony has started.'

'Hmph, well I've seen that nonsense often enough without wanting to see it again. Come on, take me to the mother to be.'

He pronounced her all right for the next few hours and said that she could have one of the other women convicts to attend her. 'One who knows about these things,' he said briskly. 'I don't want anybody fainting in my sick berth. And that goes for you as well, Mr Linton. You'd better keep well out of the way.'

'I'll be glad to,' Philip began, when a midshipman dashed into the sick berth without knocking.

Clavell looked annoyed, but the young officer apologized. 'I believe, sir, that it's naval regulations that the surgeon should witness a lashing?' His face was red and sweaty and he looked nervous. 'I hope I'm doing right, sir?'

'A lashing? Who's being lashed and why?'

'One of the convicts, sir, for assaulting Mr Boyle, and I think maybe one of the women.'

'What?' Clavell's face turned purple. 'Women are not to be lashed! Whose order is this?'

The officer licked his lips. 'Mr Boyle's, sir.'

'Is it, by God?' Clavell snatched his coat from the chair. 'We'll see about that.'

When they reached the upper deck, Johnson was already tied to a grating by the wrists with his arms above his head and his ankles ironed. Philip was appalled to see Meg fastened up also and mouthing abuse at Boyle, and Emily being held by two guards. He stepped forward, but Clavell stopped him. 'This is my business, Mr Linton. Leave it to me.'

He confronted Boyle. 'I'm here to attend the lashing. What is the man's punishment?'

'Twenty lashes.' Boyle's voice was surly. 'Less than the regulation permits.'

'Why is the woman tied? She is not to be lashed?'

'Assault and insubordination! She's to be given five strokes.'

'I think not, Mr Boyle,' said Clavell. 'The flogging of women ceased some time ago.'

'The charge is serious. These women have to be shown that they cannot behave as they wish.' He glared at Clavell. 'I am the most senior officer here whilst the captain is sick and I say the woman is to be flogged. You may watch to ensure that she does not suffer unduly.'

As Philip listened, he knew that Boyle was within his rights as the ship's master. He could decide on the punishment for an offence. Clavell could only supervise the lashing to ensure that the prisoners did not die of their injuries.

The lash was held by the bosun and the prisoners were ordered into a semi-circle in order to watch. 'Leave the woman alone,' Johnson shouted. 'I'll tek her lashes.'

'How very noble.' Boyle grinned. 'Begin!'

The lash spat and then spat again until ten strokes had been given. 'Stop,' Boyle shouted. 'Mr Clavell, perhaps you would like to examine the prisoner?'

Clavell stepped forward. Ten weals criss-crossed Johnson's back but the skin hadn't broken. He stepped back and nodded for the punishment to continue, but Boyle put up his hand and called for a bucket of sea water. He took it from the seaman and threw it over Johnson. They heard him gasp as the salt licked his back and saw his hands clench.

'Swine!' Meg shouted. 'You're enjoying this.'

Boyle said nothing, but indicated that the

flogging should continue. Five more lashings and the convict's fair skin started to bleed. Clavell stepped forward to examine the wounds. 'I think that's enough, Mr Boyle.'

'Five more,' Boyle ordered. 'Is he a woman that he can't take more?' Again he ordered a bucket of sea water to be thrown over Johnson's back and they saw him flinch, though he made not a sound. 'Continue.'

The bosun hesitated, but had been given his orders; to disobey was an offence. He took a step backwards and launched the whistling cat for the final five, which opened up the wounds into a bloody, sticky mass.

'Put him below and iron him,' Boyle began, when there was a movement from the companionway and Captain Martin appeared. His face was sallow and his eyes heavy, but he greeted Lieutenant Boyle and the other officers and asked, 'Have I missed the ceremony? Has Neptune departed?' then, glancing around the deck, said sharply, 'What's this? A flogging? On my ship!'

'Yes, sir,' said Boyle. 'One of the convicts. He became abusive after taking part in the ceremony.'

'Indeed? Bring him to me,' the captain ordered and Johnson was pushed towards him. 'Do you not agree with tradition?' he asked him. 'Crossing the Line is an age-old ceremony.'

'Not when it means half-drowning a man, sir. But that isn't why 'officer had me lashed. He had me lashed because I objected to him giving 'same treatment to one of the women.'

'I was attacked by the prisoner, sir,' Boyle

began, but was interrupted by the captain.

'Mr Linton, take the prisoner and dress his wounds, then put him in the cramping box to reflect on his misdoings. You must realize', he addressed Johnson, 'that you can't take the law into your own hands. That is why you are here on this ship and not enjoying the comforts of your hearth and family.'

Johnson opened his mouth to reply, but was marched away with Philip following and anxiously looking over his shoulder at Emily, who was still being held by the seamen.

The captain conferred quietly with Boyle and Clavell to ascertain what had happened and to ensure that Boyle didn't lose face before the prisoners. 'I'll see you in my cabin, Mr Boyle,' he said, 'and in the meantime, put the woman below and keep her fettered for the rest of the day. As for the other woman,' he looked towards Emily, 'put her in the cramping box for a couple of hours, she'll not cause any trouble after being in there.'

Clavell started to object that the heat would be too much, it was so hot that the deck planking was scorching.

'An hour, then,' the captain conceded. 'That should teach her not to interfere.'

Two cramping boxes for the punishment of the prisoners stood side by side on the upper deck and an immense heat almost knocked Emily over as the door was opened and she was pushed inside. There was no room to sit or crouch but only to stand and after ten minutes she felt as if she was being baked alive. 'I need water,' she called. 'Please! Fetch me some water!'

'You can't have water,' a voice shouted back, 'but if you're not quiet you'll get a bucket of sea water over you.'

She hammered on the door. 'I'll die,' she shrieked. 'I must have water.'

'Give her water, then,' she heard a voice say and a moment later a hatch in the roof opened and a bucket of sea water was thrown in, drenching her through and making her gasp and although for a moment she was refreshed by its coldness, the salt dried instantly on her skin and her clothes, making her itch and scratch. She heard voices again and braced herself for another bucket of water to be thrown in, but it was the guards bringing Johnson into the other cramping box.

She peered through the slats. 'Are you all right?' she whispered. 'Is your back very painful?'

'Aye,' he said. 'More than it would have been if that bastard Boyle hadn't thrown sea watter at me.'

'You were very brave,' she said softly. 'I would have hated to have been thrown into 'sea.'

'I was terrified,' he admitted. 'I'm not used to watter. I'm a countryman, used to 'earth beneath my feet.'

She listened. Meg was right. He did sound like a northern man. 'Where are you from?' She kept her voice down so that the guards didn't hear.

There was a hesitation and she peered again through the slats and saw a pair of eyes looking back at her. ''North of England.' He was brief. 'Nowhere tha would know.'

'I might,' she said. 'I'm from 'north too. Did you come from York county gaol?'

Again there was a hesitation. 'No. I've travelled a bit. I got caught pinching stuff in London.'

'Oh!' There seemed nothing more to say and it was too hot for the effort of conversation.

'Is tha feeling all right?' he asked after a long silence.

'No,' she whispered. 'I feel ill. My legs are giving way and I'm so thirsty.'

'Not so long to go now,' he said. 'There'll be a bit of a breeze now that we're under way again. Bear up if tha can.'

A tear trickled down her cheek and into her mouth; she licked her lips and tasted the salt. The sound of his northern accent brought back so many memories. Of her father and mother, her brother Joe and of Sam, who had been like a brother to her.

'Is tha from York, then? Is tha a Yorkshire lass?'

'Yes,' she wept as she answered, 'I am. But I'm not from York, I'd never been there before until I was sent from Hull to go to 'county court.'

'Tha's from Hull?' There was a note of surprise in his voice. 'I know it!'

'Do you?' She stopped her crying. 'No, I'm not from Hull. I worked there, as a servant,' she added. 'I'm from a place called Holderness. You wouldn't know it, even folk in Hull don't know where it is. It's very isolated, there are great tracts of marshy land and hummocky plain which stretch right towards 'sea. I used to live near 'River Humber,' she said huskily, finding it difficult to speak because of her dry throat. 'I used to watch the big ships go downriver towards Spurn and wished I could go on one. I never dreamt that one day I would and sail to the other side of 'world.'

'I know it,' he said hoarsely. 'I know Holderness! That's where I'm from – but no-one here knows it, I never telled 'em.'

'Oh!' she breathed, amazed to think that out here in the middle of the ocean could be an alliance with home.

'What's thy name?' he asked. 'Or did tha change it like I did?'

'Emily,' she said and felt shame that she had sullied her family name by her misdeeds. 'Emily Hawkins.'

There was silence from his box and she could hear the sound of running feet out on deck, the hails and cries of the helmsman and the boys up on the yards. 'White squall approaching, sir,' and heard also the order to get the prisoners below. The great ship plunged and quivered, the sails and masts creaked and groaned as the *Flying Swan* and her seamen battled with the sudden storm and Emily would have fallen if she hadn't been so confined within the box.

'Emily!' Johnson called huskily.

'Yes?' she answered. 'What?'

'No, I mean – that's thy name? Emily Hawkins?'

'Yes.' She was too exhausted to speak. The heat was blistering and she felt as if she was being battered to pieces as the ship dipped and plunged between mountainous troughs. Was the hour almost up? Was the ship going to sink? She could see through the slats that the deck was awash with water.

'Em!' His voice sounded strained and tearful. 'Not little Em? Not our Emily who went to live wi' Granny Edwards?'

She didn't answer, but put her face close to the slats to see him staring back at her. 'Yes,' she whispered. 'That's me!'

'Then doesn't tha know me, Em? Doesn't tha know thine own brother Joe?'

Chapter Thirty-One

It appeared as if they had been forgotten in the cramping box and so brother and sister rediscovered each other as they were buffeted from side to side and the sea water washed over their feet. Emily told of how she had come to be convicted and Joe raged as she revealed her ordeal at the hands of Hugo Purnell. 'I swear on the soul of our ma, if I ever could lay my hands on him I'd kill him, Em.'

He spoke of when he and their mother went to the workhouse after their father died. 'All she could think of was that you were safe, Em. She allus said that Granny Edwards would look after thee. She said she had a way wi' bairns.'

And he confessed to her about the time when their mother had died, which was the start of his thieving. 'She was tekken to a paupers' graveyard and they let me go wi' 'coffin. I marked where it was and when I eventually left 'workhouse – I was about eleven, I think – I stole some flowers from a garden to put on her grave. Onny I got caught and was put in gaol for a month. After that it was a downward spiral and I had to steal to eat and I decided to go to Hull, 'cos I'd heard that 'vagrant office sometimes gave out money. Onny they wouldn't give it to me 'cos I wasn't from 'district. I was starving, Emily,' he said. 'I sometimes didn't eat for days unless I could pinch summat from bakers' bins.'

Emily thought of the masses of food which had been thrown away at the Purnell house and grieved for her brother. 'If only you'd come to find me at Granny Edwards's,' she said. 'She would have taken you in. She wouldn't have turned you away.'

'I decided to travel and look for work,' he shouted to her above the crashing of the storm and the shriek of the wind through the rigging. 'I'm strong, though I might not look it, but I got with a gang and was led into thieving. I was caught several times and went to gaol. I'd changed my name by then 'cos I had a bad record and I allus thought how Ma and Da would have been ashamed of me. They were allus so honest.' He paused. 'And, as well, I didn't want you to hear of what I'd done, of the life I was leading.'

She heard his voice lift as if with a smile. 'I allus imagined you being in service somewhere, a lady's maid or summat and I wouldn't have wanted you to hear of your brother being in gaol! We had good memories, Em, I wouldn't have wanted them spoiling.'

'We had,' she answered. 'Do you remember when we went to catch tiddlers in Lambwath Beck and you got a hiding from Da when we got home because I was covered in mud?' She felt tears gathering as she remembered. 'I often thought about you, Joe. I passed Skirlaw workhouse once and wondered what had happened to you and Ma.'

She heard a voice calling that the wind was dropping. 'And now here we both are, sailing to 'other side of 'world. But I'm glad, Joe, that I've found you. I won't feel so far from home if I know that you are near.'

'We shan't be able to stop together,' he said. 'I'll be put in a road gang I expect, and you,' he hesitated, 'well, I hear all sorts of things that happen to women. Worst ones get sent to Parramatta and others, well, they say that some of 'em are sent as housekeepers to settlers or soldiers. Onny – onny, they're not really housekeepers, they're sort of – wives!'

'You don't have to conceal what happens, Joe,' she said. 'I've heard so many stories. I'm not an innocent girl any more. I know that women are used as whores and I know that they don't go home again, not like the men can.'

'I don't want to,' he said sharply. 'I'll never go back. England doesn't want me and I don't want England. When my time is up – and I've onny three years to go, I've spent four already doing hard labour, I'll hire myself out. I've heard that new settlers want hard-working men and I'll save up to buy a bit o' land. I'll graze a few sheep and grow some corn and I'll become my own man, Emily. I'll not be behodden to anybody ever again. And you can come and live wi' me when your time is finished. We need never be parted again.'

The doors were unbolted and they fell out onto the deck. They faced each other and Emily looked into the eyes of her brother. When she looked at his face through the beard and matted hair, she saw that he was the same Joe that she remembered. They each put out a hand and smiled and touched fingers before being parted by the guards and Joe was led away below decks. Emily sat on the wet deck with her head bowed and wept, her shoulders heaving with sobs until a shadow fell across her. She wiped her eyes and looked up. It was Philip Linton standing there and he bent down to help her up.

'You'd better come to the sick bay,' he said softly. 'Don't cry, there's no need to be frightened. It's all over now. It was just a sudden squall.'

She dared not tell Philip Linton that she was crying because of her meeting with her brother. Joe had been convicted under another name and she felt she must respect his decision about changing it. She gratefully accepted the water which Mr Linton gave her and he urged her to drink it a sip at a time.

A woman was in labour in the sick berth. She was pacing up and down and it brought back more memories for Emily of her own lonely labour. 'Will someone stay with her?' she urged. 'Don't let her stay alone.'

'A woman is coming up to be with her, and Clavell will be here. He'll look after her.' He bent towards her to whisper, 'Come to my cabin, you can rest there.'

She shook her head. 'I must go below to see Meg. She's been shut up too and fettered.'

'Then come later,' he persuaded. 'It's cooler on the main deck.'

She said that she would and made her way below

into the putrid heat of the 'tween decks. The other women were coming back up on deck, but Meg was lying on a bottom bunk, fettered by the ankle to a ring on the bulkhead. She lay quite still and perspiration ran down her face. Her clothes were sodden with sweat. She turned to Emily as she bent over her. 'You all right, Em? Was it very bad in 'box?'

Emily nodded. 'Bad enough. I was desperate for water, but they wouldn't give me any. Only a bucket of sea water, and then my feet got wet from the storm.' She passed Meg a drink of lukewarm water from an uncovered jug.

'It's putrid.' Meg spat it out. 'I'd rather die of thirst! Isn't there any clean?'

'No, but I know where I can get some. I'll go back to Mr Linton's cabin, he asked me to.'

Meg turned her head away. 'Huh,' she griped. 'It's a bad business when women have to sell their bodies for a sip o' water.'

'Sell their bodies! What do you mean?'

'What I say!' She gave a bitter laugh. 'I offered myself to him to save you, and he still got what he wanted in 'end, in spite of his fine words and promises!'

'I don't understand.' Emily was bewildered. 'Offered yourself who to? You mean Mr Linton?'

'Aye, 'first time he sent for you,' Meg said wearily. 'You were asleep and I went up in your place. I told him that you were still an innocent and would I do instead. He promised me, *promised* me that that wasn't what he wanted. But I should have known! Should have known that all men are 'same. They're

338

all snakes, you can't trust anyone of 'em.'

Emily sat down beside Meg and took her hand. 'Meg, you are my dearest and best friend and I wouldn't lie to you. Mr Linton has never laid a finger on me and neither has he told me of your suggestion. I'm –'. Emotion choked her. 'I can't tell you what it means to me to know that you'd do such a thing for me.'

Meg raised her head. 'Never touched you? What? Never?'

Emily shook her head. 'Never! He gives me money so that it looks as if I'm his mistress and so the other officers will stay away. I sleep in his hammock whilst he works at his desk.' The recollection of seeing him working in his shirt-sleeves, with one hand ruffling through his hair, came to mind and she smiled. 'And sometimes if he's on duty I look at his books. He says that I can.'

Meg leaned on her elbow and stared at Emily. 'There's nowt wrong wi' him, I suppose? And he doesn't seem 'type to be of other persuasion.'

Emily was shocked. 'No! Of course not! He is simply a gentleman.'

'Well!' Meg lay back on the bunk and pondered. 'I'll have to think about this,' she muttered. 'It isn't summat I've come across afore.'

'I've something else to tell you, Meg, and this must be a secret too.'

'I don't feel so good, Em. Will it keep?'

'No, I have to tell somebody or I shall burst. Listen.' She lowered her voice, though they were the only ones left in the women's quarters. 'My brother is on board! You know that convict John

339

Johnson that you said sounded like a northern man? It's Joe – my brother Joe! I can hardly believe it! We've not seen each other since we were bairns and we were locked up next to each other in 'cramping boxes! He says that he won't ever go back to England and that he'll work to buy some land in Australia and that I can live with him.'

Meg squeezed her hand. 'That's incredible! I'm so glad for you, Em.' She turned her head away. 'I wish I had somebody to belong to. I've got nobody.'

'You've got me, Meg,' Emily comforted her. 'We'll try to always stay together.'

That night as she swung gently in Philip Linton's hammock, she put the question to him. 'Will the women be separated when we arrive, Mr Linton? I've heard rumours that some will go to Parramatta, the women's factory, and others will go to – er, houses as maids.' She baulked at mentioning the real object.

She thought he turned pale about the mouth, but he said that he didn't know, but would find out. He got up from his desk and put on his coat. 'If you will excuse me, Emily, I must go to the sick berth.'

He hurried across to find Clavell. He would know, he had done this trip many times.

'We've got a fine boy, Mr Linton.' The surgeon pointed to the bunk where the mother lay with her newborn son. 'And the mother is calling him Ralph after me! And God help him and her, for nobody else will,' he muttered as he washed his hands in a bowl, then calling for a boy to take the bloody water away, he drew Philip to one side. 'She'll go to Parramatta unless somebody takes her on.'

'I wanted to ask you about that, sir. Where do the women go after we dock?'

'Worried about your little friend are you, Mr Linton?' The surgeon smiled wryly at Philip's embarrassment. 'I doubt if she'll go to Parramatta, she seems a better type than the ones who go there. She'll probably get picked for a housekeeper by one of the settlers.'

'Picked?' Philip said. 'Do you mean like at the Martinmas fairs?'

Clavell laughed. 'Come with me, young man, and I will tell you about it. I need a drink anyway after that ordeal.' He turned to the woman lying on the bunk. 'Try to rest. Tomorrow you have to go back to your quarters.'

'I didn't know that you knew, sir,' Philip said as they entered Clavell's cabin, 'that Emily Hawkins came to visit me.'

'I might seem like an old soak,' Clavell poured himself a drink and one for Philip, 'but there's not much gets past me. How do you know her?' he asked abruptly.

Philip, taken by surprise at his directness, said, 'I met her when she was a servant girl in Hull. She has been ill used by someone I know. There was no need for her to come to this,' he added bitterly. 'She is a very gentle person.'

'Fond of her are you, Philip?'

'Yes,' he said simply. 'I'd gone to Hull especially to seek her out when I found that she had been in trouble and was already in gaol. She was quite innocent,' he said fiercely.

'Yes, yes. Of course she was,' Clavell interrupted.

'In your eyes at least, so what do you propose to do about her? You can't take her back with you on your next ship!'

Philip looked down at his feet. 'I want to protect her. That's why I came out. I also want to obtain a free pardon for her, but I don't see how I can do that when I'm over here.'

'You can't,' Clavell said bluntly. 'You have to be in England to pull strings. Listen to me. I've been doing this trip for years and years and years, and I can tell you that conditions for the felons have improved immeasurably. I could also tell you some horrific tales of the old days; of convicts dying in their hundreds on their journey out, of the whole-sale rape of the women when they arrived; of the whippings and scourgings, of the humiliation and degradation which men and women have endured.' He took another drink and muttered, 'We have much to be ashamed of. Many forgot that these people were human beings too.'

He shook a finger at Philip. 'Things have improved, but they are still bad. Parramatta, if your friend goes there, will destroy her. There are some women in that place who are the worst possible kind, dissolute and abandoned. Believe me I know, and they influence others who, if they were in a better situation would improve on their former selves.

'That is where I am going,' he sighed. 'I'm going to Parramatta.'

'I thought this was to be your last voyage, sir? That's what I'd heard.'

'So it is.' He gave a thin sad smile. 'I'm not

going back. I've said goodbye to England once and for all.'

Philip was silent, there was obviously much, much more that Clavell could tell him, but he would only do it in his own good time.

Clavell took a pipe from his desk drawer, opened a tin of tobacco and put his nose to it to smell the aroma. 'Ever wondered why I'm a drunk, Philip?' he asked. 'Yes, of course you have!' He tamped down the tobacco into the bowl. 'I've been sailing on convict ships for more years than I care to think of and it can strain a man's conscience. It's condoning the system, you see, even though indirectly. I took my wife out one year. A good country, I thought; we could make a life out there.'

He stared into space. 'She loved the country, hated the penal system and became involved in trying to have it abolished, like so many others did. I was the medic at Parramatta then and saw some terrible things, but I never told my wife. Then one day,' he drew on the pipe and a cloud of smoke enveloped him, 'she decided to come and see the place where I worked. She came on the day there was a riot; the women had complained about their conditions and rampaged all over the building. Caroline arrived as they were being rounded up. The soldiers had been brought in and they and the warders were beating the prisoners with rifles, sticks, bricks, lashes, anything they could lay their hands on. Some of the women were half naked and there was blood everywhere.

'I was the only doctor and she helped me to clean them up and bandage their wounds.' His pipe went out and he laid it on his desk. 'From then on she started campaigning for the abolition of the convict system and the rights of those who were already convicted. She formed committees, petitioned the governor, Members of Parliament, wrote to the English newspapers and she gained the support of the wives of officials who were out there.'

'Well, she has almost succeeded, sir. I read in the newspapers that the settlers won't accept the convict ships any more, that they are blocking the harbours.'

Clavell nodded. 'But it has come too late for her.' He looked up and there was something in his eyes, some sorrow lingering that made Philip pause. 'She continued to come to Parramatta, she used to visit the women and talk to them or sometimes just listen, and – and when she died, they said how they missed her, that just being with her made them feel like human beings again.'

'I'm sorry, sir. I didn't know,' Philip began.

Clavell brushed away his apologies. 'She caught typhoid fever from one of the women, but before she died she made me promise that I would do something to improve their conditions. But, coward that I am,' he sighed, 'I've been sailing the high seas in a drunken stupor all these years, never daring to set foot in the place. Until now,' he added, 'now I shall stay. I have burnt my bridges in England, settled my affairs. I won't go back. She's still here, you see. Waiting for me. Waiting for me to go back to Parramatta.'

They both had another drink and Philip didn't like to intrude on Clavell's thoughts to ask what he should do about Emily. But Clavell hadn't forgotten. He suddenly looked up and said, 'So this is what I think you should do, Mr Linton.' He had become formal again. 'You must stay awhile in Sydney. If you can afford it, buy a small farm. If you can't, then rent one, but better to buy, land is cheap. Then set her up as your housekeeper or wife or whatever name you choose to give her. That way, in effect, she gains her freedom, even though she can't go back to England. Then find someone you can trust to keep an eye on her and then you head off home to petition for her pardon. If she goes to Parramatta she will always have the stigma of convict on her.'

Chapter Thirty-Two

They were all on deck a few days later, men and women, when the order came that they were to go below, that another squall was brewing. A light wind was blowing and the sky was clear.

'What's happening?' Meg asked one of the seamen as she went below. 'Why can't we stop on deck? A drop o' rain won't hurt us.'

'Because you'd be in the way and you might well get washed overboard.' He roughly pushed her down the companion ladder. 'We're in the doldrums. It'll be more than a drop o' rain, believe me. It's for your own good,' he shouted through the grating before closing it completely. The doors were firmly fastened and the hatches closed so that the atmosphere was stifling.

'In 'doldrums!' Meg grumbled. 'I've often thought that's where I was and now he's telling me I am!'

Emily wiped her face with a rag. It was so hot and already some of the women were starting to retch as the ship rolled and pitched.

'Next time you go to Mr Linton's cabin,' Meg said, 'do you think you could borrow some scissors?'

'Whatever for?'

'Tell him you're mekking a new frock,' she said ironically. Some of the women had been stitching up the tears and rents in their clothes. They had been given needle and thread when on deck but always had to give them back before returning below decks. 'I want to cut my hair,' she said. 'Lice are driving me mad. I thought 'tar would have killed 'em off, but it hasn't.'

Meg's thick hair was still streaked with the sticky tar which Lieutenant Boyle had plastered over her and her hands were blackened with it where she had tried to pull it out.

The squall hit suddenly, a strong gale sprang up and heavy rain lashed down and even below decks they could hear the crash of thunder.

The woman and her new baby were now below and he had started to cry. She put him to her breast, but still he wailed. 'I've got no milk,' she said, rocking him in her arms. She looked up at some of the women. 'What can I do? How can I feed him?'

The ship pitched and plunged and many of the women and children fell to the floor screaming. The woman and her baby fell too and the baby cried even more. 'For God's sake, shut him up,' a voice shouted. 'Give him a bit o' pap or something.'

Someone gave the woman a piece of bread and she put it in her mouth to moisten and then placed a morsel in the child's mouth. He coughed and spluttered and started to scream; the ship heeled and they were flung over once again and first one and then another of the women started to be sick and they heard the sound of the men retching from behind their barrier.

'We're going to die,' a woman shrieked. 'We're trapped like rats in here.' She pushed her way towards the locked door and started to hammer with her fists. 'Let me out. Let me out!'

Meg strode forward and smacked the woman across the face. 'Stop that,' she roared. 'We might be going to die, but shouting and screaming isn't going to help. Now get back to your place!'

As she passed the woman with the baby, the mother held him up towards her. 'Have you any milk?' she asked pathetically. 'He's hungry.'

'Me?' Meg held onto the bunk as the ship rolled. 'I've got no milk! I've never had any bairns.'

The woman continued to hold him up. 'Please,' she appealed. 'Somebody! My milk's gone.'

Meg took the child from her, nestling him on her shoulder. 'Rest on your bunk,' she said. 'Mebbe it'll come back. I'll tek him for a bit.'

The child feeling another presence stopped his mewling, but sought with his mouth towards Meg's cheek. 'No use searching, young fella, I've got nowt that you'd want.' She took him back to the bunk and sat with him next to Emily, who was lying flat on her back. Some of the other women were sitting or lying on the floor to reduce the effect of the ship's pitching and rolling.

'Give him a drop of water,' Emily suggested. 'There's some clean in the jug and it might pacify him.'

'How?' Meg asked. 'I can't give him a cup!'

'Dip your finger in the water,' another woman

348

said, 'and put it in his mouth. I used to do that with my bairns.' She nodded her head as if remembering and then started to weep.

Meg wiped her hand on her skirt and dipped her finger into the jug of water, then put her finger to the baby's mouth. 'Hey, he's tekking it,' she said. 'Ha, it tickles!'

The vessel pitched again and Meg clutched the child to her. They heard a crash above deck and water trickled in through the seams of the ship, soaking their blankets.

Emily watched Meg as she held the baby and thought of the child she had lost. If he had lived, I wonder how things would have been? Would we both be starving somewhere in the streets of Hull? Would I have had to live on charity? She thought of what Mr Linton had suggested to her, that she live with him as his housekeeper. I didn't think that he would stay in Australia, I thought he would be sailing on to some other land or else going back to England. But he says that he is going to buy a small farm! I find that so surprising. He was disappointed, I think, when I told him that I had promised to stay with Meg.

'He's gone to sleep,' Meg said. 'Fancy that. I've settled him.' She picked her way through the women lying on the deck, back to the child's mother. She was lying with her back to her. 'I've brought 'babby back,' she whispered. 'He's gone to sleep.'

'Keep him, will you?' The woman turned towards her. Her voice was weak and breathless. 'Just for a bit. I feel that bad. His name's Ralph,' she added.

'Well, I don't feel too good myself,' Meg began, but the woman turned her back again, so there was nothing Meg could do but take him back to her bunk, where she lay down and held him in the crook of her arm.

The ship shook and groaned and they heard the rattle of anchors as she rode out the storm. The bilges overflowed and the convicts prayed and cursed and all were sick, so that the stench of vomit and the oppressive heat became intolerable until, when they thought they could bear it no longer, the door was opened and a glimmer of light appeared from the deck above.

'What a stink!' The guard who opened the door retched as the stench came up to meet him. 'Get a gang together and get this lot cleaned up.' He gave out terse instructions. 'Come on, all of you, up on deck. We'll have to hose you down.'

Buckets of sea water mixed with disinfectant were thrown over the prisoners as they came up. 'Poor pathetic wretches,' Clavell said as he stood next to Philip watching them. 'And worse to come when we land.'

Philip was watching for Emily, he hoped that she had withstood the storm and hadn't been ill. But he couldn't see her for the crush of women and now the men were coming out too. He cast his eyes around the deck and saw a woman edging her way towards the forecastle, part of the deck which was out of bounds to the convicts. He lifted his head and saw her clamber onto the bulwarks. 'Ahoy there,' he shouted and started forward. 'Stop her!'

The woman turned for an instant and he thought

he recognized her, then she lifted her arms high and hurled herself over the side.

'Man overboard! Man overboard,' came the cry and the crowd rushed to the side. 'Who was it? Did you see? I didn't see anybody. What happened?' The sea rose and fell as the great ship with its press of canvas billowing, drew on, but the woman had gone.

The captain was called, but there was nothing to be done. A report would have to be written, but who was she? No-one seemed to know, though there were three people who had an inkling. Philip said nothing, and Emily and Meg looked down at the baby. 'Poor bairn,' Meg said softly and touched his cheek. 'You're going to need a new Ma now.'

'Mr Linton,' Emily asked later, 'would it be possible to have fresh goat milk for the new baby?'

'I should think so, you will have to ask the storekeeper. Can the mother not feed him herself?'

She shook her head and looked away. 'No, her milk has gone.'

'Is she sick? Perhaps Mr Clavell should see her!'

'She's resting,' she said quickly.

'Ah!' She saw perception in his eyes. 'Yes, I see. Well, see the storekeeper. Tell him to come to me for authorization if he needs it.'

She smiled. 'Thank you. Meg and I will look after him until we land.'

They were more than half-way through the voyage and the days stretched in boredom. The captain and his officers organized the convicts into groups in which they could learn to read and write; the women were given old sheets to make petticoats and bonnets and clothes for the children, and the younger convicts played leapfrog with the crew as a form of exercise, but still the days dragged on. Then one day came the cry, 'Land ahoy,' from the men on the yards and everyone rushed to see their first glimpse of land in weeks.

The coast of Rio de Janeiro was in sight and many of the convicts thought that they had reached their destination and started to gather together their meagre possessions. 'Not yet! Not yet!' The officers laughed. 'You've many weeks to go before your feet touch land.'

They encountered more storms and the winds became hurricane strength, the rain lashed down and the convicts grew sicker and more weary of their confinement in the dungeon-like accommodation. The ship wallowed for days as the seas ran high and a northerly rain squall blew. The port anchor was let go, and the *Flying Swan* hove to as she rode broadside to the storm, dipping and bucking, the decks awash with the waves and her masts bare of sail.

Finally the storms abated and the convicts crept out like rats from a hole, too exhausted and sick to do more than lie on the deck. The skies cleared, the sun grew hotter and they rounded the Cape of Good Hope into the Southern Ocean and the last leg of their journey.

Chapter Thirty-Three

The baby thrived on the goat's milk and Emily became increasingly anxious as she saw how attached Meg had become to him. 'You might not be able to keep him,' she said, as she wielded the borrowed scissors on Meg's tangled hair.

'Cut it short,' Meg said fiercely. 'Go on. Shorter. Shorter! And I'll worry about 'bairn when we reach land, not afore.'

Meg's hair dropped to the deck and some of the women gathered round to watch. 'Cut mine, will you? I'm lousy,' one of them asked; they were all scratching with head lice.

'It'll look as if you've been punished,' said another scornfully. 'That's what they do to the women in Parramatta if they've misbehaved.'

'Well, I don't care what anybody thinks.' Meg ran her fingers through her short curls. 'I feel better already.'

Emily stood back to admire her handiwork. Meg looked taller and more dignified now that her unruly dishevelled hair had gone, and her strong features and fine eyes stood out, making her look quite regal. I'm tempted to cut my own, she thought, but she had secretly borrowed Philip Linton's hairbrush when he wasn't in his cabin and the shine was coming back to her long hair.

'Emily,' he said, when she returned the scissors to him, 'have you thought any more about what I asked you?' He flushed slightly. 'I mean about you coming to be my housekeeper?'

She looked down at the floor. It was what she wanted to do more than anything, just to be near to him. These last few weeks had been an awakening to her. He had been kind and considerate, much more than he needed to have been, and each waking moment when she was away from him, her thoughts had only been of him. But I'm being foolish, she thought as she strove for an answer, it will only end in heartache when he returns to his ship.

'What would I do when you return home to England?' She raised the question which had been bothering her. 'Where would I go then?'

'If I went, it would only be for a short time, nine months, a year at the most. You would stay to look after things.'

'Alone?' Fear was in her eyes. 'I'm a convict woman, Mr Linton, it wouldn't be allowed.'

'You can't go to Parramatta!' He stepped forward and gripped her hand urgently. 'I've heard such terrible things!'

The ship heeled to starboard and she fell against him, putting her arms up to steady herself. She saw him swallow hard and she disengaged herself from his grasp. 'I can't leave Meg,' she whispered. 'She's my friend.'

'You must!' He shook his head. 'I can't take two women as housekeepers.'

'The women are saying that Sydney is full of black savages.' She changed the subject, embarrassed by his intense gaze. 'Why would you want to live there?'

'Once it was, but not now. I'm told it's a fine town with magnificent buildings; built by convicts it's true, but there are many respectable people there. Business people, traders, sheep farmers and landowners. Australia is a growing country with a lot of potential.'

'So,' she said slowly, 'do you intend to give up your naval career to live there, and not go back to England?'

He looked at her and there was a depth of feeling in his eyes that she couldn't understand. 'No.' His voice was low and steady. 'I didn't say that.'

She left his cabin feeling confused and miserable. She desperately wanted to go with him. She knew that he would take care of her, he had behaved admirably, as a gentleman should and she thought of how firm his arms had felt as he'd caught her from falling.

'Meg,' she whispered as they lay side by side on the planking that night. It was after ten o'clock but the women had been allowed to stay on deck. 'Have you ever been kissed by a man?'

Meg turned towards her in surprise. 'Kissed by a man? Me? No, 'course not! Men don't kiss women like me. They kiss their wives or mistresses. Not whores!'

'Oh!' she said softly.

'Why?' Meg asked. 'Have you?'

'No. I just wondered what it would be like, that's all.' She lay dreaming, thinking of Philip Linton and how she thought that he had almost kissed her when he'd caught her. But I suppose that I'm quite glad that he didn't, she mused reluctantly. It might have spoiled everything.

'Land ho!' This time as they heard the call from the masthead the next day and gathered to see the dark smudge of land on the horizon, they knew that at last here was their final destination. Some of the convicts, men as well as the women, wept as they viewed their new homeland and full realization came that they might never see England, their friends and family ever again.

'My poor bairns,' wept a woman with small children clinging to her skirts. 'What'll become of 'em?'

'Me poor old ma!' A boy, no more than fourteen, brushed away the tears that coursed down his cheeks. 'She'll die and I'll not know of it.'

Emily wept too, even though her brother and her friend Meg were there on the ship with her. She wept for her childhood, left behind by the deep muddy waters of the Humber. She wept for the humble cottage that she had shared with Sam and Granny Edwards; for her mother and father and for Mary Edwards, who had a special place in her heart, and she pictured her amongst the flowers in her sweet-smelling shop in the heart of Hull. I want to go back, she despaired. I belong in those hummocky plains of Holderness, I belong under the wide cloudy skies which seem to stretch on for ever. Not out here in this foreign land.

Meg stood with her chin held high, clutching the child who wasn't hers. She had told Emily that she was glad that she was here, that England had done nothing for her and that perhaps in this new country she had a future.

She's like Joe, Emily mused. He says the same. Perhaps they will do well, if they can endure it, for she was under no illusion that there were terrors ahead and that only the fittest and strongest would survive. And they are both fit and strong, life has made them so. They will take a few falls and still get up again. But will I? Am I strong enough to outlast my sentence?

The wind blew strongly and they shivered on deck and below it, for here at the other side of the world it was almost winter when they had expected summer. The women had only their cotton dresses and few had shawls, and the children amongst them were mostly in rags. Emily and Meg had made the baby, Ralph, some gowns and bonnets out of cotton sheeting which they had begged from the sick ward, and when they were up on the upper deck, Meg tucked him inside her bodice to protect him from the elements.

'Look,' she whispered to him as they sailed past Botany Bay towards the bay of Sydney. 'Here is your new country, your new land.'

Captain Martin had taken the decision to sail into Sydney Harbour even though he had been warned by other ships' masters that there might be trouble from the residents. For two years transportation to New South Wales had been halted as the immigrant residents and free settlers and the critics in England argued against the barbaric transportation system. The transportees had been re-directed to Van Dieman's Land and Western Australia, which were crying out for free labour. Now because of pressure from Lord Grey of the Colonial Office, transportation to New South Wales had resumed under a different name, assisted exiles; but the people of Sydney had blocked the harbour against the transport ships and had refused to let the convicts land.

'English law is a labyrinth of confusion,' Captain Martin muttered as the ship drew towards Port Jackson. 'And transportation is one of the worst iniquities of all. Worse even than slavery, for the black savages were ignorant and many of them probably had a better life after they were captured, than they had been used to. These are white people we are condemning to a soulless life.'

Philip glanced at his commanding officer. Not for him to disagree with his superior, but he couldn't help but say, 'How do we know the black slaves were ignorant, sir? They may well have had a superior life to ours, and it should be on the conscience of all white men that such cruelty was administered.'

'Wait until you meet up with some of these Aborigine fellows before you make up your mind, Mr Linton. You will find that some of them barely speak English, even after fifty years of English rule.'

Philip excused himself and went to find Clavell. When he wasn't drunk, he was the most intelligent, articulate man Philip had ever come across and he had a different opinion entirely from Captain Martin.

He wasn't drunk now, but quite sober and was busy packing his medicines into his portable medicine chest. 'No real problems on this trip, Mr Linton. One birth, three deaths, and only a few with fever, including the captain. That's what happens if you keep a clean and healthy ship. Plus the lemon or lime to keep down the scurvy, I'm a big believer in that, plenty of citrus juice, clean water and not too much meat.' He straightened up and cracked his head on the ceiling. 'Shan't be doing that for much longer!' he winced. 'Come and see me in Parramatta will you?' he said abruptly. 'I don't suppose I'll get many visitors. That's if you're staying?'

'I don't know what to do, sir. Emily – Emily has promised to stay with her friend and she'll probably end up in Parramatta.'

'Mmm.' The surgeon pursed his lips. 'Well, I'll keep an eye out for her as best I can if she does go there, but you know, I'm inclined to say to you buy or rent a small farm anyway. If she goes to Parramatta she won't want to stay!'

'And could I bring her out?'

'Good Lord, yes.' He snapped the lid of his box closed and strapped it with a leather strap. 'The place was always besieged by men wanting a wife. Of course, what the authorities are wanting now are families, men with wives and children, even though they may not be married in law. They want to change the image of a country filled with convict labour. They want families here to create the next

359

generation. They want to be seen as respectable! That's why the immigration scheme is opening up. The country is massive, Philip, it can't ever be filled. There's a great future for people who are prepared to work hard. There's land by the thousand acres waiting for young men and women to snap it up.'

'You make it sound exciting, sir, but what about the Aborigines, don't they object to their land being taken over?'

He nodded. 'They do! But on the whole they are a peaceable race and I'm afraid, I'm very much afraid, they're going to get swamped.'

Philip made up his mind. As soon as they were docked and before the convicts left the 'tween decks, for they had been put below again as soon as they were within reach of land, then he would ask permission to leave the ship and go ashore. Clavell had given him the necessary information on purchasing a homestead and had given him a reference if he should need one. If Emily should change her mind once they had disembarked, then he would have the papers to hand, and hopefully a house where he could take her.

He felt churned up with apprehension. He couldn't bear to think of her confined in the women's factory. It would be worse than gaol and she would be incarcerated there for many weeks before work was allotted to her. He could sense trouble ahead for her if she stayed with her friend Meg, for from what little he had seen and heard of her he realized that she would not take the brunt of authority lightly. However did Emily come to befriend her? he asked himself for the hundredth time, yet the woman was loyal and protective of Emily. That much was obvious.

An image came into his mind, an image of another woman he had seen by Emily's side. A woman with short dark hair nursing a baby. At least, was she nursing a baby? Had there been another baby delivered below decks? Officially there was only one baby born on board ship, and he was sure, almost sure that it belonged to the woman who had jumped overboard. The woman had not been named, they would find out who she was at the end of the voyage after the roll-call. So who was looking after her child? Emily had asked for goat's milk initially and after that it was collected regularly by various women.

But he had no time now to think about it, they were coming into harbour and there was a party waiting for them on the quayside who didn't look very welcoming.

'No more convicts!' The cry went up from the waiting crowd as the first of the men were rowed to the quay. 'Take them to Van Dieman's Land,' they shouted. 'They're happy to have them. Lord Grey reneged on us!'

The deputy governor was there to accept the transfer of the convicts from the captain and he turned to the crowd. 'The Legislative Council has agreed in principle to take these assisted exiles and an Order in Council has been secured. These men have served most of their time already. They are now here to work, on the roads and on the farms.'

There were mutterings and grumblings, but the

crowd knew they couldn't win this time unlike a previous occasion when with a mass show of public indignation they had turned away the convict ship the *Halshemy.*

Captain Martin sent a boatload of women next, including Emily and Meg. Some of the women collapsed as their legs gave way beneath them when they touched firm ground, but Emily and Meg stood up straight and proud, Meg clutching the baby close to her chest. There were a few whistles of approval from the men as the women convicts stood there and some shouts of derision from the women settlers. 'Whores! We don't want you here!'

But the women immigrants were outnumbered as well they knew. There was a shortage of women in New South Wales and although some immigrant men had brought their wives, there were many single men on the lookout for women to share their beds, clean their houses and cook their food.

'I'll take the blonde one,' a man in the crowd shouted. 'How much do you want for her?'

Emily's neck and face flushed in shame. This was worse than she expected. She moved closer to Meg, then lifted her head to look for Mr Linton. She saw Captain Martin talking to officials with Lieutenant Boyle and several other officers. The surgeon was there also, looking extremely smart in his white trousers and waistcoat and his dark dress coat gilded with braid, but she couldn't see Philip Linton. Surely he would come to say goodbye, she grieved. He wouldn't just stay on board. Was he angry with her for not agreeing to go with him? Or perhaps he is on duty and can't leave the ship. She looked round at the male convicts to try to find Joe and spotted him within the crowd. He had a worried frown as he looked across at her and was rubbing his hand across his beard.

The crowd started to disperse as more convicts came ashore and soon the quayside was full, over three hundred in all, men and women, shackled by the ankle irons once more and assigned to their new prison homeland.

'Some of these men are ticket of leave men.' An official, primed by the deputy governor, spoke up. 'If any of you need help on your farms come to see me to arrange a contract.' He turned to Lieutenant Boyle. 'If any of these men are agricultural workers, put them together in a group, otherwise they'll be put to the roads.'

Emily could see that Joe was straining to hear what was being said and he edged nearer to the front of the crowd.

'Some of the women will be taken on as house-keepers,' said the official. 'Those with children will be accepted first. Children can't go to Parramatta.'

Emily drew in a breath. Meg had the child and she had said that she would swear he was hers. 'Meg,' she whispered, 'we'll be parted. I'll have to go to Parramatta alone!'

Meg turned to her. 'What do you mean?'

'I just heard them say that they won't take children to Parramatta. You'll go somewhere else. Not Parramatta.' She was frightened. What would happen to her?

Meg stared at her. 'But, you'll go with Mr Linton! You said that he'd asked you.'

She shook her head. 'I told him that I couldn't. That I'd promised to stay with you!'

'You idiot, Emily! You know that I can look after myself. You must go with him, it's 'best chance you've got!'

'I don't know where he is! I haven't seen him.' She started to shake. Suppose, just suppose she was made to go with some other man, some settler who wanted a woman. Scenes of Hugo Purnell's assault on her filled her mind and she felt faint. Blackness filled her senses and she clutched Meg's arm. I'd rather go to Parramatta. Parramatta. Parramatta. The dreaded name which had been talked of by the women convicts in such hushed tones, hammered in her mind before she fell to the floor in a dizzy spell.

Only Meg and some of the other women came to assist her. She heard voices and names being called, hers being one of them, and she was hauled to her feet and shepherded to one side along with some of the other women, all young like herself, but Meg wasn't one of them.

'All women with children step forward.' The order came and with irons clanking the women shuffled forward, Meg amongst them. A roll-call was held and names called. 'You,' an official shouted at Meg, 'what's your name?'

'Margaret Johnson,' she answered.

'It doesn't say here that you have a child!'

'I hadn't when I was put on board,' she answered boldly.

He looked down his list. 'There's only one birth

registered.' He looked at Clavell. 'It's not the same name.'

Clavell shrugged. 'Perhaps I didn't deliver it.'

'Is it your child?'

'Yes.' Meg stared straight at the official. 'He was delivered below decks.'

The official again glanced at Clavell and then at Meg. 'Then who delivered it?'

'I did!' Emily, listening to what was being said, spoke up. 'I delivered it.'

'And I helped her,' said another woman who had shared their bunk.

Lieutenant Boyle moved forward with a sly smile on his face. 'Lies,' he said. 'The woman's a whore! It's not her child at all. She's after going with a family instead of Parramatta, which is where she belongs.' He outstared Meg with a cynical glare. 'Look at her with her shorn head. I remember her insolence. She's a whore, she's been with every man on this ship.'

''Cept you, Mr Boyle, and I wouldn't touch you wi' gloves on,' Meg replied sharply and there was a ripple of laughter.

There was a sudden movement among the male convicts and Joe pushed his way forward. 'You're speaking of my wife, sir. The child is mine.'

Chapter Thirty-Four

Philip hired a mount to take him back to the harbour. He had the deeds of the purchased property in his pocket. It had been remarkably simple. He had given his guarantee and Clavell's recommendation, signed a few forms and the property was his. He had also been persuaded to accept a grant towards an additional two hundred acres of land on condition that he maintained a convict. 'Welcome to Sydney, sir,' the government clerk had said. 'You won't regret it.'

I hope not, Philip thought as he rode back through the town. I've never before purchased something without seeing it. But he had been shown a drawing and plan of the farmstead and land, which was small in comparison to some he had been offered. But he reckoned it was enough. I'll get an overseer to look after it and he can hire some hands, and then when I return to England they will be there to protect Emily. Already he was churned up in anticipation of taking her to the farm, of planning the arrangement of the house and furniture. And then, he mused, when she is used to having me around we can look to the future and I can tell her that I am returning to England to obtain her pardon.

If she comes with you, a small voice hammered in his head. She said that she wouldn't. He shuddered. What would he do if he was rejected? He would have a house and land that he didn't want, although the clerk had said he would be able to sell it easily should he want to.

He rode down the wide streets and noted the variety of houses, some brick, some stone, some whitewashed. Most were of a simple structure and huddled together in groups as if for protection. Nearly all of them had a garden, though there were few flowers growing, but there were exotic-looking trees with thin grey leaves, and he thought of home, up on the Yorkshire Wolds, where it was now early summer. The blossom would be fully out and the birds singing in full trilling throat.

The public buildings and administrative offices, the Public Library, the hospital and churches were grand and impressive and many were built in the English architectural style. On the streets he rode through, new buildings were being erected and the air was filled with dust and the sound of hammering and sawing. The Domain had been laid out as a public park, where elegant ladies emerged from their carriages to stroll arm in arm with their companions, whilst the free settlers sat in small groups on the grass to eat mutton pies and drink ale, listen to the regimental bands or watch a game of cricket or gaze at the magnificent harbour view.

There was a snake of wagons and carts moving away from the harbour as he rode towards the quayside and only a few groups of convicts standing in desultory fashion awaiting their fate. Poor devils, he thought. There's hard labour on the roads for the men and God only knows what's waiting for the women.

He tied the reins to a hitching rail and walked across to where Clavell and Boyle were standing. Boyle's face was flushed and angry and Clavell's was pained. Boyle gave a cynical grin when he saw Philip. 'You've just missed your little lady.' He emphasized the word lady. 'She's gone off to Parramatta.'

'No!' He was horrorstruck. I can't be too late. I've ridden so hard.

''Fraid so. They've sent all the single women.' Boyle pointed to those who were left. 'Though there's one over there who should have gone. She's claiming to be married with a child and I'd bet a month's salary that she isn't.'

'The name's the same, Boyle,' Clavell said idly. 'What difference does it make to you whether she goes to Parramatta or gets sent to a farm?'

Boyle sneered. 'Because she's a street woman and they never change. She'll be running around the rookeries of Sydney plying her trade within a month. She should be sent to Parramatta to finish her sentence. They know how to punish in there.'

'Who are you talking about?' Philip was busy working out how he could get to see Emily. If only Boyle would take himself off he could talk to Clavell.

'The tall woman with the child.' Clavell nodded

towards Meg, who, with a male convict, was arguing with an official. 'She claims the child was delivered below decks.'

'And your little friend said she delivered it!' Boyle laughed.

Why would Emily say that and why didn't she mention it to me? He stared hard at the woman. Was it Emily's friend Meg? Yes, he was sure it was. But why was she keeping the child?

He turned to Clavell. 'Don't they take children at Parramatta?'

'Not any more.' Clavell shook his head. 'I told you that the authorities want families here. They'll be assigned to a farm if someone will take them.'

Philip took off his hat and ran his fingers through his hair. Damn! Am I too late again? 'Excuse me,' he muttered and raced across the quayside towards where Meg, the convict and the official were standing.

'Are these people free?' he burst out. 'I urgently need a farmhand and a woman for the house.' He stared hard at Meg. 'So you were delivered of your child safely? You didn't need the help of the surgeon?'

Meg opened and closed her mouth. 'No, Mr Linton, I didn't,' she said firmly. 'He was delivered below decks. An easy enough birth.'

'Good. Good!' Philip rubbed his hands together, then shook a finger at her. 'But you should have notified us, you know! We're supposed to log births and deaths.'

'Sorry, sir. I didn't realize.' She eyed him warily. 'You've not met my husband.' She turned towards

Joe. 'I didn't realize he was on 'same ship 'till we were well out at sea.'

The harassed official looked down at his notes. 'Well, if you can vouch for these people, sir, you can hire them. He's an assigned man, so if they're married like they say, she gets her freedom. He says he's a farm worker.'

'Was, sir,' Joe interrupted. 'I've been doing hard labour in 'dockyard for 'last few years.'

So how are they supposed to have conceived a child? Philip quizzed himself. I could be taking on a footpad or murderer. He rubbed his chin. I'll have to risk it. If Emily will only come if Meg is there too, then I'll have to take him as well. He looks a villainous fellow with his shaggy beard and long hair, but then who wouldn't after being incarcerated below decks?

He signed the necessary papers and as the official took his leave, Philip said to Joe, 'These papers give your address as London, but your wife's is different!'

'Yes, sir. I was caught thieving in London but I'm from 'north of England, same as my wife, Margaret, here.'

'Yes.' Philip wondered how they had managed to meet to concoct a story. 'I know. I can hear it in your accent.'

'Can you, sir?' The man seemed astonished. 'How's that then?'

'Because that's where I'm from too. But that's not a Hull accent like your – wife's!'

Joe put his head up and looked at him frankly. 'No, I'm not from that town. I'm from a country district, but I'd rather not talk about it if you don't mind, sir. That's a life behind me. This is a new one.'

Philip called for the irons to be unlocked from their ankles and noticed that Johnson walked with a limp, throwing his leg as if still shackled.

He sent a boy to hire him a horse and wagon. 'The farm that I've bought is a few miles out of Sydney.' He studied the map of the area that he'd been given. 'I've no idea what it's like. It's a shot in the dark.' He looked at each of them squarely. 'I've taken it on trust, just as I have taken both of you. If you let me down then I won't hesitate but send you to the road gang, Johnson – and you, Meg,' there was a threat in his soft tone, 'will go to Parramatta without the child.'

Meg hugged the child closer to her, there was fear in her eyes. 'I won't let you down, Mr Linton. I promise.' Then she looked at him pleadingly. 'When will you go for Emily, sir?'

There was a cool breeze blowing and the seagulls shrieked their shrill cries as they swooped over the cove as Emily was bundled into the cart with the other women. I seem to have spent my life getting in and out of carts and wagons, she thought wearily. Is there to be no end to it? She looked despairingly to where her brother Joe and Meg were standing next to each other and they too were staring across at her as she was driven away. She felt desolate and so alone.

The road to Parramatta was sixteen miles long, rough and laid with broken stone, and as the wagon trundled and shook on its journey, she gazed about her at the countryside. Strange grey trees climbed the high ground and as she looked back the way they had come she saw an old, crumbling fort overlooking the bay. The town had been filled with townspeople, not only convicts in their dull grey uniforms, but women in bright cotton dresses with baskets over their arms; others in silk and muslin stepped into carriages. There was a scattering of colourful uniforms, the dark blue and white of the naval men and scarlet and grey of the military. What a strange place, she pondered. I thought it would be dark and dismal like a prison, but most people seem cheerful, although perhaps they are the free settlers. But there were shops and warehouses and green squares and a stream running through the middle of the town and a market where dark-skinned natives were selling fresh fish, and farmers, just the same as at home, were wearing thick cotton smocks and straw hats on their heads.

Parramatta too was a lively town, whereas she had expected only a prison, and the sky was filled with the sound and colour of budgerigars as they flew over their heads. But as they drove through the open gates set in the high brick walls of the female factory, she felt that her worst fears were about to come true and that here life would be as dark and dismal as she had expected.

'Everybody line up! Come on. Jump to it, I haven't got all day.' The orders were barked out by a military-looking man. By his side stood a clergyman. There were women prisoners milling around the yard and as Emily watched them she thought that some of them looked drunk. Some of them were hanging onto the arms of soldiers who were lounging in doorways, whilst others were walking out of the gate and no-one appeared to be stopping them.

'You will find', the official shouted, 'that there are grave punishments here for those who misbehave. We no longer lash women, but we still have the treadmill,' he added with a thin smile. 'And heads are shaved and food is withdrawn for the serious miscreants. But those who obey the rules will find there are special privileges.'

Some of the younger women who had just arrived began to weep, but Emily stared straight ahead. I will cry no more, she vowed. I will not let them get to me.

They were taken to their quarters by a supervising woman convict, who ushered them into a large bare room, and Emily was glad that she had had the forethought to pick up her blanket from the ship, for on the floor were thin straw mattresses but no blankets or pillows.

'If any of you have money,' the woman said, 'I'd advise you to keep it safe. You'll get supper and breakfast, but if you want anything else you have to pay for it.'

'How?' Emily dared to ask. 'How can we pay if we have no money?'

The woman stared at her. 'Work for it,' she said harshly. 'Or sell that blanket you're hanging on to,' she grinned, 'or anything else you have to offer.'

Emily sank on to a mattress away from the door. The door was open on to the yard and she didn't want everyone staring in at her, for this appeared to be an open house with other convict women coming and going to inspect the new arrivals.

A group of these came and stood in the doorway and made jeering remarks at the newcomers. Some of them retaliated and abuse and foul language were hurled from one to another. One woman leaning on the door jamb spotted Emily and shouted across to her. 'Hey, you. I know you!'

Emily looked up. She saw a bedraggled old hag with scanty grey hair and dressed in rags. She turned away and ignored her, but the woman came across the room towards her.

'I remember you.' She dropped down onto the mattress and Emily shuffled away. 'We drove from York gaol together. Don't you remember?'

Emily cringed and shook her head. She would surely remember such a miserable creature with her sore face and misshapen black teeth.

'Yes!' The woman poked at her with a dirty finger. 'In the coach going to London! You remember me – Molly?'

Molly! Yes, now she did remember. The vile woman who had offered –. Emily shuddered. To meet again with such a woman on the other side of the world!

Molly leaned forward and Emily pressed against the wall in order to get away from her sickening stench. 'Listen,' she poked Emily again and whispered, 'do you remember I said I'd get you fixed up with an officer or somebody, so's we could eat? Well, the offer still holds. I've been here a few weeks now and I've seen what goes on. Soldiers and farmers come and go as they please, but they're getting a bit particular. I can't do business with 'em, they won't look at me.' She appraised Emily. 'But you, now, you've still got bloom o' youth on you. I could get a good price for you! We could have a regular little business going. What do you say?'

Emily jumped to her feet and grabbing the end of the mattress she tipped the woman off it so that she sprawled onto the floor. 'I say get out of my way with your filthy mouth,' she screamed. 'I want nothing to do with you!'

Molly looked up at her from the floor and wiped her dirty hand across her mouth. 'Think you're too good for 'likes of us, do you? Well, you'll soon find out you're not. I've onny to put the word about and you'll wish you'd never been born! You've not seen likes of some of these women in here, they're worse than men some of 'em, and they're not averse to using leather or a knife on a pretty face.'

Emily started to tremble, but she would not be intimidated. 'I said – get out of my way,' she hissed, her eyes wild. 'Get out!'

There was a sudden silence in the room as two men appeared in the doorway. One was the clergyman, who stood nervously twisting his hands together. The other was a tall, thin man in naval uniform whom Emily recognized. Mr Clavell, the surgeon from the *Flying Swan*.

He came into the middle of the room and slowly turned around so that he looked at each of the women in turn. There were about thirty of them. 'Good afternoon, ladies.' His voice was authoritative, but not unkind. He looked down at Molly and pointed with his finger to the door. 'I wish to speak to the new arrivals.'

Molly shuffled off, casting a look of loathing at Emily. The surgeon waited until she had gone and then spoke again. 'My name is Clavell. You may not know it, unless you were sick, but I travelled on the same ship as you, the *Flying Swan*, though I have to admit to having had a trifle amount more comfort than you did.'

The women glanced at each other, here was a man speaking to them as if they were human beings. 'I am here on a permanent basis, much as you are,' he explained. 'This is my prison as much as it is yours. The difference is that I chose to come here.'

He waited for this to sink in. 'I have been here before and I didn't like it. Nor did the women who were here, but some of them made it worse for themselves than it needed to have been. There have been improvements since then, but you wouldn't notice. Now what I aim to do, with your help,' his words were chosen carefully and precisely, 'is close this prison down!'

Chapter Thirty-Five

First of all Clavell made them take all the mattresses outside and shake them. Then he appointed groups of women from the newcomers to brush down the walls and windows of their dormitory and wash the floor with antiseptic. He then turned his attention to the old hands, those who had been in Parramatta for some time and who looked at him suspiciously as he went to speak to them.

'Some of you are set in your ways,' he said. 'You have established a routine for yourselves which you may find difficult to break. But I am telling you that from where I am standing, you are a disreputable lot! You are dirty and lousy and you have forgotten what it is like to be a woman. Except,' he added, as some of the whores of the prison grinned and nudged each other, 'except for those who sell their bodies in a vile trade and have given this prison its name of whorehouse! It may be too late to do anything about any of you, but I aim to stop you staining the reputation of those who have not yet sunk so low.' His voice was firm and they were left in no doubt that he was determined to do exactly what he had stated.

'For those who are diseased,' he went on, 'you can come and see me in the sick bay. But first of all,' he said forcibly, 'you will take out your mattresses and pile them in the centre of the yard, where they will be burnt. You will scrub and clean your cells and dormitories. Then you will be given water to wash yourselves and your clothes. If your minds are dirty then you may cleanse them through the parson here, who will hear your confessions.'

Emily heard some of this as she came outside to empty a bucket of dirty water and felt a glimmer of hope. Some of the other newcomers felt it too and spoke in whispers that perhaps it wouldn't be long before they would be allowed to leave.

But the soldiers, settlers and farmers appeared at the gate to ogle the new women and offer them their freedom and other inducements if they would go with them. Some of the women were tempted, for they had no money to buy extra food or blankets and the nights were cold, and they had no reason to know that when their services were no longer required they would be turned out on to the streets. Emily pulled her blanket over her as she lay down that night on her mattress; it was scratchy and tore at her skin, but the floor looked and smelt cleaner than previously, though she could hear the scurrying of mice beneath the floorboards. Then she heard one of the women scream. Everyone sat up. 'A snake,' she shouted. 'There's a snake by my bed.'

The women started to scream and shout and run to the corners of the room. Emily got up, and picking up a broom that was leaning against the wall, she brushed the creature towards the door. The door was locked, but there was a gap beneath it and she propelled it through it. 'Was it poisonous, do you think?' someone asked. 'I've heard say that snakes in this country are deadly, and that there are spiders and beetles as big as your hand!'

Emily shook her head. 'It wasn't a snake. It was a lizard, I think, and it was probably more frightened of us than we were of it!'

The next morning she smoothed her hair with her fingers, for she had no hairbrush, and plaited it into a thick braid. She left the dormitory and approached the sick bay, which was nothing more than a wooden hut. The door stood open to reveal a row of beds, which unlike the mattresses the prisoners slept on were raised from the floor on wooden legs. Mr Clavell was standing by a sink washing his hands. She knocked on the door and entered and as he turned, she dipped her knee.

'I'm sorry to bother you, sir,' she said quietly, for she saw that two of the beds were occupied, 'but could I speak to you?'

There was a flicker of interest in his eyes which lasted for only a second, and he nodded.

'I wondered if you needed any help in the sick bay? I need something to occupy my time whilst I'm serving my sentence. I'm clean – as a rule, though I have head lice at the moment – and I'm a hard worker. But', she finished in a rush, 'I don't want to stay in the dormitory with the other women.'

'Too good for them, are you?' He echoed Molly's words, a trifle cynically she thought. 'A touch above them?'

She hung her head. 'No, sir. I'm here to be punished for a crime just as they are.' Then she raised her head and looked at him honestly. 'But there is no point in wasting my life if I could be doing something useful with it.'

He came towards her and stood with his arms folded, surveying her. 'Why did you not go with Philip Linton, Emily?' he asked softly. 'I know that he asked you.'

She put her hand to her mouth in surprise. 'How –?'

'He confided in me,' he answered. 'And he said that you had some loyalty towards another prisoner, that you were going to come to Parramatta together. That was very foolish, surely?'

She nodded miserably. 'I realize now that it was and now Meg has gone off somewhere else with the baby.'

'Ah, yes! The infant. You helped to deliver it, I believe?'

Emily bit her lip. It didn't seem right to tell a downright lie but she didn't want to get Meg into trouble, and what if Meg had to give up the child because of her honesty?

Fortunately he didn't seem to want an answer, for he was muttering something about the stamina of women under these circumstances. 'A boy, I believe?' and as Emily nodded, he asked, 'And did she name him? Has he had the benefit of the parson's blessing?'

'Not yet,' she said, 'though his given name is Ralph.'

She thought she saw the ghost of a smile, but it was gone instantly as he said, 'Ah, yes! Very well. I do need some help in here. There are some instances when I need a woman in attendance or I shall stand accused of all kinds of misdemeanours. Fetch your mattress and you can sleep in here if you don't mind being with the sick. I shall be glad if you will come.'

'He doesn't know that you're Emily's brother,' Meg whispered, as side by side in the hired wagon she and Joe drove up the dusty road towards the farm-stead. Philip Linton rode ahead on his hired horse and in the back of the wagon there was a pile of furniture which he had collected from the stores. Two chairs, two single and one double bed, blankets and a table. The double bed was giving Meg some cause for concern and she eyed Joe with misgiving. The child in her arms stirred and she smiled down at him, grateful to Philip Linton for having the forethought to ask if she needed milk for him and collecting it from the grocery store as well as provisions for them.

'I think that's it.' Philip turned round in his saddle and pointed up the hill to where a stone-built house stood on the summit. 'Creek Farm.'

Joe shook the reins and urged the horse on and the wagon creaked and groaned under its load. 'Let me down,' Meg said, 'I'll walk up,' and jumping down she finished the journey on foot, stopping and turning from time to time to gaze at her surroundings.

'It's filthy,' Philip exclaimed as he unlocked the door of the house. 'An absolute dung heap! However will we get it clean?'

Looking at it, Meg thought she had never seen anything so wonderful in her life. A large wooden veranda fronted the house and several big rooms with windows overlooked the hillside and in the distance a view of Sydney Cove. There was a big kitchen with a wooden floor and a cooking range, and various rooms at the top of a wide staircase. It didn't look in the least dirty to her, maybe a few cobwebs, but as she had never in her life done a day's housework, that didn't bother her too much.

'Soon get it cleaned up, Mr Linton,' Joe said. 'But just as well you bought a broom.' His strength was enormous as he manhandled the furniture into the house, refusing the assistance of his new master. 'Perhaps you could have a look to see if there's a well, sir, then we can swill out all this muck from 'floor.' He looked at Meg, who was standing with Ralph in her arms, just looking around her. 'Go fetch provisions out of 'cart, Margaret,' he said in a familiar manner, 'and then you can start Mr Linton's dinner!'

She placed the baby in an empty box and glared at Joe as she passed him. 'Don't keep calling me Margaret,' she hissed. 'My name's Meg!'

By the time they had unloaded the wagon and brought everything inside, lit the fire under the range and Meg had somehow produced a simple meal of eggs and ham, dusk was starting to fall and Philip decided that it was too late to ride to Parramatta. The road was unknown to him and he had no idea of the hazards which might be waiting; he just hoped that Emily was all right and not afraid. Surely she will come back with me, especially now that I have a house and Meg is here?

The double bed they put in a back room at the top of the house and Philip said that he would sleep on a single bed downstairs for the time being. 'We will sort everything out eventually,' he said. 'I shall need more furniture, but I'll leave it until – until later.' He caught a slight smile on Meg's lips as he hesitated, but which disappeared when he said, 'You and Johnson can have the room upstairs.' He wanted to be downstairs in case anything untoward happened. He had his pistol strapped beneath his jacket so that if they were attacked by escaped convicts or unfriendly natives he was well prepared, and he also had full view of the stairs, should Meg or Johnson decide to take their leave during the night.

That night Meg eyed the double bed and then Joe, who was also standing looking at it. 'I can't remember 'last time I slept in a bed,' he said softly.

'Well, that's all you'll be doing,' she said harshly. 'Sleeping in it! Don't think, because we've passed off as a married couple that you can have 'same privileges as such.'

'It never entered my head,' he said sourly. 'It was onny when I realized that couples could be assigned together on a farm that I came forward. It would have been 'road gang otherwise.' He gave a sudden grin. 'Stroke of luck though, that our names were 'same.'

''Cept that yours isn't,' she griped. 'So don't expect owt.'

'Changing thy spots?' he said harshly. 'Or is it because I've no money? Whoring was your living, wasn't it?'

'It was!' She glared at him. 'But not any more.'

'You don't have to worry about me. I've not been wi' a woman in years. I can wait a bit longer, till I meet one I fancy.' He picked up a blanket from the bed and lay down on the floor giving a deep sigh. 'I feel as if I'm home at last. Get into bed, Meg. I'll not trouble thee, have no fear.'

The next morning Philip hammered on their door to waken them. It was six o'clock and the sun shone brilliantly through the uncurtained windows. He had gone outside and swilled himself under the pump, eaten some bread and cheese and then saddled up the horse ready for his journey to Parramatta. Thing is, he pondered, will they both be here when I get back or will they have taken themselves off in search of real freedom? He thought that Meg would stay because of Emily, but he had no inkling of Johnson's motives. He has no ties with Meg in spite of what he claims, I'm not such an idiot that I don't know that, and he could go off.

Many convicts in the past had absconded from their employers, some had become bushrangers, living a wild life and terrifying decent citizens, others had disappeared into other parts of the New Territory, never to be seen again.

Philip confronted Johnson as he hurried down the stairs apologizing for having overslept. 'I can't remember when I slept better,' he said. 'Not since I was a little nipper anyway, safe in my ma and da's bed.' And in truth, although the floor had been hard, at least it was stable and not prone to dip and plunge as his bunk on board ship had done for the last few months. Tonight, Joe vowed, he would move his blanket to another room along the landing.

'Where are your parents now?' Philip asked casually and saw the veil of secrecy drop over his face.

'Both dead, sir, many years ago. Ma died in 'work-house and that was 'start of my downfall.'

'And no other relatives?'

He hesitated. 'Onny a sister, sir. Nobody else.'

'I'm going to Parramatta, Johnson. I know that if you have the mind to you can take yourself off as soon as my back's turned and I'll never see you again.' Philip was blunt. 'But I'm putting you on your honour to stay. I'll be gone all day and I want you to stay with Meg to protect her until I get back.'

'What makes you think I'll protect her?' he said defiantly. 'If you think I'm likely to go off as soon as your back's turned, why should Meg make any difference?'

Philip challenged him. 'She's supposed to be your wife, isn't she?'

Johnson's eyes shifted away from him. 'Aye, she is. But I wouldn't be 'first husband to go off and leave his wife to her own devices.'

'But you won't?'

'No. I won't!' He stared at Philip defiantly. 'I'll onny leave here if I'm treated unfairly, otherwise

I'll stop and serve my time. I intend to make a life out here and I don't mean to start off on 'wrong foot by absconding. Besides, I have another reason for stopping.'

'Yes?' Philip queried. 'And that is?'

He shook his head. 'It's a private matter, sir. But I'll be here when you get back wi' Emily.'

Strange fellow, Philip mused as he swung himself into the saddle and then looked back as Johnson ran towards him.

'Permission to look over 'land, sir, just to see what we've got?'

Philip nodded and as he dug in his heels turned once more as Johnson called again, 'Sir! Mr Linton. Can tha lend me a razor?'

Chapter Thirty-Six

There were two occupied beds in the sick ward. One held an old woman sick with fever, the other a girl who was pregnant and lay semi-comatose with her eyes staring into space.

'Her child is probably dead,' Clavell said in a low voice to Emily. 'And she's not far off, her body is full of poison.'

'Can you do anything for her?' Emily whispered. 'Will she suffer?'

'Give her something you mean? Laudanum? Yes, I have already.'

'You didn't give me enough.' The girl's voice, low and husky, came from the bed. 'I need more to pass from this world into the next.'

Emily went across to her. She was young, as young as she was herself. Her hands, red and puffy, lay on top of the sheet above her swollen belly and Emily stroked them. 'You're not ready to go yet, surely?' she said softly.

'Why should I stay?' she whispered. 'There's nothing for me in this life. Nobody who cares and nobody who I care for. Babby's gone, I know. It's so still I know it's dead.'

Emily pulled up a stool and sat by the bed. 'I'll stay with you if you like.'

'Please,' she said. 'I'm frightened. Frightened of being alone.'

'Would you like the parson to come?' Emily asked. 'Would he be of any comfort?'

The girl gave a hoarse laugh, which set her coughing and wincing. 'Last time I saw a parson he said I was wicked and would go to hell! I was wicked 'cos I went with men. He doesn't know what it's like to be hungry.' Her eyes became bright with tears. 'Mr Clavell brought me in. He found me outside the gate. He's the onny man that's ever shown me kindness.' She clutched Emily's hand. 'Do you think I'll go to hell?'

'No.' Emily's voice trembled with emotion. 'I think you've been there already.' She urged her not to distress herself and to try to rest.

The girl sighed. 'I'll be getting plenty o' rest soon, more than I bargained for just yet. But I don't mind,' she added huskily. 'I'm ready. I'm sick of this life. It's given me nothing but misery.'

She fell asleep shortly as the laudanum took effect and Emily went to look at the other patient. There was a great heat emanating from her, and as she muttered and sighed in her delirium, Emily saw that her mouth and tongue were swollen and her eyeballs were yellow. She fetched a bowl of water and a cloth to bathe her face, and then becoming more anxious went to find Mr Clavell, who had gone off somewhere.

She found him with the governor of the prison outside in the yard. 'I'm sorry, sir,' she said, 'but could you come? The old woman is very sick.'

'Don't let her come into contact with any-body,' the governor boomed. 'We don't want an epidemic.'

'It's what you'll get, Morrison, if this place isn't cleaned up,' Clavell barked back. 'And the women who are punished for offences work too hard. That woman is sixty and she's been on the treadmill for three days! There's no wonder she's sick!'

The governor shrugged. 'She's a troublemaker. In the old days she would have had the cat and then she would have behaved!'

Emily shuddered as she looked at the governor. His eyes gleamed. He would have enjoyed seeing the women lashed, she was sure of it.

Clavell looked at the young pregnant girl as he passed the bed and pressed his hand to her neck. Then he bent low and listened to her chest. 'She's gone.' He pulled the sheet over her head and turned to the other bed, leaving Emily staring horrorstruck in the face of death.

'Already! But I said I would stay with her,' she whispered, 'and I didn't.'

Clavell shook his head. 'She wouldn't have known. Be thankful for her that she went when she did. At least she has been spared the trauma of childbirth, for she would have died in agony then, without a doubt.'

He turned his attention to the old woman. 'Did you wash your hands after attending her?' he asked.

'Yes,' she said, feeling tears gathering. 'I did.'

He looked down at the woman. 'Then wash them again, up to your elbows. Scrub them until they

389

hurt. I'll have to warn the governor. We have gaol fever here. Typhoid!'

Emily poured water into a bowl and took soap and a brush and started to scrub her hands. She felt so miserable. The poor girl, lying still and silent in the bed across the room, who had died unloved and unwanted. Perhaps if she had kept the baby things would have been different. At least she would have had someone to love. But in her heart Emily knew it wasn't so. The woman on the ship who had had the child, Ralph, had known how difficult life would be with two mouths to feed. And I, how would I have coped had my child lived?

What kind of life is this? Her shoulders heaved with sobs as she scrubbed vigorously and angrily at her hands. It's no better here than it was in England. I don't know if I can go on. I don't know if I want to.

'Emily!' The voice was low and she thought that it was Clavell come back into the room. She turned and with wet, soapy hands she brushed away the tears which streamed down her cheeks.

'Mr Linton!' Relief and happiness flooded over her. So he hadn't forgotten her after all.

'Emily!' He took hold of her hands with both of his. 'Are you all right? Why are you crying? Have you been ill treated?' His face was suffused with anxiety.

'No, no, no! I'm crying because – because people keep dying and babies are abandoned by their mothers, or they die before they have lived.' The tears ran unchecked down her face. 'And the woman over there has typhoid and – oh, Mr Linton, this is such a dreadful place and Mr Clavell is going to try and close it down!'

He took out a handkerchief from his pocket and wiped her eyes and patted her face, then gently hushed her and led her to a stool and sat her down. 'Emily! I've bought a house and Meg is there with the child and the man she says is her husband. Will you come back with me? Please!'

She stared at him and her mouth trembled and her eyes were so awash with tears that she couldn't see and had to close them. She shook her head. 'I can't,' she sobbed. 'I've told Mr Clavell I'll help him here. He needs someone to help with the sick women.'

Philip banged the heel of his hand against his forehead and swore. 'Emily! For God's sake! What more can I do?' he burst out. 'I travel half-way across the world! I buy a farm I don't want. I employ a woman of the streets because you want her with you, and *still* you say you won't come!' His face was flushed and angry. 'If you won't come I shall take the next ship back to England. I'll not stay in this God-forsaken country!' He turned on his heel and stormed out of the room and across the prison yard.

She sat dumbstruck and watched him through the doorway. She saw Clavell stop in his tracks and stare and then chase after Philip, where they spoke briefly before Clavell turned towards the sick bay.

'What did he mean', she said vacantly as Clavell entered, 'about travelling half-way across the world?'

'You mean that you don't know?' Clavell was astounded. 'He hasn't told you?'

'What?' She lifted her head to watch Philip going out of the gate and untethering his horse.

'That he believes in your innocence. He obtained orders to sail on the *Flying Swan* for only that reason,' Clavell looked down at her, 'and you have just sent him off saying you can't go with him because you have promised to help me.'

'No,' she breathed. 'I didn't know.'

He put a finger beneath her chin and lifted her head. 'Foolish girl,' he said softly. 'Go after him. He needs you more than I do.' Then gently he patted her cheek. 'Take happiness whilst you can; it is so fleeting. Go on.' He suddenly became brisk. 'I'll make it all right here, fill in the necessary papers. Hurry, before he leaves.'

She jumped down from the stool and with a quick glance over her shoulder at Clavell, who was now standing with his back to her staring out of the window, she raced across the prison yard towards the gate. Philip was already riding away up the hill and as she reached the gate she called his name.

'Mr Linton! Mr Linton!' Philip, she echoed in her thoughts. Please turn around. Don't leave me!

Some of the other women gathered against the railing as Philip stopped and turned in the saddle, some of them whistled and called, but Emily hardly heard them, concentrating only on him. He wheeled around and trotted back and sat regarding her.

'Hey!' a woman shouted and her voice had a

desperate ring. 'Can I come with you, mister? You won't regret it!'

If I go with him, thought Emily, I will be regarded as his mistress, his 'wife' in everything but law. Regarded by whom? A small voice echoed in her head. Is there anyone here whose estimation you care about? No, she debated, there isn't, but I care about my own. What value do I set upon myself? Am I being proud in spite of all that has happened to me?

She looked up at him and felt a deep emotion welling up inside. I care so much for him and I need his good opinion of me.

He dismounted and put out his hand and she walked slowly towards him. 'Trust me, Emily,' he said gently. 'I would never hurt you.'

She put her hand into his, affirming to the watching crowd that she was leaving to become a 'housekeeper', a 'wife'. 'I know,' she said. 'I would trust you with my life.'

She rode behind him on the road back to the farmstead, her arms about his waist, feeling the nearness of his body and crying in her heart because of the gulf between them. He too was silent for most of the journey, then he started to tell her about the house and the land.

'The house is in a mess,' he began, 'and I'm not sure if Meg knows how to go about things. But the fellow Johnson, I think he'll be all right.' He turned his head sideways towards her and smiled. 'I know that they are not married, of course, and that the child isn't theirs. But it seems to me that out here in this country it's everyone for himself. There are opportunities waiting for those who can see them and I think Johnson saw his when he realized that he and Meg had the same name.'

Emily didn't know whether to tell him that Johnson wasn't Joe's real name, and that he was her brother, but Philip continued, 'He could be gone when we get back, of course, though he said he wouldn't abscond. Strangely enough, he said he had a reason for staying, though he didn't say what it was. Some scheme he has in mind, perhaps.'

They rounded a bend and he pointed upwards to the house on top of the hill. A line of washing blew in the breeze. A shirt and trousers, a skirt and a blanket and some small things belonging to the baby. 'I take it back,' he laughed. 'About Meg, I mean. She's been busy already.'

A man was standing in the doorway watching them approach. He was clean shaven and his hair was trimmed neatly. He was also bare chested and had a sheet tied around him. 'Who's this? A squatter?' Philip muttered. 'And where the devil is Johnson?'

He reined in and Emily slipped down from behind him. She hesitated for only a moment. 'Joe,' she murmured. Gone was the bearded, wild haired man she had met on the ship who had borne no resemblance to her brother, even though she had known that it was he. But here was the brother she recalled from her childhood; the same fair hair and complexion, the same cheerful, winning grin on his face as he stood there to greet her. 'Joe,' she called and ran towards him with her arms held wide.

* * *

'I was going to tell you, Mr Linton,' Emily said later as she served him supper. 'I was only waiting for the right opportunity.'

Thank God he is only her brother, Philip thought, for when I saw her run towards him I thought for a moment I had been duped and that it was Emily that Johnson wanted to be with and not Meg. He had been totally surprised by Joe's appearance. He had changed from the ragged, wild man of the convict ship to a young man near his own age, shorter, sturdier than him, a countryman with iron muscles formed from the hard labour of the road gangs and not from the plough. Meg had trimmed his hair and he had shaved his beard and bathed in the creek, where he had also washed his clothes. He had apparently persuaded Meg to take off her skirt so that he could wash it, and she too wore a blanket to cover her, showing a prudishness which was surprising considering her former trade. The child, Ralph, gurgled in a wooden box filled with straw and moss which Joe had gathered from the land, and he had washed his clothes too and fixed up a line between two trees where they would dry.

'Joe won't let you down,' Emily said nervously, 'and nor will I. We'll both work hard for you, Mr Linton, to make your farm a success and to thank you for your kindness.'

He put his chin in his hands. For heaven's sake, Emily, he wanted to say. I'm only here for you. I don't want this damned farm. If I'd wanted a farm I could have stayed at home in England! But he didn't say it, only nodded as he ate his soup.

'I – I need to know my duties, sir, and so does Meg, though Meg knows nothing about running a house. But I can teach her what I know, what I've been taught, and I think she might make a good cook. She made the soup,' she added.

'Emily,' he sighed, 'do what you think best; run the house as you wish. I didn't bring you here as my servant.'

So why did you bring her? he meditated. To bed her? No. To make her your proper wife? No, not that either, not yet. To rescue her then, from the terrible fate which was undoubtedly hers had she remained in Parramatta? He shuddered as he thought of the women who had clung to the railings at the gaol. Those women with dirty hair and scabby faces in their drab prison garments who had made obscene suggestions as he had come in through the gates. Have they always been so low or has life made them like that?

No, I can only ask her to be my wife when I have obtained her pardon. Only then can she once more hold up her head and know, as I do, that she is a modest and respectable woman. One who can choose independently whether or not she wishes to become a man's wife and not be beholden to him. And I can only do that by returning to England.

Chapter Thirty-Seven

The creek ran fast and strong and Philip and Joe stood side by side looking at it. 'You've done well to get this land, sir. If you've got water for stock you've fewer problems. I reckon', Joe said, looking about him, 'that nobody wanted this property because it's small. Everybody is going for a vast acreage and they don't seem to realize that just because the land is large it's not necessarily all good.'

'I agree entirely, Johnson. Some of the properties I was offered had acres of scrub which would need to be cleared before you could put a sheep or a cow on it.'

Joe rubbed his chin and looked thoughtful. ''Course, come high summer this creek might dry up. They get terrible droughts I do believe. I wonder if –?' He looked up the creek and then down to where it flowed towards the outskirts of Sydney. 'Just suppose we dug a pond, sir. We could divert the water to it while it's in full flow and we'd have water during 'drought.'

'Yes.' Philip was interested. 'That's a good idea. I could get some of the government men to do the digging and we could be ready before the spring.'

So it was agreed and Joe accompanied Philip into Sydney to arrange for labour and buy stock. 'I don't know owt about buying sheep, sir,' Joe admitted. 'Pigs, yes, and wheat and barley, but I don't know one sheep from another.' He grinned. 'Unless they're black sheep!'

'Well, I know a little, even though I'm a sailor. My family have kept sheep up on the Yorkshire Wolds for decades and I remember my father talking about the sheep going to Australia and saying that Merino were the best. So that's what we'll buy.' Though what Father will think of his son buying and tending sheep when he ought to be sailing the high seas, I can't imagine, he mused.

Joe remarked that the Sydney market reminded him of the markets in England. There were ducks, geese, chickens, cabbages, potatoes and hot mutton pies for sale. There were also melons and other exotic fruit which he hadn't seen before. There were fine carriages with liveried servants, and gigs and phaetons trundled along the wide streets; but beyond the fashionable part of town was the area known as the 'Rocks', where the first convicts had built their shacks and living accommodation, and which now was a broken-down, dissolute place filled with cheap lodging houses and brothels.

Whilst in town Philip went to a gun shop and bought a rifle and a lady's pistol, for he intended to teach Emily to shoot. There were dingoes about, the wild dogs of Australia which caused considerable damage to flocks, and he had been warned that there were occasional attacks on farmsteads by bushrangers and squatters. The settlers too complained that the Aborigines were wild and dangerous and camped on their land and wouldn't move unless by force.

A dozen men arrived a few days later with an armed soldier and digging began. Philip put Joe in charge of the men and told him to unlock their anklets. 'I can't expect men to work when they're hampered by chains,' he said, even though the guard protested, and he gave Joe the new rifle. 'I don't expect you to use this.' Philip looked at him keenly. 'It's only a precaution.'

'Just as well, sir.' Joe took it from him. ''Cos I don't know how. I'm not a violent man, never have been.'

'Then I'll give you a lesson later, as well as Emily and Meg. Just hold it as if you know what you're doing,' Philip added.

Two of the convicts disappeared the first afternoon they were freed, but on the third day one of them returned, saying he was hungry.

'You'll all get fed while you're here,' Joe told them. 'As much soup and bread as you can eat, but we'll expect you to work for it. Tha knows 'penalties just 'same as I do,' he stressed. 'If you abscond, your sentence is extended and you lose your privileges if you're caught. If you stay it means you'll have a better chance than you ever had in England.'

Within three weeks the pond was dug. Stone, old bricks and rubble were laid in the base and an outlet was dug towards the creek. As the last spade of earth was removed and the water gushed towards the pond, the men gave a cheer, elated with their efforts and achievement.

Philip bought sheep in the spring, a small flock of Merino as he had been advised; he also bought pigs, on Joe's advice, so that they would have bacon for the table and Emily asked for a cow and calf and a clutch of hens.

She stood looking down at the hens scratching in the dirt as Philip and Joe hammered nails into a hen coop they were building. 'Do you remember, Joe?' she said softly. 'Ma swapped me for a hen and a dozen eggs.'

Both men looked up. 'What?' Joe's forehead furrowed. 'What do you mean?'

She gazed into her distant memory. 'When Sam came to take me to Granny Edwards.' Her recollection was only hazy, but she said, 'He'd been sent to fetch you, only Ma wouldn't let you go. She said, "Leave me a dozen eggs and yon hen and you can take Emily."'

Philip was aghast. 'What a dreadful thing to do! Your own mother!'

Emily shook her head. 'I didn't know it at the time, but Ma knew that my father was dying and she must have realized that we would have to go to the parish workhouse. She sent me off to save me from that.'

Joe pushed his hat to the back of his head. 'Aye, she did. It was that same day that I lost my job on 'farm so we had no money coming in.'

'What happened to the hen?' Emily asked curiously.

'We ate it!' Joe said. 'She was a good layer as well.

But 'day after Da died, Ma wrung its neck. She said that it would be 'last good dinner we'd have in a long time. She was right an' all. We packed what was left of it into little parcels and ate it as we walked to Skirlaw workhouse.'

Later as Emily sat hemming a sheet by the kitchen fire, Philip came in and stood over her. She looked up and made to rise. 'Don't get up,' he insisted. 'There's no need.' He continued to gaze down at her, then he put his hand briefly on her head and stroked her hair. 'You've had a hard life, Emily.'

She looked startled for a moment and then bending her head, said, 'No, sir. Not until I met Hugo Purnell. It was after meeting him that things started to go wrong. It was all right until then. It was 'kind of life that I expected.'

'I'll make it up to you, Emily,' he said quietly. 'I swear to God I will.'

'You have already, Mr Linton.' She smiled at him. 'You have made my life so much better. And Joe's,' she added, 'and Meg's too.'

He sat in the chair opposite her and leaned towards her. 'When this place is up and running, I have to go back to England.'

'Oh!' Dismay showed on her face. 'Must you, sir? What will we do?'

'I must because I have things to attend to. I need money for a start. I'm living on bank loans out here and as to what you will do, you will carry on as if I am still here. Joe will look after the sheep and you will run the house.' He grinned. 'And Meg will do whatever it is she does besides play with the baby.'

'She's becoming a good cook,' Emily began.

'I know,' he agreed. 'I'll give Clavell authority to act on my behalf and any problem you can't deal with yourselves you can refer to him. He'll be a good friend.'

He noticed her anxious expression. 'Don't worry, it won't be yet. Not until the end of the summer anyway. And I'll be back as soon as I can.'

The summer was hotter than they ever imagined. Hotter even than when they had been on the ship. Emily spent most of the day indoors, for her fair skin burned and she only ventured out in the early morning and late evening. Meg, being darker, was not affected so much, though she always wore a hat and she took to doing things outside which previously Emily had done, such as feeding the pigs and chickens. Ralph, learning to crawl, stayed on the veranda or inside the house and Joe rigged up a fan above him to keep him cool.

Early one morning Joe came indoors looking for Philip, who was sitting at the kitchen table going over his accounts.

'There's an Abo wandering about. Shall I see him off?'

'What's he doing?' Philip looked up.

'Nowt,' Joe said. 'He's made himself a camp at 'top end of 'high field, just by some scrub. He's old, seems harmless.'

'By himself?' Emily asked.

'Aye, there's nobody with him.'

'Leave him then,' Philip said. 'He'll probably move off in a day or two. I don't think they stay in one place for long. They're too afraid of being shot at by the settlers.'

But about a week later, when Emily ventured out one evening as the heat of the day dispersed, she saw the native sitting cross-legged in a pair of cotton trousers and a worn cotton shirt, where Joe had said. His skin was wrinkled and dark and he did seem very old. She walked across to him and asked, 'Are you hungry?'

He nodded and patted his stomach. 'Empty belly, missis.'

'Come with me, then,' she suggested. 'I'll get you some food.'

He followed behind her. His back was bent and he loped along in a lopsided way. In his hand he carried a stick, but he seemed to have no other possessions. Joe and Meg were standing on the veranda as she approached and Joe stepped forward in some alarm. 'What do you think you're doing, Emily?' he said angrily. 'The fellow might be dangerous!'

'No more dangerous than some white men I've known,' she retorted. 'Meg, is there some of that salt beef left or any rice?'

'Yes.' Meg looked warily at the Aborigine. 'There is. I was going to use it for supper.'

'Give him some,' Emily said, 'and some bread. He looks half starved.'

'Oh well!' Joe said caustically. 'Invite him in to dine! We'll have all 'tribe arriving now and we'll not get rid of him if he knows he's going to be fed.'

'He's old,' Emily insisted. 'And he's alone. Be charitable, Joe!'

The old native took the food and touched his head to Emily and took himself off back to his place and didn't disturb them until three days later, when he arrived at the veranda trailing a dead dingo. He had his stick in his hand which he held up. 'Dingo kill sheep,' he muttered. 'Me kill dingo.'

'You mean he killed the dog with his stick,' Philip said incredulously when they told him.

'Aye,' Joe said. ''Said he did, and I found a dead sheep at top of 'creek. It had been well and truly savaged, but the others are all right. They must have scattered.'

'Better give him the dead sheep then if he wants it,' Philip said, then looked at Meg. 'Unless you were planning on cooking it, Meg!'

'I'll cook it if somebody'll skin it,' she said.

'Get the Abo to skin it,' Joe suggested. 'He can keep 'fleece and we'll share 'meat.'

When the native produced a knife from his pocket to skin the sheep, they looked at him in alarm. 'So he was armed all 'time!' Joe muttered. 'He didn't just have his stick.'

'He's all right,' Emily insisted. 'How else would he live without a means of killing his food?' She had seen feathers and the remains of rodents near to the Aborigine's camp. 'There's nowhere else for him to go.'

'Emily's right,' Philip said. 'The natives have been hounded off the land. They've been hunted like dogs or else been plied with liquor so that they've drunk themselves to death. There's not many of them left. Leave him. He'll go when he's ready.'

Towards the end of the summer when the pond was almost empty and the creek was running dry,

Joe came to Philip and said, 'Mr Linton, if you don't mind me saying so, this farm isn't going to make a profit if you don't get more stock. You could get a licence for running them into the hills outside your boundary.'

Philip took stock of Joe as they stood on the veranda. His face was brown, his bare arms were strong and muscly and he looked every inch a farmer. 'Come outside,' he said. 'I want to talk to you.' The two women were in the kitchen preparing the evening meal and Philip and Joe strolled through the paddock at the front of the house. 'I need to discuss something with you. I've seen how you work and I know that the one reason you work so hard is to obtain your freedom.'

'That's right, sir, and I might say that I wouldn't have had such a good chance if you hadn't come along. I couldn't have had a better master. But I'll leave when 'time's right. I want to be my own master so it's onny fair to warn you.'

Philip nodded. 'That's what I guessed and now I'll explain to you why I won't be buying more stock or expanding the farm. The reason that I am here at all has nothing to do with me wanting to become a landowner or starting afresh in a new country. The only reason I am here is because of Emily.'

Joe turned and stared. 'Emily, sir? Well, I knew that you wanted her for your housekeeper, Meg told me that, but Emily can come wi' me when I start up on my own, you don't have to feel behodden towards her!'

'No. You don't understand. I only came to this country *because* of Emily! I only discovered what had

405

happened to her when it was too late to do anything about it. I obtained orders to sail on the *Flying Swan* when I heard she was on it.'

He looked squarely at Joe, who stared in astonishment. 'What are you telling me, Mr Linton? That Emily means summat to you?'

'She does.'

'But you're a gentleman, sir. Emily's onny a servant lass. She's a good lass and a bonny one, but there's no getting away from 'fact that that's what she is! Course I know that some gentlemen do tek servant wenches for their mistresses, but –.'

'That's not what I want for Emily, Joe. And here's the crux of the matter. There's a ship sailing for England next week and I've obtained orders to sail with her. When I'm in England I shall stay until I've obtained Emily's absolute pardon. Then I shall return and ask her to marry me.'

Joe's mouth remained open. Finally he said, 'Well! I don't know what to say! Does that mean you'll tek her back or stop here? It'll be no life for her in England. An ex-convict woman marrying above herself! No.' He shook his head. 'It'll never work. You'll have to stop here.'

'That would be up to Emily. Besides, she might not have me.' He smiled as he spoke, but his eyes looked anxious.

'Not have you! She'd be a fool not to!'

'I'm telling you this in confidence, Johnson.' Philip became brisk at Joe's comment. 'Emily doesn't know of my intentions or why I'm returning to England. I shall tell her that it's to sort out my affairs. No point in building up her hopes.'

'So why are you telling me, Mr Linton?' Joe asked frankly. 'There was no need.'

'I'm telling you so that I'll be sure that you'll stay to look after things here, and to take care of Emily. You obviously have an affection for her.'

'Aye, I onny want what's best for her after all she's been through. I'm not a violent man as I've said, but I could kill that bastard who destroyed her.'

Philip gave a thin smile. 'I have him in mind, never fear. He won't escape lightly.'

'I'll stop, Mr Linton. I'll look after 'farm as if it was my own.' He put out his hand. 'You have my word on it.'

So can I trust a convict's word? Philip pondered as he walked back alone to the house and Joe went towards the creek. But he has nowhere else to go. He's a bit like the Aborigine, turned out of his own land, but unlike the native he has the chance to do something with the rest of his life. Should I have told him about my intentions towards Emily? And I didn't like the implication that Emily would be a fool to turn me down, as if I was her best offer.

Emily was sitting on the veranda and she got up as he came towards her. 'I wish you wouldn't do that, Emily.' He was nervous over what he was going to say and spoke sharply.

She looked startled.

'You don't have to get up every time I approach!'

'It's what I was taught, Mr Linton. It comes naturally now.'

'But what if you were a lady?' he admonished. 'What would you do then?'

'Why – I would remain seated, sir.' She had an

apprehensive expression as if she wasn't sure whether he was serious or not. 'And wait for the gentleman's bow.'

'Quite so!' He gave her a quick smile to show he was teasing. 'Come and sit over here with me. I have something to tell you.'

They sat on either side of the table and she poured him a cool drink of lemonade from a jug. He drank and then, putting down the glass, said, 'I saw Lieutenant Boyle in Sydney the other day. He told me of a ship sailing for England next week.' A flush spread across her cheeks as he added, 'I've obtained orders to sail with her.' He looked away from her, across the land towards the creek, where Joe was striding back for his supper. 'I've given Clavell the necessary authority to take decisions should there be any trouble here and Joe has promised he will oversee the farm in my absence.'

'I didn't think it would be yet,' she whispered.

He turned towards her and seeing her distress he impulsively reached across and took hold of her hand. 'It has to be! It's a fast ship and I might wait weeks for another. I have a special reason for returning home,' he appealed. 'I will come back as soon as I can. I promise.'

'You may not want to when you see England again. It will be spring there, you'll see the green fields and the blossom and the leaves curling open on the trees,' she said wistfully. 'I know I wouldn't want to come back.'

'But I also have a special reason for returning.' He held fast to her hand and absentmindedly stroked it.

'Ah, yes. You said you had to sort out your affairs at the bank. You'll be able to expand the farm if you come back. Buy more land and sheep.' She still looked pensive.

'Do you think that's the only reason I came here, Emily? Do you think that that was my design in coming here?'

She lifted her eyes to his, but would not give an answer to the hidden question. 'I have no right to question your motives, sir. I only know that you have changed my life.' Then she looked away. 'And I have given you nothing in return. You never asked,' she said softly.

Chapter Thirty-Eight

Philip thought of Emily as the ship sailed out of harbour and around the Heads and wondered if she was watching from the veranda as she had said that she would. One of the best things about the house was the magnificent view of Sydney Cove far below; to see in the harbour the crowded shipping fleet looking like toy ships, gathered from different parts of the world, from London or Shannon en route for China or New Zealand to trade in tea, silks, wool and other commodities.

He thought of her as the ship battled around the Cape and the seas washed over the decks and the canvas sails ripped into shreds from the tenacity of the trade winds. And as they passed the Canaries and felt the heat he was glad that the ship had no passengers below decks but only a cargo of tea and Australian wool for the English market. He remembered tenderly the brightness in Emily's eyes as he'd said goodbye and the startled flush as his emotions had got the better of him and he'd kissed her cheek. He'd said goodbye to Meg, who told him that he mustn't worry about Emily, that she would look after her, and he'd tickled Ralph under his chubby chin and thought of how he would have changed by the time of his return.

They've all been like family, even Meg and Joe, he mused, when three months later they sailed into Portsmouth, and after being released from his duties he travelled first by coach and then on horseback to his parents' home on the Yorkshire Wolds.

'Such a relief to have you home, Philip.' His mother beamed with delight. 'It's more of a worry, you know, when a son goes away than it is with one's husband.'

His father humphed at that and said, 'Your mother's done nothing but worry since you sailed, in spite of your letters!'

'Mama thinks you went off in such a hurry because you were lovesick, Philip.' His sister Anna smiled wickedly. 'She said you were either running away from a lady or chasing after one.'

He had the grace to blush. 'You might well be right, Mother, but I don't want to discuss it just now.'

'You always were so stubborn, Philip,' his mother said. 'Just answer one question and then I will question you no further. Is she of good family?'

'She has no family.' Only a convict brother, he deliberated, and no point in telling of him.

'Is she foreign?' his mother persisted.

'That's two questions, Mother,' he smiled. 'But no, she is as English as a rose.'

'Oh. So she's fair!' Louise said delightedly. 'Is she as fair as me?'

'I said I do not want to discuss her.' Philip was firm, he knew well how his sisters could cajole and persuade if they had a mind to.

'If there was a wedding I would wear blue,' Louise said dreamily and Philip shook his head in resignation. When he took his leave of them he told them that he would come back as soon as he could.

He took lodgings in Hull at the same house as previously, where he was sure of a warm feather bed and good food from his landlady. He then made his way to Mary Edwards's florist's shop in Whitefriargate.

'Mr Linton! How good to see you.' Mary Edwards took him through to her sitting room at the back of the shop and it was just as he remembered it, with a bright fire burning and a kettle humming on the bars. 'Do you have any news?' she asked anxiously. 'Mr Francis has written to you through the naval office, but you may not have received his letter.'

'Indeed I haven't,' Philip replied, 'and I regret I have been remiss in not writing to him or to you, but events seemed to take over. But perhaps you realized that I took the same ship as Emily out to Australia?'

'Indeed? How fortuitous!' said Mary. 'The Navy Office would only say in reply to Mr Francis's query, that you had gone abroad and they would send on the correspondence.'

There was an appeal in her voice as she asked, 'And what news? Did Emily withstand the journey? Is she well? We cannot contemplate the conditions these poor people have to suffer.'

He shook his head. 'I couldn't begin to tell you of the privations, Mrs Edwards, nor would I want to, though I am told that conditions are better than they once were.' He took a deep breath. 'But, thank God, transportation is coming to an end. There will be no more convicts going to New South Wales at any rate, and I managed to make Emily's journey a little more comfortable than it would have been.'

'At no cost to herself, Mr Linton?' He heard the hidden query beneath her words.

'None, I assure you, Mrs Edwards.'

Her face cleared. 'Forgive me. It isn't as if I distrust *you*. It's just that there are some very wicked people in this world which makes one question innocent motives.'

'I do understand; but I promise you I only have Emily's well-being at heart. And so,' he enquired, 'what of the villain? Has he been found? Is he to be brought to account?'

'He has been found. He is back at his house in Hessle. But he will not answer enquiries, neither will he let Mr Francis see his daughter and he – Mr Francis – is extremely worried about her. Even Mrs Purnell has not seen either of them, though I rather think she has washed her hands of her son altogether. That is what I have heard. I have also heard that he is in debt. He is spending Deborah's allowance as fast as his own.'

'Can Mr Francis not stop the allowance?'

'I don't think so. I believe it was written into the marriage contract. The only way it could be stopped is if Deborah could leave him and the marriage be annulled. But', she sighed, 'as no-one gets the chance to see her there is little hope of that.'

'What a worry for Mr Francis,' Philip murmured.

'So it seems that Emily's case is at stalemate too.'

She nodded. 'Mr Francis has been quite ill with the worry of it, I am very anxious about him.' She looked down and linked her fingers in her lap. 'There is something more. Mrs Francis has left. She has gone to live with her sister in Hampshire and says she is not coming back.'

'Not even to see her daughter?'

'No. There was never anything much between them. Mrs Francis cannot cope with any kind of illness. She hasn't seen her son in years.' Her eyes clouded. 'And she has had every opportunity.'

'I will think of what to do, Mrs Edwards. The matter has to be resolved.'

He rode out to the village of Hessle that evening to ascertain the whereabouts of the property and to enquire if there was anyone at home. On finding the house he discovered several carriages in the drive, lights flickering in all the rooms and the sound of music and laughter. He dismounted and handed the reins to one of several grooms waiting by the door and mounted the steps.

'Do you have an invitation, sir?' A footman barred his way.

'I've just got in from abroad,' Philip said in a jovial manner. 'I didn't realize I needed one.' He put his hand into his pocket and brought out a guinea, which he slipped into the fellow's hand. He winked. 'Purnell's going to be surprised to see me!'

The footman slid the money into his pocket and invited him in. 'I'm sure he'll be delighted, sir.'

He wandered around the various rooms. Card

games were being played in the library and a hard drinking session was obvious in the smoking room. He opened another door and found Hugo with his arms around a woman.

'Linton! What the devil! How did you get here?' Hugo's face was flushed, either with drink or lechery or possibly both, Philip assumed, for the lady was hastily adjusting her dress.

'I thought I'd pop up to see you,' Philip said heartily. 'I'd heard there was a party and as I've just got back from abroad –. Nice place,' he added, looking around at the sumptuous furnishings. 'Must have cost you a fortune!'

Hugo slapped the woman on the rear. 'Off you go, darling, I'll see you later.' He waited until she had gone out of the door. 'You should get yourself a rich wife, Linton. That's where all of this has come from.'

Philip raised his eyebrows. 'Really! I must take a leaf out of your book. I'm looking forward to meeting your wife. I haven't yet had that pleasure.'

'Er – she's indisposed at the moment. She won't be joining us tonight.'

Philip expressed his disappointment. 'Will she rest with so much going on?' There were great shouts of laughter, the crash of piano chords and the splintering of glass.

'Yes, she's at the top of the house, won't hear a thing. She prefers it up there,' he added. 'It's much quieter.'

'I've heard the most extraordinary rumours since I came back, Purnell!' Philip accepted a glass of wine and watched as Hugo spilt some over the carpet as he attempted to pour himself more. 'I heard from someone that – well, in very bad taste of course – but this fellow said that since no-one ever sees your wife, everyone thinks that –'. He dropped his voice to a whisper. 'They're saying that she's either dead or in an asylum.'

'They're saying that, are they? Well it isn't true!' He shook a finger at Philip. 'She just doesn't go out, that's all. She is a bit –!' He put a finger to his forehead and wiggled it. 'You know! I didn't know when I married her, of course, but seeing as we are married then I'll have to put up with it. I'll look after her.'

'And spend her money!' Philip gave an enforced shout of laughter.

'That's it!' Hugo roared. 'I knew you'd understand, old fellow.' He slapped Philip on the shoulder. 'I need the money!' He took another drink and drained his glass. 'God knows how I need the money. Do you know,' he poured himself more wine, 'that my mother, my very own mother, has cut off my allowance at the bank. Says I have to wait until she's dead.' He lifted up the bottle and shook it to get out the last drop. 'I hope I don't have to wait long!'

Philip cringed, then said, 'Can I go up and see your wife? I could scotch the rumours for you.'

Hugo looked at him through bleary eyes. 'I'd never get up the stairs, old fellow, and I don't know where Alice is.'

'Alice?'

'Alice who looks after her.' He gave a loud

hiccup and grinned. 'And me as well.'

'I'll go up on my own then, shall I? I'll tell Alice you sent me.'

Hugo had slumped into a chair and closed his eyes and didn't answer. Philip opened another bottle of wine which was standing on a table and refilled Hugo's glass, placing the bottle beside him, then slipped out of the room and up the stairs. He passed several rooms where he could hear peals of laughter and went up again on to another floor. He listened at several doors, but couldn't hear anything and came to one at the end of the corridor. He put his ear to it and heard the murmur of voices, one petulant and the other impatient. He knocked softly.

The voices stopped then he heard the pattering of feet across the room. 'Get back,' he heard someone say. 'You mustn't go near the door.'

The door opened a crack and a pair of eyes looked out at him. 'Yes?'

'Alice?' he said softly. 'Hugo sent me up.'

The door opened a little wider and Alice's face looked into his. Behind her he could see another slighter figure hovering. 'He said would you like to join him downstairs.'

Her face brightened, then she said, 'But what about her? She'll kick up a fuss. Unless I give her another dose?'

'No. No, don't do that. I'll stay and talk to her until you come back. There's no rush,' he grinned. 'Go and enjoy yourself.'

She slid out of the door and locked it, putting the key in her pocket.

'Shall I have the key?' he asked brightly. 'I could go in and talk to her.'

'Not likely,' she said. 'If she gets out there'll be no catching her. I know that madam!' She looked at him keenly. 'I don't think I know you, sir.'

'I'm an old friend from a long way back,' Philip lied. 'I've been abroad.'

'Ah!' She nodded and moved away down the corridor. 'Come and fetch me if she makes a row.'

When she had disappeared down the stairs he again knocked softly on the door. 'Mrs Purnell,' he called, 'can you hear me?'

There was no answer, but he was sure he could hear the sound of soft breathing against the door. 'Miss Francis.' He tried again. 'Miss Deborah!'

He heard the intake of breath and then a low voice. 'Who are you? Are you a doctor? Are you going to lock me up?'

'No!' He was horrified at the thought of her fear. 'I'm a friend of your father. He asked me to find out if you were all right. If you were well.'

'I'm not all right.' He heard the sob in her voice. 'Why doesn't he come for me? Papa! I want to go home!'

Philip rubbed his hand over his beard. What should he do? 'Miss Francis, Mrs Purnell –.'

'Don't call me by that name!'

This time he could hear hysteria in her voice. 'Miss Francis, are you sure that you want to go home to your father?'

'Yes, but Hugo won't let me. He says that Papa doesn't want me any more and I have to stay here with him for ever.' She started to cry. 'If I don't, he says he'll lock me up with all the mad people.'

Philip swore under his breath. What a hellish fiend Purnell was. Not content with ruining one young woman's life he was now ruining another's.

'Can you ride, Miss Francis?' he whispered and glanced down the corridor.

'Ride? Of course I can ride. What a stupid thing to ask.' Her voice was haughty and imperious and he was glad to realize that her spirit wasn't completely broken.

'If I can get you out of here, will you ride behind me and I'll take you to your father? You will have to trust me, even though you don't know me.'

There was a moment's hesitation before she said, 'The door is locked, how will you open it?'

Like this, he thought for only a second and slammed his boot against the lock. The wood splintered and he kicked again, breaking the panel and pushing the door open. 'That was easy, wasn't it?' He smiled reassuringly at the pale-faced young woman standing there with her hands clenched tightly together. 'Don't be afraid,' he said. 'If we can get out of the house I'll take you to your father. He's been very worried about you.'

She shook her head. 'He hasn't,' she whispered. 'He hasn't come to see me, not since we came here. Hugo and Alice said he didn't want to see me ever again, that I had been too naughty because I spit my medicine out at them.' She fingered her cheek. 'Alice hit me last time I did it.'

'Your father does want to see you and you haven't been naughty,' once more he reassured her. 'I'll take you to him. But I'm not sure how we can get out.'

'Oh, I know,' she said eagerly, 'we can go through the coal cellar. I tried once before, but Alice caught me.'

'Take what you need, then,' he said swiftly. 'A cape or coat and we'll go. It will be a big adventure,' he smiled and was gladdened to see a childlike expression of pleasure on her face. 'Come along, be quick.'

There was no need to use the coal cellar as, when they crept down the backstairs towards the kitchen, they saw the outer door wide open and one of the maids with her back to them trying to draw the fire on the range. They heard the sound of laughter coming from the servants' dining hall and crept silently through the rear passage and out through the back door. He took Deborah down the drive and bade her wait in the bushes whilst he went back to fetch his horse. He tipped the groom and rode away, collecting Deborah from where he had left her. Crying silently, she swung up behind him.

Chapter Thirty-Nine

He took Deborah to Mary Edwards's house. It was late and dark and he wasn't familiar with the road to Holderness where her father lived. He could also still hear her crying as she rode behind him and he was anxious regarding her welfare and state of health.

'This is a friend's house,' he said as he dismounted outside the florist's shop. 'A friend of your father's as well as mine. She will look after you whilst I ride to fetch your father.'

She looked at him with suspicion, but as Mary Edwards came to the door, her face honest and friendly, the distrust melted away and she became like a child who has been hurt and is looking for comfort.

'Come in, my dear.' Mary was all warmth and sympathy and led her to the fire. 'Come and warm yourself. Don't be afraid, everything will be all right now.' She took off Deborah's cloak and sat her by the fire and wrapped a shawl around her. Then she warmed a cup of milk and sprinkled nutmeg into it.

Deborah sniffed at it, then gave a sad smile,

'Betty Brewer used to give me this whenever I was unhappy or ill.' She wiped a tear from her cheek. 'I wonder if I will ever see her again?'

'I'm sure that you will,' Mary soothed. 'She's still housekeeper at your father's house.'

'Do you know her?'

'I did,' Mary answered. 'A long time ago.'

She turned to Philip. 'Mr Linton, I think that Mrs Purnell will be better staying with me tonight. She's chilled through and could not withstand the journey to Holderness. May I prevail on your good nature and ask if you'll ride to Mr Francis in the morning and ask him to come for her?'

'Of course. That was my intention. I will ride at first light.' He lowered his voice. 'I'll ask him also if he would bring a doctor with him. I think she has been on some kind of medication or substance. The effect may wear off with who knows what effect!'

Philip found Roger Francis the next morning with his farm beadle. He was just about to mount his horse and inspect the estate, but on Philip's news he immediately changed his plans. He ordered the carriage to be made ready for their journey, and called for the housekeeper to prepare for the return of his daughter. He looked pale and spoke in a breathless way, and rubbed on his chest nervously.

Philip refused a ride in the carriage and took the journey back slowly. He noted the vast landscape and tried to see it as if through Emily's eyes. The wide sky was painted with streaks of sunlight and masses of cloud formed and reformed as it was gently buffeted by the north-east wind. He stopped for a glass of ale and bread and ham in the bustling market town of Hedon and wondered if by any chance he could be following in Emily's footsteps, for this would have been the nearest town to Elmswell Manor, where she had once worked.

Roger Francis was so anxious about his daughter that he hadn't mentioned Emily, and Philip mused as he remounted and took the turnpike road towards Hull, that the question of a pardon lay in his own hands and his alone.

Philip called at Hugo Purnell's the following day and reminded him that he still owed him fifty guineas. 'The fact is, Purnell, I need the money now.'

'I don't even remember borrowing money from you,' Hugo said sullenly. 'When was it?'

'A long time ago! I consider I have been very patient.' Philip fished in his pocket. 'Here's your IOU. I've presented it at the bank but they won't honour it.'

'I can't pay it!'

'Nonsense!' Philip was scornful. 'You have this splendid house, beautifully furnished. You must have some money.'

'It's my wife's money that bought the house,' he growled, 'and I don't expect her allowance until the end of the month. I tell you I haven't got a *sou*.'

'Sell something, then.' Philip hardened his voice. 'Your wife's jewellery or a piece of furniture.'

'Can't.' Hugo slumped into a chair. 'The furniture's not paid for. I'm being pressed for payment and my wife doesn't have any jewellery. Besides, she's not here.'

'Not here?' Philip dared. 'Where is she, then?'

'God knows, I don't. She got out of the house and has disappeared.'

'What do you mean, got out of the house? Did you have her prisoner or something?'

Hugo poured himself a whisky, but didn't offer Philip one. 'She's off her head, you know. Got out the other night while I was entertaining a few friends.' He looked up at him and frowned. 'Weren't you here?'

'Was I invited?'

'I can't remember.' He ran his hand over his eyes. 'I don't know who was here. I've got rid of half the staff anyway for letting her get out. And I've just told that bitch Alice she can go. She was supposed to be looking after her.'

Philip had wondered at the absence of footmen and maids. A nervous kitchen maid had answered his knock on the front door. 'Well, be that as it may, Purnell. I need the money pretty badly and although we've known each other a long time, I'm very much afraid that I'll have to go to law to get it.'

Hugo stared in astonishment. 'You wouldn't?'

'I would. I consider I've waited long enough.'

'But I could go to gaol if you press!'

'Yes. And if I press then so will your other creditors. You'll lose your house and your possessions. Perhaps you should speak to your father-in-law,' he said, knowing he was rubbing salt into the wound. 'Surely he'll help you out?'

'You'd press me for a measly fifty guineas!'

'It might be measly to you but not to me!' Philip replied nastily. 'I'll expect to hear from you by the end of the week, otherwise I see my lawyer.'

He trotted briskly along the road towards Hull and saw a woman in front of him struggling with a large bag. He turned to observe her as he passed and then reined in. 'Hello. It's Alice, isn't it?'

She looked up. Her face was flushed and angry. 'What's it to you?'

'I've just been to the Purnells'. I didn't get a very warm welcome.'

She scowled at him and then said curiously, 'Weren't you there 'other night? Yes! You were. Did you let her out?'

'Her?' Philip asked smoothly. 'Of whom are you speaking?'

She tossed her head back towards Hessle. 'Mrs Purnell. Somebody broke 'door and let her out. It was you, wasn't it?' She spoke roughly, there was no respect in her voice and Philip guessed that she had probably been encouraged to be harsh with Deborah Purnell.

'It might have been. Do you know what the punishment is for keeping someone prisoner and under duress?'

'I only did what I was told,' she said sharply. 'I was only obeying him.'

'And I expect he paid you well for doing so. You were Hugo Purnell's accomplice in keeping his wife locked up.'

Her face paled and she began to look nervous. 'No. He made me do it!'

'But you enjoyed it, didn't you? You enjoyed

having someone of a higher class in your power. It won't look very good when it's brought to court, and I expect that Hugo Purnell will blame you entirely. He does that with people, doesn't he?'

She shifted uncomfortably and looked up and down the road as if for a means of escape. 'I don't know what you mean.'

'I was thinking of Emily Hawkins,' he said harshly. 'You know that she was transported to Australia because of Purnell? You wouldn't like that, would you?'

'I never meant anything.' She bit her lip. 'It's just that he persuades you. He promises everything. He said I could have some of her jewellery, but I never got any. He sold it to pay his debts.'

'Have you proof of that?' His voice was terse, his manner cold. 'When Mrs Purnell comes to claim it back, he'll probably say that you have stolen it.'

She looked up at him and he could see the beginnings of fear. 'Will she come back?'

He shrugged. 'She might not, but her father most certainly will. He hasn't been allowed to see her for weeks. Something is very wrong. I'd like to talk to you,' he added, softening his tone. 'I might be able to help you in this difficulty, but I would need something in return.'

'Huh,' she said derisively. 'That's what they all say!'

He viewed her with distaste. 'Don't misunderstand me! I need to know if you have any knowledge of what happened to Emily Hawkins. Of the child she gave birth to and the picture that was damaged.'

'I'll tell you,' she said slyly, 'if you'll help me. I've no job and no reference 'cos he wouldn't give me one. Give me a ride into town, I know an inn where we can talk.'

She was happy to talk once he had given her a glass of ale and a meal of meat pie and peas and had put a guinea on the table. 'I'll need more'n that,' she said with her mouth full.

'Not until I hear what you have to say,' he said firmly. 'First of all about Emily and the child.'

'He raped her. He told me that he'd taken Emily on his wedding night. Boasted about it. Said as he couldn't have his wife he'd have Emily.'

'Couldn't have his wife?' Philip recoiled at approaching such a delicate subject, but Alice, it appeared, had no such scruples.

'Never been near her,' she said, mopping up the gravy with a hunk of bread. ''Cos she's not all there and there's madness in 'family he daren't risk having any bairns! I know', she pointed a greasy finger at him, ''cos I slept in next room to hers with 'door open. Anyway,' she picked at her teeth with a fingernail, ''bairn that Emily had was stillborn. I said as much at 'time but he told me to keep quiet, and as for that picture –', she gave a coarse laugh, 'he said it was valuable, didn't he? Well, he'd got it from one of 'street artists in Florence when he was visiting there one time. He pointed them out to me when I went with him and his wife. There was hundreds of 'em, pictures of women I mean. Some were nearly naked, some were getting out of a tub, and some, well, I wouldn't tell a gentleman like you what they were up to. But he didn't pay more'n five bob for it, I know that for sure.'

He gave her the guinea and promised her two more if she would verify what she had said in court or in front of a lawyer. She agreed and told him that she was going back to live at her mother's and gave him the address. When he saw where she lived he knew that she would soon be glad of the further payment, and had no doubt that she would be willing to earn it. Now all he had to do was wait until the end of the week and hope that Purnell had no means of paying off his debt to him.

There was no money and no message by the weekend, so on the Monday morning he went to his lawyer to instruct him to press for the payment of debt.

'You may not get your money, Mr Linton,' the lawyer said ponderously. 'I have heard through various channels that Mrs Purnell's allowance has been stopped by Mr Francis.'

'I didn't think he could do that!'

The lawyer cleared his throat. 'It appears that the marriage may not have been consummated. This I must say to you is only what I have heard through chambers, and I tell you in confidence. If it is so, then the marriage could be annulled.'

Philip thought of Alice's words on the matter. So Deborah Purnell is free, he thought jubilantly, and she cannot be forced to go back. 'Go ahead', he said determinedly, 'and press the lawsuit. I want my money back and if I don't get it I want to see him in the debtors' prison.'

Chapter Forty

'There's somebody coming.' Meg narrowed her eyes as she looked down the hill. 'Somebody in uniform.'

'Mr Clavell?' Emily joined her on the veranda; she had just come in from feeding the hens. 'No,' she said, 'it's not. Who can it be?'

They watched as the rider came nearer. He didn't sit easily on his horse whoever it was. 'It's that beggar Boyle,' Meg said suddenly. 'What's he want with us?'

'I don't know,' Emily said uneasily and went inside to take off her apron.

'Good morning. I thought I'd drop by to enquire if everything is all right.' Boyle sounded quite pleasant as he dismounted.

'Come to see if we're still here, more like,' Meg muttered beneath her breath.

'Everything's quite all right, thank you,' Emily said calmly. 'Mr Linton made every provision for us before he went away.'

'Unusual situation.' Boyle's glance took in the house, the vegetable plot, the hen coop and the pigsty and the sheep grazing in the far pastures.

'I mean to leave a place like this in charge of a convict!'

'He didn't,' Emily said abruptly. 'Mr Clavell is in charge. He comes regularly. In fact we expect him today.'

'Oh.' Boyle looked disappointed. 'So where's Johnson?'

'Tending the sheep.' Emily didn't volunteer any more information and Boyle turned his attention towards Meg.

'And how is the child?' He grinned as he spoke as if he knew of something amusing.

'He's well,' Meg answered brusquely. 'Did you want to inspect him to make sure he's still here?'

'Not my place,' Boyle said dismissively. 'Nothing to do with me what Linton does. He can collect as many women and children as he wants.' Then he addressed Emily. 'I'd like to have a look around.' As she hesitated, he added, 'I'm thinking of buying a place of my own and bringing my wife out.'

She stepped down from the veranda and joined him and walked towards the creek. She felt uneasy, remembering his cruelty towards Meg and Joe and his attention to her at the beginning of the voyage.

'How does it feel, then,' he smiled, looking down at her, 'being almost free? Though of course you'll never be completely free will you, not when you're *housekeeper* to a gentleman?' He put a particular mocking emphasis on the word housekeeper.

'I've been a servant girl before, Mr Boyle,' she answered solemnly, not rising to his bait. 'I know my position and what is expected of me.'

They were approaching the creek and a small

copse of trees. 'You know your position, do you?' he asked. 'And what position is that?' He came closer to her and she edged nervously away. 'On your back, is it, Emily? Is that how Linton likes you?'

She felt a sudden terror and his round, flaccid face seemed to transpose into the thin-cheeked, gloating features of Hugo Purnell. In her fear she cried out and swung out at him and caught him on his chin. He grabbed her arm and held her tightly. 'What a little firebrand! Who would have thought it? Looks so sweet and innocent too.' He put his face near to hers and wet his lips with his tongue. 'Give me a kiss, Emily, and I'll say nothing about you assaulting me.'

She struggled to pull away, but he held her fast, leaning over her and straining for her mouth. Suddenly he gave a sharp exclamation and let go of her, putting his hand to the back of his head and dropping down to his knees. 'Ow! What the devil was that? I've been shot!'

But there was no sound. Emily looked around, there was no sign of Joe, who had a rifle, neither was Meg on the veranda holding the pistol as she might have been. She moved out of his reach and glanced at the other side of the creek and saw a movement amongst the trees. Boyle looked at his hand. 'I'm bleeding,' he gasped. 'I've been shot!'

'You can't have been shot, Mr Boyle,' she said hurriedly. 'We would have heard it.'

He made to get up, but was immediately struck again on the side of his forehead. This time they saw the weapon. A small sharp stone dropped to the ground. Boyle looked up. 'There's somebody in those trees. Look, over there. It's a black. A native. I'll have him whipped for this!'

'I don't see anyone,' she lied and the words died on her lips as the old Aborigine appeared in full view, with his stick held high in one hand and the other clasped as if holding something. Boyle put his hand for his pistol, but before he could draw it was hit on the hand by another stone.

'Don't,' she cried. 'Don't shoot him, he's harmless!'

'Harmless!' Boyle held his bruised hand in the other. 'He could have killed me!'

'Yes, he could,' she said nervously. 'But he didn't. He was protecting me.'

'Protecting you! Does Linton know there are dangerous blacks on his land?' Boyle backed away towards the house.

'Yes, as a matter of fact he does. He keeps an eye on the flocks and he kills the dingoes.'

'With a stone?' he said sarcastically.

'No, with his stick.'

As they approached the house, another rider was seen coming up the hill. He too was dressed in uniform and he swayed unsteadily on his mount. It was Clavell and Emily greeted him with relief. At least she would now be safe from Boyle.

'How de do, Miss Hawkins, Mrs Johnson.' Clavell slipped down from his mount and held onto the saddle to steady himself. 'Just thought I would pop round to see if there were any problems. How de do Boyle, what you doing up here?'

'Same as you, Clavell, visiting. But seeing as you're here perhaps you'd take a look at my head.

432

A damned black has just aimed a stone at my head. Damned near killed me!'

'If he'd wanted to have killed you he would have done. What was it? A warning shot?' He gave Emily a sly wink and she smiled tremulously at him. 'He probably thought you were trespassing on his land.'

'His land!' Boyle blustered, and winced as Clavell poked at his scalp. 'It's not his land, it's Linton's land!'

'Ah, yes, but he tolerates Linton because he doesn't move him off it. Not that he would think of it as his own land, mind. The natives don't claim the land, they consider the earth is free for them to roam just as their ancestors did.'

'Well, they'll soon be wiped out,' Boyle griped. 'And not before time.'

'It's just a graze.' Clavell turned away impatiently. 'You won't die from it.'

'You will excuse us, Mr Boyle?' Emily said, her voice calm though she was shaking. 'I have something to discuss with Mr Clavell.'

Boyle looked astonished at his dismissal, but as Clavell was already walking up the steps to the house, where Meg was standing with the baby in her arms and Emily was half turned away, there was nothing he could do but mount his horse and ride away.

'I'm drunk!' Clavell said as he sat down at the kitchen table, then he got up again and removed a flask from his coat pocket. He waved it in the air. 'I'd offer you a tipple except it's empty.'

'I don't drink spirits normally, Mr Clavell,' Emily said. 'Would you like a cup of tea?'

He shuddered but said yes, he would. 'Did you enjoy a drink, Mrs Johnson?' he asked Meg. 'Before you came to this pleasant land, I mean.'

'Yes, sir, I did. It was onny way I could forget about 'life I was leading.'

'That's it,' he nodded. 'That's what it does. Makes you forget.' He sighed. 'Except that it doesn't.'

'No, sir,' Meg agreed, 'it doesn't. Nothing makes you forget until you find something else to replace 'memory.'

'And for you it was the child?'

'And Emily, sir.' She smiled across at Emily, who was scalding the tea leaves in the pot. 'When I met Emily I realized there were some good people in 'world after all.'

He leant over and took the child from her. 'And this young fellow confirmed it. What will you tell him when he grows up, Mrs Johnson? What will you tell young Ralph about his beginnings?'

She looked startled and a little afraid. Then she put her head up. 'He'll be a free man in a young country, sir. There'll be no stigma attached to him. He'll be able to do whatever he wants.'

'And of his mother? What will you tell him of her?'

She hesitated. 'I'll tell him that there is no blame or shame attached to him regarding his mother's character. That she only did what she thought was right.'

He gave a gentle smile. 'Quite right, Mrs Johnson. The sins of the parents should die with them.'

She stared at him and her mouth trembled. 'It's all right,' he said softly. 'It's all right.'

He stayed and had something to eat with them and as he was leaving he asked Emily if she would like to accompany him on a journey the following day. 'I'm visiting a clergyman friend in Port Macquarie who has done much to improve the convicts' lives. He would welcome you,' he added, as uncertainty clouded her face. 'He likes to hear other points of view. You will be away one night and well cared for.'

She had no qualms about accompanying him and welcomed the chance of seeing another part of the country, but with a proviso. 'Providing that Joe is back tonight,' she said. 'I won't leave Meg alone.'

'Not even with your faithful native?' he asked.

She smiled and shook her head. 'Not even then.'

After he had left, she and Meg sat on the veranda as the afternoon cooled. Ralph was asleep in his cot and they could see far off a figure approaching from the pasture land. 'Clavell knows, doesn't he?' Meg said. 'He knows that Ralph isn't mine.'

'I think so,' Emily agreed, 'but it doesn't matter. He won't tell anyone. Here's Joe,' she said. 'Do you mind if I go with Mr Clavell tomorrow?' She rose as Joe approached and didn't see the doubt on Meg's face as she said that, no, she didn't mind.

Meg saw Emily off at dawn with Clavell and two escorts and busied herself during the morning while Joe went up to the pasture land. He came back for breakfast and she cooked bacon and eggs, then whilst he worked outside she tried her hand at making bread. Emily had told her how the cook she used to know had made it and she tried to remember what Emily had said. She made one batch which was heavy and leaden and then she made another which was only a little better. Then Joe came in and told of how his mother used to do it, so she made another batch, and by the time she had put it to prove for a second time and made some soup and cooked a chicken, the day had gone and it was time to put Ralph to bed.

'You're getting 'hang of it.' Joe poked the rising dough with his finger. 'It needs a hot oven if I remember right.'

'It's hot all right.' Meg wiped the sweat from her forehead. 'Just like me.'

'Why don't you tek a dip in 'creek while it's cooking? I'll keep an eye on 'bairn.'

'What and have that Abo staring at me!' She glared at him. 'Not likely!'

'He's not there,' he said mildly. 'He went off last night. Probably out of 'way after tekking a pot shot at Boyle. He hasn't been around all day.'

'Oh!' She was tempted. 'Perhaps I might then.'

'I'll bake 'bread if you like,' he grinned. 'Then we can have it for supper.'

She gloried in the coolness of the creek and walked back as the sun was dipping, casting long shadows over the land. She'd draped a fustian sheet around herself and washed her skirt and shirt, which she hung over the washing line.

'Here we are.' Joe placed the hot bread on the table and served up the soup. 'Come and sit down. Food fit for a king – or a queen,' he added as he glanced at her.

'I – er, I'd better get dressed first,' she said lamely.

'Who's to see thee? Tha's all right.' He didn't like to stare, but he thought her a fine-looking woman with her broad bare shoulders and the damp sheet clinging to her. She had lost the convict aura.

She smiled and sat down. 'It's very – comforting I think is 'word,' she said, 'to hear your accent. It sounds like home.'

'But thank God it isn't,' he said harshly. 'We might still be prisoners of 'Crown, but would we be sitting out on an evening in England eating fresh baked bread and soup? No, not us. In England I'd be trying for work and not getting it, going to 'soup kitchens and begging for some sustenance. And you, what would you be doing, Meg?'

She looked away. 'I'm shamed to think of what I'd be doing. Selling my body to some stranger for a crust or a drink.'

'Don't be shamed, Meg.' He leaned over and put his hand on her arm. She flinched, so he removed it. 'It wasn't your fault that you had to live like that.'

'No, I know,' she muttered, 'but it doesn't make me feel any better knowing that that's what I did, and my mother before me. I thought of summat Mr Clavell said yesterday, that 'sins of 'parents should die with them and I hoped that it was true.'

She looked across the table at him. 'I've never in my life had a conversation with a man until now, except for negotiating a price.' She gave an angry grimace. 'What do you think of that, eh?'

'I said, it wasn't your fault!' He tore at a piece of

bread. 'No more than it was Emily's for being raped by that bastard Purnell.'

'She's lucky is Emily, having you to care for her. And Mr Linton, he cares for her as well, you know, in spite of what happened to her!'

Joe nodded. 'He wants to marry her. He told me, but don't tell Em. He's gone to England to try for her pardon.'

'And she doesn't know?' Meg said in astonishment. 'So, if he gets her a pardon –.' She stopped, as if thinking. 'Then – might she go home? And if she does –'. Her face creased as if she was going to cry and she pushed away her dish of soup. 'I'll be left alone except for Ralph and it'll be just like England again.'

'If she wants to go back with Linton, then that's what she'll have to do,' Joe said softly. 'We can't hold her here if she doesn't want to stop.'

'We?' she questioned, looking at him with wide brimming eyes. 'You're a man! You can do whatever you want once you're free. I can't go back to England, how would I pay my passage? Not that I want to anyway,' she said defiantly.

'Don't you, Meg? Do you want to stop here?'

'I want to stop in this country, but –'. She swallowed hard. 'If I'm on my own I know what'll happen. I'll finish up on 'streets again like them whores down on 'Rocks in Sydney!'

'No,' he protested. ''Course you won't, there are more opportunities here than at home.'

'Huh! You're talking just like a man!' There was a frightened anger in her voice. 'I'm a whore! What else could I do but go back to my trade?'

'And I was a thief,' he said quietly, 'but I don't intend to become one again.'

They both sat silently and Meg gave a shiver. 'Here, you're cold, put this on.' He picked up a shawl which was draped over his chair and, standing up, put it around her bare shoulders. He looked down at her. 'You're a right bonny lass, Meg, and your tongue isn't as sharp as it used to be.'

She gave a half-smile. 'It's onny blunted 'cos I've not had 'chance to sharpen it lately. But I could.'

'On me?'

'Aye. Like when you come in 'house with your muddy boots on.'

He grinned. 'Why didn't you say summat then?'

She shrugged. 'Not my house – or my place.'

'You know that once I'm free I'm going to work for my own farm?'

'Aye, Emily said so.' Her voice was low and her expression cast down.

'Wilt tha come wi' me?'

She looked up at him. 'What do you mean?'

'I mean we could get married proper. Have our own place. Give Ralph a good start.'

'You're not feeling sorry for me 'cos of what I've just said?' Her tone was sharper, more like it used to be.

He laughed. 'That's more like it. More like 'woman I met on 'ship. And no, I don't feel sorry for you at all. I think I know what sort of woman thou art, Meg Johnson. One who'll work to get what she wants, given 'chance. Besides,' he looked away, 'you're an 'andsome woman like I said. A right bonny lass and you'd probably do better than me in different circumstances. I'm not much of a catch,' he said sheepishly, 'and I'd better tell thee now, I've not had much experience wi' women. I've not had 'chance,' he added, 'seeing as I spent most of my growing up in gaol.'

She gazed at him, a blank expression on her face. 'You mean it? You're asking me to marry you even though you know what sort of woman I was?'

'We've nowt to hide from each other,' he said quietly. 'We've no secrets, we couldn't start better than that.'

'Aye, that's true,' she agreed, then added, 'I've not been with a man in a long time, not since I met your Emily. She put me on 'straight and narrow.' She looked down as if she couldn't meet his eyes and he saw a soft flush on her cheeks, which made her look young and vulnerable. 'I've got no disease, no clap or owt, and it's not true what Boyle said about me going with every man on 'ship.'

'Don't think on that, Meg,' he pleaded. 'I've had chance to get to know you while we've been here, and I hope that maybe tha'll take me wi' all my faults, 'cos I've just as many as you.'

She raised her head and he saw there were tears in her eyes. 'Aye. All right then. Do you want –? Shall we –?'

'Aye,' he said softly and taking her hands in his he drew her to her feet. 'We can do. I could do to sleep in a proper bed again.'

Chapter Forty-One

The following morning Meg was awakened early by someone banging on the veranda door. She turned to Joe, who was still sleeping and gently touched his cheek. He smiled and turned towards her, reaching out to hold her.

'There's somebody at 'door,' she whispered.

'Damn! It's all right, I'll go,' he said as she threw back the blanket. He slipped into his breeches and after checking that Ralph was still sleeping, she put a shawl around her nightshift and followed him to the door.

The old Aborigine was standing there. He looked at them and then muttered, 'Young missus?'

'She's not here,' Joe answered gruffly. 'What do you want?'

He shook his head and turned away. 'See young missus.'

'Come back later,' Meg called after him. 'After dinner.'

'I wonder what he wants,' Joe said as they went inside. He bent to pick up the water pail.

Meg ran her hand gently over his back where his

441

skin was scored by lash marks. 'Is this what Boyle did?'

'Aye.' He put down the pail and put his arms around her. 'Him and a dozen others.' He nuzzled into her neck. 'I didn't know it would feel so good,' he whispered and kissed her lips.

'Nor did I,' she whispered back. 'I feel as if I've been reborn.'

'Come on.' He took her hand and led her back upstairs. ''Sheep can look after themselves for once.'

Emily returned later in the day, tired but brighter for the excursion and full of the happenings of the journey. 'Mr Clavell showed me which were eucalyptus and gum trees, and we saw a strange creature by the river called a platypus. Oh, and at night there were koalas climbing in the gum trees, and we saw kangaroos, such funny animals, and great masses of parrots in the trees. And the sea was such a beautiful colour, not grey like the sea at home sometimes is,' she added, always comparing, never forgetting the landscape of her birth.

'And Mr Fowler, the clergyman was such a nice gentleman, and so kind that I didn't feel inferior at all as he asked my opinion on so many things. And, what's more, I ate supper with him and his wife and Mr Clavell!' She related all of this with such excitement that both Meg and Joe laughed.

'Well, you're not inferior, Em,' Joe said. 'You were born to good, hard-working parents. Nowt wrong wi' that, in my opinion.'

'That's what Mr Clavell said. He said that such

people were 'salt of the earth and that I shouldn't have so much humility.'

She didn't tell all that Mr Clavell had imparted. That he had heard from Philip Linton; a letter had been delivered from a ship just arrived in harbour. She had at first been disappointed that he had not written to her, but she was immediately wreathed in smiles when Clavell had handed her a sealed letter which had been enclosed with his.

'He is always circumspect, our Mr Linton,' he said as he handed it to her. 'He wouldn't want a letter to you to be delivered into the wrong hands.'

She had opened it with trembling fingers when she was alone and although it was brief, it was to her like a breath of English air.

'My dear Emily,' he wrote. 'By the time you receive this letter I hope to be on the journey back to Australia. I have obtained orders to sail and providing my business here is completed satisfactorily, I shall be back in Sydney Harbour by the spring. I have great hopes of good news to bring with me, but will not impart it in case I raise your hopes too high, so will beg of you to be your usual patient self and be assured that I think only of your safety and preservation at all times.

Your sincere friend,

Philip Linton'

He had put a postscript at the end. 'I visited Roger Francis in his home at Elmswell Manor and found it to be in a fine country.'

My dear Emily! Your sincere friend! she'd breathed joyously, and he has been to Holderness! She shed a few tears at the thought of him being where she longed to be, but a spring of joy kept pushing up as she thought of him crossing the ocean towards her and that soon she would see him. Mrs Fowler remarked on how well she looked at supper and although she could eat little as she was shy in such splendid company, she felt quite at ease when she was included in the conversation.

'You know that Mr Linton cares for you, Emily,' Clavell remarked on the journey back, as they bumped along the road in the hired chaise. 'Do you consider that at all?'

'I believe that perhaps he does, sir.' She'd bent her head to hide her embarrassment. 'I have not treated him as well as I should.'

'You mean that you have not been more than a housekeeper, even though it is accepted by the world at large that you have?' he'd said bluntly. 'Come, my dear, I know you are of modest nature, but these are enlightened times. You must follow your heart to achieve happiness.'

'My heart is happy that I have his consideration, Mr Clavell,' she'd replied honestly. 'It's what I wish for more than anything else, to have his regard for me.'

There was something in the atmosphere when she arrived back at the farm. She had been worried about leaving Meg alone with Joe in case they quarrelled. There had been a few sparks fly between them recently, but now they seemed pent up about something.

'Have you two been arguing?' she asked. 'If you have, you must settle it. You know I can't abide it when you quarrel!'

'Us?' Joe put his hand to his chest. 'Who? Me and Meg? Would we do that, Meg?'

Meg too looked equally astonished. Then she said, 'Well, yes we did, Joe. Be honest. We did have that small argument.'

'Ah, yes!' he said. 'So we did. Do we ask Emily her opinion or do we fight it out between ourselves?' He couldn't hide the huge grin on his face.

'Joe Hawkins!' Emily warned. 'What have you been up to? Have you been upsetting Meg?'

He shook his head. 'We couldn't agree on whether we should ask 'parson to marry us now or wait for Mr Linton to come back. What do you think, Emily? What should we do?'

She flung her arms around the two of them. 'I thought you would always be at loggerheads,' she said. 'I'm so happy for you!'

'We probably will be,' Joe grinned. 'Meg's not going to be 'meek little woman I allus thought I'd marry.'

'Oh, you need a strong woman to keep you right,' Meg laughed, and Emily thought how lovely she looked. So regal and handsome, her sun-browned skin glowing with health, no sign of the scabs or gaol sores that she had once had.

'Please wait for Mr Linton,' Emily said. 'I've had a letter; he hopes to be back in three months.'

They were interrupted in their conversation as the old Aborigine came across the paddock. 'I forgot to tell you, he came looking for you, Emily,' Meg murmured. 'He wouldn't say what he wanted.'

Emily signalled for him to come onto the

veranda, but he preferred to wait below the steps, so she went down to him.

'This is for you, missus.' He held out his hand. In it was what looked like a lump of dried-up mud.

'Thank you,' she smiled politely, turning it over. 'You're very kind. What shall I do with it?'

He shrugged his shoulders. 'White folk collect it.'

'What is it, Em?' Joe stepped down beside her. 'What's he given thee?'

She opened her palm to reveal the brown mud with yellow staining. She scratched at it with her fingernail.

Joe took in a deep breath. 'Gold! He's found gold! Emily – tha could be rich!'

'But where did you find it?' Emily asked the native. 'Is it yours?'

He spread his arms to encompass the land. 'All mine! My father's, my sons' and grandsons'.'

'Where's 'old devil found it?' Joe was trying hard not to show his excitement.

'Thank you,' Emily said. 'Thank you very much. Are you sure I should have it?'

The old man nodded. 'More in the creek. You want some?' he asked Joe.

'Yes! Yes. Please! Will tha show me?'

'But Joe, it's not our land. We're not entitled –', Emily began.

'Everybody's entitled if it's not on somebody else's land,' Joe said decidedly. 'And if it's on Linton's land then we'll dig it for him.'

'But you must keep it quiet, Joe,' Meg broke in. 'If 'authorities find out about it, they'll take it from you. You're still a convict, remember? Nobody will accept that it's yours. They'll say you stole it.'

'Aye, that's right, they will.' Joe's enthusiasm abated a little. 'But I'm still going to look and I don't have to tell anybody. Will you take me?' he asked the native.

He shook his head. 'My grandson. He take you. Tomorrow, for three days. I mind sheep for missus.'

The old man brought his grandson Benne before daybreak the following morning. Joe was ready and waiting for them. He'd packed a shovel and a pick and a roll of chicken wire for a sieve into a sack. He also had the rifle, but the young man, handsome but sullen, shook his head when he saw it. 'Soldiers shoot us if they see rifle,' he stated.

'Will there be soldiers?' Joe asked.

Benne shrugged. 'Soldiers everywhere. Looking for bushmen and crappy convicts.'

Joe wondered why the old native had offered them the gold. There was no love between the Aborigine and the English, and the natives considered the convicts to be the lowest order on earth, even below themselves, who had been hounded from their hunting grounds, to be beaten and tortured and their women taken into slavery and prostitution.

Meg gave them bread and cheese for the journey, which Joe put into the sack and they set off, the old man going with them to the boundary of Philip Linton's land. 'He look after you good,' he said. 'You do what he say.'

They followed the creek, climbing ever higher, the watercourse wide in some places and running through meadow-like land with patches of scrub, then narrowing through ravines, where the water rushed down in great torrents, falling over hidden rocks. By dawn Joe was sweating and he was thankful that it wasn't high summer, but even so there was heat in the sun when it came up and soon the flies were swarming around them. He felt the bite of mosquitoes and saw the dart of lizards and heard the screech of cockatoos and the chattering, coloured cloud of budgerigars flying above them.

They stopped at noon beneath the grey-green foliage of tall eucalyptus which gave them shade and Joe brought out the bread and cheese and handed it to Benne. Surprise showed on his dark face as he was offered it, but he tore off a piece of bread and ate it. 'It's good,' he said as he chewed. 'Is that your missus?'

'Yes,' Joe replied with a grin. 'She is.'

'Are you crappy convict?'

Joe shook his head, knowing that he meant the Irish, whom the Aborigines hated even more than the English. 'No. Assigned man.'

'Ah!' Benne chewed thoughtfully on the bread and then went to the creek and drank, cupping his hands to collect the water. Then he bent down and scrabbled with his hands in the mud at the side of the bank and brought out two grey-brown eggs. He cracked one of them and tipped it into his mouth, then handed the other one to Joe. 'Eat,' he said. 'Good.'

Joe hesitated. The shell looked old. 'Is it duck?'

Benne shrugged. 'Eat,' he said, so Joe cracked it,

looked to make sure that nothing was about to hatch from it and swallowed it whole.

'I come and work for you?' The question was direct. 'My grandfather said I can – if we find gold.'

Joe made his decision fast. 'Yes. Until master comes back.' Then he asked, 'Don't you want gold?'

The boy shook his head. 'No. Can't keep it. I want sheep.'

Joe grinned. 'If we find gold you shall have as many sheep as you want and so will I.'

They rested until the afternoon and then moved along again. They heard the sound of voices and up on the skyline saw the flash of red tunics which denoted soldiers. They flattened themselves on the ground beneath the shelter of bushes and ferns until they had gone, and then moved up once more, until Benne called a halt by an outcrop of rock which hid in its hollows nests of snakes and enormous spiders. The creek ran through a gully, here at only a trickle, and Benne crouched down on his haunches. 'Here,' he said, running his fingers through the water. 'Here grandfather says he find gold.'

Joe put down his sack and he too let the water run over his fingers. He scooped up the mud from the bottom and let it trickle through his fingers. It was only mud and grit, no yellow staining. 'Can't expect to find it straight off,' he muttered and bent to open up his sack. He took out the shovel, the pick and the chicken wire and threw the sack against the rock. A snake, disturbed by the movement, slithered out of one of the hollows and down the rock, where it disappeared into the undergrowth. Joe grimaced.

'Poison!' Benne said. 'Don't touch it.'

'I won't.' Joe took a step towards the rocky hollow where the snake had been resting. It was lined with dried leaves from the gum tree and where the snake had slithered out there was a line of yellow staining running down the rock. 'Look!' he called to the boy. 'Look here.'

He felt a great well of excitement rising up inside him as he followed with his eye down the rock across the rough earth and rock towards the creek, where Benne was still crouched. A seam! 'Thy granda was right,' he beamed and shook his arms in the air. 'It's gold!'

Chapter Forty-Two

The old Aborigine stayed away all day after Joe and Benne had gone, but as dusk fell he arrived back and sat on the veranda steps. Meg gave him soup and cold mutton, which he took without thanks, but when Emily came out he grunted, 'Master get dog, look after sheep, keep dingo away.'

'That's a good idea,' Emily said. 'I'll see to that.' The Reverend Fowler had a house dog she remembered, he would probably know where to get one.

The Aborigine stayed all night on the veranda steps. Emily got up before dawn and, looking out, saw his dark figure merging with the shadows and felt safe because of his presence. Anyone coming to the house, not knowing he was there would not have seen him, but as the morning broke he had gone, slipping away to the pasture and the sheep. He did the same thing that night, blending into the darkness and shadows of the veranda like a chiselled wooden sculpture.

'I wonder why he comes here,' Meg said as they ate breakfast. 'Do you think he has any other family but the boy?'

'Mr Clavell said that the natives are being wiped out,' Emily pondered. 'I think that perhaps there's just him and Benne left of their family and that the old man wants Benne settled with someone before he dies. He looks so very, very old.'

When he returned that evening to his customary place, he said to Emily, 'Tomorrow they come back. You keep Benne here? He help with sheep till master comes on ship?'

Emily agreed. She didn't think that Philip would object, the boy wouldn't cost much to keep and he would be useful to have around the place.

It was late evening when Joe and Benne were seen in the top field. Joe was running and the boy was following after. Emily and Meg stood waiting for them. 'Something's happened!' Emily exclaimed. 'I can sense the way he's running, just the way he used to when we were young.'

He was waving his arms in the air and had a huge grin on his face. He met the old Aborigine first and took him by the hand, shaking it vigorously, then on reaching Emily and Meg, who had come down the steps and into the paddock to meet him, he took hold of each of them and swung them round. 'We found it,' he said breathlessly. 'We found gold!'

'Where is it?' Meg asked eagerly. 'Did you bring it back with you?'

'No.' He shook his head. 'At least onny a scraping, just for proof. We're going to have to do some thinking about this. It's not on Linton's land but just above it. We're going to have to buy it and then stake a claim.'

They gave the old man and Benne some supper and then went inside. 'We can be rich!' Joe said. 'But it needs thinking about. The seam isn't far from a main track; we saw soldiers up there and if word gets out 'place'll be swarming wi' folks.'

'You're off your head, Joe,' Meg said. 'How can we possibly buy it? We haven't a penny between 'three of us! And even if Mr Linton buys it when he comes back, it still won't be ours!'

'And if we wait for him, somebody else might get to it before us.' Joe looked at Emily. 'Who would you trust apart from Linton, Em?'

'Mr Clavell,' she said softly. 'He's the only one. I could talk to him about it. But we'd have to wait until he comes again and it might not be yet, he's going to be busy. He told me he's trying to get the women organized into work groups.'

'If we could onny get to him,' Joe said thoughtfully. 'But I can't go. I'd be picked up as an absconder. What about you going, Em? What's 'road like? Could you ride so far?'

'On my own?' She was horrified.

''Course she can't!' Meg was sharp with him. 'She might get robbed or beaten or owt with all 'villains that are skulking about in this country.'

'I didn't mean on her own,' he argued. 'Would I suggest that to my own sister? No, I meant wi' Benne. I'd thought of Clavell when I was trying to work out what we could do and I asked Benne if he knew 'road to Parramatta. He does, but he also knows another one across country, where there's little traffic. He'd take you if you'd go.'

'I'll think about it,' she said and went early to

bed. She tossed and turned all night, thinking of the journey she had made with Philip Linton when he had brought her out of Parramatta. I rode behind him with my arms about his waist, she sighed. If only he was here now. But he's not and I have to make a decision. I'm not a horsewoman, I've only been on the horse's back half a dozen times. Suppose he throws me or Benne runs off and leaves me on my own? I could get lost and the hills look so wild.

She rose at dawn, heavy eyed and tired, but she had made up her mind. If one of us was ill, perhaps the baby, she had thought, then somebody would have to go for help into Sydney and it would have to be me. Parramatta is no further in distance. I'll speak to Benne and ask him if he thinks I can manage the journey.

Benne nodded when she asked him. 'You'll be all right with me, Missus Emily. I know good way to Parramatta. No soldiers, no crappy convicts. Maybe bushrangers, but they'll not see us.'

How will they not see us? she thought. I'd better wear dark clothing. But as they set off the next morning she realized that they wouldn't be seen because Benne had insisted they set off before dawn, when the sky was still dark but lit by a million stars and the trees and shrubs beside the track where he led her horse were dark and forbidding. She was terrified and kept her head and shoulders hunched down as tree branches tore at her hair like demented fingers.

They travelled up steep hills and then descended into scrubland before rising again towards woody paths. She could hear the screech of nocturnal animals and a croaking and chattering in the trees of animals and birds and creatures, which she only glimpsed as they fled or hid within the shadows, and had no idea what they were or if they were dangerous. 'A bear!' she hissed as a lumbering creature crossed their path.

He shook his head. 'Wombat,' he said and continued on, seemingly tireless as he jogged along beside her. As the night sky started to lighten, they entered a clearing where below them was the main road to Parramatta and beyond that the Parramatta River and Emily realized that they were probably more than half-way there. Benne went first towards the road and checked that there was no-one else travelling along it. It was still too early for most travellers, unless for some reason, like them, they didn't want to be seen, and they crossed the road undisturbed.

Benne took her to the edge of the town, where trees had been felled and a clearing opened up to make a parkland. Fine houses had been built and through the windows Emily glimpsed muslin curtains and Chinese ornaments set on the windowsills, whilst working outside in the gardens were men with chains around their ankles.

'I wait here, Missus Emily, and take you back when you are ready.'

She nodded nervously, but putting her shoulders back and lifting her head, she urged the horse on towards the Female Factory beyond the town.

She found Clavell where she had expected him, in the sick ward. 'Whatever are you doing here,

Emily? You never came alone?' His astonishment was great.

'I came with an Aborigine,' she said. 'Benne, the old man's grandson; he guided me across country. We couldn't come on 'main road because I'm a woman, an ex-convict and might have been molested, and he's a black native and would probably have been arrested on some made-up charge for accompanying a white woman.'

'Then the reason for your being here must be very important,' he said slowly, pulling out a chair for her. 'If you travelled all that way in the dark, for it is still early, and risked God knows what on the road.'

She sank gratefully into the chair. 'It is,' she said. 'Is someone ill, or – have you had news from England?'

'No-one is ill and I regret I have no news from home.' She glanced towards the door and then towards the beds. 'But we need your help, Mr Clavell. Can you come back with me?'

'If it is urgent I can.'

'Mr Clavell,' she said earnestly, 'are you a rich man?'

He laughed. 'Rich! Certainly not. In fact I have never been poorer. I'm living on my late wife's money because I cannot live on what I earn. It will just about last until I die, providing I don't live to a ripe old age!'

She smiled. 'Then I think it's important that you come back with me, sir. You are the only man we can trust and that trust we have in you could earn you a lot of money.'

He laughed again. 'What jest is this, Emily? Come along, tell all.'

'No jest, Mr Clavell.' She lowered her voice. 'I'm talking about land and I'm talking about gold!'

He borrowed a horse, telling the governor that he had to attend someone who was very sick, and travelled back with her and Benne, again across country. This time they travelled in daylight and Mr Clavell carried a pistol and, he said, he knew how to use it. It was dusk by the time they arrived back at the farmstead and Emily was almost dropping with exhaustion, but Benne jogged along as easily as he had done during the morning.

Clavell talked with Joe right through the night, whilst Emily dozed by the fire and Meg went to her bed. By the morning it was settled. Clavell refused the offer to visit the seam to see for himself. 'If you trust me enough to tell me,' he said, 'then I trust your word that the gold is there. Gold has been found from time to time over the last decade, somewhere by the Blue Mountains and also by the Fish River, but there was no real prospecting done. However, if there is a seam, we must keep it quiet; if the word gets out the whole place will be over-run by diggers.'

He stretched himself. 'I'll go down to Sydney straight away and apply for a grazing licence. I'll buy two flocks of sheep –.'

'Make it three, sir,' Joe interrupted. 'If we fill the area, nobody'll come on it.'

'Right. Then I'll apply to buy the land if it's for sale.'

'That's it, sir. Then I'll take down Mr Linton's fence in 'far field and we'll let 'em all graze together.'

Clavell looked at him. 'What do you have to lose in this venture, Johnson?'

'Nowt, sir. I've been at 'bottom. I can't go no further down.'

'As I thought.' Clavell stood pondering. 'I have everything to lose. If this fails I shall be left with nothing. Yet I have a hunch that it will work.' He turned to Emily. 'Come along then, Miss Hawkins. Put on your bonnet.'

'Am I to come with you, sir?' She was so tired that all she wanted was to go to bed.

'Of course. We need two signatures for this partnership and as your brother can't sign due to his present situation, then you must. You, to all intents and purposes are free!'

She gazed sleepily at Joe, who noddingly agreed, so she went to swill her face and brush her hair and as she came back into the kitchen she heard Clavell say, 'So, the name as agreed. You're quite sure?'

'Quite sure, sir. I'll be glad to have it back.'

'Very well.' They shook hands on the agreement. 'Clavell and Hawkins it is.'

Chapter Forty-Three

Philip rode up to Hugo Purnell's house and saw men carrying furniture, mirrors and beds from the house and placing them in a wagon outside the open front door. He dismounted and approached one of the men.

'I'm looking for Mr Purnell,' he said. 'Is he at home?'

'Everybody's been looking for him, governor,' the man answered grimly. 'And now they've found him. If you want him he's in gaol – debtors' prison in Kingston Street. Don't expect any money, wilt tha, sir?' he called after Philip, as he turned away. 'There's a line of folks before thee as long as 'road between here and Hull.'

'In that case, I'll pay him a visit.' Philip couldn't help but feel a sense of satisfaction that Purnell was in the same gaol where Emily had been confined.

'Linton! Thank God!' Hugo Purnell clung to the bars of his cell. 'Get me out of here, there's a good fellow. I promise I'll pay you back every penny.' There was a look of anguish on his face, his shirt neck was undone without a cravat and he was huddled into his greatcoat. 'I don't even know where my mother is, she'd get me out if she knew I was here.'

Philip gave a grim smile. 'I've heard around town that your mother has gone abroad. The house is shut up with only a skeleton staff.'

Hugo groaned and put his head in his hands. 'Where are all my friends when I need them? They were willing to drink my wine and eat at my table before this happened. Now the beggars have gone – don't want to know me.'

'Could it be that you owe them money?' Philip said cynically. 'And what about your wife? Do you know what happened to her after she ran away? Has it crossed your mind that she might be in trouble?'

'Hah, good riddance to her! Do you know, her father wrote to me saying he was stopping the marriage allowance and that we were not man and wife in the true sense. Hah, how would he know?' His face creased into laughter. 'Do you know! Deborah spun them such a tale about us being together on the ship, that when I asked to marry her they couldn't agree fast enough. 'Course, her father was most disagreeable, claimed I'd taken advantage and all that.'

'And had you?' Philip asked, stony-faced.

'What! She's loony, old boy. Would I risk that? No, as far as I'm concerned she's as pure as driven snow and who wants a woman like that? Besides,' he shivered and huddled into his coat, 'I prefer a woman with a little more flesh.'

'Someone like Emily, perhaps?' Philip felt his anger rising and he clenched his fists.

'Emily? Oh you know Emily, do you?' He gave a

grin. 'Now there *is* a woman!' He leaned towards Philip. 'Come on, old fellow, you've always been a good sport. Get me out of here. I'll pay you back as soon as I can.'

'I'm not interested in the money.' Philip stared at him through the bars. 'I just wanted to see you in here, where you belong.'

'What?' Hugo blustered. 'A man like me, of my standing?'

'You're a liar, a braggart, a libertine, a seducer of innocence.' Philip spat at him. 'I could think of a dozen other names, but I don't want to waste my energy. But I wonder if you have ever given thought of the effect you have had on that young woman's life? Have you ever thought what it must be like to be chained up on board a convict ship?'

Hugo turned away. 'I've changed my mind about you, Linton. You are the most boring fellow I've ever met and if you're not going to get me out of here, you might as well leave.'

Philip grabbed hold of him through the bars and pulled him towards him. 'Go to hell! I hope you rot! But I'll tell you this before I leave; the only way I would try to have you released is if you retract your statement about Emily having damaged your painting and to say that, against her wishes, you fathered her stillborn child.'

'What's she to you?' Hugo glared at him. 'Fancy her yourself, do you? You'll have to travel a long way to find her!'

'I hate injustice, Purnell, and if you don't retract I shall go to the magistrates and state that there has been a grave miscarriage of justice. The case should never have been brought and I consider that the court was given false information. If there is an appeal, you may well find yourself following in Emily's footsteps.'

As he released his hold on him, he added as if in afterthought, 'Oh and by the way, I understand that your wife's father is about to sue you for the return of her dowry and her jewellery. There is a witness who is prepared to swear that you sold the jewels to pay your debts. That will add to the case against you.'

Purnell said nothing, but slunk to the back of his cell, where he curled up into a corner on his bench. Philip turned away and walked to the end of the corridor, where the warder was waiting. Then he turned and retraced his footsteps. He stopped at the cell gate. 'If you should change your mind about retracting, Purnell, I shall be at my lodgings until tomorrow evening. Then I have orders to sail. I won't be back in this country for at least six months.'

By midday the next day a message was brought that Purnell wanted to see him urgently. Philip waited until the following morning, just to give Purnell a fright, and then took his lawyer with him to the gaol.

'All right! I'll retract the charge,' Purnell said. He looked even more haggard than the day before. His eyes were heavy and he had a dark growth of beard. 'Say anything you want, but get me out of here.'

The lawyer took a statement and Purnell signed it, with Philip and the governor of the prison as witnesses.

'So, can I go?' Purnell asked the governor. 'Will you call me a cab?'

'I'm afraid not!' The governor observed him coolly. 'That isn't the procedure at all. There are other considerations which will keep you here a little longer apart from Mr Linton's dues.'

'What? But Linton – you said –.'

'I said that I would try to have you released. I will return the IOU to you as settled as soon as Miss Hawkins receives her full pardon. You have my word on that. But I have nothing at all to do with the other charges made against you.'

'You've tricked me, Linton!' They heard his furious shouts as they walked away down the corridor and even as the gate clanged shut behind them.

Philip shook hands with the governor. 'Thank you for your help in the matter. I am much obliged.'

When he returned to his lodgings that afternoon there was another message waiting, this time from Mary Edwards, who urged that he visit her with all possible speed. He walked quickly down Savile Street and across the Junction Bridge to Whitefriargate and knocked on the door of her shop, which surprisingly had a closed notice on it.

Mary Edwards lifted the door curtain and on seeing him, opened the door. Her face was pale and her eyes red-rimmed. 'Please come in, Mr Linton, and forgive me for involving you, but I have just learned some tragic news.'

He followed her into her sitting room and was surprised to see Deborah Purnell sitting by the fire in almost the same position as when he had brought her from Purnell's house. She didn't look up as he entered, but stared into the flames. Behind the chair with her hand on Deborah's shoulder stood an older woman, who inclined her head in greeting.

'Mrs Purnell you already know, Mr Linton. This is Mrs Brewer, Mr Francis's housekeeper and former nurse to – Miss Deborah.'

He glanced at Mary Edwards anxiously. She was obviously under a great strain, her voice trembled as she spoke. 'I – we have terrible news to impart.'

Mrs Brewer stepped forward and, taking Mary by the elbow, led her to a chair, where she sat her down. 'Mr Linton,' she said, 'perhaps I might be permitted – I have had a little more time to digest the news. Mr Francis – Miss Deborah's father and my most benevolent employer – died yesterday.'

Philip stared, stunned, at the three women in turn. Mrs Brewer continued. 'I've sent messages to Mrs Francis and to the lawyer and to everyone I thought should know.' She glanced at Mary Edwards and then at Deborah. 'Miss Deborah, I fear has not yet grasped the significance, but when I told her that her father had gone, she insisted on coming to stay with Mrs Edwards.'

Mary wiped her eyes. 'We formed a friendship when you first brought her here, Mr Linton. I think she felt secure under my roof whilst she waited for her father.'

Mrs Brewer nodded. 'You were always warm-hearted, Mary, even when you were young. Miss Deborah would sense it.'

Deborah lifted her eyes; they were glazed as if she wasn't seeing properly. 'I told Papa that I would like to live with Mary Edwards in her lovely shop and he said that perhaps one day I could.'

Philip crossed over towards her, took her hand and gave a slight bow. 'I will do what I can to help you, Miss Deborah,' he said, using her old name familiarly, then turning to Mary Edwards he said, 'I am so sorry. So very sorry for your unhappiness. He was a kind, honourable man and will be greatly missed. Just tell me what I can do, and I will do it.'

There wasn't a great deal he could do apart from wait with them for the lawyer and help with the funeral arrangements. Mrs Francis wrote to the lawyer that she would not be attending the service and that she should only be contacted by letter. To her daughter she made only a passing reference in that as she was now a married woman, she was her husband's responsibility, and to her son, incarcerated in an asylum, she made no reference at all.

Mary Edwards, against her instincts, was persuaded to attend the funeral service at the chapel in Elmswell Manor. She shrouded herself in black and walked with Deborah, who was prostrate with grief. The house servants, the farm labourers, the tenant farmers and so many people from the surrounding villages attended the service and Philip, standing at the back, looked at the people filing in and wondered if Mary and Roger Francis's son, Samuel, was there.

He said his farewells to Mary and Deborah and left to attend to the most important matter of his life, that of acquiring Emily's pardon. As he stepped into the hired chaise, Mr Francis's lawyer came hurrying towards him.

'Mr Linton, I understand that you are returning to Australia and will be in contact with Miss Emily Hawkins?'

'Indeed. I am under orders to sail but must first attend to the business of obtaining a pardon for Miss Hawkins.'

'Then please attend me at my chambers and I can expedite matters for you. I know of this case already as Mr Francis has consulted me. You will be pleased to know that proceedings have already been started.'

Philip heaved a great sigh of relief. Thank heavens! If proceedings have begun then hopefully I can sail very soon to give Emily the best possible news, he thought. I can bring her home. She will be free at last!

Chapter Forty-Four

As his ship sailed through the Heads into Port Jackson and Sydney Cove, Philip thought that it had seemed to be the longest voyage of his life, though they had had good winds and an uneventful voyage. On board they carried supplies and a hold full of immigrant passengers, eager to brave the seas and come to a new country with the opportunity to make a good living in trade or on the land, and without, as they thought, the petty bureaucracy of England, not realizing that the laws of England still applied. The difference was that in Australia the laws were not as easily regulated, owing to the Crown's inability to manage the scattered inhabitants in that vast country.

He took leave of the ship as soon as he could and hired a mount to ride up to Creek Farm. It was almost nine months since he had left, it was spring and he could smell the blossom on the trees and the new grass after the winter rain, and as he climbed higher he heard the squalling voices of the cockatoos and saw a flash of white plumage as they swooped overhead. They were big birds with loud voices and a curl of yellow feathers on the top of their heads and beneath their tails. He turned in the saddle to view the Cove, shimmering in the sunshine below him, and wondered if Emily would still want to return to England.

I could stay here, he thought, if she wanted to. It is a beautiful country, though the seasons are not so gentle as at home. He rounded the last bend and looked up as he had done before when first he had ridden up with Meg and Joe. The farm had looked shabby then with peeling paintwork on the windows and an untidy drive leading up to it. Now it looked different, someone had freshly painted the woodwork and the neatly clipped hedges were underplanted with spring flowers.

As he reached the front of the house, he heard the sound of a woman's laughter and the squeal of childish chatter and Emily came into view running down the veranda steps in chase of Ralph, who was tottering unsteadily into the paddock in pursuit of two puppies. She scooped up the child and swung him round, and as she did she caught sight of Philip and stopped in her tracks. It is such a happy family scene, he thought as he gazed at her, her face flushed and animated. One that I want to be part of.

Emily put Ralph back on the veranda and shooed him inside, calling to Meg to come as she did so. She walked slowly towards him, her fingers partly raised to her lips. He dismounted and stood waiting. 'Emily!' He put out his hand.

She put her hand in his and he closed his fingers over hers. 'Mr Linton,' she breathed. 'I've watched for your ship every day. I'm so glad to see you at last.'

'And I you, Emily. So very glad!'

He was vaguely aware of Meg coming out on to the veranda and picking up Ralph, then going inside again, but his eyes were only for Emily. Her skin was golden from last summer's sun with a faint flush on her cheekbones, and her hair was streaked even blonder than he remembered. Her hand as he held it was brown and firm and strong.

'Emily,' he said softly, 'I have missed you so much.'

She gave a hesitant, gentle smile and replied in no more than a whisper. 'And I've missed you, sir. More than it is seemly to do.'

Do I tell her now that I love her, he worried, or is it too soon? Do I tell her the news of her pardon first? The fact that she is now a free woman and can make her own decisions as to what she wants to do or where she wants to go and with whom?

She took her hand from his and, as if making a great effort to be practical, she forestalled his decision. 'There have been so many things happening in your absence, Mr Linton. I trust that what we have done will meet with your approval.'

'Emily!' He reached for her again and turned her towards him. 'I don't want to talk of mundane matters just yet. I have so many things to tell you.'

She lowered her eyes. 'And I have things to tell you also, Mr Linton, if only I dare and if I don't lose your regard for me.'

'You can never do that, Emily. You have my regard for ever.' He lifted her hand to his lips and kissed it. 'But first, before I say more about my feelings for you and therefore influence you, I am the bearer of good news. Excellent news.'

She looked up into his face. 'Yes?'

'Yes. You are a free woman, Emily! I have an absolute pardon in my pocket. Hugo Purnell withdrew his evidence against you and the charges have been dropped. The magistrate who heard them initially has been forced to retire, being considered an unsuitable person to carry out his duties.'

'Free!' Her voice was choked. 'Free! To go home?'

'If that is what you want. Is that what you want?'

She continued to gaze at him. 'I want –'. She hesitated. 'Where will you be, Mr Linton?'

They were interrupted by a sudden shout from the top field and, turning, they saw Joe and Benne and a dog coming towards them.

'Who's that with Joe?' Philip asked. 'And we seemed to have acquired several dogs.'

'It's Benne,' she said. 'The old Aborigine's grandson, and we've three dogs, two for the sheep and one for the house and two puppies, oh, and two cats to catch the mice and rats.'

He laughed. 'Is there room in the house for me?'

Joe took off his large-brimmed hat and stood in front of Philip. 'Welcome back, sir. Hope you had a good voyage?'

He seems more assured, Philip thought. Being in charge has done him good, given him back his self-esteem. 'I did, thank you, Joe. Everything all right here? Everything looks in good order.'

'Aye, sir. Meg and Emily painted 'house, and, well we've a few things to talk about. This here is Benne, he's been helping wi' sheep. He's not had any wages, but we've just fed and kept him, same as his grandda. I doubt we could have managed without 'em.'

Philip looked up into the hills beyond the pasture land. 'Is it my imagination or are there more sheep than I remember?'

Joe glanced at Emily. 'Just a few, sir. We've done nowt underhand. Mr Clavell has given his approval and he'll be up to see you, I expect, as soon as he hears that you're back.'

Philip started in surprise. 'You're not telling me that Clavell is going in for sheep rearing?'

Joe grinned. 'In a manner of speaking, sir. In a manner of speaking.'

'Well, shall we go inside? And then perhaps Emily would like to tell you of her good news!'

He had brought a bottle of cognac and they gave a toast to Emily's freedom, and then Philip said, 'And one more piece of news which I'm sure you will be glad to hear before we get on with the happenings here.' He glanced at Meg and Joe standing together. 'Meg, you are already a free woman simply by the fact that you are, to all intents, married to Joe, an assigned man. And you, Joe, would have been free anyway, in – what? One year? Two?'

'Would have been? What's would have been?' A flush touched Joe's face. 'I will be! I'll have served my time.'

'You are!' Philip's face broke into a grin. 'Whilst I was talking to a lawyer about Emily's pardon, I mentioned you and the life you had led as a child and how you came to be transported. With his influence we obtained a conditional pardon for you! It means that although you can't go back to England – you are now free! You can do whatever you want within the rules of this country.'

'Free?' Tears ran down Joe's face. 'A free man? Does tha hear that, Meg, Emily? I'm free! I can buy land, graze sheep –!' He crossed the room in two strides and grasping Philip's hand shook it vigorously. Then he put his face into his hands and wept.

Meg rushed towards him and put her arms around him and Philip looked enquiringly at Emily, who, as she brushed away her own tears nodded her head. 'They're going to be married properly,' she said, her voice choked with emotion. 'They've been waiting for you to come back.'

They sat long into the night as Joe told of the discovery of gold; of Clavell's involvement so that the adjoining land could be bought in his and Emily's name, and that Joe and Benne had already started work on the seam.

'Mr Clavell has been listening around Sydney and says rumours are rife that gold has been found at Wellington and along 'Macquarie River. Men are leaving their jobs on 'farms to start digging and 'stores are running out of picks and shovels and you can't buy a wheelbarrow for any price. They're also saying it won't be long before Crown licences'll be issued. I won't be able to apply for one as I'm a convict and Benne being an Abo wouldn't be able to keep any gold anyway.'

'Clavell?'

'Aye, he could, but all 'gold will belong to 'government eventually and we'll have to sell it to them, so what we thought, Mr Clavell and me, was that we'd do some prospecting first, just to see if it was worth continuing. Trouble is, you see, that I can't take it for testing, being a convict – I'd probably be flogged for stealing it, and Mr Clavell doesn't want to show his hand, so what we'd thought, Mr Linton, is that maybe you would take it to England on your next voyage and get it tested there.'

He grinned. ''Course, now I'm a free man, things'll be different. I'll be able to apply for a licence and 'tek gold down to Sydney myself.'

Philip sat back in amazement. 'So – you did find gold?'

'Oh, aye! We've got a bagful inside 'mattress and Meg and Em have got their old boots stuffed wi' it and Mr Clavell's got some under a roll o' bandages at Parramatta.'

'So, you're a rich woman and a landowner, Emily,' Philip smiled at her. This puts a different complexion on things, he mused.

'Not at all, Mr Linton. Mr Clavell has taken the risk. It's his money that bought the land and the sheep and it's only in my name because it couldn't be in Joe's. It belongs to Mr Clavell and Joe, not to me.'

Joe and Meg both protested. 'It's for 'family,' Joe said. 'We'll have no squabbling ower it. It'll be shared out equal just as soon as we can sell it, which won't be yet. It'll depend on whether Mr Linton is willing to tek it.'

'Or even if I am going back,' Philip said, glancing at Emily. 'And that has yet to be decided.'

The decision had to be Emily's and as he and Emily sat on the veranda long after Joe and Meg had gone to bed, he put the question to her. 'Will you stay in Australia now, Emily, or will you return to England?'

She hesitated and then said softly, 'My whole heart tells me that I want to be in England again, in the country where I was born. It has such a strong pull for me and although I could settle here if – if I had to, my dearest wish would be to return home.'

'If you had to? You can go wherever you want, Emily. You are free! Are you thinking of Joe? Of Meg?'

She shook her head. 'No. I'd miss them of course, and Ralph too, but – most of all, and please forgive me for being so forward and presumptuous, but I've thought long and hard over this whilst you have been away.' She took a deep breath. 'Mr Clavell said that we must take our happiness whilst we can. I want, Philip, to be wherever you are.'

He was by her side in an instant, kneeling down and grasping her hand and showering it with kisses. 'Emily! Emily, I am lost for words. You can't imagine how I have been waiting to declare my love for you, and you – I cannot believe that you feel the same way!'

'But I always have.' She smiled at him. 'Since we first met. 'But –'. Her smile faded. 'I knew that I was spoiled, that no man would want me for his wife after what happened with Hugo Purnell, but I have buried my pride. Philip, if you will have me as your mistress, your *housekeeper*, I will serve you well and love you more than any wife could.'

He rocked back on his heels. 'How can you speak of such a thing! That is *not* what I want!' He drew away from her and paced the floor, running his fingers through his hair in a way which she remembered so well. 'I want you to be my wife! I don't want to hide you away like Mary Edwards has been hidden away all these years.' Through his flash of anger he suddenly realized that he had not yet told her the news of Roger Francis's death.

'It was her choice,' she said appeasingly. 'She told me that Mr Francis had wanted to marry her, that he was willing to leave the country if she would go with him.'

'These strong women,' he muttered. 'But I will not have you hidden away,' he said firmly and drew her towards him. 'I want you as my wife, to bear my name and my children. I have no obstacles in my way, no estate to lose, no loss of face. In fact,' and he felt a shiver of doubt run through him, 'it seems that if you agree to marry me, you may well be marrying a poor man in comparison to the riches that are in front of you.'

'It is not a matter of riches, Philip,' she said quietly. 'It is what I am, what I have been.'

'What you have been is in the past and was not of your making.' He kissed her gently, regretting his outburst. 'And what you are is the same as always in spite of the humiliations and privations you have endured. You are still the pure, gentle woman I have always known.'

Meg and Joe were married by the Reverend Fowler in his tiny wooden church. Joe gave his name as

Joseph Hawkins and Meg as Margaret Johnson. Philip gave the bride away and Mr Clavell and Emily were witnesses. After the ceremony Ralph was baptized with Ralph Clavell and Emily as godparents.

'So you knew all the time that Ralph belonged to that poor woman who threw herself overboard?' Meg said to Clavell as they sat in the Reverend Fowler's house, where they had been invited to tea.

'I did.' He stroked the little boy's head. 'But I reckoned that he stood a better chance with you than he did in an orphanage or workhouse.'

'Thank you,' she said softly. 'You have no idea the difference he's made to my life.'

He nodded. 'I can imagine, my dear. My wife and I were not able to have children and they were sadly missed.'

'I haven't told Joe yet,' she whispered. 'I wanted to wait until after 'wedding, but', she put her head down and looked quite bashful, 'I'm going to have a babby. I never thought that I would – it's like a miracle!'

Emily joined them. She looked very happy. 'I have made up my mind,' she said. 'I'm going home to England.'

'Oh, Emily.' Meg was distressed. 'I'll miss you so much.'

'But you and Joe have each other and Ralph. You can build a life together. You love this country, it has so much to offer you, whilst I – I must go home to try to remember who I am.'

'And Mr Linton?' Meg asked. 'What about him?'

'He's been talking to Joe, they've been discussing

the sale of Creek Farm. Joe wants to buy it, but he has to sell the gold to do so.'

'I didn't mean that, as you well know,' Meg said bluntly and Clavell smiled and moved away. 'I mean about him and you. You know how he cares for you, how he has always cared. Everybody can see it, why can't you?'

Emily smiled and glanced across the room to where Philip was in earnest conversation with the parson. He looked up and caught her gaze; he ceased talking and it was as if there were a tenuous thread linking them and drawing them together.

'I do see it,' she said softly. 'At last. And it is because I care about him that I must protect him from himself.'

Chapter Forty-Five

Emily had said a tearful farewell to Meg and Joe and she had waved and waved from the ship until the figures on the harbour side were no more than dark specks. Around her waist and beneath her shift she had small bags of gold hidden away. Joe and Benne had cracked open the rock and splintered out several small nuggets. Now she and Philip were taking them to England to be sold.

As she'd stood on the veranda for the last time, a flock of budgerigars flew over, filling the sky with their noisome chatter. She looked up and watched them as like a green and yellow cloud they whirled and spun above them. There would be nothing like these in England, but oh, how she longed to hear the song of the blackbird and the song thrush, to see the bright flash of a kingfisher by the dykes and hear the hoot of a tawny owl from a deep wood.

'Meg,' she said, 'do you remember the Lark?'

Meg looked puzzled for a moment, then her face cleared. 'When we were in Kingston Street gaol, you mean?'

'Yes,' Emily nodded. 'How beautifully she sang, even though in such a terrible place.' She took hold of Meg's hand and said softly, 'Whenever I hear the skylark's song I'll always think of you, Meg.' Her eyes filled with tears. 'I shall miss you so much, my dearest friend.'

'And I'll never forget you.' Meg hugged her and wept. 'You made my life worth living.'

'Come on, no more tears,' Joe said gruffly. 'When you've sold 'gold, Emily, you'll be able to afford to come back and see us.'

She wiped her eyes. Of course. Joe had trusted them with the gold so that they could get the best possible price in England, whilst Mr Clavell was making other discreet enquiries about selling it in Sydney and Melbourne. But she hadn't quite grasped the notion that she might no longer be poor.

The sea voyage was rough for the first few weeks and they passed through hurricane-force winds and violent storms of lightning and thunder. Yet, as Emily clung to her cot in the cabin which she shared with an officer's wife, she thought that nothing could ever be so bad again as the journey coming out from England, when she and the other women prisoners had been locked in the forbidding, frightening darkness below decks. When they'd thought that their last hours on earth had come.

When the weather cleared she came up on deck and watched the schools of whales and threw crusts of bread to the albatross and petrels which followed in the ship's wake. Philip took her ashore in the Canary Islands, where they bought fresh fruit and vegetables to take back on board and she walked in

479

the hot sunshine with a newly purchased parasol over her head and Philip's arm protectively on hers.

Philip had told her of Roger Francis's death and it was this above all that had made up her mind that she wanted to return to England. 'I want to see Mary Edwards,' she had told him. 'She's my kinswoman after all and will be so lost without Mr Francis. If I can be of comfort to her in any way, I will, and I'd also like to see Sam and try to bring them together at last.'

He had nodded and a smile played around his lips and she thought that he was humouring her, but she had worried over Sam quite considerably and wondered what would happen to him without Mr Francis's protection. They are fond of him at the farm I do believe, she had pondered. But there could come a time when he might not be needed there and would have to look for other employment.

Philip had taken orders to sail on this ship, a slender, four-masted American clipper built for carrying cargo at top speed. 'I need to earn my living,' he had told her. 'I don't want to live only on my father's allowance.'

She was puzzled. She had always thought that he was rich, but then he had been compared with her. His family had money, Ginny had told her so. Ginny! How lovely it would be to see her again. But then her mind clouded. What if she should meet Hugo Purnell? She suddenly felt sick. He might have dropped the charges against her, but to be confronted by his arrogant face and overbearing manner would remind her of the torment he had put her through.

Philip called for her to escort her to supper and commented later, as they strolled the deck, on her quiet demeanour. 'You're not sorry about going back to England?' he asked. 'Are you missing Joe and Meg already?'

She shook her head. 'I do miss them and little Ralph. No, it's just that, it's just that – well going back and starting life over again I realize might be difficult. I want to see Mary and Sam and Ginny, but –', still she hesitated. Then she blurted out, 'I'm so afraid of meeting Hugo Purnell again!'

He stopped and looked down at her. A breeze ruffled her hair beneath her bonnet and he moved a wisp from her cheek with gentle fingers. 'I have an absolute pardon in my pocket. Hugo Purnell is in gaol and has withdrawn his evidence against you. He's probably still there, for although I removed his debt to me on condition he withdrew the charges, he still owed money all over town.'

'He's in gaol?' she breathed. 'A gentleman such as him!'

He admonished her. 'He is not a gentleman, Emily! Your brother Joe is more of a gentleman than Purnell.'

She gazed at him. 'And the money he owed you, was that the money that was stolen from me when I was bringing it from Mrs Purnell?' When he affirmed it, she said softly, 'So I am truly in your debt?'

'Indeed you are, Emily!' And as they were alone on the deck, he bent and kissed her, his lips lingering gently on her cheek. 'However will you repay me?'

Her voice was only a whisper as she replied, 'I have told you already that I will love you as much as a wife would, is that not repayment enough?'

'No. It is not! Not without a gold ring on your finger and a ceremony in church.' Then he added seriously, 'But perhaps we should wait until the gold is valued. When you are very rich you will have eligible men queuing up at your door.'

'Now you are teasing me,' she smiled.

'Indeed I am not. There are many matters which you will have to consider after we arrive in England. Matters which I am not at liberty to discuss as they were told to me in confidence.' He kissed her hand, holding it against his lips. 'You will need to be very sure of your love for me before making any kind of decision.'

She need never know, for he wanted her love not her gratitude, how he had spent his time in England working for her release; of the statement gathered from Alice, who swore that Emily's child had been stillborn, and that the damaged painting was merely a product from a street artist and not of great value as Purnell had claimed. And of the sworn statement from Mrs Anderson that her niece had been seduced and abandoned by Purnell and that she too had been threatened violence by him if she didn't keep her silence. And finally from Mary Edwards, who affirmed that Deborah Purnell had told her that she had been forcibly medicated by her husband and locked in her room. All of this he had gathered to give proof of Purnell's unreliability, his lies and treacherous behaviour.

They docked in Portsmouth and after staying overnight in an inn to enable Emily to recover from the voyage and buy some warmer clothes, they took a coach to London, where they stayed several days to sell the gold and open bank accounts in the names of Ralph Clavell, Joe Hawkins and Emily. Her eyes opened wide as she saw the amount that was deposited. It was more money than she had ever dreamed existed and as they were ushered out of the bank by the effusive banker, she felt as if she was living in a dream.

'So what do you want to do now, Emily?' Philip was amused at her air of bewilderment. 'Buy new gowns and bonnets? Buy a fine carriage to take you back to Holderness?'

'I must write straight away to Joe and Meg to tell them,' she said breathlessly, 'and I would like to buy something for Mary and for Sam. I wonder what he would like? I can get something pretty for Mary, a shawl or maybe a piece of jewellery. But for Sam? A new suit of clothes – but no, he wouldn't know when to wear it. A stout walking stick perhaps or some leather boots, yes, those he would appreciate.'

Philip burst out laughing. 'Oh Emily, you are beyond price. Something for you, I said!'

'I don't need anything more.' She took hold of his hand. 'I have everything that I ever wanted.'

They travelled by train to Leeds and then hurried from one station to another to catch the train to Hull. It was a tiring, dirty and noisy journey, yet Emily was thrilled as she gazed out of the window and saw the countryside rushing by. She had been delighted when Philip had suggested that they travel by train rather than coach; until he added that for propriety's sake, railway travel would be more appropriate than the coach.

'We shall not have the opportunity to be alone on the train,' he said gravely. 'We are back in England again, Emily, with all its prejudices and hypocrisies and I have your reputation to think of now that we are travelling north.'

'But my reputation is shattered.' There was a note of bitterness in her voice. 'It was gone for ever even before I was transported!'

'It will be rebuilt,' he said quietly, 'now that you are back home again with a pardon in your possession.'

But where is home? She had pondered this as with a great rush of steam their journey had begun. Do I do as Mary Edwards has done and set up a little shop to occupy me? Or do I buy a house in the country and act out a lady's life? But no, she sighed. Perhaps not. Who would visit me when they know my reputation? That once I was a servant and a convicted prisoner. And will Philip's parents ever accept me, or will they disown their son?

She glanced at Philip and he smiled reassuringly. 'Don't worry about anything,' he said. 'It will all come right.'

He had booked rooms at the Station Hotel in Hull and after Emily had washed and changed from her sooty travelling clothes she went down to the foyer to meet Philip for supper. 'Is it too late to visit Mary now?' she asked eagerly. 'I think she wouldn't mind, she will be so thrilled to see us.'

'She won't be there. She has let the shop to someone else.'

'Oh! I was so looking forward to seeing her!' Emily was bitterly disappointed. She had so much to tell her and things to ask too. Important things which would affect her own future.

'Tomorrow,' he said firmly. 'I will take you first thing tomorrow.'

'But where? Where has she gone?'

He shook his head and smiled in a maddening way and would not be drawn.

They had supper and then called for a hackney carriage to take them to the riverside, where along with others who had come to watch the busy river traffic of steam packets, tugs and ferry boats, they walked to stretch their legs and felt the briskness of the breeze coming in from the sea. Emily drew in a deep breath. She could smell the salt, she could even welcome the smell of the whale blubber and the seed oil. She sighed it out. 'It's so good to be back,' she said gratefully. 'Especially when I was told that I could never come back. That I was banished for ever.'

He remained silent until she whispered, 'But I can't get rid of this feeling that Hugo Purnell is behind me. I won't ever be able to come into Hull without thinking of him.'

'I told you that he was in gaol and that is where he will remain for a very long time. You don't need to be afraid of him!'

'But I am! I can't rid myself of his image. He's like a spectre haunting me!'

He looked down at her. 'Then we must confront the spectre,' he said firmly and put up his hand to signal another hackney.

'Where are we going?' She was helped in and Philip took his seat beside her.

'We are going to confront Purnell once and for all! You cannot spend the rest of your life thinking of him. I want you', he said softly, 'to think of me sometimes.'

'But I do,' she pleaded. 'Always. But', she shuddered, 'he is always there.'

The cab came to a halt. 'You sure this is where you want to be, sir?' the cabbie asked. 'I know some folk come for entertainment, but it's not a suitable place for your lady.'

Philip nodded in agreement and asked him to wait for them and as Emily got down she trembled and shook. 'Not here, Philip! Not here. I can't go in!' In front of her, its walls as forbidding as ever, was the Kingston Street gaol.

He took hold of her arm and firmly propelled her towards the octagonal building. 'You must, or Purnell will always hold you fast.'

Two wards were kept for debtors, one for male and one for female, and as Emily took reluctant, dragging steps down the corridor to the male cells, she was reminded forcibly of her time spent incarcerated deep in the depths of one of the other buildings.

'This fellow doesn't get many visitors.' The warder rattled his keys as he led the way. 'He did at first. Some of his friends were very curious to see him locked up. They used to give him a shilling or two, but he was very abusive so they stopped coming. Purnell!' he shouted. 'Purnell! Visitors for you.'

Emily clung to Philip as she looked over the crowd of men in the communal cell, but couldn't recognize the tall figure of the man who had so humiliated and debased her. The men in here were bent and sullen looking and simply looked up in a desultory fashion as Purnell's name was called.

A man in a dirty old coat got up from the floor and shuffled towards them. 'Who wants him?' he whined. 'Have you brought some liquor – or money?'

'It's Purnell we want, old man,' Philip said. 'Can you point him out?'

The prisoner looked from Philip to Emily, then back to Philip again. His face was grey and lined, his hair long and unkempt. He narrowed his red-rimmed eyes. 'I know you,' he said hoarsely. 'What's your name? I went to school with you.' He clutched the bars of the cell. 'Don't you remember?'

Philip stood back from the stench of him. 'Purnell! Is it you?'

Emily was horrified. This was never Hugo Purnell! This shabby, uncombed, dishevelled figure was not the figure who had haunted her sleep.

''Course it's me!' Purnell snarled. 'Come to gloat have you? None of my friends come any more, so why have you come? What's your name? I can't remember.'

'Linton,' Philip reminded him. 'I came to see you about a year ago.'

'Ah,' Purnell said vaguely, his mood changing. 'Yes. So you did. What was it about? Something about a servant girl? Do I still owe you money?'

'Not any more, the debt was repaid.'

'Was it? Hah! You were lucky then. Nobody else's has been. I get letters every day asking me to pay.' His face flushed and he became angry again. 'How do they expect me to pay from in this hell hole, I ask you? I've got to work to pay for my keep in here, you know! I've been on the treadmill, I've ground up whiting.' He showed his hands, which were ingrained with dirt and lined with white powder. His mouth worked and trembled. 'But I can't do it, old fellow. I'm not cut out for it, you know.' His head drooped and he put his hand to his eyes. 'Now I sweep out the cells, sweep up other people's filth.'

Philip and Emily were both silent and Emily pressed her hand to her mouth and closed her eyes tightly. She fought hard not to feel sorry for him. Remember, she deliberated, what he did to you, how he made you suffer.

Purnell lifted his head. 'So why have you come, Linton? And who's the lady? Your wife?'

'Er, yes,' Philip agreed cautiously.

Purnell stared at Emily. 'Well, you're a very lucky dog, Linton, but then you always were! I'm delighted to meet you ma'am – delighted.' Some of his old charisma returned and it was obvious that he didn't recognize Emily. He turned his gaze to Philip. 'You're the only one who ever comes you know. Nobody else does. My wife left me and so did my mother. None of my friends come. They've all left me to rot.'

Emily stifled a sob. How often she had wished that bitter thought on him, and Meg too had many times voiced the hope that he would rot in hell, for it was indirectly because of him that she too was transported.

'Is there anything you need, Purnell?' Philip asked. 'Food? Blankets?'

Purnell shook his head. 'Nothing, except a bottle of whisky maybe. There's nothing else that can ease the misery or the humiliation.'

Emily spoke softly. 'Do you ever think of why you are here? Of the events which brought you here?'

He stared at her blankly. 'It was something to do with owing money, I think. I kept borrowing I suppose and not paying back.'

He doesn't even remember me, Emily thought bitterly. After all I went through and he doesn't remember, therefore he can't feel any remorse.

Philip took her arm. 'Come, Emily, let us go,' he said.

'Emily!' Purnell said suddenly. 'I knew someone called Emily once. She was a servant girl, but very beautiful, too beautiful to be a servant. But I hurt her.' His eyes grew thoughtful and he scratched his chin. 'She had my baby, but it was dead. Poor Emily! I wonder what happened to her.'

Emily turned away. There was nothing more to be said. They reached the top of the corridor and she turned around. Purnell was still clutching the bars of the cell and watching their progress. He painted a forlorn figure of misery, she thought.

As they reached the waiting cab, she looked back. It was dark now, but the moon, which lay half hidden behind cloud, cast a daunting, ominous shadow of the high walls over the courtyard. The only lights came from the top of the gatehouse in the north wall and the governor's house, which overlooked all the buildings. She shivered and hoped that never again would she see the inside of this dreadful place.

'Pay off his debts, Philip,' she whispered as they drove away.

'What?' he said. 'What do you mean?'

'Pay off his debts on my behalf. I have money enough.'

He gazed at her. 'You can't mean that? The man who brought you so low?'

'Yes. There's no sense in him being there. He can't ever pay off the claims against him and he'll die in there otherwise.'

'Do you forgive him?' he asked quietly.

She hesitated. 'No. I don't think so. Nor will I ever forget. But I'm not afraid of him any more. He can't harm me, he can only harm himself. I want to let him out and perhaps – just perhaps there's a chance that he will redeem himself.'

'All right,' Philip agreed, though privately he thought that there was little hope of Purnell becoming a reformed character. But it was ironic, he meditated, that the one person who owed him least, should be the means of offering him that hope. 'I'll ask my lawyer to find out who his creditors are.'

He leaned back against the cushions. 'But not

just yet. Purnell will have to wait just a little longer for his release. Tomorrow I have a surprise for you. Two surprises, in fact.'

'Yes?' She heaved a deep sigh. She felt as if a great weight had been lifted from her shoulders. 'Tell me.'

'No, you must wait. But –', he relented a little, 'I will tell you some of it.'

From the glow of the carriage lamp he saw the anticipation on her face. 'Tomorrow', he said, 'I am taking you for a carriage ride into Holderness.'

Chapter Forty-Six

The morning was bright and there was just a hint of spring in the air as they came out of the hotel. Waiting on the forecourt was a spanking smartly painted four-wheeled chaise drawn by two horses and attended by a liveried coachman.

'For us?' Emily drew in a breath. 'Oh, it's so handsome. So very elegant,' adding anxiously, 'but expensive?'

'Yes,' Philip agreed, 'indeed, but you must accustom yourself to a different lifestyle, Emily. I told you that you were a rich woman.'

'But I can't spend money in such a fashion,' she whispered, not to be overheard by other hotel guests who were arriving or departing. 'There will be nothing left if I do!'

'You're forgetting the seam,' he urged. 'Joe hasn't even started yet. Once he gets all the equipment together and he can now that he's free, there will be gold in plenty.'

'But it's not mine,' she insisted. 'It belongs to Joe and Mr Clavell.'

'All right,' he said grumpily, 'if you want to give it all up, then do so. Perhaps I'll stand a better chance of marrying you if you are penniless and only living in a poor cottage in Holderness?' He sighed. 'My mother will be so disappointed. I wrote and told her that I was trying to win the hand of an heiress.' He shook his head in mock sorrow. 'It's what she has always wanted for me.'

'You are so silly, Philip,' she laughed. 'I'm seeing an entirely different side to you from the one I thought I knew.'

'That's because, Miss Hawkins,' he said with slight irony as he led her down the steps, 'you are no longer conscious of our different situations. You no longer a servant girl trying to do the right thing for her so-called *betters*. *I* haven't changed. You are the one who has!'

'If I have changed, it's because of you,' she murmured. 'If you hadn't taken orders on the *Flying Swan*, I dread to think what would have become of me.'

He shook his head. That prospect didn't bear thinking of. 'Miss Hawkins,' he continued in the formal manner as he handed her into the carriage, 'I said yesterday that we must be careful of your reputation now that we are back in your home county, and to this end I took the decision that it would be more circumspect for you to have a female companion to accompany us.'

'Oh!' she said in dismay. 'Is it really necessary?' She had planned to tell him as they travelled of her childhood days in Holderness, of times by the river, of Sam and Granny Edwards. All those memories she knew would come flooding back now that she was home. The day will be spoiled now if there is a stranger with us.

'It is indeed necessary.You must know that,' he said severely, yet she caught a glimmer of mischief in his eyes. 'I have made the arrangements so if you would excuse me for one moment?'

She sat back against the cushions and waited whilst he ran up the steps and back into the hotel. If being a rich woman means that I have to be careful over everything I do or say, then I don't think I shall like it, she pondered and even the velvet cushions and the rich smell of leather did not dispel her disappointment. Perhaps there is something to be said for being poor after all.

She glanced out of the window and saw Philip appearing through the doors and ushering out a young woman. She sat forward. There was something familiar about the woman's bearing, though she had her head lowered as she came down the steps and her bonnet obscured her face.

She lifted her head and Emily took a deep, deep breath of joy, of recognition. 'Ginny! Oh, Ginny!'

Ginny jumped inside the carriage, not waiting for Philip's help and wrapped her arms around Emily. 'I'm so glad to see you back, Emily!' Her eyes were bright with emotion. 'I never gave up hope, not after that day I met Mr Linton. I knew, I could tell how he cared for you and I was certain he would bring you safely home.'

Philip, who had been standing outside the carriage doors as their greetings were made, put his head inside. 'Well, ladies! Shall we drive?'

As they travelled out of Hull and into the

countryside it seemed to Emily that there was so much to tell Ginny and yet so much that couldn't yet be told. She remained silent over her journey to the London gaol and about the convict ship which took her to Australia. That was something which would be told only piece by piece; yet she shyly told her of Philip Linton's concern, of Creek Farm and of Meg and of her brother Joe, but not of the gold, for she didn't want to lose Ginny's friendship now that she had wealth.

'How ever did you find Ginny again, Philip? And how ever did you get Mrs Marshall to give you time off, Ginny?'

Ginny glanced at Philip Linton, who said, 'Oh, all the better people know Ginny, she was easy enough to track down.' He smiled as he spoke and Emily felt that they were hiding something from her.

'And I no longer work for Mrs Marshall,' Ginny said. 'I gave up on her just after your trial. I was sick of her questioning and wanting to know every detail. I had no trouble finding other employment. As Mr Linton said, everyone knows me. And', she added, 'I was given today off as it was such a special day!'

They travelled in silence for a while until Emily, looking out of the window, exclaimed, 'Oh! I know this road! We're not very far from Elmswell Manor, where the Francises lived!' She recognized the wooded area which surrounded the house and estate and sheltered it completely from the road. 'I was so happy there until Miss Deborah became too attached to me and I had to leave. It was such a beautiful house,' she mused. 'What I would give to see it again.'

'Then let's do that,' Philip said and drew down the window and, putting his head out, gave instructions to the coachie.

'Oh, but it will be all shut up, I expect, until Mrs Francis decides what to do with it.' Then Emily became thoughtful. 'What has happened to Miss Deborah, I wonder? Will Mr Francis have made provisions for her? I'm sure her mother won't want her. Perhaps Mrs Brewer will look after her again, though she is getting too old to cope with Miss Deborah's tantrums. Oh, she surely won't be sent to an asylum like her brother! Mr Linton,' she said formally, 'I think I must enquire.' She suddenly felt anxious. 'I hope that someone is concerned for her, for her mother never was and neither was Hugo Purnell.'

Philip nodded in an absent-minded way and she gave a small frown at his apparent disinterest over her former young mistress.

'And whilst we are here in the district I must enquire about Sam.' She gave a sudden smile of happiness. 'He will be so surprised and he won't recognize me! I was not quite fourteen when I left Granny Edwards's cottage.' She gazed out at the familiar landscape. 'So much has happened,' she said softly. 'I feel as if I have packed a lifetime into just a few short years.'

'So you have, Emily.' He roused himself and, she thought, he is listening to me after all. 'But there is still so much of life ahead of you.'

Ginny looked discreetly out of the window as

Emily said softly, 'What kind of life is ahead of me? I seem to have forgotten who I am.'

'I know who you are, Emily.' He gazed at her earnestly as he spoke, almost forgetting Ginny's presence. 'You can always ask me – or your friends.'

I am so afraid, she thought. I know I have his esteem, his love, but can I live up to his estimation of me? And I am so afraid that he would eventually regret his commitment towards me.

She turned her gaze to the window. They had turned up the drive of Elmswell Manor, the long drive where once she had walked with her childhood friend, Jane, to enquire for a position as maid. They were approaching the gatehouse and as they drove through, they saw three figures standing by the entrance of the main house. A woman of middle years, dressed in black, a younger woman who was holding her hand, and behind them standing on the steps was a tall, well-built, fair-haired man.

'There is someone here after all,' she said nervously. 'We'd better turn back! Perhaps someone else has bought the house. Tell them we have made a mistake, Philip, and lost our way. We don't want anyone thinking we have come out of curiosity.'

The coachman drew to a halt and jumped down to open the carriage door and fold down the step. Emily stared at Philip. 'Why have we stopped? We can't call without an invitation!'

'You know the formalities so well, Emily! But we do have an invitation.' Philip stepped out and gave her his hand to help her down. 'At least I have. You don't need one.'

Whatever did he mean? She lifted her head and looked towards the group of people who were coming towards them. Mary Edwards! But how could it be? She hadn't been to the house since she was a servant girl, and that's Miss Deborah with her!

'Oh, Mary!' she cried. 'I'm so pleased to see you at last.' Emily put out her arms to embrace her and saw the tears of joy on Mary's face.

'Miss Deborah.' Emily bobbed her knee, but to her surprise Deborah too put out her arms to hug her.

'Emily,' she said in an excited voice as if she had seen Emily only a few days before. 'Such things as you wouldn't believe. I have a puppy of my own! Sam bought it for me as a present. He's going to show me how to train her. You know Sam, don't you?' She turned to include the tall man standing behind them. 'He's my brother. Not the one who I thought had died, but a new brother and he says he will always look after me!'

Sam walked slowly towards her. 'Hello, Em.' He lowered his head and a flush touched his cheeks. 'I'm right glad to see thee back.'

At his homely words, Emily was overcome with emotion. 'I'm glad to see you too, Sam,' she choked. 'I can't tell you how much,' and she put her arms around his rough tweed jacket and held him close and felt the memories come rushing back.

'And, Emily,' Deborah chatted on, as if determined to tell all, 'you'll never guess what else! Mary – who was my father's best friend – is Sam's mother!'

498

Emily looked from one to another. So Mary and Sam had rediscovered each other after all. She saw the smile on Philip's face and realized that he had known all the time. But why was Mary here, in the house where her name was never mentioned? Had she been employed to look after Miss Deborah? But who had engaged her? Not Mrs Francis!

'Shall we go inside?' Mary asked. 'Luncheon is prepared, but first there are some others waiting to welcome you home, Emily.'

She barely heard what Mary was saying, so overcome and confused was she, but she followed her and Deborah through the great heavy doors, and Philip, Sam and Ginny followed behind.

In the coolness of the hall she could smell the fragrance of lilies and roses, which were set upon the gleaming polished table, and standing alongside it a line of servants was waiting. She gasped, not the servants she had worked with! Not Cook and Mrs Brewer! But yes, it was. Mrs Castle who had a dusting of flour on her cheek and Mrs Brewer, side by side. She grasped their hands and couldn't stop the tears which coursed down her cheeks.

'I'm so very happy to meet you again,' she wept.

Mrs Castle wiped her eyes on her apron. 'Why bless you, Miss Emily. It's good to have you back home again.'

There were other servants whom she didn't know, kitchen maids and housemaids, and rather strangely they bobbed their knee to her; but, she thought, they don't know who I am and they have been well trained to greet guests of the house. She reached the end of the line and her tears had almost abated, until she saw that Ginny had positioned herself there and had a broad smile upon her face.

'Welcome home, Emily.' Ginny kissed her and put her arms around her.

'I'm so confused.' Emily looked at all the smiling faces. 'I don't understand. How did you know that I was coming?'

Mary took her arm. 'Come into the drawing room whilst Cook finishes luncheon and I'll explain.'

She led her through to the room which she remembered so well. The room where she had once laid the fire and dusted the furniture and plumped up the cushions on the chairs and sofas, and where now she was invited to sit as if she were an honoured guest.

Deborah drew a stool near to Emily's feet and sat hunched with her hands pressed together as if enclosing a secret. Sam stood hovering near the door and after clearing his throat said, 'Deborah! Shall we take 'pup for a run before we have our dinner? Then you can bring her in to show Emily.'

She jumped up immediately and ran towards him. 'Oh, yes. You'd like that wouldn't you, Emily?'

Emily nodded agreement. How strange everything was. Sam and Miss Deborah being so easy with each other and Mary sitting relaxed opposite her in the house which belonged to her former lover and his wife. And where was Mrs Francis, anyway?

'I was going to ask Mr Francis's lawyer here today to speak to you, Emily, and explain what has happened,' Mary said, 'but then I decided that if I gave you prior knowledge, then he could explain the intricacies of the will later.'

Emily looked from Mary to Philip. 'But why should I wish to hear of Mr Francis's will? It's surely no concern of mine?'

'Indeed it is, my dear. Of as much concern to you as it is to me and Sam, and I must say here how grateful I am to Mr Linton for bringing you home so swiftly and of being so considerate and understanding when I felt there was no-one I could turn to in my despair.'

Philip inclined his head in response and Emily said softly to Mary, 'I am so sorry about Mr Francis, he was such a kind gentleman. You must miss him so much.'

'I do,' she murmured sadly. 'I shall never get over his loss, even though I have been offered so many compensations. But', she added, putting on a brave smile, 'let me tell you what has been happening.' She took a breath. 'Roger Francis has left his estate to his elder son – Samuel.'

Emily gazed at her in astonishment. To Sam? But how could he look after it?

'He realized, of course, that Samuel would not be able to attend to it himself. He's a good worker on the land but has no knowledge, nor sadly the education or ability, to be able to run it. Roger decreed, therefore, that although the estate will be in Samuel's name,' Mary gave a sudden uplifting smile, 'and he has acknowledged him as his elder son, that the finances and the running of the estate will be in the hands of Samuel's mother, that's me, and his cousin, Emily Hawkins.'

Emily gasped. 'But –'.

'There is more,' Mary added, 'and it may take some time to explain. But tomorrow the lawyer will be here to inform you officially. My dear,' she leaned towards Emily, 'Roger has left you Elmswell Manor in its entirety, but there is a proviso, which is that Deborah should live here also if she should wish.'

She broke off as she heard the sound of Deborah's voice and the yapping of a puppy in the hall, then continued, 'But Deborah has decided that she would rather live with me and Samuel in the gatehouse, which she describes as very sweet and cosy!'

'Live with you and Sam?' Emily could hardly take it all in. 'But – what about Mrs Francis? What will she do?'

Mary's face hardened. 'Mrs Francis does not want her daughter any more than she wanted her poor son, and Roger knew that. She has been left an annuity until her death, which will then expire and return to the estate. Deborah too has been left an annuity, which I, as her appointed guardian, will administer.'

The door flew open and in romped a golden bundle of legs and fur which hurled itself with licking tongue at Emily and then at Mary, but barked at Philip, who remarked that Deborah would have a busy time training it. Sam caught it by the scruff of its neck and firmly put it out again, where they could hear it scampering up the stairs and along the corridors.

Mrs Brewer appeared at the door to announce

that luncheon was about to be served and, shaking her head and smiling, said that she had never known such goings on in all the time she had worked there.

'There will be changes, no doubt, Mrs Brewer,' Mary agreed. 'There will be some joy and laughter in this house at last.'

Emily could hardly eat, though the food was tempting. Mrs Castle hadn't lost her light touch with pastry, but she was trembling so much and her senses whirled as she thought of what was in front of her. How could she manage such a great house? How could she run an estate, even with Mary? It just wasn't possible.

'The estate manager will stay on, of course,' Mary was saying. 'If we are agreeable, that is. He has been here for many years and we would be wise to take his advice. I took the liberty of sounding out Mrs Castle and Mrs Brewer and they both want to stay here with you until they retire and then perhaps you would like Ginny to take over as housekeeper. Some of the other servants left when Mr Francis died and Mrs Brewer has taken on new staff.'

Emily sighed. That at least was a relief. It would be difficult to have servants who had known her as a servant also, Jane and Brown the groom, and she supposed that Jane had long gone away to have Brown's baby. And Ginny would be her companion as much as a housekeeper.

'I'm not used to running a household,' she resisted weakly, 'let alone an estate so large.'

'But Emily,' Philip interrupted, 'don't be fearful. You ran Creek Farm whilst I was away and managed it very well. This is just bigger, that's all, and you will have plenty of people to help you.'

She smiled; how he teased. There could be no comparison between Elmswell Manor and Creek Farm. At the farm, life had been hard but casual and simple, whereas Elmswell Manor when she had known it had been so very formal. Then she reconsidered. But was that because of the people in it? Because Mrs Francis was so grand? She gazed up at the paintings on the dining-room wall and saw Mr Francis's ancestors looking down at her. What would they have thought, she wondered, of a servant girl living in their house and running their estate? She felt their pompous, arrogant gaze and suddenly laughed. They wouldn't have liked it, she decided.

After luncheon Mrs Brewer invited her upstairs to inspect the room they had suggested for her. 'You may use another if you prefer it, Miss Emily,' said the housekeeper. 'But this was always the best room with the loveliest views. The one Mr Francis preferred.'

She nodded, unable to say much. She was feeling very strange and rather lightheaded. It was indeed a lovely room and it had been decorated since she had last seen it. Instead of the heavy mahogany furniture which Mr Francis had inherited from his parents, someone, and she suspected it might have been Mary, had removed the chests of drawers and the heavy tester bed and filled it with lighter, more feminine furniture and had draped the windows with muslin and silk curtains.

She started to shake. Coming upstairs upset her,

bringing back the memory of when she had last slept in the house as Mrs Purnell's maid, and of the consequences of that visit. She sat down abruptly on a chair.

'Are you unwell, Miss Emily?' Mrs Brewer asked in concern. 'Has the shock of it all been too much for you?'

Emily shook her head. 'No,' she murmured. 'It's not that, Mrs Brewer. It's just that – well, in truth, I'm reminded of the last time I was here – at Miss Deborah's wedding and it has very unpleasant associations for me.'

Mrs Brewer gazed down at her. 'I do understand, my dear,' she said quietly. 'We were so sorry that such a dreadful thing happened under our roof, but you must try to put it behind you. Will you come with me? I want to show you something.'

She led Emily out of the room and along the corridor and up a short flight of steps to the landing where the guest rooms were and which Emily remembered so well. At least, she thought she did, yet there was something different. A door which she didn't remember was midway along the corridor.

Mrs Brewer opened it and stepped through. 'Mr Francis changed all of this after your trial. He said he wanted to eradicate all memory of that dreadful man.' She opened another door to a room which Emily was sure was the one she had stayed in. But within the room was a wall full of shelves, piled high with lavender-scented bedlinen. Where the adjoining door to Mrs Purnell's room had been was now a wallpapered wall and standing by a table next to the fire, which had flat irons heating on it, was a young and flushed maid folding up a freshly ironed sheet.

'We needed another linen room,' Mrs Brewer said by way of explanation, 'and we can get to this landing easily from the back stairs. No need for you to come through here at all, Miss Emily.'

'Thank you, Mrs Brewer,' she said gratefully. 'Thank you so very much.'

Later in the day, she strolled with Philip around the garden. Snowdrops drooped beneath the hedges but in their place tips of yellow primroses showed beneath rosettes of green leaves. 'Have you laid all the ghosts?' he asked. 'Have you rid yourself of the bad memories?'

'Yes. They are fading fast. It's as if those terrible things happened to someone else, to someone I once knew. But I am still overwhelmed by Mr Francis's generosity and I can't think why he should consider me in this way.'

'He told me once when we were discussing your predicament, that you reminded him so much of Mary Edwards that he could almost imagine that it might have been her going through the conflict which you were suffering.' He paused, adding, 'Had Roger Francis been a different kind of man, then she too might well have been abandoned with an illegitimate child.'

'So it was because of his love for Mary,' she said thoughtfully.

'Yes,' he said lightly. 'How surprising it is what men will do for love!' He looked down at her, an anxious expression on his face. 'Have you made a decision, Emily? I must know.'

She drew away from him and lowered her head. 'I know well what you have done for me, Philip, and it is because I love you that I cannot ruin your life by becoming your wife. You must think of your future. One day you'll meet someone of your own class, someone you will be proud to introduce as your wife and to bear your children.'

A sob caught in her throat. 'I will always love you, but even though I now have riches it doesn't alter what I have been, what I am. A servant girl and an ex-convict! Think of your parents and your sisters, think of how they would feel if you married me.'

He gazed stonily into the distance. 'Then I might just as well have left you out in Australia,' he said bitterly, 'for all my plans have come to nothing.'

'I am doing this for you,' she whispered, 'because I love you.'

'Do not say that you love me!' She heard the anger and distress in his voice. 'If you loved me you wouldn't put me through this torment!' He turned on his heel, 'Please excuse me,' and left her standing alone.

She felt the warmth of sunshine on her head, but there was only an icy coldness in her heart. I've lost him! She watched him striding back to the house. What have I done?

Philip sent a message that he wouldn't be down for supper, that he had some papers to attend to, and later Emily sat with Mary whilst Deborah and Sam played cards at the other side of the drawing room and Ginny stitched a piece of linen. Deborah shrieked whenever she had a winning hand and Sam guffawed.

Mary smiled at their noisy enthusiasm and commented, 'Roger told me that he hoped that one day Elmswell Manor would echo to the sound of children's voices and the patter of small feet. He was very fond of children and wished that he could have had grandchildren. But', she sighed, 'it wasn't to be.' She glanced at Emily with a question in her eyes. 'Perhaps one day his wish will come true?'

Emily felt as if she was made of ice. How could she tell this dear, kind woman that she had refused Philip for the last time?

Just before bedtime Philip appeared downstairs. 'Mrs Edwards,' he said formally. 'I shall be away very early in the morning, my parents are expecting me, and so I will wish you goodbye now and thank you warmly for your hospitality.'

'You must go so soon?' There was a note of surprise in her voice. 'But thanks are due to you, Mr Linton,' she said warmly, 'for bringing our dear Emily safely home.' She gazed questioningly at him. 'We shall see you again very soon, I trust?'

He bowed, but didn't make a reply.

He turned to Emily and taking her hand he briefly kissed her fingertips. Neither of them spoke, but Emily gazed at him with such fullness in her heart that she felt it would burst. Am I being foolish? She saw misery and hurt in his eyes. Am I making a mistake? I only want to do what is best for him, I love him so much.

She lay tearful and sleepless in her bed that night, thinking of the momentous events of the day and of Philip leaving the next morning. I am so thankful to be back and to be given so much, but without Philip beside me it will mean nothing. I will be as a pauper without him. He's leaving. He's angry with me. I might never see him again and I can't bear that! What shall I do?

She tossed and turned, dreaming and waking with a million things running through her mind. She dreamt she was back on the convict ship. She was ironed and shackled in the darkness of the hold, the ship tossed on momentous seas and she could hear the sound of women crying. She called Philip's name again and again, but there was no answer and she felt as if she had been abandoned.

She woke again just as night slipped away from day and heard the first clear call of a blackbird, a sound which she had so longed to hear when she was at the other side of the world. She listened to its crystal clear beauty and waited for the answering call from the other early birds, yet there was no pleasure in the sound as once there would have been. Then came the repeated rhythmic melody of the song thrush and the *coo-coo* of pigeons and below that she could hear the whisper of voices and the jangle of harness.

She threw back the bedcovers and padded to the window and looked out. A grey mist was dispersing above the grass and by the front door a groom was adjusting the stirrups on a black stallion and talking quietly to him was Philip.

He's going! In the cold light of day, the enormity of her decision came to her and she panicked. I must stop him! She snatched her robe from the bed and sped downstairs, past a startled and sleepy maid who was emerging from the lower stairs with a dustpan in her hand.

She struggled with the heavy front door and as she stepped outside, saw Philip trotting half-way down the drive. I'm too late!

He stopped and bent to adjust the leather on his stirrups and ignoring the fact that she was in her bedclothes and barefoot, she flew down the steps and the drive after him.

'Philip!' she called. 'Philip. Don't go!'

He turned in the saddle. 'Emily! I tried not to wake anyone. I thought you would still be sleeping.'

'You're leaving!'

'I told you I was leaving early,' he said bluntly. 'Besides, there is no reason for me to delay any longer now I have brought you safely home. You have made up your mind about your future, and mine, seemingly. Why should I stay?'

She put her hand up to his and held it. 'Because I need you. Because my life is nothing without you.' Her eyes held his, though she could hardly see for tears. 'I am so foolish. Please forgive me. I don't deserve your love.'

He stroked the top of her head and said gently, 'My parents are expecting me. What would I tell them?'

'Go tomorrow – or the day after – and tell them –', there was a sob in her throat, '– tell them that the rich heiress who loves you wouldn't let you come any sooner.'

He dismounted and wrapping the reins around

his wrist, bent down and kissed her tenderly on the lips. 'And what then, Miss Hawkins?'

She smiled and blinked away the tears and returned his kiss, whispering, 'Bring them back with you for the wedding, Mr Linton.'

THE END

A SELECTED LIST OF FINE NOVELS
AVAILABLE FROM CORGI BOOKS

THE PRICES SHOWN BELOW WERE CORRECT AT THE TIME OF GOING TO PRESS. HOWEVER TRANSWORLD PUBLISHERS RESERVE THE RIGHT TO SHOW NEW RETAIL PRICES ON COVERS WHICH MAY DIFFER FROM THOSE PREVIOUSLY ADVERTISED IN THE TEXT OR ELSEWHERE.

All Transworld titles are available by post from:

Bookpost, P.O. Box 29, Douglas, Isle of Man IM99 1BQ

Credit cards accepted. Please telephone 01624 836000,
fax 01624 837033, Internet http://www.bookpost.co.uk or
e-mail: bookshop@enterprise.net for details.

Free postage and packing in the UK. Overseas customers allow
£2 per book (paperbacks) and £3 per book (hardbacks).